SPELLBOUND BY THE SEA LORD

LORDS OF ATLANTIS

USA TODAY BESTSELLING AUTHOR

STARLA NIGHT

Copyright © 2019
All rights reserved

All product and company names are trademarks™ or registered® trademarks of their respective holders. Use of them does not imply any affiliation with or endorsement by them.

Cover by Earthly Charms
Editing by Linda Edits

For inquiries:

Starla Night
starla@starlanight.com
https://starlanight.com

ONE

Mermen never got sand in their cracks.

Until they surfaced, apparently.

Since surfacing in New York City a few months ago, mer warlord Balim had endured enough irritations to blanket a beach.

Balim raced across the hospital parking lot. He was already too hot. His iridescent heartblood-red tattoos reflected the midmorning sunlight, and his human slacks and long-sleeve gray shirt clung damply to his hard muscle.

Another irritation.

Paramedics pushed the gurney out the back doors of their ambulance. Balim's warrior lay prone. Blood-soaked bandages covered his ruptured chest plate.

A distraught human female clambered out of the passenger's seat.

"Steady your soul light!" Balim barked.

Warrior Pelan clenched his teeth. His red-and-black tattooed cheeks trembled. "I...will..."

"Not you." Balim pointed at the female. She was sniffling and smearing black eye-grease with a fistful of paper napkins. "You!"

She jolted in surprise and dropped the napkins. The coffee-chain logo fluttered to the gray ground. "Me?"

"Yes! Calm your grief. Do not leave your husband's side!"

"H-husband? N-no, you don't understand…"

"Hurry!"

Paramedics rushed the gurney through the open doors of the large, busy metropolitan hospital.

She hiccupped and bent to collect the napkins. "He's not m-my husband. Today was our first date."

Balim gripped her elbow and righted her. Touching another male's bride was forbidden, but Warrior Pelan's health mattered more. "You drank the elixir. Marriage is a formality."

She choked. "Formality?"

Balim steered her after the gurney. "Pelan needs you. Do not collapse with sadness."

"B-but he got shot through the heart."

"Now, *you* are his heart. If he dies, it is your fault."

Her soul darkened. "My fault?"

The gurney rolled into the busy emergency department and halted.

Balim released the female at his warrior's side.

Warrior Pelan, looking sicker and weaker, lifted a shaking, blood-streaked finger to his bride's grease-streaked cheek. "Do not cry. I am happy to have met you. If only once…"

"No." She sucked in a shaky breath. Her soul light dipped and darkened as tears welled in her eyes. "No…"

Pelan's soul synced with hers.

"Comfort *him*," Balim snapped. "Do not make him comfort you."

She jolted again, glared at Balim, and pulled herself together. Curling her fingers around Pelan's, she said shakily and then more firmly, "You're g-going to be all right. We're at the hospital now. They're going to stitch you up. You're going to be f-fine."

Pelan's soul brightened.

Good.

Balim focused on the obstruction in their path: the director of the hospital.

The florid male argued with the ambulance attendants. "You were not cleared to bring him here."

"Nowhere else will take him," one paramedic said. "Your hospital did patient trials with Sea Opal—"

"Limited and long ago." He lifted his palms in refusal. "None of our doctors are trained for operating on nonhumans."

"I'm willing to try." A young, olive-skinned doctor accepted the gurney.

"Hands off, Kowalski."

"This is career-making surgery, Bob. You can't deny me the chance—"

"I can and will." The director glared. "You're not even on duty. Go home."

Doctor Kowalski frowned, mutinous.

"And you!" The director jabbed his index finger at Balim. "Get this mess out of here. You were warned last time—"

"You are a human doctor. Where is your Hippocratic oath?"

The director's cheeks jiggled with exasperation. "Exactly! *Do no harm.* We don't know your drug resistance.

Your allergies. Your pathogens. We could hook up a saline drip and kill you."

"Kill an ocean-born merman with salt water? No. You will kill no one."

"That's just an example. How will you stop us?"

"By monitoring the strength of Warrior Pelan's soul light."

The director coughed so hard, he spat into a tissue. "This is the crazy I mean! We don't know the physiology of mermen."

"Warrior Pelan has shifted to human form."

"Shifted? That's another crazy—"

"Your delay endangers Warrior Pelan. His soul light dims. Do you want a dead mer in your emergency room?"

"I don't want a dead mer anywhere on my property!"

"Then assist."

The director gripped his white hair. "Get out!"

"A small metal slug pierced his chest." Balim touched the bandages. "In time, Warrior Pelan's mer body will expel it, but the police must prosecute the shooter now. A human doctor has tools and experience to remove the metal slug. That is what we need."

"He could bleed out on the operating table!"

"He will not. But, acting on your concern from our last visit, I have amassed my warriors' injectable blood."

Balim gestured over his shoulder.

Hazel, the frazzled assistant at the MerMatch dating agency, who had driven with Balim to the hospital, lugged a large red ice chest through the emergency doors. Balim's head scientist, Mitch, steered the chest from behind.

Morning heat and spilled coffee drenched Hazel's white pantsuit. She dropped her handle, yanked her damp bangs off her forehead, and pulled out her phone. "Where do you guys want this?"

"Not in my hospital!"

"You want us to take it out?" Hazel jammed a hand on her hip and nailed the director with a raised eyebrow. "After we dragged it all the way in here?"

The director sputtered. "I will not let my hospital be targeted by your terrorists!"

That was the real reason for his complaint. He feared retaliation by the Sons of Hercules.

Mermen had just emerged from the oceans, and already, a human organization hunted them. How quickly history repeated itself.

Mer and humans had once lived in harmony. A thousand years ago, a mysterious Great Catastrophe had plunged the two races into war. The mer had fled underwater until their existence had faded into human fable. Mer females had died off, and so the remaining warriors had formed an ancient covenant with "sacred brides," women from isolated islands who promised to keep their secret and populate their undersea cities.

In the last generation, modernization and rising sea levels had emptied the sacred islands. The mer had faced extinction. And so, three years ago, rebel warriors had surfaced to claim modern brides.

The modern world had been shocked and not altogether welcoming.

Fish traps in Mexico, bombs at the Sea Festival in the Azores, and shooting Warrior Pelan in front of his bride on a crowded public street was the work of an anonymous anti-mer terrorist organization known as the Sons of Hercules.

The director feared retaliation. He was not the only one.

Hazel scoffed. "If you let Pelan die, then you're letting the terrorists win."

"And if this becomes a hospital for mermen, then I risk my staff and patients."

"How can you live with yourself? Pelan's going to die."

"He can do so somewhere else!"

"I am creating a hospital for mer," Balim finally admitted, breaking into the argument. "It will open soon. We need your hospital to save Warrior Pelan's life now."

"This is the last time." The director stepped out of the way and allowed Doctor Kowalski to wheel the gurney.

Balim bowed. "I understand."

"He can't stay. Dig out the slug and leave. I'll be watching you."

Balim followed the gurney out of the emergency room lobby.

A nurse pulled Pelan's female aside. Warrior Pelan's fingers slipped free. "Are you family?"

"No." She put that hand to her forehead, her gaze locked on the fading warrior. "He's my date. First date."

"Okay, you have to—"

Balim grabbed her elbow a second time, propelling her away from the nurse. "She stays with her mate."

"What? You can't—"

"She brightens his soul light."

"Hey! Sir—"

The director stopped her from chasing them. His furious gaze followed them to the bend of the hall.

"So." Doctor Kowalski cleared his throat. "What's your plan?"

"Remove the bullet."

Doctor Kowalski pushed into a big operating room. "And?"

"That is the plan."

Medical professionals converged on them, unfurling rubber-and-tissue armor. "And for pain management?"

"Yes, Pelan will manage his pain."

Hazel and Mitch lugged the ice chest after them. Hazel retreated, covering her eyes. Mitch suited up and set Balim's tools on his wheeled tray.

One medical professional withdrew a packet of blood. "This is matched?"

"Yes."

"Really? You have the facilities for that?"

"It is Pelan's own blood. If he cannot accept it, he has a larger problem than the metal slug."

They pierced Pelan's vein and hung the packet.

"For your warrior's pain management?" Doctor Kowalski repeated.

Pelan's bride eased into the papery armor while a professional covered her spiky dark hair and dark purple lips. Another clothed Balim in thin, papery garments, sprayed him with cold alcohol, and then pushed on squishy rubber hand coverings.

They cut off Pelan's long shorts and T-shirt, removed his shoes, then covered his exposed skin with a sheet. Pelan's bride lingered at his shoulder to hold hands.

"Warrior Pelan will manage his pain," Balim affirmed.

"No, to put him under." Doctor Kowalski clicked on a headlamp with nervous efficiency. "What can we use?"

"Under what?"

"To render him unconscious. I can't have him jumping around on the operating table."

"He will not jump. He will control himself."

"The paramedics said the bullet is next to his heart."

"Yes."

Doctor Kowalski exchanged worried glances with the other medical professionals on his team. "I nick a vein, and he could bleed out on the table."

"He will not twitch beside his bride."

The doctor shook his head as if something had broken in his brain. "And so you want me to open him up, dig out a bullet, and suture him closed with no pain management?"

"No."

He sagged in relief. "Good."

"You will not suture him closed. I will smear the wound with parasite-rebuffing salve and soak it in Sea Opal-infused elixir."

Doctor Kowalski choked.

Mitch wheeled the tray he'd arranged with two large jars of elixir, a woven seaweed bandage roll, Balim's best tool set, and an empty dish to the gurney. Balim tested the consistency of his salve, poured elixir into the dish, and dampened his seaweed bandages.

Doctor Kowalski prepared his own sterile metal tools. "Ready?"

Pelan sought the gaze of his female.

She stared at his bandaged chest in trepidation.

Balim reached across the humans, surprising them, and gripped her chin through the paper. He oriented her gaze at Pelan. "You are his anchor. Do not look away."

She swallowed and focused.

Pelan's soul lightened with peace.

Doctor Kowalski shook his head. "Now, ready?"

"Yes, now."

Doctor Kowalski pulled away the bandage. His assistants held a hose and towels to the wound.

No blood spurted.

"Hmm." He probed the wound with metal pincers.

"You got lucky. Bullet to the chest and it didn't hit an artery."

The doctor's view projected onto a television screen above him. Mitch and the doctor's assistants watched the screen.

Balim riveted his attention on Pelan's chest where his soul glowed.

Pelan held the gaze of his bride, silently communing with her. The pain must be excruciating. But their souls resonated. He could endure anything now he had found his soul mate.

Balim had seen this life-saving endurance several times. First when his king, Kadir, had been stabbed through the heart by needlefish protecting his human bride, Queen Elyssa, while exhuming the wreck of ancient Atlantis. The second time, Queen Elyssa had resuscitated King Kadir from death itself.

Warrior Pelan's injury was severe. But he would survive.

Balim would never know such endurance.

"There's the bullet." The doctor pushed the surrounding skin. "I still can't believe your luck. It's taken a bite out of the aorta, and yet you're still..."

Blood seeped around the metal plug.

"Oh. Ah." His voice lowered and flattened as his fluctuating human soul darkened. He hid stress in soothing tones. "Mmm. Hmm. Prep suction."

Balim poured elixir into the injury.

Doctor Kowalski jumped back in surprise. "What are you—!"

"Elixir. Infused with Sea Opals."

The doctor put his gloved hand on the suction hose to stop it from sucking up the elixir. "That's elixir?" He peered at it. "I thought it was shiny."

"It is shiny. To mer."

Doctor Kowalski gaped under the mask. "I always wanted to see it…"

"Pelan is ready to proceed."

He snapped back to professionalism and repositioned his tools. "Warn me next time. I can't manage bleeding when you're… Hmm."

The blood had dissipated.

"I will apply more elixir," Balim warned him.

"Yes. Proceeding on." His metal tool pinched the slug.

Blood ringed the metal again.

Pelan paled.

Balim filled the wound, washing the blood and elixir into Pelan's body, sealing and healing as they worked. Doctor Kowalski rocked the slug, testing whether it was loose enough to remove.

Pelan's littlest toe twitched.

Balim stopped the doctor and addressed the bride. "Kiss him."

She dropped her mouth to Pelan's. Their lips meshed. This was not their first kiss, but it was the most heartfelt. Her soul flared bright as a sun, and Pelan's soul brightened, strengthened by her strength.

"Go," Balim ordered the doctor.

Doctor Kowalski removed the slug. Blood filled the wound and spilled across Pelan's pectoral, marring his black and red tattoos.

"Suction," Balim ordered.

The assistant jammed the slender wand into Pelan's wound. Blood spurted out, regular as a heartbeat.

Pelan tensed.

Curse it.

Balim pushed the tube away and smeared his salve into the spurting hole, then packed seaweed into the cavity. "Pour elixir."

Doctor Kowalski grabbed the jar and spilled it on Pelan's chest.

Balim sighed. "Do you have replacement elixir?"

"No."

"Me neither. Steady yourself, Doctor."

The doctor let out a long, tense breath and poured more smoothly. The spurting stopped.

Balim's shoulders ached. Tension strained his muscles, frustration gnawed on his patience, and he itched. Pelan stabilized, the doctor had collected the metal slug evidence for the police to arrest their suspect, and he would return to training scientists to see a trait they could not sense.

But something was wrong.

Was he due elsewhere? Who needed him more than Pelan?

He smeared more salve and packed the wound with seaweed. "Now, you may apply a human bandage on Pelan until we reach the tank."

"Tank?" the doctor repeated. Blood smeared his face mask, his glasses, and his paper armor.

"Aquarium tank." Balim removed his paper armor. Mitch packed his tools and called Hazel. "He will heal quickly shifted into a mer."

Doctor Kowalski glanced at the couple still kissing. "Should they stop?"

"Do not interrupt their resonance. It keeps Pelan alive."

"Mind over matter." Doctor Kowalski swirled the elixir and lifted it to the light. "This is a miracle. A true, chemical miracle."

His cheerful assistants agreed. The mood lightened from how easily they had rescued this warrior.

Balim found it irritating.

"No miracle," Balim refuted. "The elixir of concentrated Sea Opals is activated by resonance. Resonance is a wave, like sound or electricity, produced by souls."

"Electricity and sound are pretty miraculous."

"Not according to your 'electricians' or 'sound operators.'" He and Mitch sealed the cooler. "Resonance is a tool for healing. Anyone can understand and control it."

"That's great. I wish all our patients controlled their bleeding with a thought."

"Yes, the mer possess superior control. We are not distracted by any—"

A powerful wave of knowing crashed over him. *Resonance.* He gritted his teeth, trying to assert control, but the force was so strong, it was like holding on to a twig in a tsunami. His very soul shivered.

She was here.

Balim turned on his heel.

"Healer Balim?" Doctor Kowalski held the jar. "Would you mind if I kept this?"

"No."

Someone passed the operating theater. A flash of red hair captivated his eye. His chest throbbed with heat. Recognition. Knowing.

The doctor continued as if he hadn't answered. "I wanted to test it on myself. See if it even works."

"It will work." He pushed through the doors. "You have a bright soul."

"Healer Balim? Hey—" The doors shut.

Where was she?

There. At the busy corridor. Her chest glowed like the final blast from a dying star.

She turned.

He jogged down the smooth linoleum, his skin jumping, and made the same turn.

A thick crowd of people separated them. She stepped into an elevator. Her gaze focused on her cell phone.

This was his first time seeing her so close. He drank in every detail.

Lush curves. Silky red hair he wanted to grip in his fist. A plump red mouth capable of great pleasure. And a plentiful smattering of dark marks humans called freckles patterning her skin in a delicate tattoo.

She is my mate.

Her soul burned in her chest. Sharp, bright, and yet tragic.

She was powerful.

His soul mate spoke to the person pressing buttons. The doors began to close.

He must force his way to her attention.

She turned, and her gaze flitted across the crowd. Touched on the person behind him. The person beside him. And then onto—

The elevator closed.

He shoved through the last step and pressed his fingers against the warm metal.

Without her brilliant light, cold seeped into his chest.

He closed his eyes and rested his forehead against the metal.

His heart beat faster and faster. Hunger straightened his spine, stabbing him with needles of frustration. His muscles tightened.

Control. He was a warlord of Atlantis. A healer. A male

who stormed battlefields seeking the injured without flinching.

The points of his human body fought. Mer fins. Stretchy skin between his fingers. Shudder of gills in his lower back.

Resonance was a wavelength. It could be controlled.

He held his breath.

She refused these feelings. She did not resonate with him. Her soul did not resonate at all.

Because he did not deserve her.

Everyone thought he was so honorable because he was a healer. He had fooled King Kadir. The warriors of Atlantis. All these humans.

No one could see the black fracture lines of his past. He was no more honorable than the terrorists who'd shot Pelan through the heart. He was, in fact, worse.

He did not deserve a bride.

"Balim!" Hazel's voice grew louder. "Balim. For the last time. Where are you going? The director's throwing us out. We have to move ASAP."

He lifted his head. "Yes, Hazel."

"Yes, Hazel? Did you just agree with me?" She tilted her head. "Are you feeling okay?"

He let out a long sigh between clenched teeth. "Is my health not obvious?"

"Mmm. Now that you mention it, you're looking a little paler than usual. Around the tattoos, I mean."

He'd been within touching distance. His mate was somewhere in the hospital. His soul recognized their connection and reached out with all its power. Offering his emotionless self to her.

I can control this.

Ordinary warriors met their soul mates. Ordinary

warriors bonded for life. Ordinary warriors were swept away by emotion.

Balim was not ordinary.

Nor, some would allege, was he a warrior.

He tightened on that pain and faced Hazel with calm. "The human lights reflect my tattoo color. Not illness."

"If you're sure." She operated her phone using both thumbs, stabbing at the screen with single-minded efficiency. "Because it looked like you were chasing Bella."

"Bella?"

"The redhead. The one you followed around the corner. I wonder who she's visiting?"

His heart thunked.

Bella. She had a name.

"You know Bella?"

"Not personally. She designed our website. You know, for MerMatch."

"Designed our website..." he repeated.

"And she prepared all the warriors for interviews and media appearances. Don't you remember? She must have met with you."

He shook his head firmly.

"No? Huh. Sometimes she justs drops by. She's actually been around a lot, I think."

"I have never seen her."

"Dannika's always meeting her. Or, they *were* always meeting. I manage the office calendar, Balim, so I know."

Dannika. The manager of MerMatch, the dating agency that united mer warriors with their soul-mate brides.

Balim continued to shake his head. He had never seen his soul mate's face or body. Not her skin nor her hair. Nothing physical until today. And Hazel insisted this Bella journeyed to MerMatch—and therefore could have met Balim—frequently? Impossible.

Hazel pursed her lips. "Mm, now that you mention it, Bella came around the office almost daily a few months ago, but then her visits stopped. Her work on the website must have finished before you surfaced. Oh, and she did spend the majority of her time prepping Faier for interviews because she said he had the most presence."

Faier. The quiet, heroic, scarred warrior who had gone missing just after Balim had surfaced. Faier had met Bella and Balim had not?

Hazel spoke to her screen. "Oops. We've got to go. Pelan's at the front getting loaded into the ambulance. The director's threatening to call the cops. And Dannika wants to see us as soon as we're done."

Dannika knew Balim's female, Bella. Dannika knew everyone.

The intensity of his compulsion to chase Bella lessened. Balim stepped back from the elevators. He would master this craving. "Then why are we waiting here?"

Hazel rolled her eyes. "Let's go."

Balim forced himself to walk away.

Dannika would find her. They should have met many times already yet they had not. Clearly the female felt no stirring in his presence, but still, Balim would offer himself.

No matter the consequences.

A week later, shortly before midnight outside the nonemergency entrance at the same hospital, Bella Taylor poisoned her body with cheesy chips, faux apple pie, and canned coffee.

No strange compulsion forced her to descend the steps, circumnavigate the hospital, and sneak into the emergency entrance.

Not like last weekend.

She gulped the sugary coffee and tossed the can.

Why that uncontrollable urge? The need had driven her like a tornado siren or the impending doom of an earthquake.

If you go to the emergency entrance, you will find your salvation.

She'd made a hundred bargains with God in the last year, and so far, He hadn't taken any offers. This inexplicable urge had been her only possibility. And yet it had faded as soon as she'd gotten into the elevators last weekend. Now it was gone.

She lingered for a few more minutes in the chill of the

early fall evening, but the only insistent urge was the blinking of her phone messages.

Work. Chaz. Debt.

God didn't leave phone messages, so she wasn't too excited.

Bella crumpled her junk food bags into the trash, climbed the dark hospital steps, and rode the elevators to the children's wing. The metallic aftertaste of the fake food grimed her tongue and hunger remained unsated, but she didn't have time to buy real meals. And the chips were so addictive. That cheese substance ought to come with a Surgeon General's warning.

"Bella!"

Tonight's floor nurse was a grandmotherly angel who clasped Bella's cold hands with familiarity. "He's been waiting for you all day. How are you doing, hon?"

"Better now. You've been such a support in this difficult time."

The sweet nurse pshawed her. "I do what I can."

"I appreciate it." Bella watched the nurse's smile widen. She needed to be the favorite visitor so everyone would love her patient. "How's Jonah?"

"No big changes." She patted Bella's hands and then passed over the visitor sheet. "He still hasn't opened his present."

"I'll hurry in. Thanks so much."

"You bet, hon."

Bella signed in and entered the familiar women's locker room, stowed her crumpled work suit in her locker, showered, and ripped off the tags of today's "hospital outfit": a new, unworn blouse and slacks torn straight from the plastic.

Jonah's room was the last plastic bubble on the floor.

Her heart grew heavy and her palms sweated as she made the nightly walk.

Her purification routine was more extreme than other visitors', but she didn't trust the air of the New York subway system; the germs, like the rats, were vicious survivors.

At Jonah's plastic-covered doorway, she dumped an entire container of alcohol sanitizer into her hands and smeared it over every exposed bit of skin. She doused her cell phone and crammed it, still damp, into a Ziploc bag. Then, she unzipped the door.

A fan blew the air of the room outward, cleansing her in a cool wind.

Inside the aperture, the yellow visitor gown hid her body in a hospital burqa with headscarf and veil. She selected an envelope off the shelf and tore open the paper, unearthing her specially fitted face mask and plastic gloves. Bella tugged them on and checked for stray hairs in the mirror.

She looked like a scuba diver. Plastic covered almost every inch of her body. A bit of speckled skin showed around her eyes.

Now she was sterile. She hoped.

Bella zipped up the external door, opened the second, interior plastic door, and entered her son's room.

It was dark. The TV displayed monotonous, flickering cartoons; the volume was too low to hear over the fans.

Jonah's lumpy shape shadowed the flat, hard bed.

She moved his stuffed bear out of the hard plastic seat next to his bed and let herself sink.

His eyelids twitched. He didn't awaken.

Fans muffled the sounds of the room like ocean waves crashing against implacable cliffs.

On the table, nurses had left his birthday card, a

drawing of a cake with ten candles, and the Nintendo Switch she'd bought weeks ago to sterilize it.

The present was still neatly wrapped. He'd waited for her.

A hard lump formed in Bella's throat.

She'd always made Jonah wait. Just one more client, just one more project, just one more marketing campaign.

Just one more email. Then they'd go to the park. Just one more phone call. Then they'd go out to dinner. Just one more workday scrambling to pay bills and keep the medical insurance while they waited for a miraculous cure. Then he could open his birthday present.

The sun had gone down, the restaurant had closed, and Jonah's birthday present was unopened. He had always waited.

Bella tilted back in the chair and rested her head against the hard wall. But there was no rest for the wicked. She pressed her phone to her ear.

First message. Work? Debt? Chaz?

"Bella, your latest brand redesign proposal has notes."

Work.

"The company likes how you glossed over the wars they started, pollution charges, extortion scandal, and child slavery allegations. 'Progress: It's A Process' is a good campaign slogan for them." Her boss's voice dipped into the tone where she knew she was asking for something unreasonable and she still expected Bella to comply. "They complained that you didn't play up a 'clean energy' angle. They once bought a wind farm."

And dismantled it.

"And dismantled it," her boss conceded, reading her mind on the voice message, "but they still want 'clean energy' in the television spot. Can you stay late tonight?...

Looks like I missed you. Come in early tomorrow. If we pull all-nighters all week, we should finish by the deadline."

Bella pulled the phone away from her ear to check the time. Tomorrow was a Saturday.

"Don't make me give away another client. Your portfolio's slim. The sick kid isn't forever, okay? Your career is your future. Call me when you get this."

Bella did *not* call her boss and listened to the next message.

"This is the Collections Agency calling again about your outstanding medical bills at—"

Skip.

"Bella, you won't believe this. The company just got nailed for bribing congressmen. It's on the late night news. We have to switch out half the images. On the plus side, there's more room for 'clean energy.' Call me."

She reviewed the client proposal on her tiny phone screen while the next message played. Softly, so it couldn't project over the fans.

"Hi, Bella, this is Dannika from MerMatch, trying to schedule a meeting with our handsome, eligible marine warrior, Balim."

The strange compulsion returned. *This is your salvation.* Certainty filled her veins. Hairs on the back of her neck lifted and goose bumps tingled down her arms. Her heart thudded, hard, and awareness tugged her nipples into hard peaks against her braless new blouse.

"I think Balim is the only one you haven't met! Ironic, isn't it? After the hours you've spent with us, it's so funny how life works out. Balim is eager to meet you, and I just know you'll be great together."

Bella paused the messages.

The tattooed warriors were hot. She'd never met Balim,

but cozying up to Faier, Ciran, and Pelan between coaching sessions hadn't pained her.

Sadly, their elixir hadn't cured Jonah. But while she'd been trading skills and wooing it away from the mermen, she'd learned the ripped, honest, powerful males' future brides would be well-satiated ladies.

She could be one of them...

Balim. What kind of a warrior was Balim? Bossy like serious Ciran, awkwardly hopeful like Pelan, steady and powerful like scarred Faier? Or any of the other warriors she'd worked with all those weeks ago?

He could hold her in his bulging biceps, lay her across a rose-petal-strewn bench, press one muscular thigh between her legs. Give her nights of pleasure while he wooed her to drink that same elixir, gain the powers to shift into a mermaid, and travel to the sunken mer city of Atlantis.

And as a mermaid, she'd keep her figure. The half-fish thing was a fable. Only her toes would extend into fins. The warriors were human-shaped from the tops of their dominant heads to the heels of their feet—and indisputably male.

She could be his queen.

The fantasy deepened as she imagined tracing this mysterious Balim's tattoos with her tongue. He would sweep her away from this life, and they would escape together into the deep blue—

Jonah jutted a bony, pajama-clad leg out of the sheet and sighed.

Bella ran a soothing, glove-clad index finger along Jonah's leg to let him know she was here. He didn't react.

His pajama flannel must be soft. The plastic gloves blocked all sensation.

Bella tugged the thin hospital blanket over Jonah's exposed leg and tucked it in, smoothing the fabric.

Then she erased Dannika's message and the merman fantasies that accompanied it. She would not be happy for one moment until Jonah was healthy. *Hear that, God? Not a single moment.*

She listened to the next message.

"Bel— Guess you only call when you want something."

Acid tainted with powdered cheese burned the back of her throat.

Her ex-husband, Chaz, dripped scorn with self-righteous indignation. "You can't demand my bone marrow just because you never asked for alimony or child support. The answer is no, and you can go to hell for asking. Do you know how big that needle is? It looks painful. Don't call me again."

Bella stopped the messages, clenched her phone, and swallowed.

Chaz thought the procedure *looked* painful?

Did he understand how many times Jonah had been *through* it?

How dare Chaz—

Jonah moaned and opened his eyes.

She composed herself and put on a soft, welcoming smile. "Hey, Jo-jo."

He fixed on her. In the jittery TV light, bruised rings and hollow, sunken cheekbones looked like a skull. His dry, cracked lips tugged into the ghost of a smile. "Mom."

"Happy birthday." She put on her best enthusiastic voice. "Did the nurses remember? They promised to sing."

He nodded slowly. Every movement took a heavy effort.

"I asked them to blend up your birthday cake and put it in the IV. Can you taste it?"

His light-colored brows drew together, and he frowned at the clear dangling bag of liquid. Didn't he remember this was their joke? She used to joke all the time about injecting his favorite snacks and meals into the IV when he couldn't keep anything down. His illness was making his brain fuzzy.

Her throat closed and her chin wrinkled.

She rubbed her chin and made her voice extra bright to disguise her feelings. "Can you just taste the cake? It's Funfetti, your favorite."

His brow smoothed, and he tried to smile again. He remembered. "Yeah."

Even when he was feeling so bad that he probably had forgotten what birthday cake tasted like, he humored her to make *her* feel better.

She cleared her throat. "This is a pretty sucky birthday, huh?"

He nodded with more feeling.

"Where do you want to go next year? We could have a huge party with all your friends, and we could go to Ninja Warrior House or Luna Park or even, you know, Disney World..."

He thought about all his options and then said, "Home."

Her throat closed again. She cleared it once more. "Next year for your birthday, you just want to go home?"

He nodded.

She gently rested her hand on his blanket-covered leg, nodding because she couldn't trust her voice. "Okay. That'll be...that'll be great for us. It will be so much fun. We'll have a big party, dress up in our best, have your favorite lasagna and salmon rolls and daal, and play games at home."

He smiled tiredly. His eyelids drooped half-closed. Her window of time with him was closing.

"Right." Bella pulled herself together, turned to the

bedside table, and picked up the unwrapped present. "Did you want to open your..."

His eyes had closed.

While she'd been looking away, he'd gone back to sleep.

Bella rested the present on her lap, crinkling the paper, and then returned it to the table.

Jonah used to sneak in late at night while she was working, and she'd pretend she didn't see him. He'd fall asleep at the end of her desk, snoring softly, until she finished her work and carried him back to his bed.

She should have noticed he was sick. She should have protected him.

Hadn't she been selfish long enough?

A wave of sadness crushed her in its fist. She closed her eyes.

She'd been so scared he'd never reach his tenth birthday. And here they were.

Will he reach his eleventh birthday?

She choked on the stabbing pain. This could not be endured. She could not endure.

The clock beeped. Midnight.

Her boss wanted her to come in early on a Saturday to redesign the client proposal to redeem a company she very much doubted *could* be redeemed, but her job was to do the impossible. Advertisers controlled the narrative. The company wanted to tell its lies. In her hands, a lie would become "truth."

So Jonah could keep his health insurance. So they could search for a new cure. So he could stay alive.

She rested both hands on his bedside. Silent prayers raced through her head.

I will save you. I don't know how. But I will bend heaven and earth to find a cure. I will not enjoy one single moment of happiness until you're healthy and well once again.

And if God won't answer, I'll chase down the devil.

Jonah slept, his chest rising and falling.

Bella rose and whispered, "Good night." She did not kiss his cheek before she left, not even through the plastic.

Her kiss could be poison.

Outside his plastic-encased room, she peeled off her gown. Gloves and mask went in the trash, gown and fabrics went in the linen bin for sterilization. She stormed down the hall to her locker, changed, and dropped the used outfit into the donation bin on her way out the door.

A deep breath of dark fall air emptied her lungs of the hospital stench. She checked the subway schedule. Should she go into work now and start the redesign?

An unknown number rang.

She swiped her schedule and accidentally answered the call.

"Bella Taylor." A weirdly feminine, possibly distorted voice spoke through phone interference. "You have been selected for a one-on-one date with the merman Balim."

God, dating sites were aggressive these days.

She ran a hand through her limp red hair. "Yes, thanks so much. Tell Dannika I need to cancel."

"You can't cancel."

"Oh, I'm so sorry. Now's not a good time."

"But don't you know the mermen have drugs that could cure your son?"

What?

Her brain pinged, and the pebble dropped.

No dating site would call her after midnight on a weekend.

She pulled the phone away and double-checked her recording app. Yes, it was recording.

Bella put the phone back to her ear and donned her client voice. "May I have the pleasure of asking who this is and how you know about that?"

"I know a lot about you," the distorted voice replied, smug. "As for you, you can call me 'Herc.'"

"Okay, Herc." Bella paced. Working closely with the mermen had taught her a few things. Including their enemies. "It's thrilling to meet you. Your name wouldn't be short for 'Sons of Hercules,' would it?"

"Well..."

"You're famous. If it weren't for you taking a stand against mermen despite your busy finals, the world would be a very different place." She gave a pause that she hoped would let him bask in her almost-compliment. "And you're so dedicated. Inventive. Really ingenious. I doubt anyone knows I got selected for that one-on-one with Balim...unless the employees have been talking?"

"Oh, they've been talking, all right. They don't know I've been listening."

How very helpful.

"And I should go on this date to get their medicine," she continued, using her favorite strategy to pull information out of a client. "But I heard they don't have it to give out."

"They have tons. A whole aquarium full in their plague-infested 'hospital' building."

"Ew, I can't give my son used aquarium water."

"No, no. They have more in vats. They make it all the time."

"Well, I'm so impressed you know these secrets, Herc. Nobody can get into the mermen's hospital building. It must have been so hard."

"It was easy until they moved. But we'll get in again. We have to drive the monsters back to the ocean trenches before they steal our women."

"Wow. You're so set up. Why are you calling me?"

"Of course, you can't imagine," the distorted voice continued, smug. "Because I haven't told you."

"That's true."

She let the silence elongate, testing his ability to withstand subtle negotiation pressure.

"So I'll tell you." He raced to fill her silence. "The mermen are keeping a flower from their underwater Life Tree in an aquarium behind their reception desk. You're going to steal it."

She coughed. "You want me to walk into the merman office alone and steal the only Life Tree blossom on the surface of the planet? Okay. What's your plan?"

"You'll figure it out."

So, he had no plan.

"And why would I accept this extremely dangerous task?" she asked pleasantly.

"Because you're not helping your son, Jonah, by pacing on those steps. Especially if you slip on those slimy leaves and break your neck."

She halted, the tips of her boots on the edge of the pile of autumn leaves. Her heart beat hard in her throat.

Few people walked on the street, heads down, occupied. Even at midnight, visitors climbed the steps of the hospital or rushed into the emergency room.

"Now I have your attention, call the monster office back and accept the date. You will wear our necklace, and—"

"Your necklace? I'm sorry. You're giving me a necklace?"

"Yeah, so when the monster's back is turned, you stick the flower inside the necklace to steal it."

She envisioned some kind of water-filled locket. Not exactly subtle. "Hmm."

"And if you tell anyone about this, you will be sorry."

"Sorry? I'll be sorry?"

"You'll be very sorry."

Right.

An off-duty police officer she recognized exited the hospital. Bella flew down the steps and hiked to the subway station a few strides behind the officer. "What if the necklace doesn't match my dress?"

"You're not taking me seriously."

"Oh, no. I'm taking a threat against my life very seriously. I would hate to have to give the recording of this call to the very nice officer I'm following to the subway station."

"Recording?"

"New York being a one-party consent state, I record my business calls, and I can't possibly do business with someone who made me fear for my life. But I'm sure the implied threat was a misunderstanding...?"

"...Yeah. It was a misunderstanding."

"Oh, good. I want to help you, Herc, I really do, but I prefer honey over vinegar. If you'll forward me just a small token of your regret, I'm sure I can put this awkward misunderstanding behind us."

"What small token?"

"Say..." Bella calculated. The instant she found herself operating above the law, one person came to mind. Her half sister, Starr, had contacts all over the security industry, and a wire transfer had to be something she could trace. "Five thousand dollars."

"Five thousand!"

"I'm a highly paid executive, and I have a lot of medical bills. The five minutes you made me worry about my life is worth at least that much."

"What makes you think we have five thousand dollars?"

"Did you really expect me to risk my life for free?"

"But...I'm not authorized..."

"How sad. Even my community college debate team had over five grand kicking around in our student activities account."

A long silence answered her demand.

"Herc?" she prompted. "Are you listening?"

The line was dead.

Bella hung up and rotated the phone as her recording saved into the cloud.

This domestic terrorist was inexperienced. She'd flipped on him so fast, he'd reeled.

Bargain with the devil...

The offices of MerMatch had a security leak.

Bella would plug it.

She was sick and tired of life's blows. Jonah's flat-lined status reports. Watching the mer warriors experience cruelty and violence on the news. Planning redemption campaigns for companies that had no intention of redeeming themselves.

Ooh, she hoped the idiots would call back. What would she make them do?

Transfer money to an investigation account. Incriminate themselves in a thousand traceable ways. Scramble when she rolled over the rock and exposed their wriggling, black souls to the court of public—and legal—opinions.

She had no choice but to wait for Jonah's match on the bone marrow registry. No real choice about her work clients. But unmasking the antisocial college students who'd perpetuated hate-filled acts of violence? Oh, she'd manipulate her busy schedule of schmoozing, lying, and grieving to fit that right in.

Her phone rang. A new number.

Oh, goodness.

She took a deep breath, blew out her nervous excitement, and answered. "Are you ready to pay?"

"Our funds are liquid, but I'm less convinced of your motivations." The strange not-female, distorted voice tsked at her. "You're energetic for a grieving mother, Bella Taylor."

Although the distortion was the same, the way of speaking sounded brusquer. Businesslike. She was dealing with an experienced negotiator.

"My motivations are simple." Bella grinned into the streetlight. "To be honest, I could really use the money."

"I trust no one who begins a sentence with 'to be honest.'"

"Who do you trust?"

"Hmm."

"Skepticism is a strength in your profession, but so is risk-taking. You'd be a fool to ignore this opportunity." She splayed her hand across her chest. "Herc, when it comes to opening up a box of trouble for the mermen, I'm your personal Pandora."

"Your face launched a thousand ships?"

"Absolutely," she said, although he was obviously confusing Pandora with Helen of Troy. A compliment, even if it was a mistaken one. "Now, tell me about the floral heist."

THREE

A week later, Balim received the most incredible news. "Bella has agreed to meet at the office building for your date tonight."

Dannika announced Balim's future via speakerphone. He needed his hands free to wave in the delivery truck.

"You already know what she looks like, but I'm sending you her picture."

He looked away from the backing-up delivery truck to glance at the photo.

Silken red hair. Seductive curves. A plump, red mouth. Intricate freckles.

It was *her*.

His heart stuttered and stopped a second time. The band that always constrained him tightened to the breaking point. His hand jerked up.

The delivery truck stopped with a hiss, and the engine died.

Balim held the cell phone screen so close the picture blurred. "She agreed?"

"Of course she did." Dannika's voice sounded tinny.

"Bella's a great friend to the mer. Besides designing our website, she was a regular visitor at MerMatch before you surfaced. She coached everyone for media appearances. Mostly, she coached Faier."

Just as Hazel had said. Faier had disappeared during a routine Coast Guard mission weeks ago. He had leaped into the ocean to rescue a female and been sucked into a storm.

Again, surprise struck Balim. Faier had met *her*. Bella Taylor. And he had complained of never finding a bride?

The driver opened the truck and wheeled a stack of boxes down a ramp. "Where do you want these?"

"Over here." Balim showed him the storage room.

The driver shook loose the stack and returned to the truck for more.

Balim opened the lid of the top box. Thick plastic covered the Sea Opals, but he could still hear tinkling chimes deep within.

Van Cartier Cosmetics had purchased multiple Sea Opals to create skin-care products that made resonant users miraculously young. Then, they had tried to take more Sea Opals by force.

Queen Aya had ended their reign of terror, dismantled the company, and retrieved their old scientific materials.

He carried the box of Sea Opals into the room they'd repurposed into Mitch's laboratory.

Dannika prompted him. "Balim? Finish up and meet us at the office so we can prep for our date."

He found his voice. "I do not need to 'prep.'"

"We do. Hazel's making a food run right now, and I need to secure the rooftop garden. After the attack on Pelan, we don't want to take any chances."

Balim agreed to her request and ended the conversation.

The delivery driver held out a pen and a clipboard. "That's everything. Sign here."

Balim crossed an X on the paper. "You have eye strain. Would you like a cool washcloth?"

"You got me. I stayed up for Ninja Mud Warriors." He grinned and elbowed Balim. "You don't have any of that miracle drink, do you?"

The driver's chest barely glowed.

Balim shook his head. "Elixir will not help."

"Ah, well. Only ten more deliveries. I'll grab a coffee when I gas up." He carried away his clipboard and reentered his van.

Some humans had dark souls because they were angry, sick, or dangerous.

This driver was not angry, sick, or dangerous. He was a fine human who simply had no resonance with the sea.

Balim closed the delivery door, passed by the conference rooms where he tried to explain this concept to visiting scientists every day, and again through the lab.

Mitch pored over the old Sea Opal research.

"Look at this." He lifted a paper marked with human writing squiggles. "*How to See Shiny Sea Opals* by Best Friends and Cousins Elyssa and Aya. How cute." He set the paper aside and reached back into the box. "Even as kids, they were doing great things for mermen."

Yes, long before mermen surfaced, the future queens of Atlantis had championed Sea Opals.

"Whoa." Mitch pulled out a heavy rock encased in paper and bubble wrap. He clunked it on the desk. "Heavy."

This was not a Sea Opal. It made a strange mechanical ticking noise like a human clock.

Balim continued through the lab to the main hospital recovery room.

In the center, a steel frame enclosed a giant glass aquarium with bubbling aerator and heat lamp. Mitch had taught him about aquariums, both saltwater and fresh. A ladder was affixed to the side.

Although most mer lived in the oceans, they did not suffer from freshwater, and it was easiest to get. Balim used it in the large pressure cooker machines in the next room. With Sea Opals lining the bottom, he simulated steeping the gemstones for centuries to create the elixir in huge batches and then dispensed it into this tank. He'd created a surface rehabilitation chamber for mermen.

Pelan was his first test case. The black-and-red warrior floated in the center, sleeping. Alone.

Normally, his bride entwined with him. She had partially transformed the first time she'd entered the water and spent the week trying to heal him using her resonance as his bride. Floating as a mermaid with gills in her back, she had dangled her still-human toes between his mer fins. But not now.

Now, the hospital coordinator, Roxanne, rested her fingertips on the glass.

Balim stopped in the doorway. "Where is Pelan's bride?"

"Hmm?" Roxanne's long, crinkly brown hair stuck up in wild abandon, her glasses nestled on her worried face, and her clothes were disheveled from spending all day pricing, negotiating, and coordinating the delivery of essential equipment to set up the hospital. "Oh, I think she said she was going to take a smoke break. Not that she smokes, but she needed personal time, so I said it was no problem."

Whenever Pelan's bride left, she endangered Pelan's healing. "She—"

"Don't worry. I do know that he mustn't be left alone, and yet sometimes a woman needs her personal time. Nora's been a champion. I can't imagine what she must be going through. Meanwhile, I get to go home at night, even though it's so hard to concentrate, and I don't do well here either. Something's wrong with me."

She rubbed her chest.

Pelan's soul glowed brighter as well. He resonated with the Sea Opal delivery? Balim's protest evaporated.

Roxanne glanced at him, and guilt flashed across her features. "I'm not letting it interrupt my work. I'm still concentrating on tasks. If you must know, I'm waiting on a call back from Singapore on an MRI machine."

He inserted his question. "We need this MRI?"

"Since we can't send warriors to a better-equipped hospital, I'm afraid we do. And technicians to operate it. This isn't an immediate purchase. I'm still compiling research for the doctors we hire to know their options." She rolled her lips, worry tugging at her usually cheerful features. "Pelan will be okay, won't he?"

"Yes." Balim stood beside her. "He is improving every day."

His tank had accomplished much. Pelan's two separate mer legs bent at the knees, his long fins unfurled and waving.

Roxanne touched her lips with her other fingers. "Oh, I hope you don't think I'm staring at him because he's naked. He is great-looking, I'm not going to lie, but I'm not only looking there, so please don't you tell him I did that. I'm just being present. Like a canary in a coal mine. You know. If anything goes wrong with him, I'll scream."

Balim could have that healing with Bella. Closeness. Connection. Resonance.

He shook himself. "Good."

Mitch entered the room, hefting the ticking rock. "Hey, Balim. What do you suppose this is?"

"A human clock or other mechanical device."

"It looks like a mineral, but it's not on the inventory sheet."

"It is human made," Balim insisted.

"Why do you say that?"

"The ticking."

"Ticking?"

Mitch held it up to his ear and shook it. The rock rattled. "I hear nothing. Oh, wait. There's a piece of tape. I suppose you could be—"

Roxanne's voice dropped. "Put it outside and call the police."

Mitch looked up. "The police?"

She spread her arms across the tank to shield Pelan with her body. "An unidentified ticking object not on the inventory? The Sons of Hercules are trying to kill Pelan again. Put it outside, far away, and call the police."

Mitch looked as flummoxed as Balim felt, but he shrugged and meandered out of the large room.

As he passed Balim to enter the back hall, the ticking stopped.

"Roxanne, what does it mean when the ticking stops?" Balim asked her.

She paled and shrieked. "Mitch! It's going to blow!"

"What?" His voice echoed around the corner.

"Throw it! Now!"

Mitch's running footsteps echoed down the hall.

Balim ducked into his office and looked into the parking lot.

Pelan's bride jumped up from his office chair. She wore a white hotel bathrobe and clenched her phone in both hands. She had been typing onto it.

"Oh! Balim, you startled me. I was just taking a quick break, I swear—"

"Yes, Roxanne told me." He held up his hand to quiet her.

Mitch shoved open the outer door, lobbed the not-ticking rock across the parking lot, and yanked the thick emergency door closed again.

The rock landed on the concrete with a loud thunk.

She let out her fright in a long sigh. "Look. I know you want me to spend every hour with Pelan. And don't get me wrong, I do appreciate catching up on my sleep. But I'm getting so bored, and I don't think a break is too much once in a while."

He ignored her. The rock was just sitting there. Perhaps they were mistaken.

"Hey, will you listen when I'm—"

Boom!

The ground beneath his loafer-clad feet jumped.

Pebbles spattered his office window, cracking the glass. He ducked. Pelan's bride shrieked and huddled under the desk.

In the main room behind him, water sloshed out of Pelan's tank and slapped the floor.

"What was that?" Pelan's bride demanded, shaky. "Are we under attack?"

He stood again.

In the parking lot, a large chunk of concrete was missing. A new hole sizzled. Mitch creaked open the external door and stared at the hole in shock.

"Yes." Balim strode to check on Pelan. "We are."

The warrior was still sleeping.

Roxanne hugged the tank. "We need to quarantine the rest of that shipment. Quarantine it until the police can send in the bomb squad. Call 911."

"On it." Mitch held his phone to his ear. He rubbed his head. Although he looked okay, he was shaken. "Operator? I need to report a small bomb that destroyed a chunk of our parking lot."

"Bomb!" Pelan's bride squeaked and hurried after Balim as he next checked the pressurized tanks. "I thought you said this place was safe!"

The tanks remained pressurized. No flaws or weaknesses. Good.

"We bought this property unlisted," Roxanne said.

"We need a gate. Wait, we have a gate. Who let him in?"

"I did," Balim said.

Pelan's bride covered her mouth as though to stop herself from saying any more. But fear pinched her word. "Why?"

"Because I did not expect a bomb in this delivery."

"To be fair, it might not have been the driver's fault," Roxanne piped up. "We spoke on the phone, and he seemed nice enough, if a bit tired. The police will undertake that investigation."

Pop.

A crack crossed the glass wall of the aquarium.

Roxanne moaned. "Balim..."

Irritation burned in him. The tank had been difficult to build and nearly impossible to fill.

"Climb up the ladder, Roxanne. Mitch, get on the desk." Balim herded Pelan's bride as she gaped at the crackling glass. "Your wish has been granted."

She climbed up a few rungs behind Roxanne and clutched her bathrobe collar. "What?"

"You will now aid Pelan's recuperation in the air."

The tank collapsed. Water gushed out and knocked him over. The warm elixir swept him across the floor.

His lungs shifted to gills. He stared up at the human ceiling before the water flooded out and left him beached on the wet floor alone.

He had let the dangerous rock into the building. He had carried it himself surrounded by the disguise of other Sea Opals. The Sons of Hercules had counted on him not identifying the danger as Roxanne had.

How would the enemy trick him next?

FOUR

Britney Spears's "Toxic" played on Bella's cell phone as she repeated her mantra in the mirror. "I am beautiful. I am scintillating. Clients can't take their eyes off me."

Bella sucked in her gut to smooth the black fabric corset. Her figure filled the dingy hall mirror with dismaying proportions. She hadn't dressed up since Jonah's diagnosis. After all the junk food, she was lucky the dress still fit.

Her breasts oozed out the sides.

She shoved them in. They oozed out the strained fabric. She applied under-bra tape.

There.

Rolls of fat puffed out the back.

She forced them in, grunting with every word of her mantra. "I. Win. Every. Marketing. Contract."

The tape held.

Quickly, she stepped into and zipped on her emerald-green dress. The dress hugged her like the ribs in an anaconda. Her body jiggled. Jelly under pressure.

The dress held.

Thank goodness.

She let out her breath cautiously, then in a whoosh.

The fat, frumpy, freckled woman in the mirror sagged with exhaustion.

Oh, dear, her mother would say. *Time to lay off the margaritas.*

As if alcohol was Bella's problem.

She spackled on a heavy mix of expired makeup and affixed an emerald feather in the twist of her red hair. She'd been living off convenient chips and dollar-menu items for a year. Limp hair, gray skin, and spilling out of her dresses were the natural results.

She swiped her lips with gloss.

It tasted like bitter almonds.

Well, the gloss was a year out of date. *She* was a year out of date. Bella tossed the tube in the trash and wiped off the gloss.

Only one year since the nightmare had started? It felt like much longer.

And tonight's client was the most important she'd ever courted.

She snapped the fist-sized red heart necklace on and positioned it over her collarbone. It was exactly how she'd imagined. A tacky, plastic-looking, water-filled "locket" that hung around her neck like a weight. The top screwed off. How was she supposed to shove the Life Tree blossom through the tiny mouth without crushing it or tearing the petals off? Good thing she would not have to find out. But, just in case they had spies photographing her leaving the apartment, she had to make it look real.

The Sons of Hercules thought she was working for them.

They thought wrong.

And it felt good, so good, to be *doing* something again. Slaying dragons. Punching bullies. Security-auditing MerMatch.

She crossed the tiny, run-down studio crammed with leaking cardboard and half-opened moving boxes, shouldered a thin stole, and checked her purse for emergency cab fare. Her credit cards were maxed. She stuffed one maxed out card inside her bra to be used in a little theater performance later, and then fished for a real card that still allowed charges. Somewhere... Here? No...

Jab. "Ow!" A plastic edge stabbed her cuticle, ripping the skin and spotting blood. She stuck her finger in her mouth, eyes watering.

She turned the purse upside down and splayed the canceled cards. Didn't she still have a store credit card from—

A heavy fist hammered on the door. "Bella! I know you're in there."

She jumped, tiny cut forgotten. Her landlord.

On her feet in an instant, she cut the music on her cell and eased to the window. The ladder rested against the side of the building beside cans of dried paint that had been abandoned years ago. Were her downstairs neighbors home? The country music was silent.

"Don't sneak out the back ladder again," Harv's rough bark stopped her. "That thing's older than you are, and the Steves aren't home."

Right.

She repacked her purse, checked her appearance one last time, and gave her mirror image a test smile.

Not a million dollars, but a nice flash of teeth and assets. It would have to be enough.

The hammering started again. "I can serve this three-day Demand for Rent whether or not I see you."

She opened the door and leaned on the jamb. "Good evening, Harv."

"Bella." The heavy-weight retired construction-worker-turned-landlord dropped his fist and stepped back, his gaze drinking in her figure.

His hands were empty. No official forms. Whew.

She eased her weight onto her front heel to give her profile more of an hourglass.

His thick, gray-speckled brows rose appreciatively.

Nice to know she still had it. "What's this about three days?"

"Er, yeah. That." He gripped the back of his shaggy brown head. "You haven't paid rent in a few months, and it's what I have to do, you know...it's in the rent agreement..."

She channeled a wounded look. "You know I will pay in full."

Her expression hit the mark. He swallowed. "I know. It's just, the guys..."

"What about you?" She rested her hand on his rough, construction-scarred forearm. "We've been through so much together."

"Yeah." He coughed, no longer able to meet her eye. "You were there when my dad went through the chemo. But, uh, the guys are getting antsy, and I didn't know what to say."

"You don't believe me?"

"I believe you. It's just the guys. And, ah, you know, ah... I was just thinking...if you and I went to, uh, dinner sometime, then I could tell the guys I was, uh, taking over the payments. Just for until you're back on your feet."

She ought to agree. If she led on terrorists, she should have no problem manipulating an emotionally vulnerable man.

But she did.

A spark of anger flared in her chest.

Harv had started her vending addiction by buying her hundreds of chips and coffees. He'd saved her money and commute by finding her an apartment in his building. He had shared her tears when Jonah had returned to the hospital a third time.

He didn't deserve the runaround. And she hated herself for doing it.

She'd sworn she would grow up different from her parents. Thanks to them, she knew fifty ways to avoid a summons, fight an eviction, and use people's kindness against them. The first time she'd snuck out to avoid Harv, she'd died a little inside.

Convincing Harv to write off her debt for two dates where she wasted his time and then let him down easy would solve this problem.

Bella stepped into the hall and kissed his rough cheek. "Harv."

He flushed tomato red. "So, uh, is that a yes?"

She smoothed away the damp spot. "You're too nice a guy to get run around by someone like me."

"Yeah, that's what the guys say too."

"I bet they do."

"Aw, geez. I didn't mean... Well, you know... You have that fancy, high-class job downtown. We don't get many of your kind here. That's why they're so nervous."

"Tell them to relax. I'm going to meet with a client right now."

"Oh." He looked relieved. "Will he give you the back rent?"

Not in cash. The warriors sought brides, not escorts.

"Absolutely." She turned away from Harv to lock her door and dropped the key in her purse. "If I nail this contract, I'll get my bonus and pay you free and clear. And I'll pay the next six months in advance."

"You don't have to do that."

"I want to. Everything will work out." She strolled to the stairs and waved, leaving the bighearted man in front of her apartment. "You'll see."

Were those words for him? Or for her?

She tripped out the door and hit the street. If Harv started an eviction, she'd earned a temporary reprieve.

But it had also cost her time at the subway. Bella checked the hour on her phone. Uh-oh. She ran.

A light drizzle broke, wilting her like a plucked flower. She ducked into the terminal and dealt with the discomfort. The new studio—she still thought of it as new, even though she'd moved in six months ago—was a fraction of the size and convenience of her old two-bedroom. But it was close-ish to the hospital and more affordable. Plus, she didn't need two bedrooms now.

A sharp pang stole her breath.

She closed her mind to it and pulled out her phone. Bella needed her head in the game. The cell searched for a network. She zoned in on the blank screen.

There were two types of men in the world: those who tolerated lies, and those who *needed* them.

Most men tolerated lies. Like Harv's partners. So long as a rent check showed up soon, they'd let her go.

Sensitive dreamers, like Harv, needed to believe the world was nice and people were caring.

She could play either like a maestro.

There was a third type—men who did not tolerate lies—but they were rare and not worth placating.

Bella shoved off that ancient history before it could poison her night. Now her first theater performance began.

At her exit, she ducked into the station restroom.

Thwarting tonight's flower-stealing mission was simple. All she had to do was *not* steal the Life Tree blossom—ie, leave the blossom in the tank at MerMatch. But the Sons of Hercules wouldn't like her to refuse. She'd have to give them a reason.

So, inside the grotty bathroom stall, she took off the Sons of Hercules water-filled necklace and shoved it into a feminine hygene products bag she'd grabbed from her office for just this purpose. She balanced the plastic-lined paper bag atop the stinking, overfilled small metal trash in the cramped stall.

If she didn't have the necklace, she couldn't sneak the blossom out or store it. That was the excuse she'd give the Sons of Hercules when they demanded why she'd failed. Hence, into the trash it went.

Bella put her cell phone beside the necklace in the bag and folded the top to seal it closed.

Dumping her cell phone like this created more problems. How sophisticated were the Sons of Hercules? Starr didn't want Bella carrying an electronics device she hadn't inspected. If the violent disorganized college students had even a fraction of Starr's technical skills, Bella's devices were endangered.

Bella didn't take any viruses into her son's hospital room. She wouldn't take any digital viruses into the MerMatch offices, either.

She left the bag balanced on the trash and exited the

stall. A gray hoodie-clad, nondescript woman entered the restroom and pushed past her. They didn't make eye contact. The woman ducked into the stall Bella had just vacated and locked the door.

Hopefully that woman was Starr's contact. But if not, who rooted around in a suspiciously used feminine hygene bag?

Bella stopped before the scratched-up mirror, mussed her hair, and "roughed up" her clothes. She put on a frightened expression, perfect for suggesting she'd just been mugged, and exited the restrooms—right into a station attendant.

Uh oh.

She bounced off the attendant and exaggerated a flustered expression—not hard—and then stood indecisively looking after the attendant. Was she being photographed by Sons of Hercules spies inside the station? She had to look mugged but she couldn't report an actual mugging.

Bella wavered, then made a show of seeking a station clock and acting horrified by the time. She avoided the station attendants and hurried outside.

In real life, Bella would be late to a date in order to get justice against a mugger, especially if her son's health was on the line, but hopefully the Sons of Hercules would buy her story that she'd been too flustered to make a report.

This all assumed the Sons of Hercules were even watching her and needed to be convinced.

The first time Bella had spied for Starr, they'd worked alone. No fancy equipment, no connections, no experience. No contingency plans. Now, Starr had a lot of everything, including paranoia. Her planning had leveled up exponentially, and even though they faced more numerous and mysterious opponents, Bella felt a lot more secure.

She continued enacting Starr's plan.

Outside the station, Bella bought a cell phone from a "random guy" on the street hawking cell phones. She pulled the "secret" credit card that had "survived her not-mugging" from her tight bra and swiped it in his reader—because in New York, even the homeless accepted plastic—and ignored the low funds alert. The man shoved a basic, pre-owned cell phone at her and walked off.

She powered the new-to-her phone on as she strode away from the station. Everything had gone perfectly. She hoped. A cute blue star greeted her on the loading screen. She input the pre-arranged password and dialed in to connect to Starr's network.

Bella hurried through more miserable drizzle the last blocks to the MerMatch office building. The repurposed tenement was only a few blocks from her work, and she almost turned the wrong direction on the pedestrian thoroughfare. Brown concrete and tinted glass rose six floors into the cloudy gray sky; between buildings, the ocean canal was a gray smudge.

Her new phone buzzed. Video recording had started, and it connected to a private network. Bella lifted the screen saver to get the rest of Starr's devices. She peeled two metal dots embedded beneath the plastic and stuck them to the backs of her ears. Their adhesive had survived being stuck to the phone and with her hair down they should be invisible.

"*Oh, hello.*" Her half sister, Starr, greeted her with the usual stuffiness. The dots made her words sound like they were inside Bella's ears. Starr suffered from allergies. "*What a gray, dismal day for a break-in.*"

"Fall in New York is supposed to be beautiful," Bella murmured.

"Great. Very clear. Now, drop the phone in your purse and speak again."

She stowed the phone as instructed. "Oh, well. Maybe next year."

"Clear as a bell. We are a go."

Bella tightened her stole around her shoulders and climbed the few steps to the glassed-in lobby. A security officer on the top step nodded at her. Another officer peered out.

Security was tighter than last time.

Her belly twinged with nerves. Butterflies banged into each other.

This was it. The mermen didn't know it, but they were counting on her. She sucked in a deep breath, straightened, and entered.

She passed her purse through the metal detector. The officer ran a wand over her tight dress. Her earrings buzzed.

Bella smiled. "Titanium."

The officer narrowed her eyes. "For jewelry?"

"Sure, why not?"

"They should have seen the fishbowl-sized necklace you were trying to smuggle in. My friend picked it up, by the way. As we suspected, he said your phone's chock-full of spyware."

Him? Good job, Starr's contact. Bella had thought he was a woman.

The officer studied the square ingots in Bella's ears and stepped back, waving her to go ahead.

She shouldered her purse and crossed the lobby.

Starr snorted. *"Titanium? Really?"*

Bella hummed the song, "I am Titanium," about enemies shooting her down but refusing to fall. She twirled as though marveling at the architecture.

"I see...security cameras. Heat sensors, motion. Good coverage, and a good brand. Windows are covered, as we expected. I looked up the building schematics and the security team is adequate to cover the general security. No audio jammers yet, but prepare to lose me in the elevator."

A caramel-brunette in a white business suit sat on a slim bench next to the elevators. She typed something on her phone with her thumbs and stood. "Bella? I'm Hazel Gray from MerMatch. You're late."

"I got mugged in the subway."

"Ugh." Hazel pulled something out of her purse and raised a fist. "That happened to me *three times* last year. This year, I'm prepared." She opened her fist to display a mini personal defense system.

"Is that mace, a Taser, *and* an air siren?"

"I like this girl," Starr said.

"For people who take personal defense seriously." Hazel packed it back into her purse. "No one's getting the drop on me now. And if they do, they'll regret it."

Bella smiled with just the right touch of schadenfreude. "New York."

Hazel pulled papers from her tan messenger bag. "Here are the forms Dannika mentioned."

"Oh, are we signing here? Not up in the office?"

"We've had too many close calls. Dannika said no strangers after hours."

"Ooh, ask her who's getting in during regular hours," Starr said in her ear.

"That's understandable. Rubberneckers must flood your office during regular hours."

"Ha! No. Everyone uses the website."

"Everyone?"

"Tourists get weeded out here." Hazel tapped her pen

on the papers thoughtfully. "You know, now that you mention it, I barely let in any strangers. It's weird."

"You never let in anybody without an appointment?"

"Yep. Not a soul."

"No one at all?"

"Oh. Well." She rolled her eyes. Not at Bella, but at her memory. "I mean, aside from us. The mer warriors. And the window washers last week. And the AC guys. Oh, and these painter guys, but they left without painting anything. You know, nothing but ordinary business maintenance."

"*Bingo*," Starr said. "*Well, the office is probably crammed with spy stuff. I bet you can't fart in there without somebody hearing it.*"

"But you had to let them in?" Bella pressed. "They were doing building maintenance, and the landlord didn't give them a temporary key?"

"The landlord can't just give out keys. Somebody could misuse it and break in."

"*Aw. So close to the truth and so far from realizing it. Bless.*"

Bella took Hazel's pen. Nondisclosures, privacy agreements, promises not to go on talk shows or write books about tonight's date. She scribbled her signature without reading.

None of this mattered.

But to pretend it did, she released a ditzy laugh and gushed. "I'm so excited. You see Balim every day. Do you have any tips for me?"

"Don't be a terrorist."

"*Hardy har har,*" Starr said.

"I'll do my best," Bella said.

"*Not that she'd know if you didn't.*"

Hazel stowed the signed forms and swung the bag over her shoulder. "Let's get this over with."

They entered the elevator. The doors closed.

"You don't enjoy first dates?" Bella asked.

"They are the most wretched, awkward, pointless wastes of time." Hazel fiddled with her phone, shaking it as though not realizing being isolated inside a solid steel box would break the Wi-Fi connection. "But if you mean do I enjoy catering dates for the mermen, getting shot at and poisoned takes the bloom off the rose. I started as a receptionist, you know. I didn't sign up for violent hate crimes."

"Yet, here you are."

Hazel blew her caramel bangs out of her face. "Yep. Here I am."

"Caring about someone changes what risks you're willing to take."

Hazel blinked and then her shoulders softened. "Well, yeah. It's not the guys' faults. It's those stupid college kids. All the warriors want is to fall in love, have warrior kids, and repopulate their cities. I can't stand by and watch some disturbed, faux-adult man-children with anger issues ruin it for them, can I?"

Bella smiled.

Hazel rocked on her heels, a nervous tic, but she was friendlier as she led the way out of the elevator onto the rooftop. "I hope that jacket is warmer than it looks."

"I'm used to putting my shoulder to the cold."

"*That's so deep,*" Starr commented.

Bella snorted.

Hazel glanced back at her in curiosity.

Bella smiled blandly. Starr calmed her butterflies.

She'd met and wooed clients a million times. All she had to do was ask innocuous questions while her sister audited their security. After a socially acceptable period, Bella would convince Balim to let her into the MerMatch office. She'd do what Starr needed to inspect, take over, and secure the space.

Starr would learn how the Sons of Hercules hacked in. With any luck, she'd ghost them back to their origin and expose their identities along with their crimes before anyone else got hurt. And if her investigation took longer than tonight, Bella would string them along until Starr succeeded.

And after having done the mermen another favor, if any new cures arose to try on Jonah, they would call her first.

Balim was a doctor. It shouldn't be too hard to pass the next hours with him.

"Here's Dannika." Hazel gestured at a willowy woman in a vibrant blue, high-fashion caftan, and designer navy-to-baby-blue ombre scarf. "Save room for dessert. I made raspberry mousse."

"Bella Taylor."

Dannika extended ring-covered hands and clasped Bella warmly, just like she had whenever they'd met—at the photo studio, the marketing conference rooms, or the kosher deli in the atrium. The socialite was good friends with Bella's boss at Vibrant Image Marketing.

"I'm so glad to see you again. How is your son, Jonah?"

"Holding steady." Bella returned Dannika's squeeze. Heirloom diamonds, rubies, and emeralds on Dannika's rings made her hands heavy in Bella's grip. "Thank you so much for keeping us in your thoughts."

"Yes, of course. You look lovely."

"I love your ombre."

"Balim's waiting for you by the pergola." Dannika's eyes gleamed with excitement. "Come. Let me show you."

The women strolled between boxed planters full of sweet-smelling sages, lavenders, chamomiles, trellises covered in blue and yellow passionflowers, and benches arranged with orange poppies and indigo morning glories. All closed up in the damp, chilly night, but the garden still glimmered like a fairy land dotted with landscaping lights like twinkling fireflies.

"That's so beautiful," Starr said wistfully. *"I wish more than anything I could see it in real life."*

"This is more extensive than my building's rooftop garden," Bella commented.

"Yes, the owner is a dear friend and allowed me to have a free hand with creativity." Dannika directed Bella to the corner of the garden where the night-blooming flowers twined around stone statues—evening primrose, wisteria, chocolate flowers, jessamine, and moonflowers.

"Hey, those are all aphrodisiacs," Starr commented.

"How romantic for a first date," Bella murmured aloud.

Dannika glanced back at her, a smile of having been caught by surprise. "I'm so glad you agree."

She led Bella around a mossy wall to a covered shelter in the center of the misty rooftop garden. Curtains of wisteria parted on a rustic wooden table set with vintage rose plates and cutlery, and lit by thick jar candles. To the side was a small koi pond lined with decorative rock.

"Wow. These mermen know what they're doing in the romance department."

Bella agreed, although she suspected Dannika had more to do with creating the atmosphere than a water-born warrior.

"And this is Balim," Dannika said.

Balim rose from the table.

His gray suit complemented his intricate red facial tattoos. With hands loose in his slacks pockets, he tilted his chin, awaiting her judgment.

She reached out to shake hands. "Hello, Balim. I'm—"

His eyes locked on hers, and her words died midsentence.

He was otherworldly, a warrior, and all male.

Shock paralyzed her. Her heart thudded loud in her chest. Sweat dampened her palms.

This could be my salvation.

Dark brown irises threaded with iridescent red matching his tattoos. Black loafers clad his human feet. Dark slacks accented hard thighs, a trim waist looped by a belt, and a flat, gray button-up shirt covered his bulging arms and torso. Short, dark hair cloaked his head.

Only when she reached his skin did the heartblood-red tattoos give his identity away.

Tattoos curled across his skeptical forehead like capillaries tapering into vine-curls against his right cheek and down his jaw. The fierce slash of his mouth warned he accepted no lies.

Uh-oh.

She could not lie to him.

He stepped toward her. Dark knowing filled his gaze. "You feel it."

Her throat went dry. She licked her lips. "Feel?"

"Resonance." His eyes raked her body, fanning coals to smoldering flames. "Our resonance."

She couldn't speak. His charisma filled her senses. A spicy, fruity scent like dark cherries teased her nose. She wanted a taste.

He took another step. "It is not only me."

The words disconnected in her head. She was struck dumb.

He leaned over her. Powerful and arrogant and so tempting. "Is it?"

Balim commanded her soul. She was stunned, flushed, hungry.

"*Bella? Bella! Wake up.*"

She blinked rapidly and struggled to regain her composure. Balim was supposed to be boring. She was supposed to charm him. Not fall helpless under his spell.

Where had Dannika gone?

Only Starr buzzed in her ear, trying to drag her back from the ledge of an uncontrollable tidal wave of sensation.

Bella cast for something, anything, to make sense.

She defaulted to an old media-training question. "What are you looking for in a bride?"

A smile of pure arrogance tilted his lips. "You."

Her? *Her?*

He lowered his head. His mouth closed on hers. Their lips united.

Tender, sweet pressure and spicy male unlocked her heart and spilled her soul out. Arousal flooded her veins. Feelings she didn't even know she still possessed—desire, innocence, vulnerability—flushed through her. Her pussy throbbed, hot and ready. She was his lock. He was her key.

His powerful hand spanned the back of her neck, commanding her to let go of her resistance and yield to his unstoppable possession.

Bella melted into Balim's kiss.

She mustn't let herself enjoy his firm lips on hers, his tantalizing breath on her cheek, or the soft brush of his hair against her forehead. The scent of the ocean and his masculine salt mixed with the heady floral spice of the night-blooming jasmine. Innocent and yet so alluring.

He was just a mark. A way for her to reach her goal. The male she had to trick—

His lips parted beneath hers, nibbling. Licking, sucking. Teasing.

Hot need sizzled into her center.

She parted, allowing him in.

He surged forward, unstoppable as the tide. Passion crashed over her, fizzing in white tingles. She felt her whole existence in his possession. His tongue thrusting into her mouth, claiming her. His even teeth nibbling on her throbbing, hot, sensitive lips. His mouth owning hers.

Accept my claim.

She wanted to.

She wanted him to push her down. Scoop her breasts free of the emerald velvet, releasing her from the too-tight corset, push her skirt above her thighs, bury his cock deep into her aching center. Forget herself and just exist as woman and man until her responsibilities floated away and she recaptured the easy freedom of her long-ago youth.

But she had responsibilities. Others were relying on her. She couldn't run away. That was how her parents had dealt with their problems. Every time she ran away, she hurt worse.

Jonah.

She broke off, gasping. Her lips were wet and hungry, and Balim also breathed as though he had run a marathon. She covered her mouth, struggling for control of her quivering body, and pulled out of his arms.

His kiss broke her. How dare he make her feel hungry? Hopeful? Happy?

When her life was crashing, how dare she let him?

"Bella! What's going on? Please answer. Please, Bella!"

She lowered her chin to keep her lips away.

He stayed near, his hard jaw smooth against her cheek.

She pulled in a deep, steadying breath. Her heart leaped and her knees shook.

Powerful rightness shook her foundation. She fought against it.

She'd met him. He was her one. Her soul mate. And she didn't believe in soul mates. He was her everything.

And she would betray him.

FIVE

Balim's soul mate, Bella, changed the color of her pale cheeks to bright pink. Her green eyes glistened with liquid. Her chest brightened with revitalization.

Good.

Pain had darkened his fated bride, and now his presence reignited her passionate inner sun.

They no longer endured loneliness and frustration. The tidal wave had crashed over her. They tumbled together on a current neither of them could control.

Her lips parted, and she risked a furtive glance up at him again as though testing herself.

He tasted her lips once more.

Her soul was hungry. So hungry. He needed to feed her.

They kissed.

He nibbled, giving more, demanding all of her.

She yielded to his wish. Her lips were plump, sweet, and the gateway to his dreams. His cock strained the human clothing, throbbing to burst. He memorized the suppleness of her lower lip, the sweetness of the upper, the damp secrets contained within. She released a sweet moan of need.

Her trusting sound made his heart clench.

This time, he ended the kiss. Not only her soul but also her body was starving for nutrients. He needed to heal all of her.

She held his soul in her hands.

No matter how much he feared that fact, he could not rip it away from her. It was already hers. From the moment he had first seen her, he'd known.

"You are my soul mate," he intoned again as she rested and breathed against his jaw.

She lifted her head. Her clouded eyes cleared. "What does that mean?"

"We are sewn together. You and I. For all time."

She rested one hand on her chest. "You're remarkably calm after that revelation." A touch of dryness entered her tone as she struggled to lighten the seriousness of his vow.

"I have had longer to become used to it."

"Oh? But we've never met." She licked her lips. "I would have remembered you."

"You pass by this building sometimes."

She glanced over her shoulder at the buildings in the distance. "I work on 37th."

"I saw you. Your soul light." He led her to the side of the garden and pointed over the rail at the walkway where, during the busy business hours, a mass of humans flowed without ever looking up. "You were the brightest sun in a sea of stars."

He leaned back. His hands clenched in his pockets to

stop from enveloping her in his arms. "And I also saw you at a human hospital."

Realization flashed across her face. "You were at the metropolitan hospital two weeks ago. The emergency department."

"Yes."

She rubbed her chest harder. A frown darkened her lips. "But I can't be a soul mate. There must be some mistake."

Fear stabbed into him.

Bella rejected him before she even knew of his dishonor. Was he bared to her because they were soul mates?

Dannika appeared at the opposite corner of the pergola holding a tureen in her pot-holder-filled hands. She cleared her throat. "Tom yum soup?"

Bella pulled away from Balim and forced a smile to her face. "Thank you. That would be lovely."

Her words were smooth and mature. Dannika's soul brightened with ease. She thought this date was going well.

But in truth, Bella's soul flared and extinguished chaotically.

Balim followed Bella's lead to take a seat at the table, calming himself as he talked through her symptoms.

Bella was sick. Soul sick and body sick.

By the end of the first date, she would become his mate.

His queen.

And he would heal everything.

Dannika ladled steaming hot broth into their bowls.

Bella commented on the appetizer plates to avoid considering Balim's truth. "Are these caramelized onion and pear crostinis from Syreno's? And Moroccan-spiced salmon rillettes from Aslan Chic?"

"Look-alikes," Dannika said with a smile. "We crafted them in-house. The soup and main course were ordered in and thoroughly tested. Enjoy."

Dannika withdrew.

Bella crunched the small bites and moaned in pleasure. As Balim had guessed, she needed this hand-crafted, wholesome, flavorful food as much as she needed the sweet, flower-strewn benches and the vibrant gardens. She rolled the bites across her tongue. "Mmm. Oh, wow. This is excellent. And what did she mean by 'thoroughly tested'?"

"For poison." Balim bit into his own crispy cracker.

She stopped mid-chew. "Poison?"

"On one warrior's first date, the food was dosed with Rotenone."

A quiet vibration emanated from a dark ridge of metal behind her ears. She swallowed, and her soul light dimmed. "Fish killer?"

"Rotenone kills fish because it enters the bloodstream through gills. In humans, consuming it triggers an explosive vomit reflex."

"Your warrior projectile vomited?"

"As did his female."

"That would be a memorable first date."

"Yes. We no longer reserve meals at restaurants."

She toyed with her soup, and after he showed no ill effects, cleansed her palate with the complex, nutrient-filled spices. "Again, you're so blasé about someone trying to poison you."

"Blasé?"

"Unconcerned. People try to harm you all the time?"

"Yes. They always have."

She tilted her head. "Really?"

"Beneath the water, raiders are a constant threat." He

picked up a shrimp and crunched it whole, consuming the chitinous brain and legs as well as the chewy inner meat. "We defend and protect our most vulnerable warriors. Above the water, we lack awareness. But with every new attack, our intelligence grows."

Her soul light dimmed again.

"Do not grieve," he ordered. "Atlantis is unusual. Warriors of many origins fight together to survive. Like a healthy immune system, attacks strengthen our bond."

"And above the water, you can't see them coming." Her soul flared with determination. "Anticipation is torture."

"Sometimes knowing what is coming next is worse."

Bella lowered her spoon to the bowl with a clink. "I suppose, as a doctor, you've often had to comfort the dying."

"No."

"When a patient has no hope—"

"I have seen many recoveries since modern brides have joined the mer world," he replied. "So long as a warrior lives, hope lives as well. I will use my skill to help him fight."

She stared at him. Her soul burned hot with resonance. Her chin wrinkled. She touched two scuffed, scratched fingers to her mouth, looked away, and cleared her throat while reaching for her water glass and a napkin. "Well, I'm sure your patients appreciate your unfailing dedication."

His chest clenched again. One patient he had deliberately failed.

No, he would not think about that.

"It's admirable. Where is dinner? Oh. Goodness." Her expression lifted and her lips affixed into a flat, close-mouthed smile. "Dannika."

"To the rescue!" The woman moved the soup dishes aside and served a large platter of Ethiopian food. "These just came out."

Balim mentioned Bella's scratches. "Your fingers are injured."

"Hmm? Oh." She ran her thumb across the ragged skin. "I jammed them on a credit card earlier tonight. It's fine. They don't hurt."

Balim's tool kit was in the office, but he did not wish to interrupt Bella's meal.

Dannika withdrew, and Bella tore the bread. She scooped a handful of green mush, savored the scent, and bit in.

He chewed his own bread-ful. The mer did not have hot foods under the water. They had few spicy dishes, though.

The yellow dish was creamy and tangy, the orange was crumbly and zesty, and the red was spicy. His tongue flared with heat.

The metallic squeak behind Bella's ear made her enjoyment flicker. Her insightful green eyes closed on him and then veered away.

"You have a question," he prompted.

She nailed him with her clear gaze. "How do you fight for a patient after you've tried everything?"

"I rest him against his city's Life Tree. Its healing sap flows in the blood of every warrior, and its resin forms into Sea Opals."

"What if his city's Life Tree isn't an option? Like, he can't get to it. He's too far away."

"That is unfortunate. In Atlantis, channeling the healing energy of the Life—"

"Just humor me."

"Do I have my tools?"

"Yes."

"I would use my tools to stabilize the warrior to reach his Life Tree."

"The Life Tree doesn't heal him," she insisted. "Put it out of your mind. What would you do?"

He wiped his fingers on the cleaning cloth. Few illnesses resisted the Life Tree. The more he considered her proposal, the more a certain illness seeped into his mind.

He murmured the nickname. "Oannes' Curse."

"Hmm?"

"An illness. A plague." He could not repeat the nickname in case it summoned the horror. "It destroyed two powerful cities. No cure was found. Not even the Life Trees averted its demise."

She sucked in a deep breath and tapped both fingers on the table. "No. I'm sorry. I'll be more clear. What would you do if a *human* fell ill? And doesn't respond to Sea Opal elixir. Obviously, he can't go to the Life Tree."

It took a long, hard moment for him to wrench away from the past and focus on her in the present. "A human? On the surface?"

She nodded.

"And he does not respond to Sea Opals... I would rely on human medicine."

That was not what she wanted to hear. She leaned back in her seat, disappointed. "So, nothing else?"

"If a human soul does not brighten with resonance, all the elixir on the surface will not cure him."

Her lips pinched together.

"Who is your patient?" he asked.

She waved his question away. "It doesn't matter. You've answered my questions."

"Explain."

"It's not important." She smiled with a closed mouth.

"Why do you do that?"

"Do what?"

"Force your smile."

She beamed while her chest light darkened. The classic human contradiction between her soul and her body. Once, he'd thought it meant she was ill, but now, he knew it indicated lies.

"Why do you think it's forced?" she asked breezily.

"Because your soul darkens."

"Soul? I have no idea what you're talking about."

"That is a lie."

She laughed, shocked, and her cheeks pinked. "Lie! You don't pull your punches, do you?"

"I do not punch. And this smile is natural."

"All my smiles are natural."

"Your lips are closed."

She covered her mouth with her hand. "No."

"Now you cover your mouth. Why?"

She studied her soup, her plates, the garden, and the koi pond without answering. Her ear metal vibrated. Her eyebrows wrinkled, and her soul light fluctuated.

"Now you contemplate more lies," he noted.

She narrowed her eyes.

"And now my words cause anger."

She dropped her hand, straightened, and rested her forearms on the table. "My front teeth are crooked. That's why I close my lips to smile. My parents couldn't afford dental care. I'm lucky I still have teeth."

Her words were light, but her soul was dark.

He'd made her angry? By speaking about her teeth?

Balim didn't want to make her angry. He spoke aloud what was obvious.

Her metal vibrated.

She took a deep breath and forced another close-lipped smile, picked up her glass of wine, and swirled it. "Sorry. I'm a little off-center by the 'resonance,' I guess." She took a sip.

"And by the communication device behind your ear."

She lowered the wineglass. Her soul light darkened to black. "What?"

"The metal bar behind your ear." He pointed. "The one that vibrates and causes you to calm."

The glass stem clinked on the table, rattled, and she settled it in place with both hands. "Vibration?"

"It vibrates now. What is it telling you?"

"You..." She swallowed hard and could not make her voice perform. "You hear words?"

"No. Only your reactions. I wonder who speaks to you." His point shifted to her ear jewelry. "The whine of the small camera in your right ear."

She bolted to her feet, stumbled back from the table, and grabbed for her covering. "I'm... I've got to, uh, got to go."

He shot to his feet as well. "Bella. Wait."

"I just remembered something."

"My observations frighten you."

"No, I just... It's not the right place to talk about..." She stumbled on her heels. "I've got—"

"*I* frighten you."

She was running away. Leaving him. His bride.

Rejection closed his chest. "My words. I do this."

She slowed and stopped. One hand lifted and rubbed her chest. "Why does your tone hurt my chest?"

"Because our souls are sewn together. You feel my pain at your rejection."

And that could not be allowed. He was a mer. A warlord. Control of his soul light should be a given.

He focused on calm.

"I'm not rejecting *you*." She half turned. "I don't want to ruin your life."

"You cannot."

"Give me time."

"I mean my life is already not what I desired. Among other flaws, I cannot attract a worthy female."

And now she was mad again. She turned all the way to face him. "What's that?"

"You have never noticed me."

"Because I never saw you. You looked down at me on the street. What could I do?"

"You never looked up."

"Why should I?"

"That question has tortured me alone for a long time."

Her mouth twisted. The small metal behind her ear vibrated. She lifted her head. "You don't know what it is to be tortured or alone."

"I do."

She hung her purse over her arm. Walking out for the first and final time.

Balim's heart squeezed.

She was leaving because he repelled her.

No.

"I did not go to you because I feared this. Overwhelming connection. Resonance I cannot control. We are destined whether or not I want it. Whether or not you want me. Whether or not it is convenient."

She lingered. "So this date isn't convenient for you, huh?"

"I cannot leave Warrior Pelan without a healer while we consummate our marriage and repopulate our race."

Her soul darkened to black, and she snapped up her head. "That's what I am to you? A means to procreate."

"Our race is dying, Bella."

"I know, and that sucks. It does. I have no wish to 'procreate,' not even with you."

Her rejection stabbed him.

"You don't know me," she continued, smacking herself on the chest. "You don't know what I'm going through. The choices I have to make. You don't even know why I'm here today."

"I know you experience deep pain," he murmured.

"You can't understand how much being here and enjoying this date and talking to you betrays my...betrays me."

"All warriors betrayed our origin cities to rebel to Atlantis. My origin city would kill me on sight. If you feel betrayal in your heart, it is only the mirror of my soul reflecting into you."

Her anger lifted to quiet curiosity.

She cupped his cheek. "Does that soul light tell you everything about me?"

"No." He savored the softness of her delicate fingers. "I sense the emotions that make you strong and whole, and the emotions that tear you down."

Her gaze dropped to his mouth.

"I will always feel this compulsion to join with you because you are my soul mate. No matter what you or I do. Because our souls resonate on the same frequency. We are the same in mirror."

She lifted her gaze back to his eyes. "I came here to heal my son. No other reason."

The metal behind her ears vibrated insistently.

But her soul clarified. Pure light. She spoke the truth, and it freed her.

This was a solvable problem. "You need elixir? How much?"

Skeptical amusement crossed her face. "I can't, Balim."

"I will give you whatever medicine you need. Whether human medicine purchased with money or the medicine of my body for your soul."

"It's not for me."

"You—"

She covered his mouth with her fingers. "I'm balancing a lot of plates right now. You make me want to walk away with you and let everything come crashing down. Don't tempt me."

He spoke around her muffling fingers. "There is another way."

"Another way to what? Hurt people who depend on me?"

He shook his head, allowing her hand to move with his mouth. "We are soul mates."

"So you better hope I never turn evil." Her plush lips folded into a sad smile.

"You are not evil."

"You don't know that."

"I do, Bella." He clasped the hand on his mouth and lowered her hand, sliding his fingers between her slender digits until they interlocked. "Whatever your reason, hurting others is not your wish, and it hurts you. We are mirrors. You and me."

She studied him for a long moment. Searching for his lies.

But he did not have lies.

The metal behind her ear vibrated.

She spoke. "I should really go."

"Not before I show you the other way."

"Other way?"

"To heal your son." Balim brought her fingers to his lips. "Become my queen."

SIX

ecome Balim's queen?

Become Balim's queen?

Bella's heart thudded harder and harder.

Desire welled up in her heart. Her soul sang. The future beckoned with gold, rainbows, and stardust glimmering as it fell between the twinkling flower petals.

No. No, no, no.

It was a trap. A lie. Another false hope presented in a long line of false hopes.

If she became a queen, she'd have to go to Atlantis, and she'd never see Jonah again.

Never.

But if it was his only chance for a cure...

"What do you mean?" Bella's voice broke on the forbidden question, and she swallowed. "How will that help Jonah?"

"I will show you." The steady warrior with the soothing, calm voice and mesmerizing eyes tugged her fingers. "Come with me."

Bella followed Balim through the gardens.

His fingers were a lifeline. His broad back and hard lines enticed her beneath the smooth suit.

This was crazy.

Crazy.

She had to tear her gaze away and breathe.

This resonance was no joke. She never reacted like this to a client. She never reacted like this to anyone.

"*Bella?*" Starr's voice was tight with worry. "*Something's wrong. Did they drug the food? You're not being yourself. Stop arguing with the guy and get out. Now.*"

She sealed her lips. Starr would have to understand.

"*Please, Bella. We already discussed this. You said yourself that you'll never help Jonah on the bottom of the sea. Remember how I tried to talk you out of marrying Chaz? This is me, your voice of reason, pleading you step back and think.*"

Dannika waited just inside the shelter, watching a movie on her tablet, while Hazel beside her typed furiously on her phone.

Dannika rose, concerned. "Is everything all right?"

"Fine." Balim pressed the button to open the elevator doors.

"Are you finished? Already?" She gestured at Hazel, whose gaze was glued to Balim's fingers linked with Bella's. "Hazel made raspberry chocolate mousse."

"I wish I could try it. It sounds delightful," Bella said, recovering herself.

Hazel tapped the cooler. "Here, you can try it right—"

"Another time."

"We are going to the office." Balim entered the elevator and pulled Bella in with him.

Dannika thrust the tablet into her seat and jogged across the short lobby, stopping the doors from closing with her hand. "I'm sorry. After everything that's happened, you know I don't think that's a good idea."

"Bella is my bride, Dannika."

"Oh!" Her face lit like a child opening a birthday present. "That's wonderful. Another successful match. I like you both so much, and I was hoping you'd feel the same."

Bella's heart hurt. *Don't be this excited for me. It's not going to end how you think.* She needed to escape this bitter-sweet nightmare.

Balim pulled Bella closer as though protecting her from Dannika's enthusiasm. "Excuse us, Dannika."

It had been a long time since a man had protected Bella. A long time.

"Hazel." Dannika clapped her hands. "We need to schedule Bella's photo shoot of her accepting Balim's Sea Opal, drinking the elixir, and—"

No.

"Not right now." Balim pointed at Dannika's hands in the elevator door. "Goodbye."

Dannika's smile faltered. She removed her hand. The door slid shut.

They descended.

"Thank you," Bella whispered.

"For?"

"Getting me out of there."

"I had to protect you. You were unhappy."

"How do you know?" She touched her face. He'd caught her business smile. She didn't trust her expressions around him.

"Not from your mouth." He lifted his free hand and slid one sensual finger across her hot skin just above the low-cut neckline of her emerald dress. "From here."

Suddenly, there was no oxygen.

"My chest?" Her lips trembled. *Smile like it means nothing. Smile!* "I don't have words in my chest."

"You do." He placed his palm over her heart. His fingers curved above the mounds of her aching breasts. "I hear, see, feel them. You want, Bella."

My name.

Heat kindled from his words and his caress. Her breasts swelled, threatening to spill from her constricting undergarments into his palms. A warm, liquid ache made her clench her thighs.

She wanted him to speak her name again in that soft, measured tone—in her ear, followed by the teasing tug of his teeth and the hot, wet slick of his tongue.

His intent gaze deepened as though he knew what she was thinking.

She closed her eyes.

Bella always controlled the conversation. But from the moment she'd walked into the garden, every fiber of her will bent to Balim's domination.

No longer.

Get a hold of yourself.

Only a short few hours ago, she'd run circles around Harv. And now this merman, this inhuman—sexy—monster was doing the same to her.

No one dragged Bella around.

She was here for one reason and one only. And it wasn't to remember, in panty-soaking detail, how many years it had been since she'd ridden a man's thick, hard, dominating cock.

That was a happy fantasy. And she would not experience happiness, not even one single moment, until Jonah was cured.

Hear me, God?

They reached the floor of the office. Balim dropped his palm and exited the elevator.

"You are killing me. There are more security cameras," Starr noted as Balim touched the keypad lock and punched the numbers. *"Why aren't you leaving? I'm having a heart attack. You know I can't get to you. There's a security guard on the corner. And the MerMatch office has a keypad lock. It must still be secure if the Sons of Hercules are relying on Hazel to let them in."*

Balim glanced back at Bella's ear.

"Gah, how does he hear me? It's impossible! This isn't even sound. My words are vibrating on your eardrums. It's inhuman."

Bella hummed "The Sound of Silence."

Starr shut up.

"How will me becoming your queen help Jonah?" Bella asked, redirecting his attention.

"Several ways." Balim pushed open the now-unlocked door and let her in. He disappeared into an interior office.

She strolled to the reception desk and then panned around the office.

The walls were a soothing sage green with accents of warm sand by the windows and peaceful blue couches. The thirty-gallon fish tank behind the desk glowed with light, and inside a single, white creature fluttered like a flower on the aerated tank current.

The Life Tree blossom.

Despite being a plant, its movements were smooth and calming, hypnotic, and it danced as though it were alive. It looked like a small water lily or extra-large cherry blossom, glimmering and catching the tank lights.

"*Ooh,*" Starr said, breaking her silent concentration. "*This entire place is hot. It's crawling with bugs.*"

Right. The job at hand.

Bella perused the office, following Starr's quiet directions to inspect or check on the different bug locations. She placed stickers on the windows, a jammer on the underside of the aromatherapy diffuser, and unplugged the phone cable to attach Starr's diverter. But the plug didn't look right.

"*Of course.*" Starr laughed to herself. "*The Sons of Hercules are already intercepting their traffic. Take theirs off.*"

"They'll know it was me," she muttered.

"*Just for a minute. Then log me on to the computer.*"

Bella sat at the reception desk computer. The password taped to the monitor caused Starr to guffaw, and then Bella followed the prompts to give Starr access.

"*All right...put their logger back on.*"

Bella did so.

"*Now I'll know the kinds of things they know, and with any luck, I'll be able to follow their signal back to the jerks who are peeping in.*"

Balim exited the office. "What are you doing with Hazel's computer?"

"Oh, I just wanted to check my email." Bella stood and lifted her cell phone. "Send a quick message, but I can do it another time."

He looked right through her.

She silently begged him not to ask her in the middle of this bugged office. Had Starr jammed all of them? She had to act as if they were exposed to the enemy.

As usual.

Balim relented as though he had read her mind. He

walked to an InstantPot pressure cooker, tapped the buttons, and changed the numbers.

"Cooking dinner?" she asked, still regaining her equilibrium.

"There was destruction in the labs. I am replenishing the water."

Destruction? Hmm.

"I will retrieve your Sea Opal at a later time." He straightened again and unrolled a damp mat filled with roots and reeds. He placed a chunk of vegetation into a pestle and ground it into a clear, gelatinous paste.

"My Sea Opal?" she asked, watching him.

"When you accept my gemstone, you become my bride." He took her right hand. His warm, capable fingers encircled her wrist and splayed her fingers. "That is how it usually works."

She swallowed. "Usually?"

Balim smeared the cool gel on her scabbed ring finger cuticle, an irritated hangnail on her index finger, and a paper cut she hadn't even noticed on her middle finger. It gelled like aloe and smelled like the sea.

"You need extraordinary healing for your son." Balim set the paste aside and wrapped her fingers in a thin green bandage. "There is one time a human female experiences extraordinary healing."

She looked beyond him to the Life Tree flower again. "And that is?"

"When she drinks the nectar of her warrior's Life Tree for the first time."

The blossom danced like a wish, like a promise.

Like a curse.

"*That's permanent, Bella. Elixir is temporary, but the nectar is permanent.*"

Balim's gaze eased to her ear and then back to her eyes. His own red threads gleamed with intensity.

She couldn't breathe.

Bella shook her head. Her heart thudded hard. A new possibility for Jonah. But at what cost? "I can't go with you to Atlantis."

"You must. To claim your queen powers and take your rightful place as—"

"My life is here." She spiked her voice with steel. "My son comes first."

His nostrils flared. His gaze intensified. "No mer would dare come between you and your young fry. Your dedication is well honored, Bella."

That wasn't what she'd expected him to say. She wobbled, off balance. "Well, I know your race isn't thriving."

"The needs of the many will never outweigh the well-being of a single young fry." He glowered, fiery with the truth. "Any warrior would give his life to protect a child."

Her heart squeezed. She wanted to drink the nectar. Fall in love with him. Her soul had committed. Why not her heart?

"But you want me to be your queen," she pushed.

"Queens channel the Life Tree's powers."

She shook her head again. "Faier said Jonah's soul was too dark."

"Faier is no healer."

"I know, but—"

"You possess powers beyond the knowledge of any warrior. Try. You may succeed."

She turned back to the flower. It danced like a mote of stardust on a dark night.

Wish upon a star. Free yourself. Leave this sad life behind and embrace a future far away as a mermaid.

She could never turn her back on Jonah. Balim's offer was too tempting.

Bella couldn't do it. She couldn't.

She swallowed the hard lump in her throat and forced her longings deep. "You said there were several ways to heal Jonah. What's another way?"

Balim was silent behind her.

"What are you doing?" Starr asked. *"He gave you a solution. Take him up on it. You can still save Jonah, Bel. And if this is the flower, imagine the whole tree."*

Yes, she was asking for something crazy. Once he realized the hard, ugly, ruthless woman she was, this strange spell would break. He would reel back from her, push her away in disgust. The sooner it happened, the better. She would no longer fight the compulsion to go to him and—

"The moment a bride transforms to mer for the first time, she experiences extraordinary healing," he mused, as though feeling his way through a problem. "The nectar enters your blood, resonates with your soul, and performs a change. Humans are fond of injecting blood. So if yours is injected into your son..."

"Then you think there's a chance he could gain the same benefit," she finished. "Get my healing with his healing."

He unfolded a stepladder behind the reception desk, opened the tank, rolled up his sleeve, and reached in with a small plastic cup. The Life Tree flower floated into the cup. He lifted it out and offered it to her.

"Drink and accept your destiny."

I will never transform into a mer.

He blinked as if he'd heard her. The silent refusal in her

heart. The sharp burden she carried and could never give up just because tonight, she'd glimpsed something different.

Balim frowned. "Bella?"

Bella needed to go to Balim and cup his cheek. Dismiss his feelings the same way she had dismissed Harv's. Say she'd already tried a similar proposal and there was no point in wasting the nectar on her when she would never become his queen.

But she couldn't.

Balim stood on the stepladder, a lone warrior with heartblood-red tattoos snaking up his wet arm, a strange contrast to his suit. Stuck between worlds, he was forever lonely because he belonged to neither.

She could not dismiss him. She'd cup his cheek and lean in for a goodbye kiss and crush her body to his, losing herself in his kiss, praying he never let her go.

So she took the cup.

Her fingers closed over the wet plastic. It was heavier than she expected, and the small flower danced with a strange light.

Her throat tightened. What was this emotion? Sadness? She had to tell him her truth. "I can't go to Atlantis."

"Yes."

"But you're willing for me to drink this anyway."

"Now, yes. And then hurry to your son."

She couldn't do this.

The desire curling around her heart, urging her to cup the flower and drink the bead of glimmering nectar within, squeezed.

Take it. Drink. Become a mermaid queen.

She gripped the cup. "How long does the 'extraordinary healing' last?"

"It has never been tested."

She got out the new phone. Her contacts were gone. She addressed Starr directly, even though it was dangerous and an outside observer would think she was talking aloud like a crazy person. "Dial Jonah's doctor."

Balim watched her blank screen.

"You're not thinking straight," Starr began.

"I need to drink it while we're transfusing, or else I could miss the moment."

"Bella, taking out the flower is what the Sons of Hercules want you to do."

"Dial. Please."

"Stick to the plan. Tell them you couldn't get him to release it. He can sneak it out. You can't."

"I have to."

Starr muttered. She had not secured the hospital or their route, and she chastised Bella for making herself vulnerable. *"You didn't even want to become a mermaid before tonight."*

"That's not true, and we'll take every precaution. How many resources can they have to stop me? They're a bunch of college kids."

"That's what Hazel thought when she let in the window washers three times."

"Then the longer we wait, the more chances they have of stealing it." Bella couldn't let that happen. "I know it's dangerous, but we need to go now."

Bella's phone lit up, and the number Starr had retrieved rang.

Fear warred with hope.

If the only way to save Jonah was her transforming into a mermaid and yielding to the tattooed warrior, she would do it. She made the arrangements with Jonah's doctor, but he resisted unless they promised another doctor would supervise and take ultimate responsibility. Balim gave her a name—Doctor Kowalski—and Jonah's doctor not only got approval from that physician but an eager offer of help. They would be ready.

This. Was. Happening.

Now they had to cross the city to reach Jonah.

The most dangerous journey began when they exited onto the street.

SEVEN

Balim escorted Bella out of the MerMatch office.

His warrior instincts pinged.

Although he had not heard the answers of Bella's conversation partner, he knew she meant the dangerous Sons of Hercules.

They wanted the Life Tree flower. They would try to take it from her.

"Can I risk the subway?" she murmured as they exited the office into the hall, the blossom secured in a hastily emptied and refilled water bottle she held as if it were life itself.

"We use a car service," he said.

Her ears squeaked. She tilted her head, listening. "Give me your phone."

"Mine is at the hospital drying in a container of rice. I am assured this is how humans repair damage caused by water."

She wrinkled her brows at him. "I'd think you, of all people, would buy a waterproof cell phone."

He did not know how to answer. "We can reenter and use the office phone."

"No. What's the name of your car service?"

"Dannika will know."

Her ears squeaked again.

"Never mind. We found it. Is there a side exit to the building? No, never mind. I have it."

She rode the elevator to the ground floor, pulled him behind a potted plant, and peered out the windows.

Balim's hands clenched for his trident. Daggers. Their agreement with the American government restricted these weapons, and they were not effective in the air against human ranged weapons such as guns, but he would prefer guarding his bride with his blades.

Bella clenched her purse in both hands and tucked it into her body. She leaned against him, her soft shoulders and hips brushing his.

His body hardened with readiness.

Never had he felt so much like a warrior.

"There." Bella focused on a yellow car parking outside and led Balim to the red-emblazoned emergency exit. She took a deep breath, noted the distant guards, and shoved the door open.

Alarms klaxoned in their ears. It deafened and staggered him.

She realized he wasn't right behind her, doubled back, and pulled him down the concrete steps. "Hurry!"

The building guards shouted behind them.

But Bella's focus riveted on a tall male in ordinary clothing near the front entrance. He dropped his bag and jogged toward them. A stony look set his face.

She yanked open the back door of the car, shoved Balim in, and jumped in behind him. "Drive!"

The driver stared at them with confusion. "But those security guards are—"

"Now!" She pointed at the tall man. "He's got a gun!"

The driver faced forward, saw the man, and scrambled for the controls. Their car veered backward, away from the jogger, and fishtailed around the corner. Balim slid off the bench onto the floor and Bella fell on top of him. Horns blared and cars squealed. His chest ached and his ears throbbed.

"Jeeshus," the driver cried, swerving through traffic. "What business was that? Did he have a weapon? I didn't see it. You calling the cops?"

"I thought he had one." Bella climbed off Balim and got into her seat, first checking the blossom still glinting in the depths, and then helping Balim up and fastening his seat belt with a click. "I'm so sorry if I made a mistake. I got mugged tonight, and I guess I'm seeing weapons whether or not they exist."

Balim's chest clenched. Again, he needed his trident. The mugging made little sense, and he could not endanger his bride.

Not while he guarded Bella.

They arrived at the metropolitan hospital. His hackles rose. Bella peered through the windows.

"You want me to drop you off at one ward?"

"The emergency doors, please." She whispered to Balim, "It will be less watched."

The driver coasted to the emergency drop-off. "This is it. You guys okay?"

"Soon, I hope. Thanks so much for asking." She pulled green bills from between her breasts and slipped them into his bucket. "For your clever evasive driving."

"Hey, yeah, you're welcome."

She took one last careful look and then exited the car. Balim followed her into the main entrance. She walked through the doors and pivoted.

One of the hospital security agents straightened and approached Balim.

"I must not cross here, or the director would call the police," he said.

"Oh, really?" Her gaze picked out the guard right away. "Hmm. You could have mentioned it before we walked in."

She grabbed his hand. "Follow me."

Bella wove between patients, ducked down a private corridor, and pushed into a small tiled room with sinks and stalls. A bathroom. She counted to twenty. Her thighs pressed his, her chest too close, and her forehead tilted forward so her fine red hair tickled his chin.

She opened the door, looked both ways, and led him into the elevators.

They stood beside each other in the small space.

The doors opened, and she pulled him through another long set of halls, turning corners with familiarity even after he was long lost. These human hospitals all looked the same. Twisty corridors, forced air, stagnant lights.

She clenched the water bottle as a shining beacon. Then she slowed at a quiet door and released his hand. "This is a locker room. I'll change and be right back. Don't go anywhere."

"Do not separate from me, Bella."

"I have to." She opened the door wider. "The room's empty. If anyone comes in, call out to let me know."

"Bella. I cannot guard you in places I cannot see."

"Jonah's doctor is waiting for us. I'm jumping out of my skin to start, but I can infect him by skipping these steps. Please, Balim."

Even though every instinct warred against it, he released her and stepped back.

"Thank you. I'll be right back. I promise."

He stood rigid against the wall.

She disappeared into the room.

Medical professionals passed. He tracked the light of their souls in their chests, noting who was a friend of the sea. Humans passed by, their souls darkened with grief or lightened with tentative hope. Sometimes the human couples experienced opposite feelings from each other at the same time.

Humans often married when their souls disconnected. They forced marriages. Forced joinings. Unwillingly created young fry.

The mer could not.

His soul aligned with Bella's. The tightness in his cock, which had diminished during her absence, was proof.

But did she understand?

He would protect Bella with his life. She was so close to drinking the nectar. So close to becoming his queen.

Bella peeked through the door crack, glanced both ways, and pushed out.

Her outfit was new, and she did not take his hand. They entered a hall lined with hanging sheets of opaque plastic.

"I'll go in," she said, carrying the water bottle with the dancing bloom in the crook of her arm. "They'll start the transfusion. I'll drink the nectar. You'll wait outside."

"We must kiss."

She stared at him. "We already kissed. Twice."

"We must kiss again to activate the nectar."

She squeezed her eyes shut. "Can it activate through two layers of plastic?"

"No, Bella." He turned her to face him, jiggling her

wrists so she opened her eyes once more. "We must experience the full connection. Skin to skin. Soul to soul. Bride to warrior."

"Husband to wife," she finished and shifted her weight onto her heels. "Okay. Okay. I'll figure out something. Come—"

A human male stepped into her path.

Balim pulled her sideways, out of the path of the young man, and put his own shoulder between them to block.

The male batted the water bottle out of Bella's arms. It hit the floor on the edge and burst like a bomb.

"Agh! Balim? No!"

She screamed and sheltered the wet floor with her body.

The male pushed her aside.

She landed on her hip and skidded. "No! No—"

Balim grabbed the male's arms.

The male slipped back, out of his coat, shedding it like an eel. He dove under Balim and reached for Bella again.

No.

Balim slammed a knee into the male's shoulder.

The male slid sideways.

He wheeled up to a crouch and glared at Balim with animalistic hatred. "Your kind will die."

"Do not threaten my bride!"

The man's gaze jerked to the hall. Someone shouted, "Security? Security!" He snapped his gaze back to Balim, curled his lip, and bolted.

Doctors raced toward them.

He shoved one out of his way and kept going.

Balim turned to Bella.

He had failed her.

Because he was not a real warrior. A real warrior would

not have failed. No wonder Bella hesitated to become his bride. Rejected him as a husband.

Why did a useless mer like him live when another, worthier prince fell?

Little pieces of his heart curled away as she sobbed.

Bella would never be his queen.

She knelt in the middle of a small pool, cupping the mashed, shredded petals of the dead Life Tree blossom in her palms.

EIGHT

Aweek passed.

Bella hunched over her dining room table, resting her feet on boxes still packed around her, and reviewed new hospitals.

Causing a disturbance on Jonah's fragile floor, smuggling in a trespassing merman, and coercing doctors to try a medically irresponsible procedure were prosecutable offenses.

But the hospital director would not pursue criminal or civil charges if she took Jonah to a facility more accepting of her radical care.

Her heart heaved like a paper boat on a storm-torn ocean.

None were a good fit. None would let her continue to live in this building with her quiet neighbors and sweet bulldog of a landlord, Harv. But she had no choice.

At least Balim had understood. He had forced himself to hold eye contact when she'd said it was better never to see each other again.

This pain in her heart was normal. She'd held Jonah's

cure in her grasp. Probably. No, it *would have* worked. And his cure had been ripped away. Her entire world crushed in like a soda can in a trash compactor. Her disappointment and self-reproach explained everything.

She would nail those Sons of Hercules jerks.

Nail them to the wall.

Her apartment call button buzzed. "Delivery."

Delivery?

She trooped outside her apartment and down the stairs to the front entrance, signed the certified delivery slip, returned to her apartment, and tore open the package.

A new cell phone. Not one she had ordered. She was still using the cell phone Starr had given to the street vendor to "sell" her outside the subway station.

Gee, what a generous gift from a mysterious benefactor. Hmm. Gosh, golly. Who could the mystery man be?

She pinged Starr and started her recording app.

A moment later, the new cell phone rang.

College students had no patience. As soon as Starr found them, Bella would ground these Sons of Hercules kids for life. What was that called? Oh, yes.

Jail.

"To what do I owe the displeasure?" she asked, keeping her tone pleasant as she seethed.

"You went back on the deal," the distorted feminine voice accused. "We told you to bring us a Life Tree flower, and you tried to use it on your sick kid."

"Shocking," she said, flat. "I don't know how I let myself get so distracted. Perhaps if you hadn't attacked me in the hall, we could have both gotten what we'd wanted."

"Both gotten—wait, what does that mean?"

"It means I had a plan, Herc. A plan to placate the

merman, use the cure on my child, and also get you your flower."

"You never told us that was your plan."

"How should I have contacted you? I got mugged on the way to my date. They stole my phone along with your necklace."

"You should have told us anyway."

"How? Using smoke signals?"

"Well, you should have followed our plan, not acted like you were betraying us."

"Oh, excuse me very much. Last I checked, I was the double agent, not you."

"You're not the only one who's put their life on the line. We need the flower or else."

"The situation is dynamic. Not only do the mermen sense cameras and recordings, but they can also tell when a person is lying."

"He can?"

"He can see soul lights. They show him when you're telling the truth." She leaned back and crossed her ankles, stretching. "I was trying to fulfill our goals without tipping him off, and I almost succeeded. But you had to attack me and ruin everything. When just a few more hours—"

"We can't wait. You need to get us a replacement."

"A replacement of the only Life Tree blossom in existence on the surface. Mmm. Where shall I get this for you? The local florist?"

"Since the monster likes you, you're going to swim to Atlantis and take it off the Life Tree."

It was an option.

She'd have to transform. Collect the blossom. And to activate the nectar, she and Balim would have to kiss.

The memory of his lips—and their taste and heat—made her belly shiver.

She examined her fingers. She'd taken the bandages off that night at home, and her skin had already healed. She rubbed her thumb over the smooth skin. No scabs or scars.

Every touch healed her.

Her every touch poisoned him.

"I don't have time." She picked up her own cell phone again and scrolled through the hospitals. Perhaps out of state. She'd have to quit her job. No way could she stay in this apartment building. "Thanks to your shenanigans, I have to find a new hospital for my son."

"That's not my problem."

"Correct. Just like your wish for a Life Tree blossom isn't mine."

Starr printed a message on her phone. *The signal is coming from the same cell tower.*

So, he was close. Honestly, he was probably the delivery kid with the messenger bag. She'd have to ask Harv for his security camera footage. Maybe they could get a picture.

"You're the merman's bride, Bella. He'll take you there."

"Balim can't offer me a single thing that would tempt me to leave all this behind, and believe me, I wish he could. What makes you think you have more to offer?"

"You need money."

"You can't pay me enough."

He turned aggressive. "Do what we want, or you'll regret it."

"I already regret it." She sighed and scrolled to the next state. "I regret thinking you were mature enough to wait for an intact flower. I regret not mace-tasing you when you attacked me. I regret leaving you the petals instead of giving it to a lab with the ability to analyze its properties and make important discoveries for mankind."

"There's nothing to discover about a moldy flower."

"Oh, I suppose you have a secret government lab at your disposal."

"Actually, we—" The line cut.

Did they have a high-level lab? Government funding? A private, rich, malevolent head behind their group pulling strings?

Or was this college kid bragging to sound bigger than he was?

And what did he mean he needed the Life Tree flower because others had risked their lives?

Mysteries upon mysteries, which the police would untangle when they arrested everyone.

She reached for her recording device to shut it off and archive the conversation.

The newly delivered phone rang again.

She started a new recording and accepted the call. "So you have a secret lab full of high-level scientists at your disposal, they analyzed the petals, and you found nothing valuable at all?"

"Bella Taylor." The distorted tone changed rhythm as though another person was speaking. "You will return to the monster. You will accept his offer of marriage. You will go to his Life Tree, and you will bring us one of those flowers with the nectar inside, alive."

This call is not local, Starr messaged her. *It's from the Financial District downtown.*

"Mmm," she said blandly. "Will I?"

"Or else your son—"

"Stop." Her heart thudded in her throat. "You do not threaten my son."

"Now, you understand—"

"You do not threaten him, or this ends." She shot to her feet and paced between boxes in the small apartment. "I go to the police. I give them everything I have on you. Everything."

"You don't have anything."

Starr had a lot, but Bella had something even more important. And the words flowed out of her mouth with fury.

"I have your threat. I take that to work. Do you know where I work? Do you know what I do?"

The caller fell silent.

"I design high-level ad campaigns." She lifted her fingers and ticked off her next steps. "I take your threat against my son, and I craft my masterwork. My mission is to end your organization. You portray yourselves as scrappy heroes fighting inhuman 'monsters who steal women' and a bunch of closed-minded, ignorant people give you a pass. But how many average people do you think will let it slide once you, in your own words, threaten a sick, helpless, adorable little *human* boy?"

The caller's tone was remarkably chastened. "I threatened nothing."

"Yes, I know. I would have hung up. Threats against me are stupid and shortsighted, but I *will not* entertain threats against my child. Not a breath, a hint, or a suggestion."

Silence met her rant.

She took a deep breath and straightened. "How would you like to proceed, Herc? As friends? Or as enemies?"

"Let's go back to being friends," the caller drawled, syllables elongated in the distortion. "How can I make you happy, Bella Taylor?"

"I'm so glad you asked." She returned to her seat with a

huff. "You realize there's only one thing in this world I want."

"A cure for your son?"

"And you ripped it out of my hands with your violent attack."

"I won't deny that staffing has been an issue, but the Sons of Hercules doesn't have a cure for leukemia."

"I want the next best thing." She drummed her fingers on the table.

Bella wanted Jonah to see his eleventh birthday. Running. Outside. At a park, between the swings and the slides, with roses in his cheeks and a smile the size of Texas, and hair. Adorable ginger-colored hair. Like hers, only lighter. Thick handfuls on his head, growing wild because he'd been cancer-free for a year.

There was one other possible cure.

Chaz.

When a human doesn't respond to Sea Opals, I would rely on human medicine.

"What is the next best thing?" Herc prompted.

"A donation."

"More money?"

"Blood," she corrected, leaning forward once more. "I'm looking for a match. With a small capital investment of a million dollars, you will help me get it."

Herc laughed. "For a million dollars, Bella Taylor, I expect the Atlantis Life Tree itself delivered to my office."

His office? This terrorist had an office. An internship in the Financial District, perhaps? Maybe he was the resident adviser.

"Help me cure Jonah, and I'll see what I can do," she returned, hoping that Starr was logging everything.

"Before I invest, let me ask you a question. It's one of those cutesy ethics questions they ask in business interviews." He cleared his throat; the distortion squealed. "A train has derailed, and the conductor can make one last choice before he crashes. On the right is a group of ten adults. On the left is a single child, your son. Someone will die. Which direction do you steer?"

"If that single child is Jonah, then I would destroy anyone else."

"Even if you killed ten people?"

"Even if I smashed into Times Square during the Thanksgiving Day Parade. It's not even a question."

He laughed again. "I believe you would, Bella Taylor, and that's why I will forward you that million dollars and watch you try."

Herc would forward the money?

Starr could trace it. The other payment had been encrypted and too small, but a million dollars should involve the FBI.

"I assume you accept cryptocurrency," Herc continued, sinking some of her hopes. "It's all the rage on the dark market."

"Ah, well—"

"But first, let me ask you just one more hypothetical question."

"Go ahead," she said, still breathless with the possibilities.

"What would you do if the only cure for your son required you to cut out the merman Balim's heart?"

Balim's face flashed in front of her mind. Sexy, dark, mysterious. Hurt and lonely. Also like her.

Heartbroken.

The forming plan didn't require Balim. She'd cut him

off for both of their sakes. The more time she spent around him, the harder it would be when they separated.

And yet she suddenly needed to go to him now.

Before it was too late.

"That depends, Herc." She leaned back in her seat again and crossed her ankles. "Do I get to use a sharp knife or a dull spoon?"

"Your choice." But as if he'd received the answer he wished, Herc's voice dropped to dark amusement. "Enjoy a lovely weekend, Bella Taylor."

The phone clicked.

Balim was in danger. Bella sat up straight and planned with Starr. Herc's wish had been more than a pleasantry.

No, it was a threat.

The Sons of Hercules were moving. This weekend. Against Balim.

NINE

Balim crossed the parking lot, past the missing chunk of concrete shattered in the blast, and scratched at the center of his back. No matter how he contorted, he couldn't reach the itch.

Just like no matter how his soul cried for Bella, he would not go to her.

He had failed her as a warrior, as a healer, and as a male.

Roxanne exited the building, waved at him, and checked her watch. It was beeping. She talked over the noise at her usual fast pace.

"I've only got a moment. I have to catch a plane to my baby sister's wedding. She's got the most beautiful ceremony planned, and her fiancé is such a doll. And I must tell you, she loves him for his personality and not his looks—just like Pelan, you know, who hasn't the best health—because despite being a sweetie, her fiancé has never seen an orthodontist, and, to be honest, neither has she. They're going to have adorable buck-toothed children."

She tapped her front teeth.

"Anyway, since Mitch has to be at his son's recital tonight and it's a skeleton crew on account of the weekend, I've made sure the night security officers will keep the place locked. Pelan's got color in his cheeks, or at least he did a few minutes ago when I was at his bedside and we exchanged a few words, and I can't help feeling like I shouldn't go, but weddings are like babies, they're on their own schedule, and this one isn't on mine."

"I will stay vigilant," Balim promised.

"Sure you will, and I'm not trying to imply differently. I know things have been hard what with the added warriors due in this week and still no hospital finished, but those vicious Sons of Hercules running around like nasty-tempered shark-mouthed geese. Oh, I have to go, that's my alarm.

"Call Dannika and check she's made the arrangements for where these warriors will stay, and let me know if anyone from Systems Tech calls; they have an offer on our data management system. The tank's repaired, and Mitch has just finished filling it, so as soon as you go in, you can move Pelan, and I'm sure he'll get better again under the water."

"Yes, we will move him right away."

"I could stay to help."

"Your wedding—"

"Oh, and before I forget, that Doctor Kowalski called. I think he's looking for a job, and although we can't afford to pay him, we sure could use a hand; especially once Pelan is up and about again, although I'm happy to give him my hands if they would help. My alarm again. I'll see you on Wednesday, and I hope things go well.

"Although, you know, I could come back early. My family has seen little of me in the past decade, and several aunts I intended to catch up with, but I can't help feeling like something's about to go terribly wrong, so if you need me, I could cut my visit short."

"Your alarm," Balim observed on her behalf.

"Yes. Well, I really must go, or I'm going to be terribly late. In fact, I already am. I can't stand here listening to you while my plane flies away without me. Unless you think I should stay for the health of Pelan."

"I will assist Pelan," he assured her.

"Okay. All right. Good day, then." She hurried away, worry still wrinkling her brow and her crinkly hair flying in the wind.

Balim continued into the building and wound through the halls to the bed where Pelan was resting. He lay alone on a bed, but his eyes were open, not seeking the hall where he might watch his bride, but instead straining for the distant road as though watching someone drive away.

Balim checked his appearance. "You look well for a warrior who has relied on human bed rest for a week."

Pelan lay back with a sigh. His voice emerged, weak, from his dry, chapped lips. "How do humans heal without a Life Tree?"

"Very slowly."

"It is terrible." He winced and rested the meat of his palm against the edge of the seaweed bandaging his chest. "I feel hollow. As though my heart has fallen into a deep hole."

"Your bride will return soon."

He held Balim's gaze. The red-and-black threads in his eyes glimmered with fear. "It does not comfort."

"She will." Balim had seen fear many times. "And once she becomes a queen, she will heal you much quicker."

He released Balim's gaze and stared out the window. "She does not wish to be here. That is why she continues to escape me. She left me on the land, and she does not wish to reenter the water."

"Of course she wishes to be with you." His own words tasted dry like salt powder in his mouth. "On your very first coffee date, she drank the elixir. She shared your kiss, and she's transformed into a mermaid. All that remains is for you to go to Atlantis, marry beside the Life Tree, and produce a young fry."

He shook his head.

"Do not give in to fear, Pelan. Your health will improve once your mind calms."

"I am calm." His soul light flamed cool but steady, giving truth to his words. "And I do not fear. Perhaps I am not destined to find a bride."

"All warriors find their soul mates."

"Faier did not find his." Pelan sucked in a breath and winced. "I have found mine. She refuses to stay by my side. And I do not care. My words taunt me when I speak them aloud. Perhaps you are right. I am unwell." He closed his eyes.

Balim's stomach dipped.

If Pelan's illness caused his soul to separate from his bride's, then he suffered an illness the mer could not repel. Some terrible curse.

Oannes' Curse. Also known as...

No, he couldn't say it.

He lifted the edge of the seaweed. A deep wound pocked Pelan's breast plate; his body had not filled in the mass, and his bone poked beneath the thin, red scar of flesh.

No telltale blue ring of death. It was not Oannes' Curse. Pelan was merely exhausted and ill in human form.

Balim sealed the seaweed once more. "Rest here. I will check on the tank and return."

Pelan faced the window once more.

He looked so vulnerable, and yet he had found his bride. What about the new warriors arriving from Atlantis? Roxanne was correct to worry. Without brides, the warriors would have no hope of healing from a traumatic wound.

He must finish the hospital.

Balim conferenced with Mitch, stripped off his clothes, and dove into the filled tank. His long separate fins unfurled from his feet. He rested on the bottom, on his knees, and took in the liquid via his gills, tasting it. It was clean and shiny. A long crack fractured his view. But it would hold water.

Mitch walked a woozy Pelan into the lab. Pelan's female helped him on the other side. They sat the warrior, shaking, on a chair. He looked ill.

Balim kicked for the surface, popped up over the side, and grasped the stepladder. His lungs pushed out the water and sealed his gills in his lower back while his fins shrank back into his toes. He put one human foot on the top step and pulled himself the rest of the way out.

"We ready?" Mitch asked.

"The water is prepared." Balim clambered down the steps nude. "Where is Pelan's Sea Opal?"

Pelan's bride frowned and patted her loose bathrobe. "I left it in my shirt."

"Keep it beside his heart. Always."

"It was," she muttered, glancing daggers at him as she hurried out of the room, then returned right away with the smooth gemstone. Her nervousness eased as she returned to Pelan. He leaned on her with his eyes closed.

He, Mitch, and Pelan's bride helped Pelan up the ladder and into the water. The bride slipped off her robe at the last moment, hung it on the upper step, hugged her chest, and dove. As usual, her gills emerged, but she could not yet shift toes to fins.

"Pelan's looking a little worn," Mitch murmured behind his hand.

"So long as he experiences no more shocks, he will recover." Balim pulled on human clothing, tugging the slacks up his dripping legs and buttoning his stuck-damp shirt. "Set the aerator and filter. The water must stay pristine."

Mitch checked it.

The InstantPot in Balim's office beeped. It had depressurized and cooled.

Balim fished out his Sea Opal and poured the last of the depressurized elixir into Warrior Pelan's tank. He poured in new water and put his Sea Opal back into the pot.

This was to say, Bella's Sea Opal. Not that she would ever return to accept it.

His chest ached.

"All marks are within specification." Mitch recorded the temperature of the tank and the other tests into his records. "Almost back to where we were a week ago. I hope the new security gate stops the Sons of Hercules from getting close again."

Balim did as well. He'd exited the hired car at the gate, limiting the number of people who gained any access.

He examined Pelan through the glass.

The warrior looked better under the water.

The week in a bed had made Pelan sunken and nauseous even with his bride right beside him. He'd received limited comfort from their connection.

Not because their connection was flawed, but because the air was harder to connect through. It was hard for any warrior, healthy or ill. For example, Balim could stand in front of Bella, offer himself to her, even kiss her, and she'd still walked away.

He rubbed his pained chest.

Balim strode into his office and sat in his chair. It was still damp from the deluge. Fans whirred.

He prioritized the tasks Roxanne had left him. *Focus*.

Bella would have rejected him after she learned his secrets. Secrets he had never told another human or mer, not even the warriors he now considered his closest friends.

But he could not have guessed how he would fail at protecting her.

Now Bella had to rely on human medicine to heal Jonah.

He fished her Sea Opal out of his pot and studied the smooth pearl.

She would never be back again.

Mitch's voice echoed in the room behind him. "Morning, Bella."

"Hi, Mitch."

Her voice clenched Balim's soul in a fist.

He leaped out of his chair and stumbled into the main room. Around the corner of the office, he could see the entrance corridor. And there she stood. Bella.

TEN

Balim could not have been more stunned if he'd been shot in the chest.

Warm confidence filled Bella's closemouthed smile. "Balim."

He couldn't breathe.

Her soul light flared and banked with inner turmoil, showing that her calm was a lie.

Blue denim material hugged her curvy thighs, and a puffy green shirt swooped low over generous breasts he wanted to bury his face in and rest.

Something had changed.

She'd had no intention of returning to him once she'd left the hospital director's office. Yet here she was. Impending doom clouded her arrival, and even though he wished to embrace her and bury himself in her kiss, he waited with caution for her to explain.

"How've you been?" Mitch divided his attention between friendliness to her and his clipboard of tank specifications. "It's been a while. Your kid's okay?"

"Pretty much the same. I came to talk to Balim about

him, actually."

"Good thought. He's never lost a patient."

"Never?"

"That's what the warriors said. He—"

"You know each other," Balim said.

Everyone knew her but him. Dannika had known her. Faier had also. Now, Mitch.

"Mitch's son is the same age as Jonah," Bella offered, as though that explained anything. "He helped me with the elixir when we were conducting tests on Jonah."

"Before you surfaced," Mitch said.

The coincidences of how close Bella had been this whole time shook Balim. Only two weeks ago, he'd thought their near-miss at the emergency department was the closest they would ever pass.

Yet she had met Mitch. She'd visited this lab. Knew security.

He'd felt her everywhere and thought she was beyond his reach.

In that time, she'd felt nothing.

He pulled himself together, calmed his shock, and gifted her his steady professionalism. Uncontrollable resonance did not draw her the way it drew him.

She would never come to him.

"Why are you here?" he asked.

She smiled with a closed mouth and set a teasing tone. "You don't sound that pleased to see me, your fated soul mate."

"The sooner I give you what you need, the sooner you will leave me again."

Mitch gave him a side-eye, then backed out of the room and escaped down the hall to give them privacy. Pelan and his bride, sleeping in the tank, would not respond.

Bella laughed, startled by his accuracy. "That's a little harsh, don't you think?"

"Am I wrong?"

Her laughter died.

"You had no intention of returning. Something has gone wrong."

"I wanted to see you and make sure you were okay."

"You are doing it again."

She put her hand to her mouth. "Doing what?"

"That. Yes." He nodded to remind her he could see her true emotions reflected in her soul, not only the falseness of her smile. "You lie when you pretend to smile."

"It's only because...fine. We'll do this the mer way. Blunt and with no accounting for social graces." She dropped her hand and rested her thumb in her pocket. "I came to see you."

His chest squeezed. He cleared his dry throat. "Now I am seen."

"And to ask something..."

"Ask."

She diverted her gaze and strolled around the tank. The devices behind her ears emitted the high-pitched shrieking.

"This place is clean. No listening devices here. It's secure."

"Aside from the devices behind your ears, yes."

She struck him with her startled gaze and then veered away again. "Are you staying here all weekend?"

"Unless I am called away."

"You might ignore any call-outs until you have better security."

"Why?"

"Here seems like a safe place to hide from the Sons of Hercules."

His failure stabbed into him again.

He clenched his hand into a fist around the pearl in his palm. Every instant she was here, he had to use his entire strength to stop himself from falling at her knees and begging forgiveness. "Ask your question, Bella."

She crossed her arms. "You're making this a little hard, you know."

"How so?"

"Do you not know?" She laughed, nerves mixing with disgruntlement. "I'm worried about the Sons of Hercules, and I'm trying to ask if you would..." Her gaze focused on his fist. Her fake smile wiped away. "Is that your Sea Opal?"

His fingers opened on the smooth pearl. Smaller than some other warriors', still tinted with the minerals of his home city, and all his.

He extended it.

She pulled it into her cupped hands.

Her fingertips ghosted across his palm.

Shivers walked up his spine. He clenched his hand.

She lifted the pearly gemstone. It looked larger in her hands than in his. Wonder and terror lit her face. She studied the Sea Opal with an uncomfortable mix of honest emotions.

"I can sense you on it somehow." She turned the palm-filling pearl over and over. "I saw Faier's once. Yours is more...I don't know. Sustaining, and capable, and yet also dark..."

"It is yours."

She closed her fingers around the gemstone tight and held it to her chest. Her soul brightened with fierce heat. "I can have this?"

"It already belongs to you."

She returned her gaze to the Sea Opal. Warriors had

been gifting them to sacred brides for generations. When a bride accepted her warrior's offering, she accepted their marriage.

Wicked light reflected in her green eyes. "Mine..."

The rush of hunger crashed over him and dragged at him, urging him forward. To take her into his arms. To own her. To unite their bodies and souls.

He set his feet, resisting.

Her calculating gaze flicked to him once more. "Would you give me anything?"

"Yes."

"Even things you don't own?"

"Those are easiest for me to give."

A real smile lifted her lips. "You're so different from Faier."

He dipped his head in acknowledgment. Faier bore heroic scars with greater honor.

Balim's scars existed only in his mind. Hidden inside, he was fractured by torture, splintered by revenge, filled with seeds of deadly evil.

Most days, he healed his warriors and supported the rise of his race. But on any day, he could flip and end them. Mer and humans.

Bella knew. She sensed it even when he spoke no words. Her amusement wavered.

The metal behind her ears vibrated.

"You wear the earrings once more," he commented.

Discomfort flashed across her face. "Oops. Caught again. How do you do that?"

"Hearing such high-pitched sound is a trait of the mer."

"That seems likely." She twirled around the room, glanced into his office, and peeked out the hall doors to the labs and conference rooms. "I came to peruse your new lab... There...and to invite you on a road trip."

"Road trip?"

"Upstate. I've got family I want you to meet."

He noted the hesitation. "Why?"

"If we're serious, it's important you know who I am."

"Serious?"

"About me becoming your bride." She clicked her boots together. "Going to Atlantis. Joining in front of the Life Tree."

He stopped.

Fear and anger showed in her expression along with resolve. Complex emotions beyond simple lies.

She intended to join with him as his bride?

The tide crashed over him again. He needed her. He wanted her.

He would destroy her.

Warrior Pelan needed him. He must speak with Dannika. Doctor Kowalski. Wait for the call of the data company. Figure out how to secure the incoming warriors from the Sons of Hercules.

"Just say yes," she pushed. "Live a little."

"I am dangerous to you."

Her brows smoothed with assurance and another touch of amusement. "I'll keep us safe. I promise."

He didn't believe her.

She reached over and took his hand.

His fingers closed around hers of their own accord. She was warm, vital, a lifeline of strength and light. With her, he could be redeemed. He could become honorable.

No. His past was too black.

"Come on." Bella pulled him, prancing backward through the lab. "I promise you'll have a...a time."

On that promise, he followed her to her matte-red car. The offer wasn't real. He felt dazed. Bespelled.

She tried to put his offering into her jeans pocket, but it was too small to contain the gemstone.

Instead, she secured it inside her purse, folded him into the passenger's seat, waved at the guard at the gate, and drove onto the highway.

He patted his pockets. He'd left everything important in the lab. His cell phone. The identification cards Hazel and Dannika asked him to take.

"I never drive," she confessed, weaving between cars and jerking hard on the wheel. "We have to make a quick stop."

He concentrated on the sounds of the engines of these strange land boats. Bella clicked on the radio. Her nail lacquer was fresher this time, as if she'd put it on when she was more composed. They exited the blaring road and pulled up in front of the metropolitan hospital.

Anger and disappointment rushed through him. He'd thought she would accept his Sea Opal. But no. She rejected him still.

"Wait right here," she said. "I just have to do something real fast."

"You give the gemstone to Jonah."

Her mouth opened and closed. She tucked a lock of red hair behind her ear. "Is that a problem?"

Only her jettisoning his offering moments after she received it.

But he was unfair. This surprise contact, this "road trip," was more than he thought he'd receive from her again. No matter the reason, she had gifted him with contact.

He folded his arms and focused on the empty cars surrounding them. "I await your return."

ELEVEN

The implacable warrior turned his dark, thoughtful gaze on Bella. The red threads in his eyes gleamed. He knew she was messing with him. Lying. She couldn't help it. Even to save his life, she couldn't be honest.

She tapped the car door. "I'll be right back."

He tipped his head back and gazed over the vacant lot.

She strode in, hurried up to the children's ward, and skipped her usual pleasantries with the nurses. They knew what had happened; everyone kindly worried on her behalf and on Jonah's.

But now, thanks to Balim, she again held a small token. And she had to give it to him, even interrupting the road trip.

She changed in the locker room and raced to Jonah's room, pushed through the strong fan, zipped the door closed again, and walked through the second door. Nothing must penetrate Jonah's safe, sterile chamber.

Jonah was asleep again.

She'd only seen him awake a few minutes this month.

He'd finished his most recent regimen of chemo after they weren't sure he could handle any more. Now, in the recovery phase, she was praying.

This might help.

She took out her contraband.

The Sea Opal.

She'd washed it and sanitized it as best she could, even though the hospital did more to purify cards, birthday presents, and the supplies intended to enter his room. There wasn't time.

Bella tucked it into his hand, but the stone was so big and he was lax in sleep. Just like when he'd been a toddler.

Speaking of which...

She dug out his ragged bear—he was sleeping on it for comfort—and opened the back. The bear, made with her own shirt she'd sent in to a custom shop in Omaha, played her heartbeat, but the battery had worn out long ago. She pulled out the dead heartbeat mechanism and put in the Sea Opal instead, Velcroing it shut. She placed it in the crook of his arm.

He tightened on it, hugging it to his chest.

She rested on her heels.

Another hope. Probably a dead end. *Please, please let this help Jonah heal.*

Exiting, she hurried to the locker room and found her way blocked by the grandmotherly nurse.

"I'm so sorry to hear about what happened last weekend." The gentle nurse squeezed Bella's fabric-clad forearm. "Jonah's a sweetheart. We're rooting for him."

"Thank you so much." She patted the nurse and edged around her.

The longer Balim was outside, the more chance the Sons of Hercules would discover him.

The nurse held her ground. "Have you found a support group for when the time comes?"

"Yes, I've met support groups for family battling long-term illnesses, but I haven't quite had the time—"

"Grief support," the nurse corrected. "For letting go. When the time comes."

Fire crackled in her heart and acid sizzled on her tongue.

Jonah was *not* terminal. There was still hope. Hope was tiny and fragile and slipping away, but it was all she had, and Bella would not relinquish it for anyone, not a megalomaniacal sociopath and not a well-meaning nurse either.

Bella took a deep breath and squeezed her hands. "Thank you so much for checking in with me. I can't emphasize enough how...much...your concern makes me feel. I am seeking support systems during this trying time. Thank you."

She studied Bella but accepted the answer, patted her hand, and stepped aside. Bella thanked her once more and escaped into the locker room.

Perhaps Balim was rubbing off on her.

Bella rested her forehead against the cold metal.

She had to face Balim. The weekend together. This road trip.

Starr had taken every protective measure to safeguard the warriors from whatever the Sons of Hercules were scheming—without revealing her existence. But Bella had forgotten something. In only a few days, she'd pushed away from the memory of how Balim mesmerized her. Made her forget herself. Made her crave a life she could never live. Made her want him.

Bella had to see this through.

She dragged on her jeans and a warm purple sweater, gave herself a touch-up in the mirror, and strode out.

Balim waited for her in the rental coupe alone.

A worry behind her chest eased.

She avoided his gaze and forced her smile, unable to stop herself even though she knew that he knew what she was doing. She buckled in and started the engine.

"Jonah is unchanged," he guessed.

"Yes." She composed herself. "Thank you for your patience."

He did not respond.

She drove out of the hospital.

The drive out of the burroughs was quiet as the Sunday afternoon should be. In a short time, she'd pushed out of the dense population. Once past Yonkers, the whole state opened up to scenic greenery—well, it was fall, so the green had turned to rustic reds, coppery oranges, and golds. Soon the trees would die back and reveal peeks of the nearby mountains.

Her shoulders relaxed.

New York State was such a strange mix. Inside the city, in the burroughs, the concrete and glass seemed infinite against the gray of canals, sea, and cloudy sky, but only a short distance out of town nestled the rural underpinnings of apple orchards, mountain villages, and the tip of the Great Lakes. Buffalo was six hours' drive from Manhattan, but it felt about six states away, instead of being within the same state.

Bella fiddled with the radio, alternating between NPR and old jazz. Perhaps they could reach their destination without her ever having to tell Balim anything.

"It cannot help," he said.

She rested her hand on the parking brake. "What wouldn't?"

"The Sea Opal. You already gave him elixir. Ingesting micro particles is much more effective for humans than skin contact with the resin stone."

Her heart crumpled into a ball of hollow tinfoil. "I'm sorry. I have to try."

"There are many gaps. Many types of illnesses humans suffer that mer do not. You received the elixir from Mitch and Faier?"

"Before you surfaced, yes."

"How much?"

"Ten gallons." Doctors had tested it for sterility and inserted it via his IV. Because there were no side-effects found with Sea Opal elixir, her doctors were fine with trying it. Her son had even drunk it. The therapy had taken weeks.

"And your son did not improve?"

She shook her head. "The myeloblast count didn't change."

"And that is bad?"

"Are you familiar with AML?"

"No."

"Leukemia?"

"Not at all."

"Your bone marrow produces three types of blood: red cells, which carry oxygen, platelets, which clot and prevent bleeding, and white cells, which fight disease. Right?"

He studied her as though he was learning this information for the first time.

"Right," she affirmed, for herself. "Well, a mutation can cause white cells to stop maturing. Stunted cells crowd the bone marrow. Healthy blood cells can't get made, which leads to problems."

"Such as?"

"Your kid gets anemia from low red cells and strange bruising from low platelets. Stomach aches from the buildup of immature myeloblasts in the liver and kidneys. Every single cold and flu overwhelms the few mature white cells. And just when you're on a deadline and out of sick leave, the doctors call you in for the...bad news."

She couldn't say death sentence.

Jonah had already fought the blood cancer into remission twice. Less than a quarter of patients diagnosed with AML survived five years. He'd been through chemo. He'd been through transfusions.

"I used to blame Chaz. No one in my family ever had leukemia. But all those stunted cells, like toxic hoarders, have a lot more in common with my upbringing."

He remained silent.

The long fuzzy silence of the intermittent radio got to her. She flipped channels seeking something good. "Well, there's personal history you don't want to know."

"I do want to know you, Bella."

"You'll regret it." She sighed and rubbed her mouth. "When I grew up, I was going to take care of myself. I was going to have an amazing job and tons of money. I'd never have to use underhanded means to get away with breaking rules or taking advantage of trustworthy people. And instead, I've turned into the very person I hate most. Manipulative, money-hungry, poor, helpless. Lying. I hate it. I hate...leukemia."

Another long silence filled the car.

He broke it. "I do not know leukemia. Mer do not have this illness."

"You're half human."

"It is not one of the one hundred seven illnesses. You called it a blood cancer? We have no cancers."

"Must be nice to be immortal."

"We are not. We have no machines to see inside a warrior or to perceive creatures smaller than the eye. Perhaps the technology of humans could ease the suffering of warriors afflicted with invisible illnesses."

"Our technology hasn't done Jonah much good." She tasted the bitterness on her tongue. "If I'm a bride, why doesn't he respond to Sea Opals? He carries half my genes. Why isn't that good enough?"

"Many brides have cried over the accidental drowning of their human children."

Her heart felt heavy.

"I understand that many humans have been resuscitated after drowning," Balim said. "So you must rely on human medicine now."

And she was.

To take her mind off their destination, she turned the radio to background level. "What's it like where you're from?"

"Wet."

She laughed, surprising herself. "Tell me something that isn't obvious."

"Beneath the ocean, the water is air. Floating is hovering. Swimming is flying. And coming onto land again is unsettling because the ground flies at you, always, with no safe cushion."

"The ground flies at you?"

"That is the feeling of losing your balance." He gestured with his hands flat. "The horizon does not remain fixed. You are caught by surprise. Experience betrays you."

"So the same way sailors have sea legs, mer have ground legs? Cool."

"It is a normal temperature, I think."

She snorted again, and they passed several pleasant hours snacking on old packages of goldfish crackers and gummy bunnies and diet cola. They reached the final turnoff into the suburb as the sun descended. Dying leaves clustered beneath large oaks and crunched beneath her tires. She parked and shut off the engine.

Chaz lived on a nice, sidewalk-lined street filled with picket fences, raked-over garden beds, and kids' trikes. Lights inside his house reflected the cold.

"Okay." She got out of the car and tightened her warm sweater around her. "Go along with me."

Balim also exited the car. "Go along?"

"This is my last hope to get a human cure. I'll play a desperate, grieving mother. You play a rich merman with buckets of Sea Opals."

He opened his empty hands. "I could have brought these if you had asked me."

It hadn't occurred to her. And she'd put hers in Jonah's bear. "It's fine. Just follow along."

"I will not lie."

"You won't have to." She climbed the steps and clanked the big knocker. "I'll do all the talking."

TWELVE

Balim had no idea what to expect.

Only the dread filling Bella's heart, which looked like darkness on her chest, punctuated by bright spots of anger. He tensed for an emotionally devastating fight.

She clacked the metal clapper.

Someone thudded inside the house, and light glowed out the window.

Bella straightened, smoothed her purple sweater, and fixed on her widest fake smile.

Balim braced for combat.

The door opened on a slim, short female with disheveled blonde hair scooped into a messy heap on the top of her head. She wore thick glasses. She squinted through them. "Yes?"

"Caro." Bella smiled broadly, her lips closed over the tooth gap. "Good evening. Is Chaz in?"

"It's dinnertime."

"I'm so sorry. This will only take a few minutes. I'll be gone before you know it."

She peered at Balim, but her gaze veered away. "You should really call."

"I did call. You know how he is about calls. And voice messages. And email." She maintained her false smile the entire time. "Please. I've driven this entire way. It will only take a few moments. It's about Jonah."

Caro reluctantly let them in. She walked in socks down the hardwood floor and left them in the subdued living room. "Don't touch anything."

"Of course not." Bella linked her fingers.

Caro eyed her suspiciously and padded deeper into the house.

Small plastic cars and miniature human clothing spread over the room furnishings. On the wall hung photos of two boys posed on human bicycles.

Balim set his feet. "Are the items fragile or booby-trapped?"

"No, she was warning me not to steal." The false smile tightened Bella's face as she tried to find amusement in the warning.

"Do you intend to steal?"

"If I could steal what I want, I wouldn't hesitate."

"Bella." A man's voice accompanied his shadow. "Caro says you brought a lawyer?"

Bella glanced back at Balim, her gaze lingering on his dry button-up shirt and jacket Hazel had told him was proper for most situations. "He's a doctor."

"A doctor?" Chaz flipped on the lights as he entered the living area. He stared at Balim in confusion. "What's the meaning of this?"

Caro lingered at the end of the hall, close enough to overhear. She crossed her arms over her chest. Her light faded. This man was bright with defensive anger.

Bella put her hand on Balim's shoulder. "Balim is a merman. He's chosen me for his bride, and he's gifted me a Sea Opal worth well over a million dollars."

Chaz lifted his chin, his arrogance and anger focused on Bella. "Did you come here to brag?"

She was instantly infuriated. Her tone sharpened and her words shortened. "No, Chaz, I came here to ask you again to—"

Two boys barreled around the corner and flew past Caro. They landed in front of Balim and stared up at him in shock.

"Wow," the older one said while the younger stared in awe. "What are you?"

He squatted to their height. "I am a merman."

"A what? No way."

He held up his hand and shifted. The thin skin between his fingers tightened and stretched to make a mitt that would scoop the water. It was the easiest way to show his powers.

"No way! No way, no way! Are you really?"

"Yes. Ask me anything."

While Balim distracted the boys, Bella spoke to Chaz. "It's not a brag, it's a bribe. He has money, Chaz. Money that could be yours. *A million dollars*. Help me, and I'll help you."

Good. He could help her accomplish this and spend time with human children. He had seen more in the past months above the surface than in his entire life beneath the sea. Young fry were innocent and bright no matter whether they were humans or mer.

Balim brushed the hair off the older one's eyebrow. A scab had formed. "Hmm. You have an injury."

"He fell off his tricycle," Caro said defensively. "He rips off Band-Aids."

Balim patted his suit pocket and pulled out his smallest kit. Removing gel, he smoothed it on the boy's cut. "Now you will have no scar."

The child wrinkled his brow, trying to stare up at the gel quickly drying into a bandage. "Wow."

The younger boy bounced. "I want one too."

Balim checked his hands. This boy was afflicted with one of the 107 illnesses: small, round growths on his index and middle finger knuckles the mer called Minnow Bites. He'd scratched several, because they jutted up from the skin. "Can you keep on bandages?"

He nodded.

"Yes," Caro said.

He sprinkled salt into his paste and wrapped a seaweed bandage around each knuckle. "Leave this on for two human days. The growths will shrink into your skin until they disappear."

The boy rubbed the slick green seaweed with awe.

"Those'll never last for two days," his mother said, pulling both her children back and away, and trying her hardest not to look at Bella and Chaz. "He takes a bath, and he just loves running his fingers in the sink."

"It is better if the bandages remain wet."

"You sure?"

"Yes." Balim stood and returned his small kit to his jacket pocket. "I am a mer."

She blinked, frowned, and ushered her children back to their food. The boys raced around the corner and disappeared into the brighter section of the house. Caro remained near Balim in the doorway to the living room, while Bella and Chaz's argument grew loud.

"I'm not taking your test." Chaz cut the air with his hand. "You know how they harvest the marrow? They stick a needle *in your bone*."

"Only if you match."

"No, Bella. I won't put myself through that."

"So take the test." She whipped a paper envelope out of her purse and lofted a small plastic tube. "One cheek swab. If you're not Jonah's match, I go away forever."

He held up both hands. "Get that thing away from me."

"It's a Q-tip, Chaz."

"I already told you no! There's nothing you can say to change my mind."

Her chest flared to match Chaz, anger to anger, while her smile only broadened. "Not even for a million dollars?"

The man glanced at Balim and then back to Bella. His greed was piqued. "What are you talking about?"

"If you match Jonah and donate bone marrow, I'll give it to you. A million dollars. For you or anyone in your family. Or anyone."

Caro stepped forward. "Chaz already told you no."

Chaz tapped his lip with his index finger, then jerked his head at Caro without looking at her. "Go back to dinner, Caro."

Her light dimmed, but she held her ground. "You always get dragged around by her."

"Caro."

She sputtered at Bella. "I won't let you touch my boys."

"That's your choice." Bella focused on Chaz. "They're only a one-in-a-million chance of matching Jonah like you or any other stranger. Chaz has a one-in-two-hundred chance."

She got more upset. "And you want him to sell off his body parts for money!"

"For *his son*. And bone marrow grows back."

"Quit asking for pieces of my husband."

Bella's smile flattened. Her true feelings flared out. She ticked off a list on her fingers. "I have never asked for alimony. Never come after him for child support. I don't even send you guys a Christmas card."

"We don't want one!"

"Jonah is dying. He needs a bone marrow transplant. I have no choice."

Chaz came to a decision. He motioned Caro the rest of the way into the room and put his arm around her, while she continued to cross her arms and glare. "Bella. I cut you out of my life a long time ago. This is my family now. No more sneaking in a surprise bone marrow registration drive at my church or my workplace. We're through."

She tapped the tube against her wrist. "Not even for a million dollars?"

He hadn't heard her. "Huh?"

"You won't swab your cheek for your firstborn son for a million dollars."

He jerked his head back and pressed a hand to his chest. "Hey, I'm not the bad guy here. Your kid has bad luck. I made youthful mistakes, but now I'm the head of a good Christian family."

"The other members of your congregation tested. You walked right past."

"Because you won't manipulate me." He gestured for her to leave. "Take your blackmail and your guilt trips and get out of here. You're giving me more indigestion than Caro's idea of pot roast."

His wife's soul light grew weaker with his insult. She squared her shoulders to make herself more in sync with her husband.

Bella stuffed the envelope into her purse. "How insensitive of me for inconveniencing you during dinner. You probably weren't a match, anyway."

"Quit your harassment." He hugged his wife. "Leave me and my boys in peace."

Bella's chest light extinguished. She turned and ran into Balim.

He held her shoulders, supporting her. Bella swallowed convulsively, regaining control. She did not show weakness, and the other couple would only see her back straight with pride.

He studied Chaz, irritated and righteous, beside Caro, threatened and scared.

"What are you looking at?" Chaz demanded.

"I do not know," Balim responded.

"Huh?"

"It is strange."

"You think I'm strange? You're the one with scary red tattoos on your face."

"Humans have so many children, yet such bounty does not increase your joy."

"Of course not." He snorted. "We've got more mouths to feed. If it's a choice between my kid and somebody else's, I'm saving my kid. You're lying if you don't treat your 'treasure' the same."

"Young fry are not one male's or one city's treasure. They are the future, and therefore the treasure of the mer."

"Her kid's not my future. I wasn't there when he was born. She's the one who screwed up."

"That is what I cannot understand. You carry such coldness in your soul."

Chaz raised a brow. "If the only way to save her kid was

to hurt yours, you'd hurt your own kid? That's not love. That's sick."

His question struck too close to Balim's bone. Long-suppressed anger, which had been leaking out along with the other emotions since Bella had first crossed his path, hissed like acid as it ate into his heart.

"You let my son die! How dare you heal your son first? He is useless! Not even a warrior! Now you will die, false healer."

Balim would never forget that shout. The grief. The screams.

Hard anger made his empty hand clench for his trident.

Bella sucked in a long, deep, calming breath and let it out. Fierce. Strong. She straightened and murmured to Balim, "Thank you," before once more facing Chaz. Her chin trembled, but her voice remained steady. "That is the difference between you and him. He heals everyone who crosses his path, even a little scrape or hangnail. You won't lift a finger to save your boy's life."

Chaz darkened.

Caro trembled, held on to Chaz's elbow, and spat at Bella, "Get out."

Bella's chest flared. "I hope your sons don't get sick. Because it's a long road to travel alone, and as you can see, he won't even swab his cheek with a Q-tip."

Caro's soul light fluctuated. She knew the truth of Bella's accusation. For the first time, she looked at her husband with a question.

Chaz didn't notice. "Go, before I throw you out."

Bella linked hands with Balim and tugged him through the front door.

They had failed to acquire human medicine from this selfish Chaz. Now what would happen to Jonah?

Once more, Balim had gone to war with Bella and failed her. Healing was all Balim had ever been able to do, and now even that was called into question.

THIRTEEN

Outside the house, Balim breathed in the crisp air and tried to focus on calming himself. The acid of his memories damaged him, dissolving his usual limits. The night felt strange. Dangerous.

He focused on Bella. "That male must have changed since you chose him to father your child."

"Chaz was always selfish."

She brushed empty food packets out of her way and settled into the car again. While he buckled in, she checked messages on her phone, made sure they were both ready, and drove down the road into the city of Buffalo.

"He was a rising salesman at the first firm I worked. We were sleek and selfish and rising stars together. Then, an accident happened. I got pregnant."

"And he did not treasure you."

"No. He did not."

Balim stared out at the strange lights in the human city. So much of the human world had become familiar, and yet so much would never make sense.

Bella made a frustrated noise. "I shouldn't have said that to Caro. I would feel bad if one of her kids got sick."

"Your words were accurate."

"Yeah, but I would hate for anything to happen to them. Or anyone. I mean, maybe Chaz is right, and he'd be in the millionth percentile of people who go healthy into a hospital and end up dead."

"You do not believe this."

"Of course I don't. I'm trying to talk myself out of going back and murdering him." She tapped the steering wheel with her palm. "Freak accidents could happen. Like the guy who went crab fishing, stuck his finger, and contracted flesh-eating bacteria."

"Crab-Cut Disease," Balim identified.

"It's a known illness?"

"One of the mer one hundred seven, also known as 'Warm Seas Disease.' It is common and terrible if untreated."

"I bet. It was terrible even when treated."

"He must drain the poison, pack the wound with astringent gel, and rest against the Life Tree until the streaking descends into the wound and disappears."

"Yeah, well, we have antibiotics. I think the guy lost an arm."

"He experienced a mild infection."

"Mild!"

"Although inconvenient, an arm will grow back."

She blinked. "No, it won't."

Oh, he had forgotten. An unfortunate problem. Humans could not regrow missing pieces. Their robotic limbs were very interesting.

"Grow back..." she muttered. "Limbs don't just grow back."

"They do with the healing sap of the Life Tree."

"I wish we had a Life Tree on land. Then we could cure everything."

He let her believe that for a short time, but it was inaccurate, and so he forced himself to say the truth. "Almost."

"Oh, so you do have cancer?"

"Rare diseases do not respond to the Life Tree."

"So what do you do?"

"Nothing. They are ancient diseases that have never left their cursed grounds."

Except once.

Never again.

To avoid any follow-up questions, he reached back into Bella's purse, removed the envelope, and examined the plastic tube. "How does it work?"

"How does what work?" She glanced over, saw the tube in his hand, and her expression flattened. "You want to test yourself for a match?"

"Yes."

Her soul light flared and her chin wrinkled. She sucked in several breaths and cleared her throat, but she continued driving one-handed, the other pressed to her mouth.

"Why does my action make you so sad?"

She answered, muffled by her hand. "You're not even Jonah's... You, an absolute stranger, would offer to help him and the people who should care refuse..."

"He is your treasure," Balim pointed out. "And I am your soul mate."

Bella dropped her hand, pulled a U-turn at the next intersection, and drove the opposite direction.

"I have upset you."

"No. No, no. This is just... I can't let you affect me like this. So I won't. You'll see."

Her soul fluctuated between bright and dark, and she ripped off her jewelry—earrings, vibrating metal piece, necklace, and hair clips. Her hair descended and brushed her shoulders.

"You must calm."

"No, calm is the last thing I need right now."

She drove to a parking lot, got out, and walked to a railing. Beyond it, mist blew off a slow-moving river and a giant bridge roared with traffic. Bella gripped the railing with hands covered by the thick sleeves of her sweater.

"Where are we?" he asked.

"We're still in Buffalo. This is Black Rock Canal. That's the Niagara River. It drains from Lake Erie over there. And that's the Peace Bridge. The other shore is Canada."

How strange that humans had no real markers between cities or countries. They bled into one another, sharing resources. Cities beneath the sea were much more separate. Above the ocean, everyone crossed between countries by a simple bridge. Such freedom of movement was impossible undersea.

"I was going to take you to the Niagara Falls because the light show is so impressive, but this can't wait." She turned to him. "The first time I transform after drinking the permanent Life Tree blossom nectar, my body will experience 'extraordinary' healing. It's not affected if I transform after only drinking the temporary Sea Opal elixir?"

"No. They are separate."

"So I could transform right now and still try the nectar trick later with Jonah?"

His heart thudded, sudden and hard, and a lump formed in his throat. He had to clear it, and his voice broke when he spoke. "You wish to transform?"

"I feel too much to stay confined within this skin." She

clenched her fists against her chest. The gesture was a horrible insult beneath the water, and it fit the intensity of her feelings. "It has to come out. Right now, right here, or else I will go somewhere with you and—"

She broke off, but her gaze lingered, hot and fiery, stroking his pectorals and abdomen and centering right on the hard, throbbing center of his rigid cock.

His cock tugged under her heated gaze.

"Go somewhere with me," he said, his voice thick with hunger.

She jerked her gaze away.

"We have no elixir here, Bella."

She turned away. Her breath emerged as fog and joined in with the mist above the river.

He stood beside her and rested his bare hand on the damp metal rail.

She glanced at his shirt. "Aren't you cold?"

"Rarely."

"Are you serious? Like, not even in the Arctic?"

"Never in the water."

"Never cold. I'm so jealous." She gazed out over the mist. Her soul fluctuated a bunch. "Jonah's been sick over a year. Do you know the worst part? Sometimes I want to escape it all. Pretend I'm single. Start over. Isn't that awful? He's my child, no one else is fighting for him, and what happens if I give up?"

Her question chilled his heart. "You have not betrayed him yet."

"Yet," she agreed and rubbed her chest. "But I will. Someday. Does that disgust you?"

He studied her. She was a mystery. "Are you trying to disgust me?"

"It would be easier."

"What would be easier?"

"If you would just go away." She dropped her head on his shoulder. Her temple was warm, and her hair caressed his cheek like ghostly fingers. "Then I could stop feeling guilty."

He allowed himself to reach up and touch the soft tickles. His fantasies from before washed over him. During the drive. Thinking about sliding kisses up her arm, resting on the parking brake, across her chest. Kiss every one of her freckles. His cock pulsed hard in his pants, ready and thrusting for her. Her long curls, her large sunglasses, her jeans. She called her dress casual, but she amazed him. He had plotted his own betrayal for years.

"I will never force you to choose between me and your son," he said.

"Yes, you will."

She straightened, pulled off her sweater, shirt, and shoes and tugged down her pants. Her curves were exposed to the chilly air, and she shivered as she stepped out in generous undergarments humans called a bra and panties.

Then she ducked between the rungs and shivered, hugging herself, on the edge of the small embankment next to the river. "I'm already betraying you."

"Wait." He leaned on the railing to grab her arm. "Do not enter this water."

She leaned out of his reach.

"Stop, Bella. You have drunk no elixir."

"Actually, that's not true." She squinted out on the water. "Your idea to have me drink the nectar and then give my blood to Jonah wasn't the first time someone suggested that. I drank half a gallon of elixir a few weeks ago." She shivered. "Let's see if it's still in my system."

"This is a dangerous test."

"Does it anger you?"

"It worries me. Do not treat yourself so savagely."

"Savage." She laughed, her teeth chattering. "But that's who I really am."

"No."

"I'm so 'nice.' Diplomacy is my bread and butter." She shook her head. "This is what happens when I break."

"Bella—"

"Am I a mermaid, Balim? Am I your destined bride? Soul mate?"

A wave of tenderness crossed over him. She shivered and pretended to be hot. The spell uniting their souls circled his heart. He was as much a prisoner as she was.

"Yes." He pressed against the railing. "We could resonate more."

Her soul light flickered as her gaze lowered, dropping down his chest, to his belt, and then up again. Her lips quirked. "Sometimes, Balim, you just have to make a leap of faith."

"You are not safe!"

"Darn right. Don't I infuriate you?" She tipped backward into the water. A splash collapsed over her body. The frigid waters cut off a horrified shriek.

She had not transformed.

Now, she was drowning.

FOURTEEN

Bella self-destructed hard.

In the moment before she'd leaped off the too-high embankment, in a moment of flawed judgment, desire to let Balim in had overwhelmed her. She'd needed to jump out of her skin before she bared everything.

Before she let him into her soul.

And if she couldn't transform, he was a doctor and a mer. He'd fix her.

"No!" he'd shouted.

Icy water slapped Bella hard. Her head rang and her lungs shuddered.

Her urge to be wild and crazy, to shake off her feelings for him, evaporated beneath the cold, hard ice of reality.

Why was she so stunned? It wasn't that far of a drop. She twisted in the black water and struggled to figure out which way was up. Her lips and fingertips numbed.

Everything was going wrong.

She had done irresponsible things in her life. Once, when a crush had asked her to be his girlfriend, she'd jumped off the back of a motorcycle in the middle of traffic because her feelings had been too intense and she'd just needed to get away from them. Another time, she'd climbed up on a balcony and spun over a sixty-foot drop, laughing at the people she'd scared.

She dropped her responsible act to throw them off. Prove she was the one in charge of her destiny. Not feelings, not their expectations. She was in control.

Now she refused to yield herself to Balim. What better way to shock him than by drowning herself? She could be vulnerable while he raised his own defenses.

This wasn't supposed to kill her.

New icicles fingered her intimate crevices.

Why was it so cold?

Her diaphragm spasmed. Ice water filled her mouth and seared her lungs. She clawed at her throat. Panic turned the world to blackness. She was dying. Literally dying.

"Hold on to me." Balim's voice was somehow echoing inside her own chest, hot and demanding, as he clasped her frigid hands with his warm palms.

She thrashed for the surface, for air—

"Hold. I am with you. Calm." His arms tightened around her upper back, pinning her arms, and his powerful thighs clamped hers. "You have gills. Use them."

Gills? She had gills?

Bella writhed. His words could not overcome the dark, deadly weight in her lungs.

He nuzzled her forehead with a gentle sigh. "Why does no patient listen to me? I am the medical professional."

She stopped writhing.

Probably people didn't listen because he promoted regrowing arms.

"It is possible now for you too," he murmured, replying to her unspoken remark, "at least temporarily.

You have transformed, Bella. Feel my fingers along your gills?"

No. Now that she'd stopped struggling, she would drown here, alone, in the dark.

"You are not alone." He tightened his hold on her and skimmed one broad, warm palm down her back to rest at her hip. "And it is not dark. Open your eyes."

She obeyed.

Balim looked watchful, cautious. A serious wrinkle between his brows hid the little vein of red tattoo. His dark hair waved, and her red hair floated in a watery, free tangle.

No...

"Do not fear."

He pressed his lips to hers. Their kiss. Hot and tingly and utterly different from the surface. More intimate, more intense.

Did his kiss give her the power to breathe underwater like him?

"You already have this power," he rumbled while his mouth continued its exploration of hers, replying in his rumbly chest to words she had not spoken aloud. "You are using it to breathe and hear me. Feel it now."

Powerful rightness filled her. He was correct. Bella was no longer cold. The water swirled over every bit of her body and invaded her intimate places. It felt wild and free and dangerous.

Just like her.

His worry smoothed. He looked at peace, and that twisted her heart into knots of tenderness she did not want to feel.

She could stay with him forever...

No. She broke away. Too much remained unspoken between them. But she no longer felt about to die.

In fact, she would finally live.

She released him and twirled, savoring this one and only temporary transformation.

The lake opened up like a massive underwater room. The surface above was opaque, with distant flat lights, a colorful drink, and the bottom spread out in perfect, rocky and seaweedy detail.

Fish wove between reeds and darted at the surface bugs, flipped, and splashed. The ground moved with crustaceans, worms, crabs, and a hundred creatures she'd never seen or thought about but were as ubiquitous as flies, pigeons, and squirrels. The world was upside down. She flew in the watery "sky" and the surface was "ground" above her.

"It is disorienting." Balim's chest thrummed, and she heard his words in a space inside her own chest. His mouth remained closed as he spoke. "Orienting is easier once you are farther from shore."

Right, because the ocean was much larger.

"That is not the only reason."

She kept hearing him in her chest. It was strange.

He tilted his head at her. "I am guessing at your words. It was frustrating on the surface, but at least underwater, I can understand enough to guess. Will you not speak and be clear?"

Her own chest cavity echoed with his words. She tried mimicking the vibration. "I'm never doing this again."

"You must. Only your passive senses have transformed. Do you feel your confidence growing? As you grow confident, you will develop your human toes into mer fins. Believe, Bella. Your soul is freed now, and your passions are rising. This is how you claim your destiny as a powerful mer queen."

She felt it. She felt it in her bones, lifting her from the

muck and rinsing off frustration, turning to beautiful connection. Vibrant life flowed through her still-human fingers, swirled around her still-human toes.

Temporary. This was all temporary.

"I will never be a queen," she insisted, even as her heart soared with the healing movements of the currents and fresh, clear water, like standing under a glacier waterfall while all else fell away. "I can't join your world."

"You already have."

"No."

His brows lifted. "Then why did you enter?"

She couldn't answer.

Aloud.

Because it was her only chance. She'd lost her mind tonight. Balim had ensnared her with his words and made her remember who she used to be. Before she'd compromised, grown up, lost her way.

He waved her protests away. "By now, your unpredictable behavior should be predictable. Stay close."

She paddled toward curious spires. "What are those?"

"Watch the riptide." Balim grabbed hold of her.

A current of water—which was visible too! Like a mist upon the water—picked them up and carried them deeper into the lake like a hand picking them up and tossing them.

It was exhilarating, releasing her control and just existing. She clamped down on her scream and gave in to its power.

Balim flowed with the current and carried her deeper to calm water.

The spires grew in size. It was the broken mast of an overturned shipwreck. "I forgot this was down here."

"Do you know this body of water?"

"I should. I grew up a few miles away. Can we see the name?"

He kept her in his arms, flowing in whichever direction she wanted. His suit bunched around his joints and water moved along his hard, masculine body. His feet below his trouser cuffs extended into long fins like a scuba diver in a casual business suit. Two separate legs pumped the water, arching them over the wreck.

She pointed. "There's the helm."

He hovered over it.

"I used to dream about going on yachting tours. I never wanted my own. I just wanted to be rich enough to be invited." She let go of his hand and gripped the barnacle-crusted wheel.

"Bella, no!" He yanked her away.

Hard barnacles sliced her hands. Blood spotted the water.

"Ow." She tried to put her cuts in her mouth.

"No. You must let them flow." He held her wrists firmly in the current to drag the blood away. "Cleanse the wound if this graveyard is infected."

"Infected?"

"The disease that cursed this battleground could still be dangerous."

Battleground?

Wrecks lay in every direction. A shadow of a hull silted over and turned into caves for animals, others preserved as if the boat had lain to rest on a beach.

No wonder he thought they had fought a war here. But the wrecks were from different eras. A steamboat, a small galleon, a paddleboat, a speedboat. Canoes. A fancy yacht with broken stained glass windows. A shallow hull.

"The disease that felled these humans could hurt you,"

he repeated, his gaze boring holes into her cuts as though he were lasering any dangerous viruses away. "A single touch—a single mouthful of tainted water—and the disease awakens, spreading its deadly name once more."

Subtle tremors afflicted the hands holding her wrists too tight.

He was terrified.

Her cuts throbbed, but Balim's caring squeezed her heart. "This isn't a battlefield, Balim. Storms rise suddenly on the Great Lakes, and this was a main port in the old days."

"Then why are these vessels abandoned?" He jerked his chin.

Beneath the rusted wheel, an overturned coffee mug was still visible. Funny little artifacts of the fishermen who had piloted the vessels that had survived, intact and unmoved, despite whatever storm or failures had sunk these dreams.

"It's more expensive to dredge the boats out than to leave them in their watery graves. You must have seen wrecks on the bottom of the ocean."

"We avoid human wreckage. They crash in barren rock."

"Disease didn't kill these people," she repeated, pulling him away from the dark memories. "This reminds you of something. What?"

"The Battle of Oannes Field."

"I don't know it."

"No human would. It was a field where the coral grew into perfect uncured tridents. Two great cities, Atargatis and Derketo, claimed ownership. Warriors fought for a generation over the same ground. After too much blood had been spilled, the warriors sickened. A chain of interlocking blue rings emerged on their chests, arms, shoulders, and legs. It ravaged the field, spread to the cities, and killed both Life Trees."

Balim swallowed and focused on her cut hands once more.

"To this day, any warrior who enters the field to honor the dead, study the disease, or pluck a trident will succumb before escaping the basin. No warrior contracts the curse and survives."

She tried to soothe him. "That place is far away."

"It is abandoned. The greatest tridents and daggers of the ages are lying out in that battlefield like these cups and plates, tempting any fool to take them."

"This is more of a too-many-sandbars or inexperience-meets-stormy-weather cursed lake. Nobody died from anything here besides drowning."

He loosened his grip on her wrists as though coming back to himself, but fears continued to battle. "There are... other illnesses even in fresh water."

She tried to meet his eye and soften his fears with a smile. "You won't let anything happen to me."

"It is not always my choice."

"Mitch said you'd never lost a patient."

"I have never *lost* one." His emphasis was strange, and his gaze diverted from hers.

Wait a minute...

"One incurable disease decimated two kingdoms. To this day, the abandoned field seethes with death."

He inspected her small cuts, unrolled the tools he'd taken from his jacket pocket, and administered medicine. "Reject me and reject Atlantis, but never reject caution. I cannot save you if I am not there."

Balim released her and, still avoiding her gaze, rotated, casting his wary gaze over the wrecks.

She gathered her thoughts. "What are you looking for?"

"I do not know this area," he said. "It is a large body of water. Do mer colonize it?"

"I have no idea."

"What animals live here? Lotar is better at evaluation. He is in Atlantis."

Cold seeped into her once more.

He felt it before she did and pulled up. "Bella?"

"Let's go back to the car."

He blinked in surprise and then collected her and flew across the lake to their exit point.

Just before he reached the rocky beach nearest her jump and clambered out, she stopped him. "When you said before that you'd never lost a patient..."

His expression turned taut.

She pushed through the fear. It was important to know him. He'd stripped her bare and yet he'd cloaked a shocking secret. "Did you mean you lost someone who wasn't your patient, or you deliberately killed one of your patients?"

His dark gaze told her the answer before his chest vibrated the truth. *Both.* But his actual words skirted her question. "I am not a human saint, Bella."

"You save lives every day. Every life, in fact." *Except one.*

"By choice. The mer follow no code like your Hippocratic oath."

"What do you mean?"

"Your doctors vow to heal. Always. The mer do not."

"You always try."

"I must atone."

He had killed someone. And not saved someone. Both. "Is this why you don't mind that I never go to Atlantis?"

"It is not surprising that your soul has sensed my darkness."

"But I'm not rejecting you."

He nodded as if she twisted the knife, rejection dulling his gaze.

It made her heart hurt. "Not because of you as a person. Because of you as a mer. I can't leave Jonah. So, it's because of me."

"I understand."

"No, you don't." She grabbed his cheeks. "Why aren't you disgusted with me? I'm trying to push you away, not hurt you. I've told you time and again I'm betraying you."

"With the metal and the cameras."

"Not—well, in a way, but not the one you think. Why don't you give up on me?"

"My soul is blacker than yours."

"I'm sure it was a mistake. An accident. Not in cold blood."

"I planned his death for a long time." He held her gaze so she could not dismiss his confession. "My blood and my mind were cool."

"But you're not speaking straight. You didn't murder someone for no reason."

"No."

"My victim could not be injured by ordinary means. It took all my ingenuity to effect his death."

She'd made it worse. Trying to dismiss Balim's crime, which darkened his heart and still tore him up inside, had hurt him more than facing it headlong. Bella tried to fix it.

"What do you mean, your victim was untouchable? If he committed a crime—"

"He did."

"See? So—"

"He committed a crime against me." Fury snarled his face. He slammed a fist into his chest. "A crime against my city. A crime against the mer. But no one would make him pay that debt, so I assumed responsibility. And I had to be clever. No one must blame me. If they did, I would be exiled from Atlantis and hunted for the unforgivable crime."

He'd murdered someone beyond the law. He sounded like he'd assassinated a president. But the mer didn't have presidents. They had kings.

"Who did you try to kill?" she asked slowly.

"My king." He confessed as if he no longer had any stakes, as if he were even freer than she was. As if he was trying to push her away.

That was it. He *was* trying to push her away.

"But nobody's beyond the law, right? Not even a king."

"A king *is* the law. And I did not try." He pressed a hard hand to his chest. "I succeeded."

FIFTEEN

Balim sat on the foot of the bed at the rental while the shower ran in the other room, washing the icy lake water off his bride's chilled body.

His confession froze his heart.

He rested the towel on his wet shoulders. The dark water bunched up his shirt and pants. They'd risen from the lake, she'd pulled on her clothes, and they'd gone to this rental house. Bella had barely looked at him.

The shower shut off. Minutes passed. She did not emerge from the bathroom.

He rested his palms on the edge of the bed.

This reaction he expected from a human.

No warrior could accept such horrifying disloyalty to a king, not even the rebels who'd escaped their own cities. He was the only one who'd escaped with a king's blood on his hands.

He should have committed suicide.

But he had lived. He'd stood before the vent into the black-night sea and offered himself to the darkness. The sea beneath the sea where the bodies of dead warriors were flung, with songs of honor, to hunt the bodiless denizens of eternal darkness. A reverse current had pushed him back like the hand of his father on his chest. A voice had whispered in his ear.

No. You must live.

And the deathly box had been prised from his fingers by that same current and dragged into the vent.

He could not return to his city, Undine, so he had carried on in search of a new allegiance. Soren had been gathering warriors to storm the All-Council prison to release King Kadir. Balim had been by his side from the moment they'd rolled the rock away from the entrance and discovered Kadir on the brink of death, mere bones and skin, kept alive only by his vision for a healthy, thriving mer race united with modern women. Balim had nursed him back to health.

He had killed a king, and he had healed a king.

But he could never atone.

The bathroom door opened. A puff of steam danced on the ceiling as Bella emerged. Her skin was pink and clean; her rounded shoulders peeked from the thick towel. Her shapely legs and bare feet padded across the carpet. Her curls dampened to red ringlets against her freckle-dotted shoulders.

His body reacted as he gazed on her. She was any male's dream, warrior or human.

The last thing he expected was for her to plop beside him on the foot of the bed. Still avoiding his gaze, she curled her toes. "You've probably seen many people naked, being a doctor."

He bobbed his head because he had.

"No big deal, then." She brushed her hair off her shoulders. "The freckles go all the way down. That surprises some people. Not you, though."

He didn't know how to answer.

She also didn't seem to know how to talk normally. "The shower's free."

Balim rose and toed off his damp loafers.

"Balim." She hooked her fingers around his wrist, stopping him. She'd just emerged from a hot shower and was still radiating heat, yet her fingertips were cool on his skin. "I'm not angry about what you told me. And you live in a strict hierarchy. Isn't it dangerous to admit you killed your king?"

"A death sentence."

She nailed his gaze with hers. "Why do you trust me? You know the person I am. If I could use you to save Jonah, I would."

She coldly and honestly announced how she would betray him. He had to stifle his laugh. "Perhaps I am beyond caring. Perhaps I am the tired one. Perhaps, knowing you will never be mine, I simply fantasize that these hours are different and outside the rest of time. Stolen, never to repeat, and thus with no consequences. Or, perhaps, this is how I wish for my death."

Her chest flickered with lights. She released his hand as though it burned and covered her mouth. "Go take a shower."

He obeyed, leaving her on the bed looking shaken while he scrubbed off the water of the lake and replaced it with the strange oils and lotions preferred by the land-dwelling humans. When he returned, she was in the same place, her chest bright and a strange resolve on her face.

She rose. "This night is outside of time."

"Bella. Do not dwell on my words."

She dropped her towel, revealing her shapely body to his hot, hungry gaze. His cock hardened and thickened with readiness. There was no doubt of her meaning. Not in her eyes, her actions, or in the glow of her soul.

Bella crossed the carpet, arms out, and unfastened his towel at his waist to reveal the full glory of his body. He was not as massive as some warriors, but he was still a warlord of the sea. Ropes of muscle bound his biceps, pectorals, lats, and quadriceps. Her hungry gaze traced them all.

She pressed the tattoo at his hip. The scar of the injury was long gone, but the two sides had cinched together off-center. "What's this?"

"My citizen mark for Undine." He curled his hands around her slim fingers and brought the cool digits to his lips.

Arousal washed over her face.

He kissed her fingers, nibbling the soft pads and the sharp nails, teasing and testing her will. Would she reject him? He tried to shore his heart against it, even knowing it was coming.

She stepped into his arms. Her full breasts that had already nursed a child displayed proud pink nipples. Her wide belly that had already carried a human child to term was rounded and ready.

Bella opened a small square packet.

He watched with curiosity as she unrolled it. "What is this device?"

"A condom." She touched the tip to his cock head. "It prevents pregnancy."

Her confession drew pain because she did not wish to bear his young fry. Her clever fingers drew pleasure from rolling the plastic over his hard cock.

Amusement won out. "Only humans would invent this device."

She looked up. "When you have ten kids, I doubt you'll complain."

"Ten young fry? I would not tax my female's precious body with more than one."

Her lips quirked, and pure laughter gleamed behind her twitching expression. "Mmm. Glad to hear you won't fight me on it."

"Fight! Never."

"Good." She rose and placed his hands on her hips. She was warm and soft and smooth, feminine, and touching her made his body clench with hungry wishes.

Knowing the battle that raged within, she cupped his cheek and nuzzled his lips. "Only tonight. Understand?"

He understood. Even though the welling of powerful need filled him with heat and hunger and denied her words. He would only hunger to claim her again. Better never to taste than to crave the flavor which could never be his.

Despite that, he lowered his head to her tipped-up lips and gave in.

———

BELLA HADN'T INTENDED for this to happen. She'd been with a few men since Chaz. Some might have developed into relationships.

No beautiful, wounded males like Balim.

She opened to his delicious flavor, and again the unstoppable feelings mesmerized her. He settled her soft vee against his firm, thick cock, and then his hands lifted, united on her breasts, rubbed the pearly nipples. Desire streaked to her center, and hot liquid slicked her feminine channel. He lifted his head, his lips damp with her flavors and his gaze wild. He kissed down her chest to her breasts and wet her nipples, worshipping first one with his mouth and then the other. Another wave of hot need crashed through her. She clung to his shoulders and moaned.

Balim walked her back onto the bed, kneed between her thighs, and kissed to her belly. He was careful of his cock, never touching the condom to her body, at the ready.

Sweet need thrilled her as his hands cupped her mons, parted her sex lips, and his skillful fingers entered her with authority.

She rested her heels on the edge of the bed, opening to his expert exploration. "You've studied female anatomy."

He lifted his head. "You are my first subject."

"Oh? Well—mmm."

He focused his mouth, tongue, and fingers on her throbbing clit.

The same way he knew to pleasure her breasts, he moved over her body, bringing her to the peak of need and then letting her float, bringing her almost to the peak a second time, and releasing her tension, and then starting on a third until she was so mindless with want for him, she needed sex, now, with him and no other. Thank goodness she'd already put on the condom or else it would never have happened.

And only then, as if reading her mind, did he release his hold on her hot pussy and turn his attention to the other parts of her body begging for his claims.

She let go of her fears, her schemes, her identity. Just as she'd promised him this one night stood outside of time. She was female, a crusader, and he was male, a warrior.

She gripped his hips and dragged his smooth rubber-clad cock to her wet entrance, begging him to take her and finish. Some men never approached a peak. None lasted to three. And if he took her now, they would share something she'd never experienced: Patient, masterful, satiating sex with a male who knew her mind.

Because he did. They were linked. Mind and, as much as she fought against it, soul.

His cock arrested at her entrance. Heat burned his gaze as he held hers. "You are mine, Bella. My bride."

Yes. But no. She wasn't doing this now. Tonight was outside of time.

"Please," she begged. Not to make her lie. Not now. Not like this.

He kissed her savagely, mixing his hard spice with her own taste, and his rubber-clad cock plunged into her channel, filling her. She gasped, and her body spasmed like when she'd dropped into the freezing water. But it was not freezing now. He was hotter than the sun, and she needed him in the depths of her core.

He ground his cock into her, finding her pleasure and chasing it, watching her with the savage need of a warrior who healed and who also hunted. Tonight, she was both patient and prey for him.

"Yes," she murmured, arching into his thrusts, reaching for the ultimate peak with every pounding wish he fulfilled.

The orgasm shook her to her core.

Her channel clenched around his cock, spasming with helpless wonder, releasing her from her worries and her fears and herself. It purified her like a confession. It cleansed her soul and remade her into the woman she wished to be again.

He dropped his forehead to her shoulder and shuddered his own release. His cock pressed against her pleasure spot for one final hit of wonder. Then, they lay together for a long moment before he eased out.

She helped him remove the condom and dispose of it, and then they finished getting ready for a sleepy bedtime. He put back on his shirt and boxers, and she wore her long nightshirt. In bed, with only the bathroom nightlight for illumination, she nestled against his side.

Too bad Balim hadn't been her first husband instead of Chaz. But she had been so selfish then. She wouldn't have appreciated him.

She allowed herself a little tenderness. In the morning, she'd drive back to Jonah, execute her strategy against the Sons of Hercules, and leave Balim.

For his own safety.

SIXTEEN

But leaving Balim could wait.

For now, for a few more hours, Bella would pretend that she was his bride and he was her warrior.

"It is funny," he said, startling her out of her reverie as she nestled against his bicep.

"What is?"

"Queen Elyssa also spoke of birthing multiple young fry. Her wish for five touched off a revolution."

"A race on the brink of death isn't excited about large families?"

"We did not believe a mother could birth so many. Even I doubted. Our All-Council representative destroyed Atlantis over this imagined torture."

She rested on her elbow. "But you weren't always in trouble. It can't have been that way in the old days."

"I do not know. The All-Council archives are forbidden. Because of this, 'how things have always been' changes often to suit a king."

He could be describing her life after Jonah's diagnosis.

"I barely remember what it was like to wake up in the morning and worry about clients. I used to plan my holidays and weekends around marketing campaigns. I can't remember the last time work was the top concern."

He remained silent for a long beat.

Then, he rose out of the bed and rummaged in her purse for the bone marrow test kit. "How do I operate this?"

Her heart squeezed in her throat. She swiped the cotton-topped sticks on his inner cheeks, placed them inside the sticky cardboard, and filled out the registration form. Who knew? Perhaps he would match someone, somewhere, and that person could gain another shot at life.

Balim climbed back into their bed, and somehow, she just couldn't follow him.

She settled on the chair and leaned on the back. "I'm sorry I can't be the bride you need."

His solemnity showed he understood that the night was already over, even though it was still dark. "You are more than I deserve."

She rested her chin on her arm. "Because you murdered your king."

"Other mer would agree with you."

She should not ask any more details. "Was he special to you? Were you related?"

"He was king." He fluffed the pillows and rested against the frame to look her in the eye. "Do not confuse me for a prince."

"I wondered what crime devastated you, like losing a father."

He stilled.

Then he rose from the bed and stalked the room. "Why did you reach this conclusion? What did I say?"

"Nothing. Until I met you, it was just me and Jonah. I had nobody else. Not even—"

Oh, she'd almost mentioned Starr. They hadn't spoken in years. Not since the first, and last, time Bella had donned super-spy stuff and set out to wreck a criminal.

"Not even anybody," she recovered. "And if anyone so much as touches Jonah without my permission, I will *destroy them*. The mer don't have mothers or siblings, so the most important person would be your father."

He faced away.

She touched his back. "I'm so sorry. Was he a warrior?"

"Healer."

"Like you."

"I was to inherit his place, but my warrior skill made me a liability on any mission. The prince overtook my training. He was the greatest, kindest, most capable warrior in Undine. In safe waters, raiders from another city surprised us."

Balim rubbed the fractured tattoo on his hip.

"I was injured. The prince fought off our attackers at great cost. When we returned to the city, he ordered my father to heal my wounds first."

"He died, and the king blamed your father?"

"He did not die. My father had stabilized me and was turning to heal the prince when the king mistook his son's stillness for death. He stabbed my father through the heart."

Her own heart hurt. "He was murdered right in front of you?"

He nodded, bleak in his memories. "The prince then awoke, but with no healer to attend him, he slipped away. I assumed guilt for both deaths."

She rose and strode to the bed.

He looked up as though awaiting her judgment.

She pulled him into a life-affirming hug. "It's not your fault."

"My father's last act was to stand in front of me and assume the blow."

"He was glad to do that." She pressed his morose head into her soft belly. "They both were."

Balim tried to shake his head in her arms.

She gripped him tighter. "Your father would have given his life for yours a thousand times. He was grateful his last act was patching you up. I'm a mother, so I know."

"You love your Jonah very much."

"He's my life. And you were your father's."

He remained silent for a long time.

Eventually, she slid down and landed next to him on the bed. His tattoos seemed a deeper tint, as though reliving these memories had forced old blood to the surface.

He took her hand and slid his fingers between hers, sensual and taking comfort. "You do misunderstand our ways. While I trained at the great hall of healers, no one tended Undine. I endangered everyone."

"Your king killed off the only doctor. He was short-sighted."

"Undine is a scholar's city of quiet reflection, but a core of emotion hides in every warrior. Once tapped, our urges are as deadly as any hot-blooded warrior from Rusalka or Djullanar."

"That still doesn't make what happened your fault."

"You will change your mind after I explain the rest."

She closed her mouth.

"After I returned, King Kadir traveled to Undine. He was only Warrior Kadir of Dragao Azul then. He preached that the ancient covenant was wrong, and the only way to save our dying race was to expose the mers' existence and join with modern women. I was, in his words, 'unappreciated,' and so he asked me to leave with him."

Emotion animated his tone as if this part were easy for him to reexperience.

"My city elders kicked him out, and the king delivered a powerful speech. I owed the city for surviving when worthier warriors had died, so if I swam beyond the city limits, even to heal a patrolling warrior, he would have me executed."

"They trapped you."

He tilted his head, neither agreeing nor disagreeing with her assessment. "During my training, I had stolen a cursed blade, and after his final ruling, I offered it as a token of my fealty."

"The diseased battlefield?"

"Oannes Field." Again that bleak tone replaced any emotions. "He rejected my offering and threatened my life."

She hugged him. "It almost sounds like he wanted an excuse to execute you."

He rested a hand on her arm. "The king confined me to my father's castle. But he must have opened the box after, because he fell ill with the blue chains. I escaped during the funeral procession, disposed of the dagger, and left."

"Did anyone else figure it out?"

"Of course not. I was the only healer. No one could contradict my diagnosis."

"What did they think it was?"

He focused on her. "I diagnosed him with curling flatworms."

She stroked his skin. "He made his own bed."

"The mer do not sleep in beds."

"I mean he killed your father and tortured you beyond your breaking point."

"Yes, my father would have kept him in excellent health." Flat again, and matter-of-fact.

"Who's in charge of Undine now?" she asked for closure.

"I hope I will never find out. The king was not the only one who believed I must serve the city through any abuse. Nothing must tempt me to exact revenge."

His cold rage did not chill her. She would salt the earth if anyone ever hurt Jonah.

It was just as well they would not cruise the oceans together.

Tonight was their truce. Tomorrow, they would return to their lives. Balim to healing his warriors. Her to pursuing Jonah's cure and destroying the Sons of Hercules.

"Hmm." He rubbed his chest with a frown.

"What?" She touched his broad fingers. "What is it?"

"I always imagined that telling another would unburden me. That I would feel absolution. But I still feel nothing." He turned his red-threaded gaze on her. "Why do you think that is?"

She was the last person to delve into grief. "Because losing your father to senseless rage is a grave injustice, and you'll never love another person ever again."

He pushed out his lower lip. "Is that what it is? The king was my second father. The prince was everything to me."

"And if you disengage your feelings, then you'll never lose yourself in grief."

"That makes strange sense." He glanced at her, and his lips curved. "I have long been horrified by my feelings for you."

She squeezed him happily. "That makes two of us."

He leaned into her comforting hug. His amusement

dipped to seriousness. "Atlantis differs from any other mer city. King Kadir is guided by reason and passion. His queens and warriors share their hearts. He is the future for our race."

He took a deep breath, and his grip on her hand tightened.

"But if he or any other warrior hurts you, I will not hesitate to strike. It may take a lifetime. I will execute my revenge."

"Luckily, you'll never have to worry about me."

He glanced at her sideways. "No?"

"You know why I can't join you under the sea."

"Yes, I understand. We will have a reverse relationship. Only on land."

She couldn't be Chaz. She'd never throw Jonah away to start a new family, not even to save a race.

But Bella also couldn't tell Balim the truth. Not after everything else they had shared tonight. Instead, she fell asleep with him on the bed, snuggled together like two lost puppies curled up in barren cardboard box under a bridge, alone in the world, with only each other for warmth.

In the morning, she drove Balim back to the lab and left him there. He stood outside, watching her drive away.

Surely, in his heart, he knew the truth.

She would never have a relationship with him above the water or under it.

Never.

Bella used her rental car for the last few hours by driving leisurely to Jonah's hospital. She had to select his new hospital before the end of the week. Might as well enjoy this last convenience before she upended their lives.

Parking in the lot, she got out of the car and checked her messages.

The phone was off.

Hmm. She'd forgotten it on the seat overnight and the battery had died. She plugged in her emergency charger as she crossed the semi-empty lot. Her phone booted. Notifications popped up from an unknown number.

Starr?

Or the Sons of Hercules?

She positioned the metal speaker at the back of her ear.

A guy reading his phone bumped into her, knocking her back a step.

"Hey!" she snapped.

He ignored her and trotted across the street.

Whatever. She affixed the metal and paired it. Her phone rang. She answered.

"Oh my god, thank goodness you're all right," Starr gasped.

"All right?" Bella repeated aloud, ignoring the looks of the others around her as she continued up the hospital stairs.

"You haven't answered since last night, and Bella, there's been a security breach."

As they'd expected. "Where?"

"Everywhere! Your home, MerMatch offices, their lab—"

"My home?" She stopped outside the front doors. "You mean my apartment?"

"Yes! Two college guys broke in and went through your things. I have it on video. Of course I called Harv. He chased them out the back window, and he reported it to the cops."

"Did they find out about you?"

"Not yet. We've been out of touch so long, and it's not like you have my picture up in your apartment."

A shaft of guilt spiked into Bella. She'd pushed everyone aside when Jonah had gotten sick. She had photos of Starr, but not anywhere that would compromise her.

"It's like they knew you were taking Balim out of town. A big crew of people went into the lab. I called right away, but I didn't know how to convince the security officers because I'm not persuasive like you. You're blackmailing the Sons of Hercules, right, Bella? How could they risk your wrath?"

She had threatened them for daring to threaten her son.

Bella's purse vibrated. Someone had snuck an unfamiliar phone into her purse.

No.

Bella pushed into the hospital lobby. She ran across the entrance and into the elevators. The metal box took forever to rise, and the ringing cut off. She exited the floor onto pediatrics long-term care.

The sweet nurse looked up from the desk and blinked. "Bella? What are you doing here? Did Jonah leave something behind?"

Bella raced past her. Her heart beat louder and harder.

"Hey!" The nurse chased after her. "You can't come back here. Only parents of patients!"

"Bella?" Starr's voice faded in. "What's going on?"

She was the one in charge. She was playing with fire, but only she was supposed to get burned.

Bella flew past the locker room, weaving between surprised staff. The nurse couldn't keep up. Bella was accelerated by the fears of a million years of parents returning to the safe cave where she'd stashed her child and finding it...

She reached Jonah's room.

The plastic was dismantled. The room was empty.

Nothing was inside it. Not her son. Not his clothes. Not his raggedy bear. Nothing.

Her heart cracked.

The nurse caught up to her, gasping, chest heaving. "You can't...come back here..."

She channeled the deepest, blackest, most murderous pit of fury. "Where is he?"

"...anymore." The nurse frowned like Bella was crazy. "What do you mean, where is he? You withdrew him yourself this morning."

"No."

"I was so sorry you had to move him when he's so sick."

"Who took him?"

"Your new private care physician." The nurse patted her arm as she caught her breath. "Did you get the transfer time wrong? It must be nerve-wracking, given the risks. He had more color this morning, and he stayed awake while we moved him to patient transport."

"Who. Took. Him?"

"The patient transport company. Here, hon, calm down. I know it's unsettling when you miss an appointment, but just breathe. He'll be settled into the new hospital now. Shall we call together?"

Her heart suspended its cracking, holding together with trembling glue. She would not break. She didn't have the whole story yet.

The nurse called on the wall phone. "Can you patch me through to an outside line? Yes. ... Hello? Yes, I'm following up on a patient transfer. His mother's here, and...what do you mean you never received a call? I talked to you myself. Jonah Taylor. He...you don't have a patient by that name?"

Bella's purse vibrated again.

She yanked out the foreign phone and pressed it to her ear. "What have you done with him?"

"Bella Taylor." The not-feminine distorted voice sounded pleased. "I hear your trip for the cure was unsuccessful. So, I have provided better care for your son than you can."

She gritted her teeth. "I told you not to threaten my son."

"And I am not. He is under private care."

"Prove it. Show me my son."

"Of course. I have left the details of the arrangement at your apartment. Conveniently enough, our expert is aboard a ship in the mid-Atlantic."

"You will not blackmail me." She lowered her voice as the worried nurses guided her to the hospital director, where, no doubt, paperwork would show her forged signature to discharge him. "I will destroy you."

"Now, now. I took your words to heart, Bella Taylor. The Sons of Hercules must be portrayed as saviors. And we will provide proof to defame any false allegations otherwise."

"You will regret making an enemy out of me."

"Bella Taylor, I thought we were friends."

She stopped outside the director's office. "Our friendship ended the moment you stole my son."

"That's funny. I thought our friendship ended when you used our generous financing to secure the merman office against our surveillance."

He had known. He'd known from her first date. They'd been spy versus spy this entire time, and Herc had just lit the dynamite.

"If you hurt Jonah, I will hunt you down and suffocate you with my bare hands," she snarled, preparing to end the conversation while the nurses beside her listened in, shocked.

"Well then, you'll be happy to know that you still have a very important role to play in Jonah's cure." Herc's voice lilted from breezy to serious. "If you want him to live, then you will bring me a Life Tree flower. Understand?"

"I understand," she snapped.

"And then, once we have this flower, you will destroy Atlantis."

SEVENTEEN

"Balim?" Mitch's voice filtered through the open doorway of the hospital lab room to Balim's office. "We have a problem."

He rose upright on his portable cot and stretched. His human joints creaked. So much of his surface life was spent sitting and staring. He rubbed his eyes. "What problem?"

"I'm not sure. The specifications are correct. But..."

Balim stretched farther and groaned.

The same slacks and shirt he'd been wearing for the past three days hung off his body. They still felt a little like Bella.

The sensation of uniting with his bride defied words.

She had used a small bit of plastic between their bodies. He liked this barrier more than he should admit. His duty to procreate warred with the ingenious pleasure of the plastic creation.

She'd dropped him off yesterday with a long, tearful kiss. The short trip with her had changed his life. His soul. And, he'd thought, hers.

But in the parking lot, her soul had darkened, knifing

him in the chest, and she'd cupped his cheek as she'd lied about seeing him sometime soon.

She would never see him again.

If he were a nobler warrior, she would submerge and mate with him...

He rubbed his pained chest. It was a good pain. Unlike the joint ache from sitting for too many hours in human form and sleeping for too few. He focused on logic. She was devoted to her child. He honored her devotion.

He'd never been devoted to anyone but ghosts. Ghosts, pride, and perhaps now her.

As soon as Pelan regained his health and Balim completed the mer hospital, he would chase her. She did not need to honor him above Jonah.

He would never demand that he be her priority.

Mitch leaned in Balim's doorway, muffled a cough into a paper tissue, and cleared his throat. His eyes were red; the morning sunlight illuminated his first cup of coffee. "The problem is the tank. Don't you think it's off?"

"Off how?" Balim followed Mitch out to the main room.

The aquarium water was cloudy and strange.

He clambered up the steps. Scum bubbled on the surface. The whole tank smelled foul.

"Yes." He requested Mitch to double-check his measurements. "It is 'off.' How long has it been like this?"

"I don't know." Mitch sneezed, blew into his tissue, and checked his logs. "I just got in."

"Where is Pelan's bride?"

"I don't know."

"We have to drain the water."

Pelan's healing would stop again.

Was the tank flawed? Balim's design simulated the undersea environment by the Life Tree. He was the first healer to design a surface crèche, and he had missed something.

He looked in on Pelan as Mitch hooked up the drains.

White foam coated Pelan's gills.

Large, dark bruises covered his entire body, and in the center of each bruise was a small dark spot. They splotched across his chest in a singular blue chain...

He jolted. *Can it be?* As if speaking aloud of his sin to Bella had summoned the cursed, incurable disease—

No. He forced himself to examine Pelan. This was not the incurable Blue Ring. It was a simple case of Crab-Cut Disease.

His stomach rolled with the memory of his fears.

Pelan floated in fresh water. Fresh, sterilized water steeped in Sea Opals. How could any disease penetrate?

That mystery would wait.

"Stop the drain." Balim hurried to his office. "Call Hazel to arrange an emergency evacuation to Atlantis."

Mitch put the phone to his ear and waited. "What's going on?"

"Pelan has contracted a rare disease you call a 'vibrio.'"

"Vibrio." Mitch's cheeks hollowed. "You mean flesh-eating bacteria?"

"Bella has told me human medicine is inadequate to fight this disease. After we evacuate, drain the water and bleach all surfaces."

"What about the bride?" Mitch asked.

"She must evacuate also."

"Evacuate where?" Pelan's bride wandered barefoot and damp into the main room.

"Why did you abandon your warrior?" Balim demanded. "You hold his life in your hands, and yet you continue to risk damaging him."

She held up her hands, irritation crossed with guilt. "I was just gone for ten minutes. Okay? I had this irresistible urge to sneeze, and I didn't want to wake him up so, yeah, I climbed out."

"Sneeze?" Mitch asked and then sneezed.

"Yeah, like that. But you can check the cameras or whatever. It was ten minutes."

His bride looked fine.

How had a saltwater disease entered the sterile, fresh water tank and afflicted only Pelan?

"Check your security cameras," she insisted. "And point them somewhere other than me. It's so gross and creepy."

"We do not have security cameras," Balim said.

"Yes, you do."

"He's right," Mitch affirmed, wiping his nose with the cloth. "What security cameras are you talking about?"

"The ones you guys had installed over the weekend and pointing straight in on naked me." She pointed.

He and Mitch wandered over and stared up at the small boxy device directed at the tank.

"Roxanne did not speak of security cameras," Balim said.

"I don't think they're a bad idea, but yeah, she said nothing about them." Mitch sneezed again. "I'll ask the night security."

"Wait. You had an urge to sneeze?" Balim gave a bottle of elixir to Pelan's bride. "This should heal your illness."

"Oh, I feel fine now."

"You have been exposed to Pelan's illness. Crab-Cut Disease. Drink the elixir to avoid losing your arms and legs."

She paled, swiped the elixir, and glugged it.

"Sneezing equals exposure?" Mitch looked at his bare hands. Dread filled his features. "What about me?"

"The disease enters through the blood. It does not affect healthy warriors, which is why Pelan's bride is healthy while he suffers."

Mitch sneezed again.

Balim stopped and faced him. "Perhaps you should visit a human hospital."

Mitch waved him away. "It started after work last night. A little tickle in my throat. It's allergies."

"Drink the elixir," Balim ordered.

Mitch moved toward the storage tanks.

"No! The ones inside my office. They should be secure."

Balim consulted the security officers they'd hired. The day security officer's nose and eyes were red and she too sniffled into a tissue. "Yes, Rick let in a crew to install the cameras you ordered."

"I ordered no cameras."

"Someone did. They had the paperwork."

"Did you recognize them?"

"Well, I wasn't here. I'll leave a note for Rick. Oh, and there's a woman here to see you."

"Me?"

The security officer pointed.

Bella stood in the atrium in the small, spare, water-damaged lobby.

Balim's heart stopped with shock and then thudded painfully. Curvy, beautiful, and tragic.

He strode to her with purpose.

Her soul light brightened, relieved, and then she darkened. "Balim, I—"

"Bella." He grabbed her around the shoulders and forced her outside, into the bright air and sunshine. "We must go."

"What's wrong?" Then, she seemed to sink into him. "You know?"

"There's been an outbreak." He stopped in the parking lot, held his phone to his ear, and began his own call to the MerMatch car service. "A freshwater version of Crab-Cut Disease."

"Outbreak?" She paled. "Oh, no. It's worse than I imagined."

He ordered the car and closed the phone. "You imagined this?"

"I'm sorry, Balim." She faced him, reckless and yet determined, and the dark hollows beneath her eyes said she'd been up all night. "Someone broke into your hospital. I didn't realize they would poison the tank."

A terrorist had broken in and sickened the aquarium with Crab-Cut Disease? With Bella's help?

"I'll explain, but you need to evacuate everyone. And then," she swallowed and lifted her chin with bold defiance, "you need to take me to Atlantis."

EIGHTEEN

"I made a mistake," Bella confessed in the conference room of MerMatch a short time later.

The staff glared.

She stood, poised as if she were doing a client proposal. An aromatherapy diffuser on the table dispersed a soothing rose-lavender scent. Peppy music played on Hazel's phone.

"And I'm here to make it right. If you'll let me."

The difference between this and the regular client proposals was that her soul mate was sitting with his arms crossed, watching her with new cynicism.

Of all the people she hadn't meant to hurt or disappoint, he was the one who mattered.

Bella pushed on. "Weeks ago, you invited me to a date with Balim. That same night, the Sons of Hercules tried to threaten me to get me to steal the Life Tree blossom. You have a security problem."

Hazel ended the song and stared at her. "We're doing fine without double agents."

"Do you mind putting on another upbeat song?"

"Seriously?"

"Anything from your playlist is fine."

Hazel started more music.

Bella went to the doorway, checked the locks and the new window stickers she'd placed, and drew the blinds. Then she opened her cardboard box, set up a conference phone in the middle of the table, and dialed her memorized number. The conference phone rang.

"This is my half sister, Starr," she said as the phone clicked. "She's a security consultant. As I said, a few hours after you called to schedule a first date, I received a phone call from the Sons of Hercules. Starr came with me virtually on my date to figure out why."

Her half sister's soft, stuffed-up voice sounded like she was in the room. "You have bugs *everywhere*."

"Everywhere?" Dannika, whose arms had crossed over her chest, looked up from her disappointed trance. "Bugs?"

"Everywhere," Starr confirmed. "Bella walked all over the office. They're under your seats, in your drawers, everywhere."

The meeting attendants shifted in their seats.

"But not in this conference room?" Dannika questioned.

"Oh, they're in here too."

"*Have* bugs everywhere," Hazel repeated. "Right now?"

"Yep. Right now. That's why I had Bella stick a jammer under your aromatherapy diffuser on her first date. Hopefully, it's going now."

The humans looked at the diffuser.

Balim studied Bella with disappointment. It needled her.

"I've also had Bella put stickers on the windows that disrupt anyone trying to listen from outside," Starr continued, "but you'll want to avoid sensitive topics on the roof, and—"

"Wait." Hazel held up her hand at the conference room phone, forgetting it didn't have a camera attached. "Stickers? For listening outside? We're on the fifth floor. No window washer's outside with a glass."

"Of course not," Starr said patiently, "although the window washers you let in this week weren't from the company and they removed the stickers, so that's why just now, before we started this conference, I had to have Bella replace them."

Hazel's mouth opened in shock.

"They protect against someone sitting on the next rooftop over and directing a beam against the windows. The displacement of air from speaking vibrates the glass. The sticker muffles it."

Her mouth closed. "Seriously?"

"It's what I would do if I was hell-bent on listening in on somebody and I couldn't get reliable intel."

Hazel frowned.

Bella put her hands on her hips. "The Sons of Hercules have invested serious resources into spying on you."

"It's just a website of violent, antisocial college students who can't get girlfriends and blame someone else for their problems." Hazel recited what the news reported. "They have a chat forum and a catchy slogan."

"And organization," she pushed, realizing how hypocritical she sounded. "You've been poisoned, shot, and bombed. You need to take this more seriously. Trust me. Making the wrong assumption will get people killed."

The receptionist looked bleak. She rubbed her face. "I work at a dating agency. Not the CIA. And now my life is in danger?"

"Not your life," Starr reassured her from the conference phone. "The mermen's lives. You'd be collateral, not the target."

Her lips twisted. "Not comforting."

Dannika lifted a finger. "Why didn't you tell us right away?"

"I wanted to know how far the Sons of Hercules had invaded." Bella tried to push through the relief of confessing and the fear of Balim's continued disgruntlement. "If I'd told you before Starr swept the office for bugs, they would know that you know. Her slightest probe showed your computer network is wide open."

"Wide open," Starr agreed. "Like an open jar of peanut butter at a nut-lovers' convention. I was supposed to send my report once I secured your vulnerabilities."

"Supposed to?" Hazel repeated.

"Yes—" Bella started.

"Yeah," Starr interrupted, "things got moved up when they kidnapped Jonah."

Bella shut her teeth with a click.

The others stared at her with shock and horror.

Hazel slapped her open palms on the table. "Why haven't you called the police?"

"I did," Bella said, "but—"

"And about everything Starr found?"

"No, that part I haven't—"

"Call!"

They drowned her out, sharing worries, tips, and demanding she act less composed giving this security presentation while her child was missing.

"Why are you just sitting around?" Hazel picked up her phone to call the police.

"Wait, wait. Just calm down, everybody," Starr said.

"We can't tip the kidnappers off to my efforts to find him. Bella kept you in the dark in case of bugs in your homes or the bad guys had gotten to family or friends. You never know when a single wrong word will reach compromised ears. Right now, we have the advantage. Bella has to make sure I keep it. So she didn't tell the police anything about my work, and I can't have you telling them about it either. Not until we have Jonah."

"And we've nailed the person directing the Sons of Hercules," Bella affirmed. "Who is not a college student. I believe he's a sociopathic mastermind."

Across the room, Balim straightened.

She needed his forgiveness right now.

And that made her choke. She had to swallow and refocus on the purpose of the meeting.

"No, you need to call the police," Hazel insisted, gripping her phone. "That's what they're there for. Solving crimes and catching criminals."

"Don't use that," Bella reminded her. "Starr hasn't checked it for spyware. It could be recording your phone calls."

She blanched and lowered her phone so the music played into the silence.

"I traced the ambulance transport route to the docks," Starr said, "so we think the leader was telling the truth and Jonah is on a boat. Plus that would make it the easiest for the Sons of Hercules to monitor Bella when she's in Atlantis."

Hazel whipped to Balim. "You can't take her to Atlantis. She's confessed to being a spy."

"A double agent," he corrected, steepling his fingers in front of his mouth.

"That's the same thing. Double the same thing!"

"I must evacuate Pelan. Bella must rescue her child."

And the plane was due in an hour. They would meet Pelan and his bride at the airstrip.

"I want to go with you," Dannika said.

Balim dropped his hands. "No."

"Pelan is my successful match, Balim. I need to reassure his future wife—"

"She is going also."

Dannika's brows rose to the ceiling. "But we haven't finished anything. We didn't have the wedding. She needs to contact her job. Her emergency leave ends next week. Her family—"

"She is a target. Her safest refuge is in Atlantis."

"But—"

"Someone broke into the makeshift hospital while Balim was gone," Bella interrupted.

"While you took him, you mean," Hazel sniped. "Yeah, the fake security-camera guys. What are we going to do about them?"

"Starr's working on that," Bella said. "The night security prevented the crew from dumping anything in the tank. But something got in. We think it was the other visitor you had that evening."

"Other visitor?"

"The visitor security didn't mention because she assumed you already knew." Bella focused on Balim. "The new merman."

"A new warrior has not surfaced." Balim looked to Dannika for confirmation.

"No," she agreed. "The boat with new warriors is due in another week. We just have our existing clients at the moment."

"But a new one showed up. Starr was patched into your

external security video. She watched the fake merman walk in." Bella focused on Dannika. "He drove in a Tesla. Starr's tracing the license plate. He painted on blackberry-vine facial tattoos with iridescent purple body paint."

Dannika covered her mouth, thinking hard.

"You know every warrior who's risen, and we think you could judge anyone who claims to be new. That's why you have to stay until Starr figures out a way to security-card the mermen and yet doesn't make the mer more vulnerable."

Dannika sucked in a deep breath and let it out. "I will stay and help until we have security."

"Great." Bella straightened. "Then Starr will move forward."

"I'll be working the New York angle," she agreed. "Bella will uncover double agents on the ocean platform. They have to contact her outside the mer city."

"Why don't the Sons of Hercules have double agents in the mer city?" Hazel asked.

Dannika tapped her lips with her index finger. "They would have to be mermen."

"Right, it's on the bottom of the sea." Hazel sighed and squeezed her phone. "It's just so unfair. The police catch the sniper, but he's an unbalanced creep looking for an excuse to hurt people. They catch the Rotenone restaurant poisoner, same thing. Nobody stops the organization that's inciting these crazies and spreading hate."

"Nobody? That's not true. There are people trying to stop the Sons of Hercules." Bella rested her palms on the table. "The people stopping them are us."

Her pronouncement echoed through the little conference room. Hazel and Dannika straightened. Balim's lips quirked into a slight smile.

"Ever since the Sons of Hercules contacted me, I

have been working double shifts on a marketing campaign to expose them for the terrorists they are. Starr has been tracing their communications back to recruiters. Once we've recovered Jonah and unmasked the head of the organization, we unleash my campaign."

Bella's announcement shifted the whole tone of the room.

Hazel clenched her fists in a fighting pose. Dannika arranged her flowing scarf and folded her hands in the picture of a determined, wise woman.

Balim rested his hands on his spread knees, a warrior at rest.

Starr detailed their plans to trick the Sons of Hercules and evade their traps, starting with Hazel pretending to take up meditation every day after lunch for Starr to check in secretly on this conference phone.

Their small but mighty crew would spread hope. They would stand against the men who tried to hurt them. And once Bella rescued Jonah, they would smash the organization from the head down.

Hazel got the call that their emergency airplane to Atlantis was ready, and so they ended the meeting.

Balim led Bella to his car service. He was on her side once more, and she needed his strength. In the elevator, their shoulders brushed.

Bella's skin heated to fire.

He glanced at her and bumped her shoulder again.

The knowledge she'd been trying to hold back ever since she'd seen him in the parking lot burst in. They'd had sex. She knew his smell, his taste, and the shape of his cock thrusting between her legs. And she wanted to smell, taste, and feel him again. Even in the elevator.

A small smile stretched his lips. He turned and pressed her into the wall. "You are aware of me now."

Her mouth went dry. She licked her lips, enjoying how his gaze heated and followed the movement. "Yes."

"Good."

He dipped his head. His mouth met hers, hungry, and their tongues tangled. Both desperate, both needing each other to complete the broken pieces in themselves.

Her nipples tightened to a painful hardness, and she gasped as they rubbed against his firm pectorals beneath the suit. She'd always been a sucker for a good-looking man, and he was both her barbaric dream and her civilized reality.

The door dinged, and she pulled away. His gaze flared on her with intensity as he released her, keeping a hand on her back.

They exited the elevator.

She didn't know how she would get through the next days without losing her soul to Balim. She needed to concentrate on finding her son. Not losing herself to the world of the mer.

Not when she might still be backed into a corner and forced to betray them.

NINETEEN

Balim rested beside Bella on the long, grating flight across the sunny Atlantic.

They rode in a converted airplane carrying six passengers: the captain, Balim and Bella, Pelan and his bride, and an employee from the human construction company. Bella had lost to exhaustion. She'd told Balim the entire Sons of Hercules plot, from the moment she'd received Herc's first phone call to the ransom demand for her son.

He could think of nothing to say that would comfort her, but just sharing her agony seemed to be enough. A short time after, she'd closed her eyes and rested her head on the window despite the bouncing, grinding plane traversing fluffy clouds and sharp sun reflections.

What to do about impossible demands? Balim did not know. As his soul mate slumbered, he checked on his other patients.

Pelan half collapsed against his bride.

In these few short hours, his bruises had blackened to

necrotic and threatened skin loss. Balim kept an eye on one foot. The toes were an unnatural green.

In human form, Pelan's breathing labored, and the growl of snot filled the back of his throat, interrupting every breath with a choking snort.

His bride had her eyes open for the longest time since Balim had met her. She looked bleak. Probably wondering what had been the point of finding her soul mate since all she'd done after the first few happy hours had been hunch over his semiconscious body and pray he'd survive.

She caught Balim's eye and held it. No longer frightened as she had been at the ER, she stared at him as though this experience had scraped the imperfections away and she was a pure instrument now. She hadn't been timid or hesitant with him since the parking lot.

He was the first to look away.

The converted oil platform appeared on the horizon.

When Queen Aya had arisen from Atlantis after defeating the All-Council armies and rescuing the city, she had arranged for a human company to rebuild the surface city of ancient Atlantis.

Based on the few carvings Balim had reviewed, the ancient city had once spanned the breadth of a large human island; carved stone could still be imagined into tall columns, frescoes, domes, and more in the styles of human cities such as ancient Athens, Carthage, and those of the Etruscans. Hundreds of pressurized coils had once lifted and lowered the city. King Kadir had planted his Life Tree seed and formed rebel Atlantis in its shadow.

Few human companies built on the ocean, much less over blue water equidistant between Florida and Senegal, but oil companies had experience with anchoring massive platforms using thrusters, partial submersion, and other mechanics.

Because the oil platform was so isolated, the Sons of Hercules had not yet penetrated. But they would.

The plane bumped across the massive swells of the mid-ocean on its large float pontoons.

Everyone roused. Bella stretched and yawned, smiling at Balim in welcome and making his heart contract, before the events of the past hours cascaded in on her and she shrank into her seat, hugging her elbows.

He stroked her back, knowing he wasn't enough to ease the ache.

Balim had felt so betrayed when Bella demanded to go to Atlantis. How could she throw her child away for an adult's desire? The question made him shake. He hadn't been able to bear to look at Bella. He'd wanted to run away.

Then he had realized she still prioritized her son. The fears had dissipated

He had never saved his father. If he saved her Jonah, would he finally atone?

The plane motored on top of the water like a bug. The platform lowered a hook and winched the floating plane onto the landing pad for refueling. It was Pelan's luck that calm ocean conditions had held for a few hours today.

The rear cargo door creaked open.

Balim clambered out of his seat and lifted Pelan. He and Pelan's bride held the warrior up as they lugged him to the ramp.

He'd lost too much weight since his first injury. They did not have much time.

Lotar met them at the bottom, and Balim gave Pelan over to his care. The tall, strong, gray-eyed warrior spoke to

Balim alone as they crossed the long platform. "You missed Queen Lucy and the twins. They visited with her family and descended yesterday."

"How many All-Council warriors harass and destroy equipment today?"

"Fewer." Fresh cuts scraped his cheekbones, suggesting he had swept the area of All-Council warriors with his trident. "We will escort you to the midpoint. I have called down to announce your arrival."

"Good."

In the past, mer had descended using currents. Thanks to the human cables anchoring the platform above ancient Atlantis, they had learned it was possible to ascend and descend directly. But their bodies did not react well to rapid fluctuations of pressure and temperature. New techniques for breathing, kicking, and even shifting forms had been developed to take advantage of the structures.

They had also installed a submersible filled with pressurized breathable air at the bottom of the ancient city. King Kadir stationed warriors to attend to the communication wire inside. Now, they could call from the surface to the sea floor in seconds and do so privately.

A human miracle.

A small group of humans blocked the entrance to the elevator.

Lotar spoke quietly. "The owner of the construction company wishes to speak with you and your bride."

Balim fell back to Bella's side.

She tried to finger comb her wild, windswept red hair, but her exhaustion and her darkening soul showed that she was losing heart.

He took her hand.

She brightened and leaned on him.

One genial man stepped forward from the group with a hand out to meet Pelan's bride. "Merrit Ryerson. Welcome to Ryerson Deep Water Construction."

Bella greeted him with a human handshake, and he repeated the same greeting with Balim and then Bella a second time. His open expression faltered, and he gestured for them to follow him into his office.

"I understand your friend is ill, so this will take no time," he murmured, sorting through cardboard boxes. His office was furnished with books and a wide wooden desk with a computer on top. "No time at all. Something came for you in the last supply shipment. We get those by the slow boat, you know. Ah! Here it is."

He emerged with a padded orange envelope marked with writing.

Bella paled and took it. "How long does it take a shipment to reach this platform?"

"Sailing from the closest port, ten days in good weather. Why?"

"Just curious."

"Are you?" He set his feet apart and folded his fingers across the belly of his button-up, cream shirt. "Let me enthrall you further. Do you have time to experience the technological marvels we're creating here with Ryerson Deep Water Construction?"

Her lips curved, closed, over her teeth. "I'm sorry. we don't."

"What a shame. I think you'd love it, Bella Taylor."

A knock on the frame of the open office door wiped the smile right off his face. He looked past them, and his tone flattened. "What?"

The site manager Balim had met when he'd first ascended long ago stood in the doorway, his nostrils just as pinched as they were in Balim's memory. "We're having trouble again with thruster A-29."

"So get to it." The owner's smile returned, tighter, as the site manager remained. "Anything else?"

"The turbine's lugging—"

"Parts are on the way." He edged the site manager out and forced a laugh. "Every project has delays. We at Ryerson Deep Water Construction are committed to and capable of bringing your dreams to life."

Then he ducked out into the hall and quietly conferenced with the site manager.

Bella ripped open the envelope. Inside was a large vial of blue liquid and a small paper scratched with human writing.

"Inject this into the Life Tree," she read, then frowned and shook the vial. "Inject what? How?"

Balim took the vial. "Mitch can analyze liquids."

"Back in New York." She closed her eyes. Her soul light extinguished. "Knowing what it is doesn't help us."

"It does. Identifying the poison—"

"Does what?" she demanded, frustrated tears shining in her exhausted eyes. "This liquid kills the Life Tree. So whether it's Roundup or bleach or another herbicide doesn't matter. I have to figure out how to steal a Life Tree blossom, get it to the Sons of Hercules on the surface, and then inject the Atlantis Life Tree with this poison, or else..."

Or else the Sons of Hercules would harm her young fry son.

Balim pressed Bella to his chest, soaking up her weakness while she battled this intolerable choice. He knew the crush of emotion and duty, where all that lay in either direction was grief. So he spoke the words he wished someone, anyone, had spoken to him.

"I will help you. Do not be afraid."

"But...I have no idea what I'm doing."

"Injecting is easy. Jam it into the stalk. The Life Tree's circulation will suck up the poison."

Her chest shuddered. She pulled back and stared at him, fear tinged with uncertainty. His coldness frightened her. "You make it sound so easy."

"Murder *is* easy." Cold spread throughout his chest. "That is why warriors cannot let an enemy enter the city. Hide the vial in my bag with your small plastic-coated picture of Jonah and be strong."

"But I can't..."

"Two times, you inject a poison. Once, to kill a person, and second, to kill something worse. The second meaning is the philosophy of your human 'chemo' medicine, yes?"

She nodded, choking.

"Then concentrate on the second and control your sadness. Your enemy has eyes here."

She put a hand to her cheek. "Okay. You're right. I wasn't thinking."

"I will help you."

"Please don't." She straightened her loose clothing, battered by the wind, and tucked the vial into her bag. "This time, I want to fail."

He knew that wasn't true. She wouldn't sacrifice her son without a plan. "What is the deadline?"

She reread the papers and checked inside the envelope. "I can't see one."

"And there is no way to ask?"

"Why?"

"The queens call it 'time dilation.' You do not sleep for months, and so you do not realize how many surface days pass."

"Hopefully, the Sons of Hercules took that into account." She sighed. "Okay. We'll figure out something."

The owner returned to the office, took in her watery eyes, and lowered his voice, solicitous. "Are you feeling well? The platform is large and secure. You shouldn't feel the ocean swells, but suggestive minds imagine them."

"No." She waved away his gesture with a false laugh. "I'm feeling sentimental. Thank you. Where can we meet our friends?"

"My site manager will show you. I'm taking your airplane back to civilization." He held out a hand to shake again. "Goodbye, Balim. Good luck, Bella Taylor."

They bid the owner farewell and followed the site manager through the metal gangways to an exit closer to the surf. Waves like rolling hills broke against the base and sprayed them with ocean water.

"I hate this." The site manager sniffed. "I wish we'd never taken this job. I never signed up for shark attacks and undersea civil wars. Can't go in the water without taking my life in my hands."

Balim noted the long scab on the back of his dominant hand. "You need a bandage."

"And whose fault is that?"

He reached into his bag, withdrew a roll of seaweed bandages, and took the man's hand. "I will heal—"

"Heal yourself!" The site manager jerked his hand away and glared. "Healing me doesn't get rid of the savages tormenting my men."

He stormed back into the platform, slamming the door behind him.

"Pleasant," Bella noted.

Balim stowed his clothing and shoes into waterproof tubs welded to the platform. Bella followed his lead, stripping down to the skin. Unlike most warriors, who strapped daggers to their biceps and thighs, Balim wore only a single dagger. He secured the small photo of her son and the vial of poison in his seaweed pouch, where he always carried his tools, and tied it to his waist.

His chest twinged.

If his enemies knew about this poison, they would take it and use it. His friends would exile him without hesitation.

For the second time in his life, he was committing an action that was treasonable. Only weeks ago, he would have prosecuted himself without mercy for risking the lives of the city and the new young fry.

But the dark part of him was capable of evil. He'd already proved it.

And he would rather bear the evil than Bella.

Balim forced it from his mind and instead focused on the dangerous task ahead. He collected his trident from the weapons storage locker beside the clothing tub. It was strangely pale and dried out. He'd never let it dry so long, and he tested the balance, tightening it to his side. It rested, awkward on land, in the crook of his elbow.

She walked into the wind. At the platform's ledge, a well-armed and otherwise nude Lotar balanced Pelan over his shoulder while Pelan's completely nude bride shivered.

"It sounds like we're diving into a war zone," Bella said, ineffectually covering her feminine places with her palms and giving a mirthless laugh.

"You are."

"What?"

"Do not think, Bella. Trust in me. In the Life Tree. In your destiny."

Her soul fluctuated, but she turned to him and gave him that trust. His heart swelled. He would protect her.

"Leap." Balim entwined their fingers, led her to the edge, and they jumped.

TWENTY

Trust. That was not something Bella did lightly.

She was not a leaper. She was a thinker, a plotter, a seducer. Closing her eyes and doing the fall backward while waiting for another to catch her? Not in her wheelhouse.

But if it was Balim...

Bella tensed up as her toes left the platform.

The cheerful way Balim announced they were jumping into a war zone distracted Bella from the uncontrolled white-water surf crashing and smashing the metal platform.

Then the seawater closed over her head and encased her in a frothing, thrashing, bubbles-and-surf fist.

Panic hammered her chest.

Unlike during her plunge into Lake Eerie that night, this water didn't chill her, although it was at least the same temperature or colder.

Balim floated in front of her and vibrated. "Release your air."

She blew, letting go of a long sigh, and then tightened against the inevitable.

Seawater hit the back of her throat, and she fought the gag reflex, mastering her response while tears burned in her eyes. Alone and cold, she struggled.

Balim's arms closed around her, and she relaxed. He was warm. Solid. Her anchor.

She didn't want to rely on him, but in this vulnerable moment, she had no choice.

Her heart thudded hard. Warmth filled her. All she had to do was trust in someone else for once in her life. Believe everything would work out, embrace being a mermaid, and pursue a new life with Balim in Atlantis...

Her throat closed.

She choked.

Cold seeped into her body. Icy water suffocated her.

It wasn't working?

"Bella?" Balim's arms tightened. "You are transforming back into a human. Let go of your fears and yield to the shift."

She'd thought she was. She'd focused on becoming a mermaid, and knives stabbed her in the back.

"Bella..." His voice faded out as the sounds of the seawater blubbed into her brain.

She spasmed.

"...your eyes. Open your eyes!"

She forced herself to look at him. The ocean was dark and frigid and heavy. His face faded into the darkness. He pushed her. The surface loomed.

But she couldn't rise. She had to save Jonah. She had to trick the Sons of Hercules into revealing themselves.

The ocean brightened as if stadium lights had turned on. And she saw a million miles in all directions with perfect clarity.

Balim's worry shone in stark relief. He was kicking to

the white water. The other warriors were shouting as they tried to keep him from being swept away by the furious currents.

"...not transforming! Quickly, Bella is human—"

"It's okay." Her chest vibrated the words, arresting him. "I'm fine now. Let's continue."

Sharp worry furrowed his brow. "When did you last consume elixir?"

"I don't know."

"It is only temporary."

"Do you have any here?"

"The nearest is New York."

Lotar appeared at his shoulder. "You must clip on the cable."

"I must examine my bride and ensure she is fit to descend."

"I'm fit," she insisted, even though she wasn't sure she was. But she didn't have a choice. Jonah's salvation lay below.

Lotar guided Balim across the underside of the platform while Balim checked Bella's vitality.

The mass of the submerged platform was like an iceberg where a part was above the water but much more anchored underneath. Lotar hauled them down through a maze of cables to a central column where four other warriors hung suspended with Pelan and his bride. They had shifted to mer; Pelan grew long fins while his bride's feet remained short and stubby like Bella's. The current dragged them away from the cable.

Lotar had to fight hard to clip on a harness. But Balim wasn't finished.

Nerves tensed in Bella's throat again. "We should go."

"You cannot change on our journey." He nailed her

with his serious gaze. "If you have a doubt, you must surface."

"I don't have a doubt. It's for Jonah."

Lotar's gaze fixed on Balim's. He seemed to be awaiting orders.

Balim released his frown and confirmed, "Concentrate on your son. And hold tight."

The warriors watched her, round-eyed in fear.

She lowered her voice to a murmur, "Are they worried about me?"

"A bride is stronger with her husband. Your reversion in my arms frightened and disturbed them."

Balim pointed down and kicked.

She held on to Balim.

Gleaming fish flitted and small crustaceans, worms, and wigglers adhered to the cable, tooting funny noises. Their chests glowed.

Her ears popped.

"Normally, we descend with the current," Balim told her, kicking steadily after Lotar. "Descending this swiftly, our bodies must adjust."

The oil platform shrank smaller and smaller as they swam away from it. But it was still crystal-clear to see it. She saw for a hundred miles. The rig, which looked so massive up close, was a tiny dot in a vast sea.

If Starr were here, she'd enumerate the vulnerabilities.

She missed her half sister talking in her ear. They'd gone years without speaking, first when Bella was ignoring her roots in the city with Chaz, and then again after Jonah's illness knocked her sideways.

Starr's calming presence, even as a young child, contrasted with Bella's constant kinetic motion.

No camera could capture her mermaid view.

"This isn't so bad." Small, see-through shrimp danced on Balim's broad shoulders like crustacean pixies. "A peaceful, if windy, war zone."

"We are at risk below," he grunted, kicking hard, "because the All-Council knows we use this column. They can attack us at their leisure. It is expedient but dangerous."

Her worry panged.

Bella held on to Balim. She had to trust in him. Let go of her own power and trust that he and the other warriors of Atlantis would fix everything.

Her throat closed in protest.

She focused on her own fingers clenching Balim. *I still have power here. I need to claim it.* Helplessness was not something she tolerated, and ever since the Sons of Hercules had captured Jonah, putting her at the mercy of others, they'd pushed her off center.

She wiggled her human toes.

His long fins whooshed the water.

"What can I do?" she asked, crinkling her toes.

"Watch for danger."

A shark swerved toward them.

She pointed. "Like that?"

He glanced in her direction and raised his voice by vibrating louder. "Lotar!"

The gray-eyed warrior unclipped from the column and floated into the current, legs splayed and arms out so his limbs formed an x with his trident stretched. He made himself look large.

Three sharks swerved and flew past, giving him a wide berth. They emitted a siren sound like emergency vehicles from a different country, impossible for her to ignore.

Balim focused on kicking.

Bella watched over his shoulder.

In Balim's arms, destiny swept her away. The water felt right. She was at home.

What would she do about Jonah if she truly did belong in Atlantis?

The choking sensation returned.

Not now. The elixir needs to work. Just a little longer.

Lotar faced the sharks as they split, circling the group.

One dove at him. He thumped it with the sharp edge of his trident. It swerved away with a snarl. He rotated to the other two as though he understood their shark communication, positioning himself just before the second one swerved at him from the other direction.

He slashed.

The trident made a *shink* sound as it slid across the sandpapery gray skin. It did not penetrate.

The shark swerved away again.

In the distance, an inhalation sounded like someone gasping in shock. It made the hair on her neck stand up and shivers of primal fear run up her spine. A giant maw lumbered toward them.

The trio of sharks swerved erratically. The inhalation disoriented them, and so they darted back in the giant maw's direction.

"Curse it." Balim clinked their harness hook on the cable. "Diran, how secure is this cable?"

The warrior closest to Pelan, long-haired Diran, answered. "A Merman Warrior has not tested it."

"Merman Warrior" was the mer name for a megalodon because it was the only creature in the ocean that could destroy entire cities—and the mer could do nothing to stop it.

He vibrated harder, calling out to Lotar. "Snap on."

Lotar obeyed, his gaze never leaving the giant hissing mammoth.

"What is that?" Bella demanded.

"A megalodon," Balim replied grimly.

The giant sharks, which scientists had long thought extinct, apparently lived on in the deep water the mer called the "Blacknight Sea" and occasionally emerged to torment the bottom-dwelling warriors.

They were significantly larger than scientists had thought too.

She tightened her grip. "What can I do to help you?"

A partial smile curved Balim's lips. "Relax."

"You're joking, right?"

He gave his head a quick shake. "When our bodies move in rhythm, a warrior and his bride can move more efficiently than a single warrior alone. King Kadir discovered this with Queen Elyssa. *Relax.*"

She tried to relax. Think relaxing thoughts. Ignore the massive, creepily inhaling megalodon hissing on a collision course.

This wasn't the worst fear of her life. A visceral fear, but not the worst one. She let go. Gave in to Balim. Yielded her body to his, his powerful thighs swishing the water, his fins kicking between her stubby human toes while awareness of his nude, hard waist heated her blood.

They moved faster, sliding up to the warriors hauling Pelan and his bride.

The choking happened again. A tickle like a terrible, deadly sneeze gripped the back of her throat. If she let herself go, she'd shift back to human, and that tickle would turn into choking while the water transformed into shattered glass.

She stiffened, controlling herself.

Balim's kicks slowed and grew heavier. "Relax, Bella."

"I'm trying."

His wide hand held her head, and his vibration turned into a private, sad question. "Can you not trust me?"

She couldn't. She couldn't. She couldn't.

Because giving in to this enchanting world, and Balim specifically, would kill her.

"The All-Council has outdone itself," Diran vibrated, glancing over his shoulder at Balim, unaware of their struggles. "Merman Warriors are creatures of the blacknight abyss and the vents. They cruise the ocean bottoms and should not rise to this column of the water."

"This Merman Warrior is lost," Balim vibrated flatly. "Want to give directions?"

Lotar eyed him as though to ask why he was resorting to sarcasm now that their lives were in immediate danger.

But Diran answered. "The All-Council has been attacking us with many distractions. We withstood their attacks, and so they have escalated to sharks and now a megalodon. When will their reign end?"

The megalodon came at them like an approaching blimp.

With her new senses, the blue column of water appeared to be vast sky, and the megalodon crossed it like a deadly Hindenburg.

One smaller shark flew too close.

The megalodon twitched. It vacuumed up the writhing shark. The shark had seemed so large close-up, but it was a minnow inside the massive jaws. The megalodon drifted toward them, crossing the miles of ocean with disconcerting speed.

"How far to the midpoint?" Balim asked, his chest vibrating with a sharp edge of fear. "Any shelter?"

"Some distance." Diran slowed, released his grip on Pelan, and unclipped as he leveled his trident. "You continue."

Balim snapped. "Do not be a fool."

"I must protect the future queens of Atlantis." He lifted his chin. "I will—"

"Diran." Lotar's tone ordered him to obey Balim.

Diran paused.

A new sound reached Bella's chest, one of gravel tumbling in the washing machine, like when Jonah had come home unbeknownst to her with pockets full of rocks, combined with a scratchy record on top making a high-pitched "we-we." Awful, tone-deaf, and yet somehow, a cheerfully defiant noise that greeted them from below.

"Praise the Life Tree," Balim murmured. Everyone kicked toward that terrible sound as fast as possible. Then, he swore again. "This is not the midpoint."

"No," Lotar confirmed.

A gigantic octopus filled the ocean below them. Standing on top of the octopus's head, arms out as if she were embracing them, was a human.

"Queen Lucy." Balim's vibrated worry mixed with awe.

"That's a queen," Bella repeated.

"She is your future."

Lucy's hands glowed with a white light that reminded Bella of the glow of the Life Tree blossom. The same gentle light glowed over them in a sphere of protection.

The octopus waved one arm in the megalodon's direction and squawked. He curled his arm like a crotchety old man shaking a fist and shouting to get off his lawn.

Across the ocean, the megalodon checked itself and then it turned away. It disappeared into the far distance.

The creepy hissing noise like inhaling snakes dissipated with it.

Around Lucy, the protective glow faded.

They descended to the level where the woman had stopped. The octopus curled one giant arm around the rope like it was hanging out, fist at the ready in case it needed to thump someone. Its noise changed to a satisfied gurgle-snort.

Lotar and the other warriors ringed Lucy. It became really noticeable that all the warriors were bristling with daggers, tridents, and blades while Lucy floated entirely nude without even a pin in her flowing hair.

Balim wielded his doctor's implements. "Queen Lucy. This is not the midpoint. You will injure yourself."

"I went slow," Queen Lucy protested, obediently holding out her wrists for him, blinking and fluttering her gills on command while he conducted an exam with Bella still within his arms. Lucy smiled self-deprecatingly at Bella while she submitted to his orders. "Patrols swore they heard a megalodon, and when we found out you were coming down, I had to risk it."

"What would you have done if your lungs had inflated?"

"Been shocked since I don't have lungs right now," the woman replied.

Flowing black hair swirled around her head like a halo as she stood with normal human toes on the generous head of the giant octopus.

"You know I used to scuba dive, Balim. I may be an idiot about mer things, but I'm more aware of the risks and symptoms of rapid decompression than you are."

"You seem well," he grudgingly agreed, bandaging a

small wound on her finger. "Tell your young fry they must stop using your fingers to teethe."

"That was Prince Kael. Stand back. I want to greet everybody."

She drifted off the octopus and kicked her feet, grimaced, kicked a few more times like she was trying to kick-start a recalcitrant motorcycle, and then her feet finally morphed into long fins. She opened her arms to Bella and Pelan's bride.

"Welcome to the middle of nowhere, the ocean! I'm Lucy. This is Octopus Kong, our resident giant cave guardian."

The octopus curled his tentacles around Pelan's bride and nudged Balim aside.

He released Bella reluctantly.

Octopus Kong curled around Bella delicately, with her safety harness still clipped to the cable. Despite his massive size, his control was expert. He held her with perfect care, the large suckers tightening and loosening.

Bella rested her hand on his rubbery skin. Aside from the raucous noise, he emitted a bright light like a lantern in daylight.

He released her, Pelan's bride, and also the cable.

Balim examined the places the octopus had touched, ensuring that no sucker had marked her, and then entwined her again.

Octopus Kong stretched his massive arms. Flying out in an exploratory manner, he acted as if he had done his due diligence of greeting them and was now off to do octopus things, creaking and groaning the whole time.

Beneath him, a squadron of warriors rose.

They'd held back, cautious of the giant, and now traded greetings with the Atlantis warriors using a subtle hand gesture of two hands touching in the center of their chests three times.

"Second Lieutenant Ciran." Lotar approached the leader. "The cable is not safe. The All-Council moves."

Just as Bella remembered from meeting him months ago at MerMatch, the studious warrior paused his orders only long enough to gain information and then returned to his authoritative role.

"If the All-Council moves, then we must also move." Ciran's coffee-and-green tattoos tangled around his cheeks like twin plants. "Nothing will turn us away from claiming our brides and reuniting the air and water kingdoms. So says King Kadir."

They repeated the gesture honoring the king of Atlantis.

Balim greeted the warriors rising to find their brides. They looked and sounded worried. Their view of Pelan, too sick and injured to greet them or introduce his own bride, gave them pause.

"And Queen Bella experienced a reverse shift after entering the water." Lotar's gray eyes met hers across the distance. He vibrated softly, as usual, but was too disturbed by the experience to stay silent. He turned his back on her and continued to Ciran. "Her transformation is unstable."

"She must drink the Life Tree blossom nectar right away."

No! No, she mustn't. Jonah's cure!

But the warriors separated into two groups.

Bella's heart ached for them. They risked so much to go to the surface, meet their soul mates, and have a child. They escaped the traditionalist All-Council trying to crush them only to run into the Sons of Hercules forcing them back into the water at gunpoint. It was hard to see Pelan looking so ill.

It was a terrible warning of what reaching for dreams could cost.

"Despite this setback, we must not give up until all warriors have found their brides." Lucy's voice vibrated with crisp hope.

The warriors straightened with her encouragement.

"We will not be cowed by fear. We will not be stopped by anger. We will not be hobbled by grief. Together, we will rise and claim our destinies. Just like Balim and Pelan have."

The warriors relaxed.

Bella's own heart lift as the fears fell away. She had already fought the Sons of Hercules. She'd made progress. Now she was relying on Starr. And somehow, she would continue to follow her destiny until she got Jonah back.

"You must be Bella." Lucy exuded a motherly warmth. "I will escort you the rest of the way to your new home in Atlantis."

"Thank you." Bella's chest twinged with the twin fears of excitement and worry. She was going to a mer city.

A sneeze threatened the back of her throat.

She swallowed hard.

And the vial of poison clinked in Balim's bag. It brushed against her as he positioned her to continue their descent.

"You will love Atlantis," Lucy exclaimed as she descended. "You'll get your own octopus friend, your own castle, and rule the ocean as a queen. It's awesome. You'll never want to leave again."

Which would be tragic when Bella poisoned them all.

TWENTY-ONE

Balim felt Bella's tension through the water.

"I can't wait to see Atlantis." She smiled at Queen Lucy with closed lips. "I've heard so much about it."

"Conveniently, two Life Tree blossoms have just bloomed, so you can both drink the nectar at your wedding ceremonies."

"Only two?" Bella questioned. "On the whole tree?"

The groups separated, and Queen Lucy waved good-bye. Lotar, Diran, and the surface warriors ascended the cable with the escort of Octopus Kong. Queen Lucy led Balim, Pelan, her warriors, and Pelan's bride to Atlantis.

"Yes. The Life Tree grows a blossom when there is a need."

Bella fixed him with worried eyes. "You had one in New York."

"It should have gone to Faier's bride. Living in a tank is unusual."

"Aya kept alive the little blossom that Elyssa gave her," Queen Lucy chimed in.

"Because she already possessed the force of a powerful queen. Another future queen staffs MerMatch. My belief is Hazel and Faier's guess was Dannika. One kept the blossom alive by her presence."

"Neither wants to become a mermaid."

"Oh, I felt the same way, once." Queen Lucy made the light crackle from her fingertips. "If my old self could see me now."

Bella bit her lip.

"Perhaps another will grow," Balim vibrated quietly. "The Life Tree senses the need. Blossoms grow when brides are located."

"How do you feel about becoming a doctor's wife?" Queen Lucy asked Bella conversationally as they descended along the cable.

"About the same as he feels becoming a marketing executive's husband," Bella replied deftly.

"Oh, you used to do marketing?"

"I've completed a marketing campaign for the mer and am waiting for the ideal timing to release it."

Queen Lucy laughed. "Right. I don't mean to be dense. It's difficult to maintain a life on the surface and also raise a family, rule a city, and change the world beneath the sea."

"Yes, and so I'm continuing your work. You did a wonderful job of introducing the modern world to the mer with your Facebook videos, but new voices have arisen, and you're not there to control the record."

"Oh." She frowned. "My friend Mel is still replying."

"Yes, but the world has changed. The narrative is being taken over by other voices who claim to have more authority—and you won't like the direction they're taking it."

Queen Lucy darkened. "The Sons of Hercules."

"The person who controls the narrative controls reality.

So that's what I'm trying to do. I'm taking your narrative back."

"But instead, here you are."

"Here we are," Bella agreed, grim once more. She swallowed convulsively.

He held her closer. *Feel my strength filling you with the power of the Life Tree...*

She stiffened.

Once she saw the city and the majestic Life Tree, she would relax. Its presence would reactivate the elixir in her veins.

He hoped.

She swallowed again hard.

Just a little farther...

The wreck of the ancient city grew across the ocean floor.

Finally.

It differed from the last time Balim had seen it.

Cables were embedded in the wreckage. Human lanterns were stuck into bits of the floor and flattened the view throughout the territory.

It gave their enemies more places to hide.

King Kadir had a great interest in the past. His warriors sifted through the ruins for information about the Great Catastrophe. They'd searched for frescoes and found ancient drinking vessels and ornamental boats. Each discovery only inspired more questions and answered nothing.

Now the descending group unsnapped their harnesses, leaving them at the base of the city. A team of warriors lifted to greet them with waves, hailing the new future queens with honor.

"There's Octopus Kong's home." Queen Lucy pointed

to the giant cave at the foot of the extended coils. "You can come with us when we go over later and leave his favorite fish."

"Did King Kadir authorize that?" Balim asked.

Queen Lucy smiled. "Since Octopus Kong is the official savior and guardian of Atlantis, he can't say no. Anyway, we don't bother him on his bad days."

They flew on to Atlantis, the reborn city.

The Life Tree twinkled like a sun in a galaxy of stars. The great castles glowed green. Beneath the floating castles, the massive ribs of a felled megalodon glimmered white and fed nutrients to the vibrant sea floor.

His throat tightened.

It had never been his wish to leave Undine, even after the horrible events that had claimed his father and his prince. He'd always felt a grateful tightening when he'd returned home. Atlantis was now his home, and he had the same reaction.

Even though treason clinked in his bag.

When the city had first been planted, only King Kadir's and First Lieutenant Soren's lonely castles had arisen from the sea floor, but now a hundred castles bobbed around the Life Tree in concentric circles. So many for such a young city. They crossed the bare rock toward the increasingly lush floor where the Life Tree and castles anchored.

Bella's chest lit along with her eyes gleaming with wonder. "It's like a fairy ring."

"It is, isn't it?" Queen Lucy twirled as she kicked her fins. "I think they look like bull kelp and Elyssa thinks little planet balloons. Balim, you'll be excited to know yours grew in your absence."

His chest twinged. Imagining Bella choosing him

wholeheartedly felt wrong. Shameful. He didn't deserve it, and yet he couldn't stop wanting it. "Thrilled."

Queen Lucy laughed again as though he were being modest. To Bella, she explained, "You'll get an octopus and grow your own garden, and it will be your sanctuary. You'll love it."

Bella returned her smile, closed-lipped.

"But first, the Life Tree." She aimed for the brilliant light in the center of the ringed castles.

The warriors shouted greetings, swirling around them. Strong hands took Pelan so that their group could move faster.

Attacks had damaged the Life Tree's protective petals, leaving it cracked open and dangerously exposed.

Queen Lucy descended through one of the large cracks in the protective petals.

Inside, calming radiance soothed his heart. Bella held him closer, and her thighs brushed him as did her forehead. She breathed. "It's not beautiful...but it is."

He knew what she meant.

Balim landed at the foot of the barren tree.

Like an oak bereft of leaves, the Life Tree's bare branches stretched toward the surface. Tiny pebbles of Sea Opal resin beaded up on its small clefts and tinkled to the dais. Two small flowers bloomed at the upper branches of the tree.

It, like its crumbled dome shelter, had been battered to its roots. A silvery trunk was embedded into the dais, and the pastel pink of rebirth tinted the upper portions. The two colors intertwined.

"The roots are the original tree planted from King Kadir's seed," Balim told her. "Queen Elyssa grew the trunk when she brought King Kadir back to life after the first betrayal."

Bella clutched a hand to her throat. Guilt and hope crossed her expression and echoed in her soul light. "Would she visit Jonah?"

"Her powers work only on her mer."

Warriors rested Pelan against the Life Tree. Now, they waited.

Queen Elyssa and King Kadir entered the sanctuary. Queen Elyssa glowed with warm welcome, her human eyes twinkling at Balim.

King Kadir lifted his silver-streaked arms, daggers bristling from regal sheaths. "Welcome, future queens of Atlantis, to the—"

"Gaaah!" Young Prince Kael wiggled out of another warrior's arms and grabbed on to his father's hair, yanking King Kadir's head. A huge smile filled his happy baby face. "Gooo!"

King Kadir winced at the tugs and tried to unwind his young fry's strong grip. "And my son welcomes you also."

"Come here, you little Sea-Monkey." Queen Elyssa tickled her young fry. The baby prince squealed and yanked his father's hair harder. "Oops! Wait, wait, don't hurt your dada..."

The two parents soon were surrounded by a cluster of warriors with advice on how to get Prince Kael to release his father's hair.

Zoan, the warrior who took care of the Life Tree and was close friends with Pelan, jangled a Life Tree citizenship seed. "Look what I have for you, Prince Kael. Much more valuable than hair."

The prince agreed because he let go with both hands and wiggled up to Zoan, his little baby feet kicking and kicking and kicking, until he captured the rattle. Zoan arched his brows at the other warriors, who had gentle envy for his superior child-rearing skills.

Beside Balim, Bella touched her hand to her throat. Was she choking? No, this emotion was different. Her chin wrinkled hard, and her soul light fluctuated.

He pulled her back against his chest, and she melted there. Her soul light steadied. She took comfort from him.

King Kadir smoothed his flowing hair. "Now then, again. Welcome to Atlantis. Let us begin the wedding ceremonies."

Bella stiffened. The hand at her throat turned to a clutching motion as if someone was choking her and she needed to pull their grip off.

But before she could speak, Pelan's bride reared her head. "Wedding? No."

The Life Tree sanctuary grew deathly still. Even Prince Kael quieted.

Queen Elyssa spoke first. "Didn't Dannika explain what happens at MerMatch?"

"She did, but come on. I can't marry a man in a coma."

"Your marriage will bring Pelan back to life." King Kadir turned to Balim for medical approval.

Balim did not know how to respond.

Pelan's bride looked between the warriors. "You can't be serious."

"The Life Tree responds to important life events," Queen Elyssa offered, "like birth, marriage, that kind of thing. Kadir's not wrong."

"Okay, but marriage is out of the question."

The warriors rumbled. How could she heal Pelan if she wouldn't marry him?

"You drank the elixir and kissed," King Kadir vibrated,

giving voice to his warriors' disgruntlement. "You had the coffee date."

"Right, exactly." She rubbed her shadowed eyes. "The instant we met, he said I was his soul mate. We kissed. I saw stars, and I felt like a contestant on *The Bachelor*."

"Like a movie star," Queen Elyssa vibrated, nodding earnestly. "That's normal. That's how you know you've met your soul mate."

"But it wasn't fun. It was all paparazzi. And as we were leaving the coffee shop..." She shuddered and brushed her chest. "Then..."

The rulers stared at her with confusion stamped on their faces.

Then King Kadir turned to Balim. "You have observed her and Warrior Pelan. Are they not destined?"

He didn't know what to say. "You have remained by Warrior Pelan for so long."

"But we've barely had one coffee. You want me to marry him? I don't know if he's even a Knicks fan." She gripped her short, dark hair. Rebelliousness welled in her expression. Although she no longer wore the dramatic purple lip coloring, black eye outlines, or scuffed jeans she'd preferred on the surface, her fierceness made her soul glow.

Queen Elyssa tilted her head. "Are sports important to you?"

"I don't know." Her soul extinguished, and she scrubbed her cheeks. "I'm so tired. I've been tired for weeks. I just don't know."

"Give her something so she can rest," King Kadir ordered Balim.

"She has been resting for human weeks. With Warrior Pelan."

"It wasn't that restful," she replied, and the dark rings

still under her eyes showed that she spoke the truth. "I lost my job. I had to give up the lease on my apartment. My friends packed my stuff into storage, and I'm pretty sure my ex-roommates helped themselves to my knife set even after I told them not to. And I had to manage it all on ten-minute breaks because otherwise, you freaked out at me for 'abandoning Pelan in his moment of need.' I've spent the last 'human weeks' wondering what the heck's happened in my life and if I would ever catch up."

"So you did not focus on Warrior Pelan's recovery."

She glared. "For the love of Pete, here I am, aren't I? I care very much about his recovery."

"Do not give your love to Pete," Second Lieutenant Ciran interrupted from the back. "You must love Pelan."

She raised one brow at Bella. "Am I the crazy one?"

Queen Elyssa lifted quelling hands. "I'll explain her expression later, but don't worry, humans can love many people and still know their soul mates."

Bella looked away.

Her rejection of Queen Elyssa's statement struck Balim hard, like a trident to the chest.

He did not wish for her to love him more than her Jonah. But would she never love him a little bit?

A healer who had committed murder should not ask such a question.

The warriors grumbled, dissatisfied.

"Humans do not always know their desires," King Kadir vibrated gruffly. "She cannot see her soul light. Warrior Pelan's must brighten in her presence."

But it didn't.

Warrior Pelan leaned with his back against the silvery base. His soul flickered weakly. He gathered strength from its nearness. But not as much as he should. He was weakening. Getting sicker. Even though he should have resonated with the healing wood.

The Life Tree could not cure Blue Ring...

Balim shuddered.

Bella rested a hand on his arm, a question in her eyes as she glanced back at him. He shook his head to imply it was nothing.

The other warriors muttered amongst themselves. King Kadir had pointed out an unfortunate fact. They had brought Pelan's bride to Atlantis, and her supposed future husband did *not* resonate for her.

He had once. Enough to declare them soul mates. His bride had drunk the elixir and transformed.

King Kadir looked to Balim, worry and confusion stamped on his features. "What is the medical explanation?"

"He is ill."

King Kadir's gaze darted over the mass of warriors behind them full of hope to claim their brides.

When warriors could only select brides from sacred islands, mismatches caused chaos. But that should not happen now. Atlantis selected brides from modern females on land—so many millions in New York alone—so how could a warrior mistake another for his bride? Balim knew that Bella was his. Pelan must have known when he met his bride, even though he could not explain himself now.

Pelan's bride rubbed her eyes.

King Kadir focused on her as if he could talk her into sensing resonance. "You must feel in your heart he is your one true warrior."

She held her forehead in her hands. "To be honest, I'm exhausted. I don't know what I want."

"But you must marry."

She glared.

Balim intervened to stop a riot. "She has healed Pelan all this time. His tenacious illness would dim any soul. Perhaps after she rests, she will know her heart."

King Kadir glanced back at his disturbed warriors. Although the decision would be unpopular, he nodded. "Very well. We will postpone their wedding until the bride has rested."

"And Pelan's conscious," she insisted.

"As you wish." King Kadir turned to them instead. "Balim and Bella. Step forward and share your vows."

Bella's soul light burned ,and she turned in Balim's arms. Certainty firmed her expression. "I can't drink the nectar."

But she *would* share vows. She would marry him. He was her chosen husband. Her soul mate. Hers.

His chest squeezed as if a fist had clenched it.

She was more than he deserved.

He laced their fingers, sealing her promise. "I understand."

"You don't mind?"

"Consuming the nectar is not essential to the marriage ceremony."

The warriors rumbled uncomfortably.

King Kadir vibrated about the strangeness of their conversation. "The Life Tree has gifted you with a blossom to make Queen Bella's transformation permanent. You reject its offering?"

Bella's mouth opened and closed while she tried to vibrate a thoughtful, smooth way of explaining herself.

But Balim spoke the simple truth. "She reserves the healing power for her ill son. Bella's vow is the only promise I need."

Her mouth closed. She swallowed, and her eyes rimmed with red as her soul flared to the warmth of a beautiful sun. "Balim…"

His chest warmed to match, and even without speaking the vows aloud, he knew she was his bride wholeheartedly. Their souls entwined. The ceremony was only a ceremony. She was already his.

As though realizing it herself, a strange black poison emanated from her chest. It extinguished her soul light and strangled her lungs. Her eyes widened, and the green color dulled.

She clawed at her face and choked. "Blub!"

"Bella!" He tugged her into his arms as she writhed.

The gills in her lower back had sealed to form smooth human skin.

The elixir had stopped working. On the bottom of the sea far from any replacement source.

She was a human.

TWENTY-TWO

The world crushed Bella in a terrifying shaker of force and darkness.

Like the one time she'd gone white-water rafting as a team-building exercise with the office before anyone knew she was dating Chaz. On the first rapid, he'd thought it would be hilarious to push her in. She'd gone from breathless excitement to terror as the dark rapid had closed over her head, tumbled her over and over, scraped her across the riverbed, and made her thrash for the brighter surface. Their guide had scooped her back into the boat, and she'd gagged up half the river while Chaz had laughed.

Red flags. So many red flags. Had she only been with Chaz because it was easy not to trust him? She'd known before he'd abandoned her, pregnant, that he'd do it some-day. Balim never would, and sometimes, knowing that terri-fied her.

On the next rapid, one of their senior VPs had pushed Chaz in. He hadn't laughed so hard getting out again.

But here, there was no surface. There was no light. There was no raft.

She was alone in a turbulent, frigid silence. Cold weight pooled in her lungs. She couldn't breathe. There was no thought. Just animal survival. She bit, thrashed, struggled. The water held her in a fluid vise. There was no escape.

This was how she died.

And all hope for Jonah, for Balim's happiness as a husband, for the warriors of Atlantis died with her.

She'd wanted to be his bride. Why did that desire cause her to transform back to human? She'd wanted to embrace the mer way. She'd wanted to marry and yield and give in...

"...more, Bella. Yes, drink all." Balim's voice echoed, disjointed, as his words vibrated through the thick, black slurry at the bottom of the sea.

The cold receded, and the weight lifted off her chest. Her belly warmed with energy. She was not dying. She was transforming back into mer.

Oh, thank goodness. She could bring hope to the warriors. She could make Balim's darkness ease and rest in happiness. She could save Jonah's cure...

The ocean lightened again, and she opened her eyes.

Balim's dark gaze gleamed with heartblood-red hope as he hovered over her.

She rested in his arms.

As she blinked and focused on him, his relief lasted only a few instants before he queried her. "Bella? Can you see and hear me?"

"Yes." Her chest vibrated. She sucked in a deep mouthful of water, and it soothed her even though it was unnatural.

"I am sorry, Bella. Forgive me." His eyes darkened. "Forgive me. I could not lose you. I am so sorry."

"No..." She tried to explain her realization. That he would never hurt her. He would protect her always. She knew it now, and had known it, and that was why she'd agreed to marry—

A Life Tree blossom rested in his hand. It wilted as the shiny color faded. The bead of nectar was no longer in its center.

Oh, but there was a second one, and she'd just have to convince or beg or trick Pelan's bride into giving it to...

Wait. Balim wasn't apologizing because he'd left only one flower. He was apologizing because the elixir had failed and he'd had no choice but to give her the nectar of the Life Tree blossom. It raced through her veins now, healing her injuries and transforming her to mer.

Her healing. Her transformation. Her cure!

"No..." she moaned.

His eyes closed tight, and he pulled her to his body, rocking her as the wave of grief crashed over her.

"No, Balim. Jonah's not here. I can't... You couldn't have wasted it."

"You were dying."

"I would have rather died."

"I know, Bella. I know."

The Life Tree faded into a blur. Balim communicated with the other warriors, explaining only enough so they understood why this joyful moment represented such tragedy to her, and then he carried her away from the sanctuary and the lost hope it represented. Flying across the city while she closed her eyes and hung on tight, willing reality to be different and for her not to be alive if only there was a way to save the cure for Jonah.

The pressure changed—no, that wasn't it. The wide-open ocean feelings narrowed to a tunnel inside one of the living spherical castles. His castle. How did she know? The castle held his subtle flavor, like sleeping in his sheets while wearing his oversized shirt.

He rested her inside a small room, and when the smooth oak-like precious wood slid against her heels and buttocks and elbows, she opened her eyes.

The room was a vibrant olive green. The aperture he'd swum through looked out onto a courtyard garden bursting with plants. They nestled at the base of a dome, and the walls were pocketed with rooms just like the one she rested in. Twisty corridors and trailing plants unveiled a fairy forest rather than revealed they were deep beneath the sea. Lavender flowers fluttered on subtle currents.

Balim rested on his knees. His hands hung useless in his lap. "There is food in the pantry. Are you hungry?"

"No." Grief bubbled up in her chest. "I'll never be hungry again."

Matching pain flashed in his eyes. "I had no choice."

She tried to cover her mouth to regain control before the sobs wracked her.

He examined her, his caring touch soothing as it probed. "We should return to the Life Tree. Married or not, it will heal you."

"No. I can't be there right now."

"Bella. You can only save your son if you are alive to do so."

"Do you have the vial?"

He pulled out the small blue vial. It seemed less sinister than on the surface.

"Get rid of it."

"What about Jonah?"

"I never want to see it again."

He touched a seamless wall and pushed out a cabinet, stored it inside, and hid it away.

She couldn't endure this pain. She couldn't.

"Please." He massaged her temples. "Do not suffer. You will resolve this. You will become a queen and—"

"Stop." She opened her eyes and leaned into him, teasing her hot nipples along his chest once more. "Make me forget everything and just exist."

His gaze darkened with hunger, and then his lips covered hers. Sweet aches twisted between her legs, tightening her pussy and making her want him. She melded his abdomen to hers. His cock pressed against her soft belly, making delicious promises if she would once more let him in.

"I wish," he vibrated in his chest as his mouth descended to kiss her collarbone, her chest, and then to snag a hot, aching nipple, "we had more of those plastics."

A sliver of responsibility returned. She couldn't just lose herself with Balim or be swept away.

Well, for a little while.

"Yeah," she agreed, breathless with arousal. "But we can still feel pleasure." She wrapped her fingers around his hard cock while he groaned and switched to her other breast. "Let me teach you."

"I must heal you." His vibrations sounded ragged. "A warrior must pleasure his bride."

"You will. Watch." She encompassed his cock in her hands, savoring the length and curvature. He watched her suck the head into her hot mouth, skepticism battling arousal, and then she sucked him in deeper, tonguing his shaft.

He groaned. "How is this pleasure possible? My mind is quiet and empty and filled with you."

"It gets better," she promised, her chest vibrating as she continued to tease and arouse his shaft. Watching him fight his arousal made her own increase. She slipped her fingers between the soft, slick folds of her feminine center. She was so ready for him, and she wanted him, but the sliver of responsibility had returned and she couldn't give in without betraying...everything. She pushed those thoughts from her mind.

Balim took advantage of her distraction to lift her, rotating her mouth around his cock, and rested his hand on her soft feminine vee. "You need this."

"Yes. I do."

He palmed her mons, massaging her and studying her, chasing her pleasure until he pressed in one finger and found her G-spot.

"How?" she gasped.

"I see your soul light." He smiled, cocky, his pleasure immobilizing her. "You are bared to me, Bella."

She shook. Waves of arousal crashed over her, the orgasm threatening. He did see her. Chaz had never seen her. No one had ever seen her. Not like Balim.

Dangerous. This was too dangerous.

No. Forgetting everything was what she wanted. Needed. Craved.

Tingles filled her fingers and lips and toes. A rainbow of happiness wrapping around her chest in happy fulfillment. Everything would be okay. She was fine and everyone else was fine too. For this one moment, her burdens lifted and she was free as she'd been at seventeen leaving her house for the first time, a future career woman with the world at her feet and fortunes waiting for her to pluck.

Just like before she'd had Jonah. That's how it was now. She was happy, as if she'd never had Jonah.

She was forgetting him.

All the nights she'd intended to put him down in his

crib and get to work—and instead found herself playing with his baby fingers, booping his stubby nose, gazing deeply into his serious brown eyes as he drifted to sleep on her chest. All the days she'd taken her weekend work to the closest park and sat in the shade while he raced around the shallow cement pool chasing wily ducks. The fearless way he tried absolutely every food she carried home from a street truck, considering each bite with quiet contemplation. His delighted laughter when she'd finally mastered the newest silly dance that he and his friends had been trying to teach her so he could introduce her as the "cool" mom at school.

All the ways Jonah had seeped into her broken heart and sealed the holes, teaching her the true face of unconditional love. "No," she murmured.

Balim held her stationary, stopping his movements, holding her safe. "Bella?"

She swallowed her sudden, uncharacteristic emotion. She was breaking inside, and yet she didn't want him to know it. "I can't be the only one to enjoy this."

"Bella, you are a female with maturity and experience. I do not have many gifts to give you. You are not frightened or confused. You know your heart and your mind. I cannot convince you to be carefree or take away your burdens unless you let me. So if I ease your tiredness and comfort, it will strengthen you to bear your burdens once again."

Was that true? Did giving in to him strengthen her?

"Let me do this."

Yes, this was about more than her. Perhaps Balim was right. Perhaps she wasn't forgetting. Perhaps she just needed to rest so she would be strong.

She just needed to let herself go...

He held his position as the orgasm exploded around her,

rainbows flying free, lifting on a cresting wave of delicious tingles and then falling. He withdrew from her, releasing her pussy as she closed her hand around his trembling shaft. He grunted in surprise and then her mouth filled with his heat and salt. They were linked on a spiritual level. Souls. Lights. And more than fate operated. She felt him in her bones.

And that was terrifying.

Bella struggled to separate. Balim helped her, again stroking her with silent support as though he knew the chaos running through her mind and he didn't judge her. He never judged her. That was also terrifying.

She struggled free and stared at him.

He stared back.

"Sorry." She touched her forehead where there *ought* to be a headache, but she felt fine. "I was thinking about Jonah."

He nodded and waved for her to come to him. "Rest."

"I just can't be happy until he's safe."

"That is correct."

Now she had to find a new cure.

Balim's normal answer somehow calmed her. He was right. As the medical professional he'd once called himself, he had restored her equilibrium and she was more able to think. This cure had been removed. Failure stung. Just like her failure to test Chaz had stung.

So long as Jonah lived, she had time. She had the will.

And deep in her heart, she knew he still lived.

He was connected to her. As a mermaid with resonance, she sensed his soul.

And no matter how she fought it, she also sensed Balim.

She returned to Balim's side and rested against the floor,

floating. She would think of a new cure. Right now. "Did you know the story of the name Jonah?"

"No."

"In ancient times, he was ordered to deliver a prophecy, but he tried to get out of it by sailing away. A storm came up to punish him and endangered the sailors. Realizing his mistake, Jonah sacrificed himself to save everyone else. He jumped overboard and was swallowed by a whale."

Balim frowned. "No whale would swallow a human."

"Some whales do. The *Moby Dick* whale."

"Sharks swallow humans. Fish scavenge the dead. No whale acts as you describe."

"It's just a story," she said. "Anyway, three days later, the whale spit Jonah out on shore, where he delivered the prophecy. Disasters were averted. Happy ending."

He listened and then prompted, "Then what happened?"

"I don't know." She sighed as the weight settled on her once more. "It's ironic. My Jonah's been swallowed by the whale of cancer. And he's been in the belly of the beast much longer than three days."

She had to stop because her chest trembled and she feared her underwater voice would wobble.

Balim cupped her cheek and stroked one thumb across her lower lip. Soothing, loving.

"Sorry." She swallowed and collected herself. "I know it's not the time for this. We have to get the blossom to the Sons of Hercules so they reveal Jonah's position and not destroy Atlantis with this poison. And then save him. Somehow."

"You will." Balim held her gaze with absolute faith. "By—"

"Healer Balim!" Ciran shouted from the entrance to

their castle, and his vibrations echoed through the long tube through the wall into their courtyard. "King Kadir assigns guards to Queen Bella!"

"Enter!" He offered his hand to Bella and floated into the main courtyard to greet the warrior.

So the working world intruded.

Ciran flew in with two warriors. The trio tucked their tridents against their elbows and saluted.

"Queen Bella," Ciran acknowledged.

"You still haven't learned how to smile," she noted.

"My soul mate does not mind."

Ciran's quiet announcement rocked the warriors and surprised Bella.

"If you have found your soul mate, why are you here?" Balim voiced the question for all.

"Because she has not chosen me." Ciran saw that his answer did not satisfy and tried again. "New York City is not a sacred island. Queen Bella evaluated my lack of smile and selected Faier as a better spokesman. As I did not need to seek my bride now she has been found, I yielded my place to another warrior."

"Who is it?" Bella asked. "Your bride, I mean."

"When she has selected me, I will tell you." He gestured to his accompanying warriors, closing the conversation. "These will be your guards until the welcome ceremony when you may choose alternates: Iyen and Gailen."

Iyen had deep maroon tattoos and a silent but capable mien. He saluted again, his fingers touching before his fit chest and his gaze passing Bella to take in the whole area as though seeking enemies.

Gailen grinned and also saluted; his thumbs couldn't bend. "Nice to meet you, Marketing Executive Queen Bella."

She straightened. "Er, thank you."

"You are welcome."

Balim made a tsk sound—which was a feat underwater—and gripped Gailen's wrists, rotating them to examine the thumbs. "No improvements to your thumbs?"

"Nope." He showed his limited range of motion to Balim. "I am as scarred and limping as Faier, but not half so heroic." For Bella's information, he added, "Faier received his injuries saving other warriors from raiders and from snatching a child from inside the teeth of a megalodon. I received mine trying to rescue myself."

Balim frowned as he rotated the thumbs. "We all broke a little when we escaped our origin cities, Gailen. Not everyone has as visual an injury."

Iyen fixed his gaze on Balim for a long, measured moment and then resumed his silent scanning of the interior.

"Your bones have fused improperly." Balim wiggled the joints. "On the surface, humans would break the bones a second time and then splint them into the correct position. We may try it here."

"How strange to break something already healed."

"Yes. Humans cannot regrow limbs, but they have adeptness at fixing the limbs that remain. You would be awed by their mechanical limbs."

Gailen looked like he was considering the procedure. "Does it take long?"

"The healing process can. You could not grip during that time."

Gailen pulled his hands away and wrapped his fingers around his trident. His badly healed thumbs rested on the metal. "I wield a trident. I complete patrols. I have battled the enemy. Make me infirm when I *am* infirm and can no longer be of use to you."

"As you wish."

"Good," Ciran said, relieved. "Queen Bella, Iyen and Gailen are your guards during the period before you have made your fins and captured your queen power, and afterward, they will serve as your messengers. They will stay with you when you separate from Balim."

She clutched Balim's hand. "I won't separate."

"I see." Ciran seemed to calculate her answer. "Balim, you did not complete the mer 'hospital,' and so you must review the health of the warriors King Kadir has chosen to surface."

"How many?"

"Forty-three warriors and one queen."

Balim's arm around Bella tightened. "That is more warriors than founded our city."

"Including the warriors who have surfaced, it is less than half of our current strength. The number remaining can continue patrols with one backup. I have calculated it." He never smiled once through the conversation, so serious and yet also somehow young and confident.

"I thought we were waiting to send up big numbers to the completed platform."

"The surface weather is changing from fall to winter, and soon we must wait another year. Perhaps two. King Kadir will not wait. Atlantis will not wait. We will become powerful with queens, vibrant with young fry, and the world will see our united strength."

His chest vibrated with conviction, and the other warriors straightened, heartened by his words.

Balim looked at Bella. For one instant, she united with

him. They both knew what dangers lurked in the surface shadows.

Bella voiced the caution of experience. "The Sons of Hercules aren't going to sit idle. And you don't have a hospital or a doctor. It's a big risk."

"We have considered every angle," Ciran said. "Another healer has surfaced from Dragao Azul. He will fly to New York as needed."

"Fly him in now," Bella urged.

Ciran frowned. "No warriors are injured."

"The Sons of Hercules are more determined than you realize. I underestimated them, and I don't want you to make that mistake. If you pop up together, you will make an irresistible target."

"We will not clump together like a bait ball," he said, still serious. "We will take the recommended precautions of the new security team Dannika has contracted."

"That's not enough."

He straightened and puffed his coffee-and-evergreen-scrolled chest. "We are warriors."

"You're literally fish out of water. How can you defend against an enemy you can't see?"

"Bella is right," Balim affirmed. "Beneath the water, we see raiders. But on the surface, the enemies are eels hiding within sea grasses. It is impossible to identify the poisoned strands until they are stabbing you in the chest."

Ciran nodded. "Balim, you will review the health of the warriors in case we proceed as planned."

"We will follow," he promised.

She held Balim back. They hadn't finished discussing how they would resolve the issue of the poison vial.

Ciran shouted over behind him, "And prepare, Queen Bella, for the welcome ceremony!"

The trio of warriors flew out to await them.

Her heart squeezed again. "Balim, I can't let them welcome me to this city."

"You must." His gaze glowed with certainty. "This is your home, Bella. You drank the nectar. The sap of the Life Tree flows in your veins."

"But the poison—"

"Must not touch the Life Tree." He entwined her in his arms and kicked. His feet unfurled into long fins and crossed the courtyard with a single stroke. "You will find another way to defeat your enemies."

"I want to believe you."

"Believe." He flew down the long, green entrance canal through the wall of the castle and exited into the city beside Ciran and the others. "And develop your queen powers."

The other warriors overheard his vibrations because they beamed—except Ciran, who remained serious, but seemed less frowny.

"Meet the other queens." Balim released her outside the Life Tree sanctuary beside Elyssa and Lucy playing with their children. "They will teach you what you need to know."

He flew to a growing group of warriors a short distance away.

She tried to smile at the women while her mind turned over the problems.

A poisoned vial. A missing child. An elusive cure.

How would she escape this mess? Without hurting Atlantis, Jonah, or Balim?

TWENTY-THREE

Balim kept Bella in his field of vision while Second Lieutenant Ciran led him to the assembled warriors.

He did not think of it often, but Ciran had come from Undine as well. He had always kept a distance from Balim, like all citizens, but he had never taken part in the cruelty. He had never blamed Balim for his role in the deaths of the prince or his father.

Since he had left the city only a short time after Balim and also joined Soren's ragtag army to free Kadir from the All-Council prison and found Atlantis, clearly he'd held many of the same values and reservations.

They had never spoken of their old home. Balim because it was too dark, and Ciran...the reason was unknown. He kept the serious mien of a scholar and represented his origin city well with his serious logic. Although aware of emotions, he did not let passions rule him. He was a true Undine.

Unlike Balim.

Now, Ciran made a strong second lieutenant. He

signaled Bella's guards. Iyen made brief eye contact with Balim before flying to Bella's area and spreading between the warriors assigned to Queens Elyssa and Lucy. Gailen saluted and twirled after Bella.

She was so well-guarded, and yet...

Balim struggled with his concentration.

She had been so close to death. The painful fears swirled up around him. He'd almost lost her. The shock, the spasm, the dulling of her gaze and the slipping away of her soul. He choked on the memories. Not Bella. Not his Bella.

Second Lieutenant Ciran glanced back at him. "Healer Balim, are you unwell?"

"No."

"But your soul..." Ciran noticed the dangerous fluctuation of his soul light. "Do you also question whether your bride is your soul mate?"

"My Bella is still upset by the loss of her son's cure." Balim reassured the listening warriors beyond Ciran. "She must acclimate to the mer world. Her confusion and distraught emotions are natural. My unsettled soul reflects this *because we are united.*"

Ciran's brow smoothed, and he nodded his understanding.

Crisis averted.

The queens—Elyssa and Lucy—played with their young fry. The twins romped, and Prince Kael trailed.

Their giggles echoed in the city center, warming the hearts of all who heard the glad noise and filling the waiting warriors with smiles.

Queen Elyssa waved at them. "Bella, come over! We'll practice fins. Tory and Yrun will show you how it's done."

"Healer Balim." King Kadir, with silver lightning bolts,

floated with him beside the gathering of warriors. "Ensure these warriors are at their peak of health."

A shadow under the king's rib cage caught Balim's eye.

He turned and inspected the king's chest. "You have stopped taking on weight."

King Kadir locked his hands over his ribs. "Queen Elyssa likes this slender form for me. Turn your eye on these warriors, healer."

Balim obeyed, muttering to himself about patients deciding they were well with no evidence, and began his inspection.

The warriors stiffened and moaned when he taped up minor scratches no matter how he reassured them small injuries would not disqualify them from arising. He understood their fears.

Nilun held his hand behind his back. "I am fine."

"Then show me your hand."

The fiery warrior growled. "I have shown you all you need to see."

"Warrior Nilun, you will not surface until I have inspected you."

"I will fight you if you say I am unhealthy!"

Balim felt his eyes rolling back in his head. "Even I could win if you cannot use your weapon."

Nilun's teeth gritted. Balim had stumbled upon his true fears.

"Just show me your hand," Balim said, irritated. "You are slowing the other warriors."

Nilun looked over at the others and jutted his hand. A skin lesion covered the back and thumb, arresting his ability to wield a trident.

Balim inspected it. No bleeding, smooth rather than ragged edges, a pinker center... "You have been hiding this."

"Because!" Nilun gritted his teeth. "I must avenge Pelan."

"The shooter is imprisoned by human justice."

"But not his leader. I must find the enemies who injured Pelan and repay their attack!"

From the Life Tree sanctuary, Pelan's bride paddled out and stretched.

She smiled at Bella and the other queens and watched the warriors with interest.

Zoan also floated at the edge of the gathered warriors. He and Nilun were the closest friends of Pelan, although Zoan's teasing was the opposite of Nilun's hotheaded impulsiveness.

Balim had never made such close friends.

"You must allow me to surface," Nilun continued, issuing his request as an order without a hint of asking. "I must exact my vengeance."

"You may surface." Balim unrolled his tools and spread healing paste on the lesion while Nilun hissed at the pain. "I would not forbid a warrior to surface who has an infected water flea bite."

His jaw dropped as his chest vibrated. "Water flea?"

"This reaction is rare. Djullanar has warmer water fleas. You are unfamiliar with Atlantic water fleas." He bandaged the paste with seaweed and pressed it neatly to make it adhere. "But you will not avenge Pelan. Keep this injury wet until the bandage falls off, and you will avoid a scar."

He tried to flex his hand. "I cannot grip."

"Correct. And keep the wound wet so it will heal."

"How can I keep the wound wet? The air is dry."

"There is water on the surface," Balim reminded him. "Ask for a bowl of water."

His face blanked. "You wish for me to keep my hand in

a bowl of water? How can I move or pursue or wield a trident?"

King Kadir floated forward. "Warrior Nilun, you will surrender your weapons at the platform. It is our treaty with the Americans."

Emotion worked his face. He looked back at Zoan, who shrugged, and then into the sanctuary, where it was impossible to see Pelan. "But I must avenge him. That is my whole purpose for surfacing."

"Consider serving your race as well as your king and search for your soul mate." Balim turned to the next warrior.

But he could not keep his mind off Bella and the vengeance they would face if anyone knew about her vial of poison.

She must develop her queen powers to destroy the poison, save Atlantis, and find and cure her son. Here, with Queen Elyssa and Queen Lucy to guide her.

Before it was too late.

TWENTY-FOUR

Bella lingered at the side of the playing area where the three young children zoomed between their moms. The sight made her heart squeeze.

Elyssa's child, Kael, was a year and a half maybe. He romped after Lucy's two-year-old fraternal twins, girl Tory and boy Yrun. Pumping their stubby legs and already-impressive fins, they flew from Lucy, avoiding her tickles, to Elyssa and back again, giggling and squealing.

Behind Bella, Pelan's bride watched with her arms crossed, her human toes dangling. "They make it look so easy."

She spoke with a dry, familiar tone to Bella even though this was perhaps the first time they'd ever talked. And she flexed her toes, twisted her ankles and jiggled her knees.

"You're practicing," Bella noted, returning the cool observations. "Any luck?"

"Not yet. I think I'm getting somewhere and then nothing." Her lips flattened, and she massaged her toes with her hands. "The sooner I'm independent, the better."

Bella would ask about that but a ruckus interrupted her.

Yrun, looking behind him and giggling, flew into Kael with a cry. The two tumbled against Tory. Elbows and knees smacked into soft tissue. Little wails crossed the city, and everyone stopped except Balim and King Kadir, both of whom homed in on the injuries.

"Ouch," Pelan's bride said, and drifted back while everyone else leaned in.

Kael flew into Elyssa's arms. She kissed his head. "There, all better."

King Kadir reached them a moment later and enveloped both of them in his arms. "I shall also perform the kiss." And he did. Then he brought out a small treat from the seaweed pouch all mer carried. "To sweeten your tongue."

Prince Kael's wails faded to a whimper, and then he stuck out his lower lip, trembling, but otherwise calmed. He took the small bit of fruit and chewed on it with his few baby teeth.

Elyssa smiled at her husband.

That closeness, that instant support, was something Bella had never experienced. Yet here, now, she could experience it with Balim. He would be an attentive father.

Bella's throat tightened.

Lucy gathered her darlings, soothing and kissing them. They cried and rooted urgently until both latched on and peace reigned.

The warriors remained on alert.

"Warlord Torun will return to support you shortly," Ciran informed Lucy.

"What? No, don't interrupt his research. It's only a playground tumble."

"He must know the condition of his young fry."

"And they're fine." Lucy insisted. "We're fine. Nothing a hug from Mom won't cure. Right, Balim?"

Meanwhile, Balim examined Kael—only a tiny scrape, which he soothed with gel while Kael watched. Then he examined the twins—who had older bruising, but which Lucy assured him was normal.

Bella could stay here, make her fins, join the mer world, and never rise to the surface. Not only Balim, but the women and the warriors would give her support. If it took a village, this whole village would be devoted to her children. It would no longer be her as a single mother and her child against the world...

Only when everyone was proclaimed fine did the warriors relax, and, with a meaningful look to Bella, Balim returned to his examination of the assembled warriors. King Kadir left them a moment later, and then Elyssa had to convince Kael not to go after his father, but that was a losing battle, and the brave prince took off after his very willing father.

"He's so independent," Elyssa sighed and cast her eyes on Lucy. "I miss that stage. I thought we'd nurse for longer, but as soon as Kael could swim, he became his father's little man."

"I keep thinking mine must be done." Lucy gazed on her children with fullhearted love. "They're only two years old. I spent a lot longer grieving I'd never have my own before the Sireno Life Tree healed me. I just have to hug them close for as long as I can."

As if on cue, first Tory and then Yrun wiggled free, satisfied with their tiny snack and energetic again.

"And they're off," Pelan's bride noted, still crossing her arms. She'd drifted away with the talk of the kids; they did not hold her interest.

Lucy folded her hands, smiling, as her twins darted and danced like little underwater jumping beans, never still, always bright-eyed and bumbly and active. "You know how fast this stage goes by, right, Bella?"

"I formula-fed," she confessed before anyone could think she had a special contribution to their weaning discussion. "I never had time to fit nursing around my career."

"The mer have formula." Elyssa frowned as she searched her mind for the specifics. "Some combination of fish protein, blubber, and plant fiber."

"Torun offered to make it for me." Lucy stretched and leaned back on her elbows, floating lazily. "But you know, it's way easier to nurse even twins when you have endless maternity leave, you're already totally naked all the time, and an entire city of fit warriors is waiting to serve you like a queen."

That made Bella smile against her will. "Yes, that might have changed my priorities."

Elyssa's optimistic smile flickered, and she rested her hands across her belly. The area grew quiet.

Everyone knew about Jonah. They wanted to be careful of her feelings, and Bella appreciated their sensitivity even though it would be easier for her not to think about him at all.

Sadness welled in her throat. It choked her, not like when her body was rejecting the elixir and the transition to mer, but like a normal painful sadness that made her choke back a cry.

Across the field, Balim caught and held her gaze. He always knew. Silently, he asked—could he help her?

No. She swallowed and searched for a better topic. Something to channel her sadness at her failures and focus on the future.

"How did you make that ball of light from your hands?" Bella asked Lucy, changing the subject. "It was amazing."

"I channeled my queen powers."

"How?" Pelan's bride asked her, interested again.

"Well, I think about how much I love Torun and then 'pop,' out they come." She demonstrated, kicking her human toes multiple times. Nothing happened. "Oh, come on now. Come on...yes! There they are." Her fins unfurled.

"It doesn't look easy," Pelan's bride commented with dismay.

"For me, it's not." She huffed and rubbed her dark hair. "Look at my kids, though."

Tory flexed her feet, imitating her mother and popping them back and forth and back and forth, fins and toes and fins and toes. Beside her, Yrun picked at his lips. One foot flexed to fins and the other held toes.

Bella calculated their abilities based on her memory of Jonah. "They were born underwater. They can't be great walkers yet."

"They're not bad. We practice surface-time with Mum-Mum and Grandada every few weeks. They're better than toddlers, but maybe not quite ready to run a relay race."

Hmm.

"Every woman finds her inner power differently," Lucy said, and Elyssa nodded in agreement.

"I think meditative thoughts." Elyssa crossed her legs in a yoga pose, closed her eyes, and hummed. "Ommm."

Then she stretched into an underwater Downward Dog, and as she straightened her body, her fins emerged, flowing like a long dress.

Beautiful.

"So you have to find your own way," Lucy finished. "First, make your fins. As you gain confidence, power will flow."

Pelan's bride closed her eyes and tried the meditation route, but she didn't have much luck.

The women chatted about their powers. Lucy sheltered others with a shield; Aya, Elyssa's cousin, pushed warriors away, and Elyssa healed. Other queens who had descended to the second rebel city, Dragao Azul, possessed similar powers.

"What we used to think were separate queen powers are the same," Lucy continued, "but everyone has a natural talent for one power over another. That's why the more women marry into the city, the more we work together, the stronger we are."

"Do you have to marry first?" Pelan's bride scrubbed her face. "It's not enough to be a mermaid?"

"So far as I know, you have to drink the nectar of the Life Tree blossom, not just elixir, and that means joining with your husband," Elyssa answered. "I don't know of anyone who's developed their powers independently."

Pelan's bride ground her teeth.

"Don't worry. Balim is a great healer. Pelan will wake up soon, and then you'll know that he's the one for you. You'll drink the nectar, we'll teach you how to make your fins, and you'll embrace your queen power."

"Yeah," she muttered, unconvinced, and drifted back into the sanctuary to Pelan's side.

Bella's spine tightened.

She had to ask Balim how they would get the blossom away. Could she just ask? The mer treasured young fry. But if Pelan's bride needed to drink it to heal Pelan, how could Bella steal away his health on a risky hope she'd defeat the Sons of Hercules?

Sickness, like a raiding party, could change everything in an instant.

Bella closed her eyes. A quiet, tinkling, holy music filling her with peace.

She didn't want to think about the surface. She didn't want to think about her son, where he was, whether he was even still alive.

Her heart filled with molten glass hardened into spikes.

"Bella." Balim's voice vibrated beside her, and his powerful arms pulled her into the safety of his embrace. "Lighten your thoughts. Your soul is sick and dark."

She opened her eyes and let her current reality filter back to her. "I'm here."

"The Life Tree sanctuary should soothe you."

"I guess my problems are larger than most. The Life Tree can't heal everything."

He did not look convinced.

She, more than anyone, wanted him to be right. The Life Tree must cure anything. Leukemia, infertility, anything.

Anything...

"Balim!" Pelan's bride burst from the sanctuary, fear on her face. "Pelan's having trouble breathing."

"What do you mean?" Balim tightened his grip on Bella. "He is a warrior of the mer."

"I know, but he's arching his back." She demonstrated. "Like he can't breathe. Come look."

Balim linked Bella's hand with his and flew into the sanctuary, keeping her close as though he could sense the ripples of danger on the currents.

Inside, Pelan arched like his bride had described. The other warrior, Zoan, huddled over him with worry. Zoan called to Balim, "His soul is darkening. He is not responding to the Life Tree."

Balim released Bella, shifted his feet to human, and knelt at Pelan's side.

Pelan's bride stood next to Bella, horror mixed with helpless inevitability. Bella knew that feeling too well.

"What's wrong?" Elyssa crowded in with the other warriors. "Why isn't Pelan being healed?"

Balim rested on his heels and straightened, a dead expression on his face. "Because he has an incurable illness."

"What? What to do you mean?"

Balim pointed to the small interlocking blue loops crossing Pelan's chest encasing him in silver-blue chains. "He has Oannes' Curse."

"No," King Kadir growled.

"Yes." Balim looked sick. "The official name is Blue Ring."

TWENTY-FIVE

Balim knelt before his patient. An unfamiliar rage twisted him.

It was as if his old king had arisen from the dead and taunted him. *"You will never succeed your father. You did not even recognize he had Blue Ring, and yet you are the only warrior of this era to have seen it with your own eyes when you murdered me."*

Warrior Pelan, the young, hopeful male who had sacrificed so much to reach Atlantis, should have a happier life ahead of him with a bride. Not be suffering and dying young from this curse.

Warrior Pelan moaned.

His bride knelt beside him and tried to take his hands. "Pelan? Can you hear me?"

He dragged his hand free. And otherwise, Pelan had no reaction to her. Just as before when she'd refused the marriage ceremony.

She grimaced, rose to her feet, and backed away. "It's not working."

Behind him, the warriors and queens discussed what to do.

"Is Blue Ring contagious?" Queen Elyssa asked. "Are we at risk?"

"Perhaps it is not Blue Ring," a warrior interrupted in the back. "No one living has seen it. Healer Balim is mistaken."

Others pressed forward, encroaching on his patient, to get their own look while the more distant warriors argued.

Second Lieutenant Ciran's vibration leveled their words. "Respect Healer Balim's expertise." He met Balim's gaze, revealing nothing. "If he says it is Blue Ring, Warrior Pelan is infected with Blue Ring."

"Then is it not too late?" An unidentified warrior asked the fearful question. "We are exposed. His sickness infects us."

Panic edged the rumbles.

"Empty this sanctuary," King Kadir ordered the nearby warriors. "Those who remain must be quiet."

Nilun covered his flea bite with one hand and stood to the side, his worry palpable. Half the warriors flew out, leaving a quieter crowd.

Pelan had to respond. Balim pressed Pelan's shoulders into the Life Tree.

The warrior thrashed. His blood had been corrupted against resonance, and he reacted as a dull human. Balim released Pelan, and the warrior collapsed in a heap.

Disconcerting.

Bella floated beside Balim and leaned over him. "Are you at risk?"

"Normally? No." He flexed his own fingers, finding no cuts or injuries, not even the tiniest break of skin. "The disease is confined to Oannes Field. It afflicts only those who touch or handle the cursed weapons. But how has Warrior Pelan contracted it?"

"No one entered the sanctuary since he arrived," Zoan affirmed.

"Then he touched the weapons before." Just as Balim's instincts had told him. "Possibly any of us touched the weapons without knowing. Or perhaps Warrior Pelan *is* the weapon."

Queen Elyssa floated forth. "Let me try."

Balim's first impulse was to deny her. She should not risk herself. Queen Elyssa was the light and hope of Atlantis. As the first queen, she had welcomed all warriors with her heart.

But she was Warrior Pelan's best hope now.

Queen Elyssa knelt and rested her hands on Pelan's feverish brow.

Pelan whipped his head back and forth as though trying to shake her off. He flung an arm. It cracked against Queen Elyssa's shoulder.

She opened her eyes and gasped. "Ow!"

Prince Kael flew toward his mother with a cry.

"No!" Queen Elyssa tried to stop him. "I'm all right. I promise! Just surprised."

King Kadir intercepted Prince Kael, soothed him, and gave the young fry to Second Lieutenant Ciran with grave instructions. "Confine the young fry to my castle until the Life Tree sanctuary is purified. Guard them with our most faithful warriors."

"My king." Ciran turned away without meeting Balim's eye. He gathered his select guard, and they escorted the young fry out with Queen Lucy's gentle but worried encouragement.

Balim checked Queen Elyssa's arm. The skin was

reddish from the contact but not broken.

She laughed, a little shaken. "I don't know if I should try again. I felt nothing from Pelan. It's like something's blocking me."

This was a nightmare.

"Healer Balim!" First Lieutenant Soren's gruff vibration called out from the entrance to the sanctuary. Warriors parted to make way. "We have grave news from your human hospital."

The massive first lieutenant was the size of two warriors and covered in black tattoos. Once he had declared that he possessed no honor, but now he quieted that declaration around his brilliant queen, pale Aya.

"We have grave news here," Queen Elyssa said, curling her hand around King Kadir's bicep. "Pelan has Blue Ring."

"Blue Ring?" The dangerous first lieutenant rested at the edge of the dais. "I heard he has Crab-Cut Disease."

"That is what Healer Balim thought also. But it is Blue Ring."

"The cursed coral field," First Lieutenant Soren murmured to his smart bride. "Where the coral grows into perfect tridents but none may harvest it because of Oannes' curse."

"Now, he has cursed Atlantis." King Kadir gazed on his injured warrior with deep unhappiness. "Why?"

"The All-Council would say we face a fit punishment for having broken the ancient covenant," First Lieutenant Soren growled. "How lucky for them we should be the new center of this legendary illness."

If Atlantis became a cursed battlefield like Oannes Field, then their rebel voice would die.

Aya kicked forward, her light even more brilliant with power. "Balim, how contagious is this Blue Ring?"

He shook his head for the second time. "There is no way to know... No. My mentor studied Blue Ring for years. He might know how it has escaped the field and whether there is any hope."

"Can Pelan travel? Where's your mentor?"

"No." King Kadir straightened. "The more important question is 'who is your mentor?' Correct, Healer Balim?"

They were both good questions. And Balim only had impossible answers. "My mentor is Dalus, Healer of the All-Council, and he lives in the great hall of healers inside the All-Council stronghold."

The warriors murmured his answer. *Healer of the All-Council.* Pelan was as good as dead.

King Kadir gritted his teeth. He had devoted much effort to sneak into the archives when he had been a bright, young assistant to his city's representative.

So they would drag the injured Pelan across the ocean, break into the most guarded All-Council stronghold, and beg the rulers to treat a rebel warrior infected with an incurable disease.

Queen Aya asked the hard question they were all thinking. "Can Pelan survive the journey?"

"I do not know." Balim rubbed his forehead. So many unknowns. "I will go. Healer Dalus studies illness, not politics. The mystery of how the disease traveled into Pelan's blood will entice him."

Pelan's not-bride crossed her arms over her chest. "Pelan was shot in the heart."

"By a human. And you swam with him, yet you are not ill."

Her soul light was strong. She did not so much as sneeze. She was healthy.

Bella made a small noise. "The fake merman. He

walked into the hospital. He could have dumped something in the tank."

"Again, no one besides Pelan became ill after the interaction with the mystery warrior."

Queen Aya glanced at Soren. Their eyes met with wordless communication.

"What is it?" he asked.

Queen Aya answered. "Just now, we were coming to tell you that your scientist, Mitch, has gone to the emergency room for strange bruising."

No.

"Another had the same flu-like symptoms, but she recovered. Mitch's just got worse."

This could be no coincidence.

"They both were exposed to the same cursed package," he said.

Queen Aya's hands clenched into fists. "So humans can get this disease?"

Balim speculated. "Many warriors fought over the small Oannes Field. Many more humans share space in New York."

"Oh." Bella covered her mouth even though her chest was vibrating. "Of course. The Sons of Hercules will love this."

"Exactly. An incurable disease transmitted by mer contact?" Queen Aya laid out the facts, and Bella agreed with every point. "This will go before Congress. It will affect the UN. We're fighting for basic rights, and now they will see us as the vector of a health panic. This is not just a disease. This is a PR nightmare."

Queen Elyssa hugged King Kadir. The other warriors endured the knowledge that humans would turn against them and deny their chances for brides. Their women would run in fear while the mainland governments made laws to hunt them. They would abandon Atlantis. No one would choose them. They'd have to go back to their origin cities and face exile.

The All-Council would win.

"The Sons of Hercules are behind this," Bella declared. "It's too convenient."

"I agree," Queen Aya said.

Balim did not.

"If I surface," Bella started, soul flaring, "I can get ahead of this. My campaign is prepared. I'm just waiting until... until..." Her soul light dimmed and she didn't complete her thought; she sensed his intense gaze and looked away. "But maybe this is more important..."

Her offer rested on the silence. No one knew what to say.

Balim was cursed with another twist of betrayal. Would she lose sight of her dedication to her son? Now she was here, would she give up and sacrifice Jonah?

It hurt his heart. He reflected her emotions like a mirror, so he knew she was hurting too, but the betrayal inside him was like a sea beneath the sea. Darkness swirling so deep, he tried to contain it to prevent her from knowing it was there.

He had murdered a king. He had plotted for years. His determination had never wavered.

He had seen the same determination in Bella and respected that she could never love him as much as her Jonah because she could never take her gaze from her son. But if she lifted that gaze...if she betrayed her son, to walk away from him...

She did not match Balim's darkness. Not because her gaze fixed on a nobler purpose, but because Balim was too horrible for her to love.

TWENTY-SIX

The bitterness of Bella's sliver of doubt poisoned the back of Balim's tongue.

Queen Elyssa broke the awful silence. "But Nora's not sick."

Bella blinked. "Who?"

Pelan's not-bride pressed her hand to her chest. "What do you mean, who? Me. Nora."

"Your name's Nora?"

"We were introduced forever ago. You don't remember? I've been here the whole time."

"Sorry. I kept thinking of you as Pelan's bride and... that's not an excuse. I'm not usually bad with names. I guess I've had a lot on my mind."

"Well, don't forget it again." Nora tipped her chin at Pelan. "And, Doc Balim, she's right. I was swimming in the water with Pelan even after it got dosed by the fake merman, and here I am, healthy as a horse."

"A seahorse," Queen Elyssa said, smiling.

"I like that." Nora uncrossed her arms to stroke her hair. "Yeah, a healthy sea horse."

Even amid tension and fear, Queen Elyssa had an ability to soften the mood, connect people, and give a moment's smile. The entire sanctuary brightened as the warriors and queens reacted to her simple statements, and the Life Tree reflected their gentle kindness outward.

Her presence was possible because of the vision of Atlantis.

The vision could not be clouded.

Atlantis could not be lost.

And there were so many ways to lose it.

He had to think. Why was Nora healthy and Pelan so ill? Why was Mitch sick with suspicious bruising when Nora had no bruises?

"You remained by Pelan's side?" Balim pressed, searching for the clues to unravel the mystery of this disease. "You left him many times for long periods."

Nora tightened her arms around her chest again. "Are you saying him getting sick is my fault?"

"Was Mitch closer to Pelan than you?"

"Of course not."

"You are certain?"

"No, I'm not certain." She hugged herself. "I've been feeling guilty for weeks. For everything I did. Everything I didn't do. Even now, this place is so beautiful. I feel guilty for enjoying it, even for one second, when my soul mate is sick."

Bella's soul light darkened. "I know what you mean."

"Do not feel guilt, my queens." Zoan floated nearer to them, trying to ease the darkness knotting around their souls. "Happiness and sadness can exist together in Atlantis."

"I've never seen it," Nora grumbled.

"One full warrior swims beside his friend who has

skipped lunch, or Nilun, who has slept long while I have flown double patrols."

Nilun reddened. "You slept in the sanctuary."

"My vigil over our mutual friend is unceasing. Unlike yours, which is divided by fights with water fleas."

Nilun clapped the other hand over his injury.

But, like Queen Elyssa, his teasing lightened the mood once more. The other warriors did not snap. They allowed Balim to mull over the clues.

Queen Elyssa kept up the light tone with Zoan. "Har har. The day you're serious, Zoan, is the day Balim examines the inside of your head for injuries."

"Healer Balim only ever examines my outside, so you have issued a good challenge, Queen Elyssa."

"It's not a challenge, it's an observation."

Zoan cleared his throat and straightened to give his faux-serious lecture. "Happiness and sadness are two warriors in your heart. They are separate, although the same. They work together, and apart."

"How generic," Balim commented.

"Look at me." Zoan tapped his scarred hand on his chest. "My twin brother was captured, imprisoned, and tortured in the All-Council prison. He was released to impersonate me and destroy our Life Tree. I am happy he was freed and sad he nearly killed King Kadir. Two emotions entwined."

His confession quieted the sanctuary. But within his tragic history lay the true hope of their city. They had endured catastrophic destruction in the past and survived.

Nora cupped her own elbow. "I guess I know what you mean. I'm happy Pelan's survived. He was hurt just because he talked to me. If I could go back in time, I would oversleep and miss our date."

Queen Elyssa released King Kadir, swam to Nora, and touched her shoulder. "What happened to Pelan wasn't your fault."

"I know, but the last weeks could have been really different in both our lives."

Zoan also lowered his vibrations to speak kindly. "Accept your burden."

"But Zoan, it's not her fault."

"Queen Elyssa, next you will say I am not tainted with my brother's badness."

"You're right. You're not."

"Roa held the same ideals as I did when he was captured and I escaped. He was tortured and I was not. I could be captured. I could be tortured. Would I not want revenge against the brother who had failed me?"

Her brows drew together. "Would you?"

He shrugged. "Have not many fine warriors broken under torture? Not everyone can hold their vision under the press of death like King Kadir."

The king's mouth twitched in a slight smile. "I was not offered any opportunity by my captors to release that vision, Zoan."

"Then my brother's badness is within me. But this truth does not define me. It is not who I am."

"It is not *only* who you are," Queen Elyssa murmured. "You're also a gentle attendant to the Life Tree, a fierce guardian of your friends, and a clever wordsmith who enjoys teasing us into thinking differently."

The warrior regarded his queen and dipped his head at the honor of her clear sight, then turned back to Nora. "You wish to take the burden of Pelan's illness onto yourself because of the actions you did not take. Very well. Accept these burdens so you too may be free."

Bella's soul lightened, and Balim felt a strange shift in his own heart. Zoan was not a warrior he expected to have deep thoughts. But Queen Elyssa had described him accurately. More accurately than the rest of them had even noticed.

His words were as relevant to Bella and Nora as they were to Balim's own history.

Zoan beamed at Nora. "And that, my future new queens, is my bid to have the inside of my head examined by our favorite healer once he has cured and restored—"

"Hey!" Nilun broke formation, something a warrior from Djullanar would *never* do, to swim toward the couple. "What are you doing, Zoan? Why does your soul resonate with Pelan's bride?"

A taut silence spread through the sanctuary.

Zoan's chest *was* glowing. And so was Nora's. They matched. Like a warrior and his bride.

But she belonged to another.

Nilun shoved Zoan's chest. "Do not steal Pelan's bride when he is ill."

"Wait, Nilun." Queen Elyssa held up her hands. "Kadir, you have to stop them."

King Kadir flew to her and pulled her back, away from the danger.

"I steal no one." Zoan shoved Nilun off, the twinkle gone from his eyes. "Your senses deceive you. Nora does not resonate with me."

"She does!" He glared at Nora. "You should have married Pelan when you arrived! Your indecision makes him sick!"

She hunched in on herself. "I already told you I'm sorry."

Zoan touched her arm. "Do not be. You are—"

Nilun bashed his hand off and gripped the pommel of his dagger. "You must not touch another warrior's bride!"

Zoan moved protectively in front of her. "Do not frighten this young bride."

"Then do not resonate with her soul!"

"How can you accuse me? She descended as the bride of our friend."

"She *is* the bride of our friend." Nilun's hand on the dagger pommel, still sheathed, shook and his chin wrinkled with fury mixed with betrayal. "How dare you lure her away, sickening Pelan for your own selfish wish?"

Zoan drew his dagger. "I would never—"

"Stand down!" Soren barked.

"Warrior Zoan. Warrior Nilun. Stop." King Kadir released Queen Elyssa and kicked forward, a deep wrinkle on his brow as this new nightmare unfolded. "Warrior Zoan, anyone who has eyes can see you resonate with Queen Nora. Warrior Nilun, we do not resolve a bride dispute in Atlantis with single-warrior combat."

Zoan frowned hard and rubbed his own chest.

"Then how do we resolve bride disputes in Atlantis?" Nilun demanded.

It had never been done. "The way...we will decide...is..."

"With death!"

TWENTY-SEVEN

"No." King Kadir held up a hand, and Nilun checked, his blade half-withdrawn. "We decide our way now."

But he looked lost.

Queen Elyssa murmured to him, "I know this is upsetting, but it's real life. On the surface, we date. We change our minds."

"Because you cannot see soul lights as we can," he replied, guided by his queen.

"Dating is messy. Relationships are messy. Part of being human is figuring it out."

"We are not humans. We are mer."

"But we're melding cultures. Atlantis has to change too. And the mess will only worsen after the finished platform entices more humans to join us."

"No." He rejected her because his warriors could not handle so much uncertainty. Not now. King Kadir swung to his most faithful warriors. "How are bride disputes handled in other cities?"

"Death to the bride stealer!" Nilun vibrated, shouting.

"Yes, in Djullanar, and I believe the same in Rusalka." At Iyen's nod, the king confirmed the common experience of open combat.

"In Sireno, the elders hear both cases and decide." Warlord Torun's astute observation rumbled across the crowd. He swam in with Queen Lucy.

Their young fry were secured in the castle with trustworthy guards, and he had returned from the ruins of the ancient city to face the multiple threats now striking Atlantis.

"But in practice, warriors fight. The current king, Jolan, lost his own father when the elders ordered the bride to return to her first husband and she would not. Good, honorable warriors died because the elders did not honor the bride's choice."

Queen Elyssa linked arms with King Kadir as Queen Lucy wrapped her arms around her husband, Warlord Torun.

"We journeyed to Atlantis because you honor the bride's choice of husband." Warlord Torun rested his hands across Queen Lucy's. She snuggled in, and both of their soul lights shone as their shared resonance multiplied, increasing not ten or a hundred but a thousand times brighter than either could shine on their own. "Your resolution is obvious. Let the bride choose."

"What of females who entwine with males on their descent?" another warrior muttered, and the grumble was taken up by others. "What of the coffee date? This is madness."

The mutters grew louder. Someone in the back vibrated a shout. "What of the warriors without brides? How will we stop them from taking rightful brides from other warriors?"

King Kadir frowned.

Queen Aya spoke for the first time. "There are no 'rightful brides.' Banish that ridiculous thought from your heads."

The mutters were shocked to silence, but it was mutinous. She had calmed them but not won them over.

"Aya is right." Queen Elyssa placed a calming hand across King Kadir's heart. "Can you imagine any situation in which it would be okay to force me away from you to be with another warrior?"

His chest blazed. "No. I would fight to the death."

"Because I *choose* you. I am not with you because I got assigned. And I would not go to someone else. I am with you because we have this."

She placed one palm over her own heart and closed her eyes. Their chests resonated, glowing brighter and brighter, until their souls were as powerful as Queen Lucy's and Warlord Torun's. The Life Tree tinkled with harmonious joy, cleansing the water and purifying the sanctuary.

Queen Elyssa opened her eyes and met King Kadir's intense, devoted gaze. "We are together because we are soul mates."

His taut shoulders lowered.

He looked over to Queen Lucy and Warlord Torun and then at Queen Aya and rugged First Lieutenant Soren, who would defy the ocean to be together, and over the waiting warriors.

Then, finally, to Nora. "Warrior Zoan is your choice?"

"What? No." Nora hunched in making herself a smaller target. "You said Pelan was my soul mate."

"But you resonate with Zoan."

"How? I just met him a day ago."

King Kadir frowned. He did not understand.

She turned to Zoan. "You seem nice. But I don't think we're meant to be."

"No," he agreed, floating to put a greater distance between them to lessen any more misunderstandings. "After I betrayed my brother, I swore never to pursue a bride. This includes you."

"To be fair, you didn't pursue me, so your vow is safe."

"You are resonating again," First Lieutenant Soren growled.

"No, we're not," Nora denied, even as the two kicked farther apart and Nora fluttered her hands in the water between them to swish away any more misunderstandings, as if their resonance was dirt motes or algae.

"You must marry Pelan right away," Nilun insisted. "Before you resonate with any other warriors. He is the warrior you vowed to be faithful to."

"He can't even say 'I do,'" Nora snapped, brightening even more at Nilun than she had with Zoan moments ago. "And are you listening? *You're* the ones who decided Pelan was it for me. I don't understand why I'm resonating with anyone else any more than you do."

Queen Elyssa floated forward to mediate. "Don't you feel something extra for Pelan?"

"No more than I felt for Zoan. You're both nice and friendly and I like you. Are you my soul mate? I have no idea."

The calmed warriors rumbled again. Mutiny. The ones who had no brides might try to woo her, Nilun would fight off any who tried, and Nora's seductive resonance enthralled all warriors.

"Perhaps Nora resonates with the sea," Queen Lucy mentioned to Queen Aya. "Everyone wanted Kadir to marry you even though it was obvious you were destined for Soren."

"Less obvious to him," Queen Aya said, digging her elbow into the first lieutenant's side.

He captured her elbow and placed a quelling kiss on her forehead.

"How could you kiss Pelan if your feelings were a lie?" Nilun demanded, furious with Nora and edging closer to her.

"He kissed me," Nora pointed out.

"You drank the elixir. You accepted his mating jewel."

"Actually I never did. It's still in a pressurized vat in your hospital. And I only kissed Pelan because Balim told me to."

Everyone swung to him.

He faced their attention, heating as the mistake pierced his chest. Had he caused this danger on top of an already volatile situation?

"Balim." King Kadir focused. "Did you force a female to kiss a male who was not her husband?"

He stiffened. "Her resonance calmed and restored Pelan when he was dying from the chest wound. Perhaps healing is her primary queen power."

King Kadir accepted his answer, but the furrow on his brow filled Balim with another pang of unease. If King Kadir knew the darkness in his past as Bella did, then how would he look at Balim?

Nora snorted.

"You find this funny?" Nilun demanded. "Torturing and now failing to heal Pelan is a joke?"

"Healing's my power. Your doc just said so." She stared down Nilun, unyielding, her soul light bright once more.

"I'd kiss anyone if I could heal them the way I helped Pelan after he got shot."

Nilun's chest flared as if she had just offered to kiss him.

Truly, she had a dangerous resonance.

Zoan pulled Nilun back. "Calm yourself, Nilun, before you injure the inside of your head. Healer Balim is busy with Pelan."

"How can you brag of your infidelity?" Nilun shouted at Nora, taking no heed of her boiling rage.

Before she could shred him to pieces, the other warriors erupted into disagreement.

"What is the point of surface matchmaking if you do not meet your bride?" a warrior grumbled.

"If you are not a bride, do not shine your bright light on Zoan or Pelan. They are not yours!"

The Life Tree sanctuary chimed a warning.

Pelan spasmed.

Balim held him down, watching the blue rings track across his chest. He had succumbed to this sickness because he was injured. Because he had no bride. Because Balim had made a mistake.

Was Pelan to be the first patient he lost?

King Kadir bellowed for silence. His vibration echoed. The warriors stiffened, and the sanctuary quieted once more.

A mistake. Balim had made a mistake...

"Everyone leave here." King Kadir motioned to the warriors to exit. His judgment rested on Balim. "Even you."

TWENTY-EIGHT

Bella wiggled out of the sanctuary after Balim.

She couldn't read soul lights the way the mermen could, but his shoulders drooped. He was devastated. All mer respected their kings. He'd just been disciplined by his. And he had to feel bad.

"Balim." She wiggled, irritated that her fins wouldn't work, but he was swimming slowly enough that she reached him and clasped his chiseled forearm. "I'm here."

He tugged her into his arms and buried his face in her neck.

They rotated in the opening to the sanctuary. Light shone out through the battered holes in the petals. Bedraggled, the tree, and even the sanctuary, was stronger because it had survived the long-ago attacks. Because now two seeds twined together instead of spinning on alone.

She rubbed his shoulders. "You will figure this out."

"Nora resonated with Pelan once. She was his bride." He vibrated, chest to chest, as he mused over his error.

Bella had meant that he would figure out how Blue Ring spread from a cursed battlefield to the tank at his makeshift hospital, but this also must bother him. "What changed?"

"Perhaps outside the ambulance, I, like other warriors here, mistook the strength of Nora's own resonance to synchronize with Pelan's. Perhaps even Pelan mistook this and reacted. But he *did* heal at our hospital. His soul glowed with the nearness of his bride. He did synchronize with someone..."

"So now you believe me?" Nora floated outside the sanctuary. Soren and Aya were escorting her out.

Balim rested Bella's shoulder against his and faced the others. "I believe you are not Pelan's bride. Forgive my mistake."

She shrugged. "Sure. Fine. Whatever."

"Thank you."

"It's fine. I mean, I can understand how it happened. Soren just told me I have a 'dangerous' resonance because I'm not guarded like Aya."

Aya elbowed Soren for the second time. "That's not necessarily a strength."

"Yeah, well, it must make it a heck of a lot easier to figure out who your actual soul mate is if you don't have guys throwing themselves at you."

Aya straightened. "Yes, that was *never* my problem."

"To tell you the truth, I was excited to meet my soul mate, and it's disappointing it turns out I haven't." Nora jerked her chin over her shoulder. "I'm sure he's worse off because of it than I am. But I get that no one set us up."

Balim stiffened. He did not tolerate mistakes well, and he needed to concentrate. He had to heal Pelan and prevent mass hysteria against mermen—or worse, hysteria accompanied by a deadly health crisis.

Bella smoothed a hand over his taut shoulders, enjoying

the muscle. "Don't give up hope. You're not here for your health."

Nora cocked a brow. "What do you mean?"

"I mean that not just anyone can transform into a mer. Everyone told me I couldn't just give Jonah elixir and expect him to transform. I had to resonate with Balim before I could transform."

Nora's gaze fixed on the open ocean. "So there's still hope…"

"For you to find your soul mate? Of course. It's possible you've met in passing without realizing it."

Her lips puckered in thought. "Sure, they say that a one-in-a-million chance happens eight times a day in New York, right? So how do you know your soul mate if you resonate with everyone?"

"You'll know."

"But these guys are certain—"

"No, Nora. *You'll* know."

Her natural skepticism faded to grudging belief. "I guess you're right. I knew I wasn't Pelan's soul mate, right? So I'll know it when I meet my soul mate. Somehow…"

Balim focused on Nora as if she'd said the missing piece of the puzzle he needed. "When did you know you were not Pelan's soul mate?"

"I've kind of felt that way ever since Pelan went to that tank in your hospital," she said. "That week he had to be out of the water, I spent a lot of time organizing my life in between times sleeping on the bunk next to him, and every time I left the room I'd come back and find Roxanne in there comforting him."

"Roxanne?" Balim repeated. A new urgency filled his tone. "Our hospital coordinator?"

She nodded. "If I centered him during the operation to

remove the bullet even though I wasn't his bride, maybe Roxanne could help him through this illness even if she's also not his bride."

"Or maybe she *is* his bride." Balim turned to Soren. "Summon her to Atlantis."

The massive first lieutenant raised a brow, but he respected Balim's expertise. "Zoan. Swim to the ancient city and send our request."

Zoan kicked past.

"I'd be a great relief if his bride *was* Roxanne." Nora wiggled her stubby feet as she tried to keep up with Aya. "Then maybe I could master these fins."

"Oh, sure, I'll show you a little trick." Aya took Nora's hand and flew toward her castle. The other warriors cleared out, and soon, only Balim and Bella floated in the sanctuary's mouth. King Kadir and Elyssa tended Pelan, while the other warriors clustered in groups nearby, but they had a pocket of privacy.

Bella felt the fire in Balim, and a tendril of hope curled around her heart. She rubbed his shoulders, encouraging him. "One mystery solved. You'll figure out the rest. Like, how long can Nora avoid drinking the nectar before she collapses?"

"Perhaps a long time," Balim mused and fixed Bella with a hard stare. "She is not conflicted like you."

His accusation slashed into her heart.

She could barely suck in a breath—no, a mouthful—of water. "Because I can't—that vial, Balim."

"Not the vial."

"Yes. My conflict is all about the—"

"Your conflict is about me." He spat the words, bitter and hurt, as if he'd looked into a well and found only brackish water and it left him reeling. "Are we soul mates?"

She swallowed. "I can't deny the compulsion."

"But we do not resonate as the others do. We do not reflect each other's souls with the strength of a thousand."

"How can I help that? You know I can't see soul lights like the mer."

"But you can feel when we are not in harmony." He glared. "All this time, I accepted that you could not reflect my soul because your son is first in your heart."

"How dare you—"

"But that is not your reason for turning away from me. You cannot develop your queen powers, you cannot discover your fins, you cannot embrace the Atlantis Life Tree with your whole heart and soul because you cannot embrace *me*."

She didn't know how to answer him. He was only making half sense.

"I warned you once that my soul was darker than you could ever know." Balim's hurt sharpened like a blade honed beyond the edge so it was twisted, nicked, and hard. "When I issued that warning, I believed you would someday synchronize enough with me it would not matter. But that will never happen. Like Nora, who I mistook for Pelan's bride, I have now mistaken you for mine."

Her heart cracked. "I'm a mistake for you now?"

"You are," he snarled, ruthless with pain. "Why else are you so conflicted? Your body rejected the elixir and it rejected Atlantis and it rejects me."

"How can I 'embrace' a city I'm doomed to destroy?" she demanded, fighting to lower her vibrations to keep their argument from leaking to the clusters of warriors across the city. "Of course I feel like splitting in half. And I've decided, Balim. I can't do it. We have to get rid of it."

"It?"

"The vial."

His face closed.

She forced him to understand. "How can I live in this beautiful city, make friends with these wonderful people, wave at their adorable children while holding on to something that could hurt—no, *kill* them?"

"Have you given up on Jonah?"

"How dare you," she hissed.

"Have you?"

"Never."

"Then where is your faith, Bella? Where is your determination? Your devotion? Or are you just as confused and manipulated as Nora?"

"How dare you use my child against me?" She jerked back, throwing the most hateful accusations back at him. "This decision is agonizing."

"Not so agonizing. You have made it."

"Yes, I have. I can't wreck a city. I can't murder people. Orphan children. Even when I was acting as a double agent, I had a backup plan if you were at risk. Plus I was a crap informant. I didn't feed the Sons of Hercules anything they didn't already know. Starr made so much progress. But I can't."

"Bella, for your son—"

"I would give my own life," she affirmed. "But not yours. Not anyone else's. That's not in me. I have too much humanity. I can't destroy a city. I can't kill anyone."

Behind Balim, in the distance, a strange "pop" echoed across the city as if contents under the intense pressures of the deep sea had burst. Thick glass shattered.

A high-pitched sound emerged. It sounded like screaming.

Like the screaming in her heart. The truth came out.

Balim thought she'd abandoned her child. She disgusted even Balim. She horrified herself and him.

Except... Wait a minute...

"Was that...?" Bella clutched her hand to the throat. "The vial?"

He looked back at her with dark eyes ringed black with horror. "It exploded?"

"I don't know. I mean, anything's possible. Maybe."

Elyssa flew out of the sanctuary. "Who's attacking? Why is the Life Tree screaming?"

"The *Life Tree* is screaming?"

"Well, it's a castle, actually." She searched the city for the source while rallying the rest of the warriors for a fight. "It's the sound it makes when it's under attack."

"There." Balim pointed grimly at the castle, which shuddered with black streaks of poison. "The castle under attack is mine."

TWENTY-NINE

Balim flew after the other warriors to his castle.

"I can't destroy a city. I can't kill anyone."

Bella's words echoed in his head. He'd collected her instinctively at the sound of danger and now they both flew behind Queen Elyssa and also King Kadir to Balim's screaming castle.

Bella couldn't destroy a city or kill anyone.

But he had. He'd done those things.

"I could never live with myself if anyone got hurt because of me," she moaned, rubbing her chest.

Ice frosted his heart as she drove needle wedges between them with her panicked words. He swallowed the lump of sharp coral.

They hovered in a circle around the shrieking castle. No one knew how to proceed. The entrance was closed up tight.

"Who is inside?" First Lieutenant Soren demanded. "Warriors, to me! Whoever emerges will face their death!"

"But no one's inside. Just my mistake." Bella's face

constricted, and she clutched her hands to her chest. "I am death to everyone."

Her words slapped his heart once more and stung. She was horrified by a murderer.

But Balim was a murderer.

The castle darkened. Black lines spread across the sphere.

Ciran shouted from the back of the sphere. "What is it? What is this attack?"

Balim's heart thudded hard. Sickness built in his throat. He had to hold it together. Losing his castle and Bella was only the punishment he deserved. He should not feel so tormented.

To speak would be to incriminate Bella. But not to speak would endanger the entire city.

"It is not an attack." He looked King Kadir right in the eye as he pronounced his own exile. "It is a substance from the surface. A poison."

King Kadir's eyes widened. He kicked back from the darkening monstrosity. "What have you done?"

"What I must," Balim said.

"What substance is this? How do we combat it? How do we heal it?"

Most likely they could not.

King Kadir's fingers clenched his trident. He wanted to shake Balim until an answer tumbled out.

"We cannot stop it."

"We must!" King Kadir flew to the black streaks and stabbed them.

The castle continued shrieking. Although his trident punctured and cut, the thick walls puckered away from his attacks. He could not gain entry, and he did not stop the poison.

It would destroy Balim's castle.

"Is it going to stop?" Queen Elyssa vibrated the question tightly beside them. "We have to cut it off here. The city is interconnected. If that poison kills the roots, it will destroy the other castles and the Life Tree."

"Sever the stalk," Balim ordered.

Queen Elyssa looked at him long and hard. "There's no way to save it?"

He shook his head. Perhaps there was a way, but he could not figure it out before it endangered the entire city.

Queen Elyssa turned and vibrated with a decisive shout. "Cut the anchor!"

Warriors attacked the base where the bulb connected to the stalk.

"Farther down. Down!"

They detached from the base and descended toward the ocean floor to attack the monstrous stalk with daggers. Two warriors flew in with longer serrated swords.

The castle collapsed in on itself like a rotted pumpkin with no interior structure. Black poison lines pooled at the base of the deflated bulb.

The warriors' sawing made a creaking, shrieking sound as the massive tree-like anchor yawned. Queen Elyssa put her hands on the cut. It glowed as did her hands.

Black poison streaked into the stalk.

King Kadir snarled at Balim. "When we stop this, you will answer for your crimes."

Balim's heart cracked. He strove to endure his king's disapproval with honor.

King Kadir chased the dark poison, slicing his trident at it as though he could force it to yield first.

Queen Aya joined Queen Elyssa and put her hands at

the upper stalk. A sharp crack made the stalk jerk away from her as if she'd shoved it back with a white bulldozer.

The warriors rallied around King Kadir and sawed on the reverse side. Would they beat the seeping poison?

First Lieutenant Soren snarled at Balim. "How unfortunate we never prepared to lay siege to our enemies. We never thought to construct a stalk-cutting saw."

He bowed his head to endure the warrior's judgment. Soren was the first warrior he had pledged his allegiance to after drifting from Undine. His fury cut a long wound in Balim's heart.

The first lieutenant slammed his shoulder into Balim. "Do not leave."

It pained him.

Of course he would not leave. "I will heal the wounded."

"They would never let you touch them." First Lieutenant Soren flew to aid. With a mighty roar, he attacked the stalk. It broke into pieces. The warriors concentrated their daggers on the last filaments.

New realizations filtered into Balim.

Of course First Lieutenant Soren was right. He was a traitor. Bringing poison into Atlantis, regardless of the reason, was dangerous, as he had proved. Such a total lack of wisdom would make many question his motives. He was too smart to be so stupid. Too clever to lack so much judgment.

Finally, he would face consequences for the act he had committed years ago.

Regicide.

"Balim. This wasn't what I wanted." Bella's fingers curled around his, seeking comfort in this disaster. "Your castle... How can we ever explain this so your friends will understand?"

"We cannot." Balim disconnected their fingers and pulled free. "You can."

"Me?"

"I must bear the judgment."

From a distance. He would not wait per Soren's request to be judged, sterilized, executed, and thrown into a vent. He still had to atone.

He had unleashed the deadly Blue Ring on the old king of Undine. Now, Blue Ring had returned to haunt him.

He could not die now. He was the only one who could understand Healer Dalus's answers.

And his absence could absolve Bella of the crime of blackmail. She was still pure. He alone had the blackened soul.

"Find the Sons of Hercules," he ordered, keeping his mind on the immediate task and not allowing the grief of his losses to pile up on top and smother him. "Free your son and live happily."

She wiggled after him. "Balim. Wait!"

Her cry dissipated in the frantic battle of the warriors as they destroyed his most prestigious and permanent tie to the city of Atlantis.

But her second, more furious cry reached him through the noise. "You said we're the same sides of a coin."

He turned on her, fury snapping in his chest. It was welcome after the pain. "But we are not, are we?"

"You're a healer. You fix things. You don't destroy them."

"To atone. I heal to atone because *this* is who I am, Bella. The one thing you could never be. I am a murderer."

She jerked as if he'd slapped her in the face. "Don't brag

about it. You had reasons, so don't lord it over me like it's something to celebrate."

Crack. The stalk of his castle broke just as the first tendrils of poison rotted it away. The whole castle collapsed, sizzling, like a broken flower.

"Don't let it touch the sea floor!" Queen Elyssa shouted. "We can't let the poison contaminate the ground! We have to drag it to the barren rock."

"A vent." King Kadir overrode her orders, and the warriors together kept it from crashing.

The withered husk turned in on itself, the poison continuing to darken its former vibrancy, black streaking across gray and turning it darker and darker. The warriors moved it en masse while the queens used their powers to buffer it, pushing it between the stalks and out of the city.

"You didn't kill it," Bella insisted. "This was an accident. And poisoning the king didn't happen because you're a murderer. You escaped from an all-powerful ruler who murdered your father and threatened to do the same to you."

"That is no excuse." Balim's vibrations sharpened as his emotions broke. "Remain here. Find your son. Stay pure. And be happy."

He turned away from her and kicked hard, leaving her in the city far behind.

THIRTY

Be happy? Be happy!

Balim's last insult played in Bella's head over and over long after he had left her behind.

Of course the selfish, damaged healer had left her to deal with the inquiry. Was she supposed to be happy about that too? Just because he'd claimed responsibility before he'd run off didn't mean the kind, trusting, generous families who'd welcomed her to Atlantis would consider her an innocent victim and move on.

The stump where the hopes of one of their most important members had once rested now reminded them of what they'd lost, like a missing leg. And Bella didn't think this limb would grow back.

It was gone.

Just like Balim.

"Betrayal." King Kadir swished back and forth in front of her in his castle while his closest elite warriors and advisers listened. "You have betrayed the ideals of trust, openness, and exchange that founded Atlantis."

Bella prepared her rebuttal speech while King Kadir ranted.

"You accepted a mystery substance from deadly terrorists to steal a Life Tree blossom and destroy the city, and you told no one. What do you say for yourself?"

"I'm sorry. I saw no other way to save my son."

"We would have moved the oceans and the earth to help you."

"I didn't know who I could trust."

"You could trust me." King Kadir's eyes flashed with silver threads. "Do you know how close you came to destroying our city? To sickening our warriors and queens? Our young fry?"

Torun juggled their sleeping twins. Elyssa pressed Kael to her cheek.

Bella felt like throwing up. "I never intended to release the poison."

"But you did not know how the poison could be released. And instead of consulting with one of our warriors to assist you, you hid it away. You betrayed us."

She endured his anger, his fear, his hurt. He wasn't wrong, and she didn't take his words lightly. But her mind kept returning to Balim's parting words.

"Find your son and be happy."

Something was wrong. Very wrong. Just like when she'd run through the hospital seeking Jonah after the Sons of Hercules had kidnapped him, she felt the same sense that someone was about to commit an unforgivable act that could never be reversed.

Maybe it was because Balim had left with such a look so stony that it sent fear streaking into her heart.

Since the first moment, she'd known in her soul they matched. Balim was hers. They were the same. And yet when he'd left, she'd felt uncertainty. He'd met her assertion that his soul was not so dark with ridicule.

She felt they were still the same. He did not. That fundamental difference made her twitchy, impatient, and needing to do something.

Bella did not handle helplessness well.

"Queen Bella." King Kadir jolted her back by using a title that was the least fitting after everything that had happened. "You have been with us a short time. We were happy to unite bride and husband for a long future. But that possibility is gone now."

She averted her gaze.

"Balim is an exile. His name must never be spoken. If he is found within our city..." King Kadir's jaw flexed, and he forced himself to continue while Elyssa floated close, stroking his shoulder and hugging their sleeping son. "...he will be judged, exiled, and executed."

Exiled and then executed seemed like overkill, but she didn't see the point in objecting.

The sharp burning pain in Balim's eyes and vibrations as he'd snarled at her to stay and have a happy life made her chest ache.

He'd tried to take sole responsibility and also thrown her distress back in her face by saying he couldn't stand to see her ever again.

She'd always thought this day would come. He'd insisted they were the same. She'd believed him.

And while leaving, he'd used her most painful mistake against her.

She hadn't loved Jonah enough, and that was why he got sick. She didn't love Jonah enough, and that was why he couldn't get well.

It was possible, right? The mystical Sea Opals and Life

Tree activated on emotions. The problem was her. Always her.

If she'd noticed Jonah was sick earlier... If she'd insisted they do more during the first treatment... If she'd loved him more, he wouldn't have gotten leukemia. He would have responded to the treatments. He would have gotten better after drinking the Sea Opal elixir instead of stopping at the same low count for weeks after they'd used up the liquid and returned to traditional treatments.

If only she'd loved him more, none of this would have happened.

And Balim knew how she felt. He was her soul mate. That was why he'd emphasized it so many times. *"Be happy. Find your son."* As if she'd given up. She would never give up. How dare he?

"Queen Bella." King Kadir jolted her out of her memories again. "Answer."

She had no idea what he had asked her. "Will you repeat the question?"

"I asked if you are prepared to surface and never return?"

"Because I...okay. I can understand why you can't trust me. But you have to let me stay. Assign extra guards."

"We do not guard females in Atlantis as if they are prisoners."

"I don't mind."

He shook his head. "You have committed an unforgivable crime, Queen Bella. The warriors will struggle to remain friendly. It is safer for you to surface."

No! "The Sons of Hercules are expecting me to stay in Atlantis."

"You will explain that their poison ended this privilege."

"Jonah—"

"We will find your young fry." He rested his arm around Elyssa's shoulder and held his son close. "But we cannot trust you in this city. You are exiled to the surface for all eternity. Go with Queen Aya to the cable and prepare to rise."

THIRTY-ONE

Balim flew out of Atlantis with the same edge of darkness and anger that had followed him out of Undine.

Queen Elyssa and the warriors had saved the Life Tree. That was all that mattered. No one had died during the attack.

He'd felt the final snap of the stalk in his spine.

His head and his chest and, for some reason, his tailbone ached. A dull, throbbing pain. Was this how Pelan had felt when he was getting sick with Blue Ring? Now, as an exile without a connection to a Life Tree, Balim's blood would sicken. He was vulnerable to the contagion.

Bella would not be punished. She'd won over her enemies. King Kadir would see the goodness in her, her innocence, and he would protect her. Atlantis was filled with worthy warriors. Many better than Balim.

The shock of her expression when they'd parted for the final time had cut Balim. He still felt her betrayal in his bones.

Balim pushed through the dull, throbbing pain. He

swam alone to the edge of the city. avoiding patrols and staying far from anyone who might intend to stop him or chat.

He had a short time to escape.

First Lieutenant Soren's horror echoed in his skull. Balim had shocked even the darkest, most disreputable warrior in Atlantis. His exile was assured. Whether or not he wanted it.

Balim must brave the wilderness. Alone.

"Hey. Wait up." Nora's voice vibrated behind him.

He was so startled, he obeyed. "Why are you here? Go back to the city."

"It's not my scene." She kicked abreast of him. Long fins trailed behind her, and her bright, shining soul propelled her through the water. "Can I come with you?"

"No."

"Why not?"

"The open ocean is dangerous. You are vulnerable. And I am bound for the seat of the All-Council, where a single female alone is the antithesis of their existence."

"There's more safety in numbers." She straightened and crossed her arms. "Besides, Elyssa said most of you guys can't tell male or female under water."

She was not wrong. Queens possessed a certain brightness in their souls. But unless they were swimming entwined with their husbands, no one else might notice.

"I am an exile. Any warrior with honor will kill me, traditional or rebel."

"So I can help you." She held up her hands and spread her fingers. Little streams of light traced between them and then dissipated. "I'll use this power to keep you safe."

"Then the All-Council will know you are a queen."

"If I have to use it in front of the All-Council, you're already screwed."

He acknowledged that and swam again; she fell in beside him. "Why do you wish to flee with me? You can surface to leave Atlantis."

"I'm not ready to go." She twirled, keeping up with him, which was convenient for his escape. "Everything happens for a reason. I can't believe I dropped my promising career in busking and food service just so I could go underwater and cause drama."

"You did not cause drama. I misidentified you as Pelan's bride. Direct your anger at me."

"You're also immune to whatever my 'dangerous resonance' is." She twirled again. "I've never been unpopular with guys, but down here, everyone looks at me twice and sticks out their chests. It's weird. You're different."

"I am a murderer."

"Warriors kill people."

"Honorably."

"Murder's kind of in the job description." She shrugged. "Bella's smart enough to stay away from losers."

"She is smart enough to stay in Atlantis," he vibrated, muttering.

"You shouldn't be so mad at her," Nora continued. "Just because you disagreed about the blackmail is no reason to cut her off. She's your soul mate."

His heart warmed, and he crushed the hope. "We had no disagreement. You are mistaken."

"Balim. I was there."

"You were where?"

"At your castle. Late castle. Floating about five feet behind you guys. I heard your whole argument."

He had thought they were being quiet. "I do not remember."

"And that's why I'm here." She grinned and stretched in all directions. "You and Bella were so wrapped up in each other, the rest of the world disappeared. Including me. Every time. I don't usually enjoy being forgotten, but considering how much unwanted attention I'm currently getting, your downright ignorance is nice."

"Perhaps that will end. My soul does not resonate with Bella's."

Nora snorted. "Oh, you think?"

"She never sensed my presence as I sensed hers. Our brief union only came about because I pursued her. Promised if she became my queen she would gain the power to heal her son." He pressed his eyes on the memory of that failure. "But now when she finds the warrior she deserves, she will sever our unwelcome connection."

"Mmm. No."

"I am a healer, Nora, and a merman. I can sense souls."

"Well, you're pretty crap at understanding women." She tilted her eyes at him. "You were pretty upset after leaving the Life Tree sanctuary, so maybe you already forgot that Bella's had a lot of chances to hook up before you. People like her and me, who attract lots of people, have a hard time not settling on the wrong ones while we're waiting to find our soul mates. But when we find our soul mates, we know."

"You will know," he agreed, confused about why this was a conversation topic.

"And *Bella knows*."

"Bella knows," he repeated and shook his head. "No, she cannot accept our connection. It is as King Kadir and Queen Elyssa demonstrated. Resonance grows in the soul."

"She knows, Balim. In her soul, she knows."

Warmth seeped out around his clenched heart because he couldn't contain this feeling that Nora was right. He knew. Just like King Kadir knew. And Bella knew too.

Yes, his soul was black. He had given in to revenge when he should have obeyed the law of the mer. Bella forgave him when he could not forgive himself. And now he'd received the punishment he'd always deserved. Exile and revulsion.

Yet he still craved Bella.

Her smile, the one where she covered her teeth with her lips and the ones where she showed that small gap. Her soft skin with its intricate pattern of freckles as natural as a mer's tattoos. Her bright, fiery spirit as she took risks over and over again to chase justice, defend others, and tried to improve life.

He wished she were here now. More than anything.

No.

Bella was *safe* in Atlantis. Those worthy warriors would protect her. King Kadir would not blame her for Balim's irresponsible actions. And once Starr found her son, she could rise and save him.

He must push on to the All-Council. Even if he wanted to go back and find Bella, he could not turn aside from his mission to cure Blue Ring. The fate of the mer depended on him.

Nora broke into his thoughts as though she thought he was still thinking about her.

"Besides, I overheard what you said. You're still trying to save Pelan's life. Not only is it my fault he got shot to begin with, but it's also my fault he's not healing. So I want to help him, and you will help me do that."

"Keep up. I will not slow for you."

"Sure." She kicked harder. "I'm ready for this."

Nora was not Bella, but Balim was grateful not to be alone as they escaped into the wild ocean.

Bella was safe in Atlantis.

Balim would find her after he'd uncovered the cure. He would atone.

If he survived.

And if she would let him.

THIRTY-TWO

Bella couldn't be exiled to the surface. She just couldn't.

She wiggled her fingers in Aya's strong grip. "Let me go."

"I can't." Aya held Bella's wrist and flew her away from Atlantis to the cable over the ancient city. "I'm sorry about this."

Her mind whirred as she tested escape routes. Aya was faster, a queen, and surrounded by an honor guard led by the unsmiling Ciran.

Aya had asked to convey Bella alone. Ciran had rejected her. "Queen Bella's guards must protect her."

"It's fine." Bella had better odds of escaping if she wasn't escorted by forty angry warriors. "I'm with Aya."

Ciran had regarded her without smiling and allowed them a lead to have this private conversation, but he flew behind them, and his warriors, swimming in strict formation, ended every escape.

And Bella begged Aya anyway.

"You can't. I understand," Bella murmured while her mind worked the problem. "You have no choice."

"Don't be ridiculous. Of course I have a choice." The commanding queen looked at Bella with two raised brows like she was an idiot.

"So let me go." Bella twisted her hand.

"What's your plan?"

Bella stopped twisting. "Plan?"

"Where is better than the surface?" Aya's brow furrowed. Her blonde hair streamed behind her as she swam efficiently toward the ancient wreckage. "The Sons of Hercules will have to contact you. Make yourself available. And when they expose themselves, then we'll capture them."

Her heart thudded out of rhythm. "You're trying to help me?"

"I understand why this surprises you, but yes. All of us are."

"The warriors—"

"I mean us queens. Lucy and Elyssa are mothers. They weren't forced to make your choices, and you're one of us now. A little espionage and near-mass murder doesn't change that."

She was at a loss for words. "I would think it would."

"We know why you did it, and that's why your 'punishment' is necessary. We tried to design a punishment that would seem appropriate and also position you to continue the fight. I can't think of any better solution than making you bait."

Bait. Again.

Could she trust that Aya was on her side? That all the queens were?

Bella rolled the word "bait" around on her tongue. "I've never done well with waiting."

"If you have a better idea, share." Aya looped her wrist, glanced back at the warriors, and lowered her vibrations. "Soren will join us to ascend to the surface. He's working out a plan with Kadir to excavate the poisoned castle. If someone snuck into the castle and activated the vial, they had no time to escape before being poisoned."

"You think the Sons of Hercules have spies in Atlantis?"

"No, but the All-Council does. Something is strange, Bella."

"Only one thing?"

"Yes, good point." Aya smiled faintly but focused on her conundrum. "We're in the center of two or three colliding plots. First, the poisoned vial and the demand for a Life Tree flower. Why would the Sons of Hercules destroy the Life Tree before they get what they want?"

"They're not the most organized."

"I now believe such thinking is a mistake. They masterminded your son's kidnapping."

"Starr and I came to the same conclusion. Someone is helming this organization, and they have resources."

"Yes, and enough sophistication they should not have activated that pressurized vial prematurely. So why?"

"Maybe we were getting too close to unmasking..."

Aya waited for her to finish, but she couldn't guess what might have triggered the explosion. So Aya continued. "Second, Pelan contracted a rare mer disease on the surface. Soren has informed me it is impossible to remove anything from the battlefield. All who try will sicken and die."

"That's not entirely true. Balim removed something."

"He didn't infect Pelan, did he?"

"No. He'd never do that."

"Someone did." Aya mused on the other loose threads. Pelan misidentifying Nora as his bride, his subsequent shooting, the Sons of Hercules's incursion into the mer hospital, the megalodon that had risen unnaturally high into the water column to attack them as they descended to Atlantis, and she circled back to the poisoned vial. "I can't see how the threads come together. What mastermind plot is this?"

Bella shook her head. When she connected the mysteries, she would find where the Sons of Hercules had hidden Jonah. "Can you question the spies?"

"We're only guessing on their identities." Aya perused the warriors following them. "They don't volunteer for surface duties because to ascend and, heaven forbid, meet a modern bride would violate the ancient covenant. Soren's strategy is to woo them over to our side. Whenever a suspect sheds the old jingoisms and makes friends, we're one warrior stronger in our goal to win over the entire undersea world."

No wonder Aya and the others were so willing to forgive Bella. They lived with known enemies all the time. She had just gotten closer to ending Atlantis than most.

"So the All-Council refuses to surface, and the Sons of Hercules can't swim down." Bella faced the ultimate conundrum. "Yet someone, somewhere, is collaborating."

"And if we find proof, maybe we can unravel the whole conspiracy." Aya changed her tone. "I'm sorry for your son. I'm pregnant right now with my first. I imagine the year even before the kidnapping has been a nightmare."

"Yes." Bella smiled despite the situation. "Congratulations. You'll never sleep again."

"I thought getting up to pee every hour came later." Aya sighed out a long stream of water. "Health for my unborn is always a concern. When I'm not plotting the demise of my enemies, I'm doing prenatal exercises, watching my diet, and practicing yoga poses."

"You should probably stop plotting the demise of your enemies to reduce stress."

"Oh, that's far too satisfying to give up. And, counterintuitive as it may be, it's the source of my queen powers."

"The source of your queen powers is plotting the demise of your enemies?"

"In great detail." Her smile widened. "Right now there's a particular senator blocking his committee from finishing their report on the humanity of mermen. I wish he would take a long walk off the viewing platform over Niagara Falls. I understand it's very difficult to survive the falls especially if you're not wearing any protective gear."

"Yes, people die that way on the regular." Huh. "Elyssa prefers meditation."

"My cousin is a better person than I am." Aya kicked hard for the ruins. "Embrace your darkness, Bella. If visualizing the light doesn't allow you to transform, loosing your demons can be an energizing activator."

They reached the edge of the old city.

Buzzing noises like a thousand out-of-tune seagulls assaulting a garbage truck floated out of a large cave at the base of the extended tower.

"Octopus Kong." Aya angled over the cave.

The giant heard them and extended a few tentacles in greeting, and Aya waved back.

"Balim said he was dangerous," Bella said.

"The warriors used to consider him a crotchety, ill-tempered guardian of the ruins. But, ever since he chased off three megalodons, he's been in a much better mood. He and I have a professional relationship."

The disconcerting giant octopus spoiled the melodies of the fish in the surrounding ocean.

Aya kicked to a metal bell surrounded by guards. Bubbles emerged from it, and an unnerving growling sound pressed against Bella's ears.

"Oxygen generator and power supply," Aya explained as she released Bella to open the hatch. It swung open, and they rose into the bell. "Ready to be human again?"

Bella wasn't sure. The air pocket was strange, stuffy, and uncomfortable. Aya threw up seawater, choking and tearing up, and Bella did as well to gasp dank air.

Aya clambered onto the metal floor.

A warrior knelt before a microphone. He saluted them with both hands touching before his chest. "Queen Aya. Queen Bella."

Aya returned his salute. "Any messages from the surface?"

"None since we contacted them about Healer Balim's treason. Bride Roxanne has passed the final mark. Since she may become Warrior Pelan's bride, should I call her queen?"

"She can tell you her preference when she arrives." Aya composed herself. "Do you wish to send a message, Bella?"

She shook her head. The cramped metal bell made her long for the expansive wilderness of the sea. "I'm just waiting, I guess."

The warrior nodded emphatically. "We will find your young fry, Queen Bella."

Her heart throbbed. "Thank you."

But now she was alone, stranded, and burdened, and she had no idea how the warriors would find Jonah when the Sons of Hercules controlled everything.

THIRTY-THREE

Aya led Bella out of the air-filled bell and back into the water.

The shift choked her hard, and then she was through it, filled with cold in her belly and radiating through her body. The last time, she'd gotten through with Balim. It was harder to shift alone.

"It never gets easier," Aya confided, gripping her hand and leading her up the cable to the anchor bolt. "Just more familiar."

"So, now what?"

"Now, we wait."

Again with the waiting.

Aya caught her expression and sympathized. "The Sons of Hercules *will* contact us. Maybe through Roxanne. Maybe they'll wait until you surface. Trust in your companions, and be ready to act."

Bella gripped her hair. "I can't take this."

Aya laughed. "It's been five minutes. When Elyssa married Kadir and was the first of us to 'live among the natives,' I had to wait a month to make sure she'd survived.

Patience."

Balim was patient. Not Bella.

She flexed her human feet beneath the anchor bolt, trying and failing to unleash the fins that everyone else shifted to so naturally. Waiting left her alone with her thoughts. And her thoughts were never pleasant.

They circled on her failures. Her missed chances. How she hadn't appreciated Jonah's good health, so she deserved only his bad. How she'd tried not to let him into her heart, but then she'd sung him to sleep with songs barely remembered from her own grandparents when they'd been alive.

They'd told her to go after her dreams, and she'd listened to them.

She'd always chased after Jonah's health, chased second opinions, chased obscure treatments, chased donors. She'd chased more money and nicer apartments and more credentials in her job title. Not since childhood at the mercy of disengaged, neglectful parents had she been forced to wait.

She flexed her stubborn feet more.

Second Lieutenant Ciran floated closer to her. He would lead the warriors to the surface and then take them on a boat to the mainland, where he would work with Dannika, Hazel, and even Starr to keep them safe while the warriors sought and wooed their brides.

Ciran drifted close.

"Can I help you?" she asked.

He addressed her. "If you do not surface, will you go to Healer Balim?"

If she did not surface?

"If you let me," she answered, still flexing her foot. "If I could find him. Are you upset?"

He looked down at Octopus Kong's lair, and then to the

glimmering new Atlantis. Still floating, a beacon of hope amidst the wreckage of the past.

She assumed he would not answer.

"Healer Balim had no castle in Undine," Ciran said, apropos of nothing. "Did you know this?"

"No. How do you?"

"Undine was once my home also."

Oh. "Were you friends?"

"He was not allowed friends. The king punished any warrior who spoke or smiled at him. Do you know why?"

"Yes, he told me how he lost his father and his trainer in one day."

"The king murdered both." Ciran spoke the same truth that Balim had told her, but he did not mince words.

"I heard the king can't commit murder," she returned, dropping her leg.

"Yes. Just as no Undine scholar acts with passion. And no warlord evicted from his castle and forced to shelter on the ocean floor beneath the city may ever woo a bride."

She tilted her head. His words were so emotionless and logical. Was he on Balim's side? He might just be reciting facts. "You followed him here."

"The elder who succeeded the throne held many of the old king's ideals. And with Balim gone, his reign would not end soon. Change is difficult to enact in a city that does not tolerate dissent."

She caught his gaze and held it.

Ciran knew. Otherwise, he would say that the elder was likely to have a shorter reign without a healer. And he was on Balim's side.

Had he ever expressed that to Balim? Both Ciran and Balim were private warriors. Balim disguised his feelings behind quips and sarcasm, Ciran behind an emotionless focus on logic. They might have benefited from sharing their feelings. Now, it was too late.

She released his gaze and her foot, straightening. "It's sad that he lost his castle here."

"It would be even sadder if he lost his bride."

Anger flushed through her like a hot flash. "He left me."

Ciran had no answer for that. "Still, it is miraculous a warrior denied every chance has found his soul mate. If even he can overcome his origin, hope shines for all warriors."

Her skin crackled with his words. Ciran was right. He lit a fire in her soul.

She could no longer wait. She had to act.

"Bella!" Aya waved her over. "Roxanne's almost here."

And Roxanne might carry a message from the Sons of Hercules or from Starr. Bella could wait a little longer.

She bid Ciran farewell and wiggled her stubby toes forever to reach Aya. She used to think she was an acceptable swimmer, but surrounded by flitting warriors, she was a heavy-bottomed ostrich ringed by graceful larks.

The group of warriors descended so slowly.

Finally, five warriors from the surface escorted Roxanne, a healthy woman with deep anxiety who vibrated an insistent flutter.

"I'm so sorry I left for that wedding. I didn't enjoy it, barely tasted the cake, and forgot I had two pieces because my mind kept returning to Pelan. I just knew he was in trouble, and boy, was I right. I should have demanded Balim try me out as his soul mate instead of that Nora, but you know she's so sweet and ambitious and hopeful, and I'm opinionated and talk too much, and it's a good day when I look any better than frumpy. Is Pelan all right? I feel like I would know if he wasn't, but I tell you, I don't feel too good right now, so the sooner I see him and make sure, the better."

"He's this way. And he's ill, so we must take precautions."

"Never mind ill. I'll be thrilled when I see him healthy. And if not, that's fine with me too. If I'm his caretaker for the rest of his life, we'll have a very nice life together; just ask my mother, which you can't because she passed away three years ago, but I let more than one promising man pass me by prioritizing her comfort. Since she brought me into the world, I should bring her out of it. Not literally, of course, but that was my way of thinking. Where's Pelan?"

"Here." Aya helped the warriors unlatch her harness from the cable and then clasped hands to pull Bella on one side and Roxanne on the other. "I see you made the shift okay."

"No problem at all. Balim had me drinking the elixir after my brief cold on account of how I got sick after I returned, probably because that false merman had left powder or dust all over everything, and that elixir didn't make me feel any better but it 'arrested' the sniffles, and I held that position for a long time rather than making me worse." She latched onto Bella. "The night watch apologized a hundred times for mistaking that faker for a merman. They were just so certain."

"Do you have any messages for me?" Bella interrupted.

"No, he just needed me to convey that he was so certain because the false merman showed his fins and—"

Her head thunked. "What?"

"Yes! Forgive me. My head's falling off with messages; I need to see Pelan right away, you see, but I can deliver the messages while we swim. That night watchman and also your friend Hazel says not to worry about your houseplants. She's watering them."

"She is..." Bella translated the code Starr had set up before she'd descended. "Did she 'find' my 'houseplants' okay?"

"No, that's right. See, Pelan's filled up my thoughts. Something about her still looking for one that's missing. What was it? A spider plant? But I didn't pay attention. I mean, my mind's been on other things; specifically, on Pelan. Don't worry, Hazel's so sweet, if she kills any off, I'm sure she'll buy you a replacement."

There would be no replacement for this houseplant, and once Starr found him, the Sons of Hercules would pay.

But Bella focused on her other shocking revelation. "I'm sorry to interrupt you again, but did you say you saw the imposter's fins?"

"Not me, the night watchman. He showed the fins. The watchman said he wasn't on the list—he didn't see the false merman had gotten out of the car like your security video or I'm sure he would have known warriors don't drive. But you see, he had those shiny tattoos, an iridescent color, and then he took off his ratty old tennis shoes that didn't fit him too well like he was borrowing them from someone else, and he flexed. I've been trying to imitate the movement all the way down the cable. Once I can make my fins, the healing queen powers follow right along, and goodness knows Pelan needs those powers now. Anyway, the night watchman swears the merman's toes snapped out into those mer fins. I had no idea you could fake that."

Bella looked at Aya. A merman *did* work for the Sons of Hercules.

Aya replied, "You can't. Let us know if you see him again."

"I haven't studied the security videos myself, but I will do my best. He wasn't like any of your warriors but everyone knows the rest don't surface, so the night watchman thought, well, maybe another had come up and wasn't in the binder."

"I'm glad you're feeling better," Aya commented, swimming them away from the anchor and toward the new city. "The sniffles are terrible."

"Mitch and I had the same symptoms, but he didn't drink enough of the elixir. Or girls don't get it as bad as boys; the night watchman's ill, but the lady who substitutes seems to be like me, nominally fine. Now Mitch is in the hospital with a fever. Mine could have been so much worse. Where's Pelan?"

"We're heading to him now. And how did you shift at the surface? Did you kiss a merman?"

"I kissed all the mermen!" She wiggled her feet, trying to help Aya along and instead causing drag. "I was so terrified it wouldn't work, and I just had to reach Pelan. I kissed them all to be safe."

Aya glanced back at the group of warriors clustered at the anchor bolt.

They had a cocky attitude. The others gathered around with rapt interest.

"I suspect escort duty will be even more popular than it already is," she murmured. "Ciran will have his hands full keeping the rotations fair."

"I know it was a bit much, but I had to see him." Roxanne swallowed, and her jaw trembled. "It was so hard seeing him and talking to him when he was so sick. I just wanted to give Nora a break. She's the real hero. But when you said that she wasn't his bride and maybe I...that maybe I could be the one..." She made a determined fist. "I had to get to him as fast as possible."

Roxanne's determination was inspiring. She'd known Pelan was her soul mate even as she'd talked herself out of it because he'd been supposed to be with another. But she'd known. And now she had to be with him.

Just like Bella had to be with Balim.

She let go of Aya's hand. "I'm leaving."

Aya pulled up. "What?"

"With Jonah, I had no choice but with Balim, I do."

Aya shook her head in confusion.

Jonah had been sick. If she could have dropped her work to be in the hospital at all hours, she would have been there.

Now Balim was sick in his soul, and she had a choice.

"What about the Sons of Hercules?" Aya asked.

"What if their next message is even more impossible? Coming down here with that vial was a mistake, and if a second one shows up, Balim won't save me. Our only chance is together. I have to be with him."

"Me too." Roxanne tugged her hand free. "You two talk. I can see the city. I'll swim on, and you catch up. I was a member of the swim team, you know."

"Oh, me too," Aya said in surprise.

"See you directly." Roxanne wiggled her human feet, not put off because she barely moved.

Aya let Roxanne go and tapped her index finger against her temple. "Balim didn't exactly save you."

"I am going after him."

"You can't, Bella. I'm sorry."

She smiled archly at Aya. "I'm not asking your permission. I am an adult woman, and I'm giving you the courtesy of my intentions so you don't worry."

"You can't make your fins yet. How will you ever catch him?"

The non-melodious sounds of the giant octopus drifted beneath their argument.

"I'll ask a friend." She jackknifed and kicked toward the sea floor. "Octopus Kong? I have a slight favor for a big, strong octopus who kicks megalodon butt."

The massive cephalopod drifted from his cave.

"How do you feel about going on a wild adventure to stop a plague, rescue a child, and save the mer-human world?"

He warbled an interested off-tune song.

Aya's lips twisted to the side. "I can't imagine a safer escort. Bella, I hope we'll have a picnic lunch with Jonah someday. Good luck."

Octopus Kong's tentacle curled around her, securing her at the level of his plus-shaped eyes.

She waved to Aya. "Thank you. Octopus Kong? Time to find Balim." Searching her heart, she just knew which direction to go and she pointed. "That way."

The giant jetted across the city, flying over the bulbs until Atlantis was far behind and they plunged deep into the wild ocean. Octopus Kong seemed to enjoy the adventure, romping through the currents, twisting and turning, swooping low over the landscape and chasing giant crabs or strange, eyeless animals and then soaring up to fly with pods of giant blue whales. Great sharks veered away and giant squid fled. No one confronted the giant octopus yodeling like wheezy bagpipes were in style.

Flying with Octopus Kong was exhilarating, like being on dragon-back. With that mindless freedom of the open road—the open ocean, in this case—Bella was left with her thoughts.

Balim was her happiness and her sadness in one. Both feelings were okay. They could exist together. She treasured Balim and Jonah. She needed them both.

The giant thundered over the distance and two small figures emerged against the backdrop of the brightly lit sea. Octopus Kong oriented on them.

The back one stopped and looked. Aha! Nora.

As Octopus Kong bore down on the pair of mer like an off-tune, tentacled cloud of doom, she focused on the warrior.

Balim spun and gaped. "Bella!"

She opened her arms wide, jumped off Octopus Kong's outstretched tentacle, and barreled into Balim. They flew end over end.

"How can you be here?" he demanded.

"How dare you make me care about you and then break my heart!"

He held her tight and trembled, wordless, as though afraid she was a dream and he was about to wake.

But she was no dream, and there was no waking. They were in it together to the end, exiled or free. "You're taking responsibility for that right now."

THIRTY-FOUR

Balim's heart soared as his beloved Bella crushed him in her embrace. Her fierce love was as brilliant as her soul. They flew end over end in the water, out of control, just like always.

Together, they had the dangerous, overpowering resonance. He needed to control it. Because Bella had let go of her inhibitions.

"What are you doing here?" he demanded for the second time. "Atlantis is safe. Your son—"

"How dare you?" she demanded. "I tried everything not to love you. And yet you made me anyway. We are soul mates. You said it. We're soul mates."

"I can never go back to Atlantis," he vibrated, a catch in his chest.

"Then neither will I."

"You were happy there."

"Being stuck there isn't happiness! I'm happy with you." Bella pulled back and looked him in the eye. "Yes, I'm sad about this. I'm sad about what you went through and what you're going through now. I'm sad about Jonah. But I'm better and stronger because I'm with you. And I'll never be happy in Atlantis without you both."

"I murdered a king."

"Did you?" She cocked her head. "Because that's not what it sounded like to me."

"Any mer would know."

"Ciran knows, and he doesn't blame you. You're the reason he left. Because what happened to you was wrong, and all he wants is for you to be happy with me."

His determination fell apart like a pulled stitch. "He does?"

"He does. They all do. Even King Kadir and Soren understand. They wanted to help us. Help you."

"But...I have a dark soul..."

No one was safe around him. Bella was compelled by resonance—destiny, fate—but no one else could accept what he had done. Not Ciran. Not anyone...

Beyond her, Nora held back stroking and cooing to Octopus Kong, who, like all warriors of the sea, basked in her bright soul light.

"I have a dark soul..." he tried again, repeating the words that had tortured him. "I'm a useless warrior. I should have died."

"First, you need this." Bella curled her arms around him and kissed him long and steady.

His pulse leaped into his jaw and his veins opened up, flooding his cock with stiff heat. She was his female and he was her male. She was his soul mate.

She deserved an honorable warrior, not a murderer.

He kissed her despite this because he selfishly needed her more than life. And she needed him too. Joined without tricks, without barriers, without plastics. Skin to skin, emotion to emotion, soul to soul.

But not in the middle of the open ocean in front of another bride and a giant cave guardian, no matter how they tried to pretend they weren't paying attention.

Bella pulled back with heated cheeks, glanced over her shoulder at Octopus Kong and Nora with a sigh, and tapped her forehead against his. "Later. Definitely later. At least twice."

His cock pulsed in acknowledgment.

"Second, I only said I couldn't murder a bunch of people who'd been nothing but nice to me, you included. I make no promises about what I'll do to the Sons of Hercules organizer when I find him."

"I did not follow your Hippocratic ideal."

"Mermen don't. You said so yourself."

"But I also did not follow the law of the mer."

"Ciran was there, and he thinks you were justified."

"But—"

"Okay. You're overly harsh on yourself." She stroked his cheek. "The king threatened you. Self-defense isn't a crime."

"I removed a cursed shard from a battlefield and tricked my king into infecting himself with it."

"You didn't stab him with it in the night. There are degrees of guilt here."

"I left Undine without a healer."

"Technically, the king left them without a healer. And there were years between your father's death and your leaving to groom another."

"In Undine, healers remain in one family line."

"So when the king evicted you from your castle, demoting and preventing you from being chosen by a bride to sire a son, this was, again, not your fault."

His stomach dropped. "Second Lieutenant Ciran told you?"

"More importantly, he told me he was happy you now have a soul mate. Me. And it's over, Balim. The cruelty you endured and the choices you made to survive will haunt you, but they're over. You're free."

She seemed serious, but how could he believe her? The accusing silence when he'd left Undine, the agony of the betrayed Atlantis warriors, and his own heart told the truth. Her words were his wish.

"Do not wish away my crime. I must atone. I will never give you happiness like Jonah. I am not pure."

"Neither am I, and trust me, you'll never replace Jonah. No one will ever replace Jonah. That's what I realized. It's why I'm here." She pressed her palm to her chest. "Stay with me, Balim. We'll be happy and sad together. That's okay."

Her soul glowed with her faith.

"You are happy now," he accused.

"Because I'm with you. Oh! Look." She flexed her foot, and her fins unrolled. Her smile glowed, brilliant. "Somehow, as soon as I said 'We'll be happy and sad together and that's okay,' I felt deep inside I could make my fins. And now I am."

"You channeled your power."

They enjoyed the swirl and flash of Bella's fins. The long trailing beauties were cream-colored and speckled with her freckle-tattoos just like the rest of her. He observed every detail. She was beautiful.

And his.

"It's impossible to imagine breathing water when you're in the air," she mused, "and it's impossible to imagine being happy when you're drowning in sadness. But both worlds coexist. You dive back and forth between them. Zoan said it best. I have faith that no matter how sad I become, someday, I will once more be happy. And vice versa. And that's okay." She pulled him close. "So long as I'm with you."

He held her.

She'd found her strength. Her queen power. He'd been wrong to think she wasn't dedicated to Jonah because of her convictions. She was dedicated to justice and never gave up on Jonah no matter how dark his chances. She would never give up on Balim either. Not even if the rest of the world did.

He'd always known he was beneath Jonah in her heart the same way he'd been beneath his father's and prince's memory in Undine. But Bella explained she loved Balim *and also* her son. He wasn't beneath anyone. Her love coexisted.

"You have changed."

"I couldn't be happy while Jonah was sick," she confessed. "It was supposed to be my last bargain with God. But really, it was the voice of my deepest fears inside me. My heart is bigger than one emotion. And so is yours."

His heart clenched.

She was right.

Confessing the truth of his past had lanced his inner wound. Earning her respect drained the infection and allowed healing.

"I may never return to Atlantis," he remembered, not able to release the last vestiges of his sadness.

"Never say never." She squinted at the distant mouth of a vast undersea tunnel. "Are we going in there?"

"You cannot. The All-Council stronghold lies on the other side. I must go alone."

"Nice try." She shook her head at him. "The warrior

who administered the disease is not a fake. He's connected to the Sons of Hercules. I promised Aya I'd find her answers. You're not going alone."

Nora pulled closer now that their serious talk had finished. "A merman, two humans, and a giant octopus walk into a bar..."

"And then what?" Bella asked.

"I'll tell you once I come up with the rest of the joke."

"That is no sand bar," Balim corrected. "It is the Under-Continental Current and is well guarded by warriors. A giant cave guardian will be noticed."

"He can cause a distraction while we sneak in," Nora suggested.

"There are too many warriors."

"Okay, so we're *all* the distraction. There's Troy. Here's our giant wooden horse." She gestured behind them at the discordant Octopus Kong. "He can hide us in his tentacles. We pop out once we're inside."

"He will never convey us."

"We don't know that until we ask."

"Giant cave guardians are unpredictable and violent."

"That helps us."

Bella interrupted. "I asked, and he brought me to you."

The giant cave guardian ruffled his tentacles, plucked a passing flounder, and crunched it contentedly.

"Such a radical plan has merit," he conceded. "Healer Dalus's training hall is distant from the main All-Council stronghold. Fewer warriors will chase after us. We could use the distraction to claim a secret audience with my mentor."

Bella approached the giant cave guardian with respect and explained their plan. "This could be dangerous."

He warbled something and curled his tentacles around

them, even Balim, gathering them into his underside as the ocean closed into thick walls of rubbery tentacle.

"He says, 'Not for a giant octopus.'" Nora grinned, squishing against him and Bella as they twined together.

"Do you truly understand his words?" Balim asked.

"No. It's a feeling."

"Bella?"

"Same," Bella said.

"There's no way this can go wrong," Nora vibrated nervously.

He held Bella closer. "For the sake of averting an incurable plague, I hope you are right."

THIRTY-FIVE

The group sat tight while the giant cave guardian flew into the massive underwater hole that comprised the Under-Continental Current.

Balim had been through it several times during his training. Never in the tentacles of a giant cave guardian pressed against his soul mate while praying for their lives.

The current forced them through, and the giant octopus navigated the tunnel, his warble changing from yowl to snarl and back again.

Warriors' shouts followed them, and Octopus Kong banged about, holding them tighter as he performed rolls and sweeps.

Bella rested her head against Balim's taut pectorals.

Nora tried to hold herself steady. "It's like riding in a barrel over Niagara Falls."

"Let's hope we stick the landing."

The longer they continued on and the more aggressive the shouting pursuers sounded, the more Balim was grateful for the giant cave guardian and the queens who had partnered with him.

Any other plan would have been suicide. The exile had clouded his mind. With Bella pressed against him, his mind cleared.

So long as her faith in him was real, someday he could vanquish the darkness in his soul and be the warrior—and healer—she and her ill son needed.

Someday.

"Once we arrive near the healer's hall, you and I will go out," Balim told Bella, because he hinged his recovery on her strong, queenly presence. Being without her was nonnegotiable. "Queen Nora, you will remain with Octopus Kong and draw off enemies or stand lookout."

"Queen?" Nora cocked a brow. "Me? As if that will happen."

"Did you not drink elixir and transform? Did you not already make your fins? A flower will bloom for you. You are a destined queen of Atlantis."

Nora's light swelled. She rubbed her mouth to hide her smile. "You're the only one not trying to get in my pants, so I almost believe you."

"You are not wearing pants."

"Yeah, okay, Doc." She dropped her hand, revealing her pleased grin, and peered through the tiny gaps Octopus Kong had kept between his tentacles to circulate water for them. "We're coming up on a cliff."

"Overlooking a battlefield?" He gripped Bella's hand. "Octopus Kong must release us and carry on with the distraction."

The giant cave guardian flung his tentacles wide. They tumbled out. Nora grabbed a sucker. "Whoa! Not me!"

Octopus Kong scooped her up.

She waved as his tentacles closed around her once more. "I'll catch up with you guys later!"

Her vibrations cut off as his protective tentacle closed around her.

A massive army of elite warriors stormed the giant cave guardian from three directions. They were efficient, well-armed, and coordinated.

And no match.

The giant cave guardian raced over the distant pursuers, driving and scattering their formations. They regrouped and chased after him. It was like watching a human wearing an impenetrable suit antagonize swarms of bees. No matter how the bees might think to sting him, Octopus Kong was barely irritated. His appalling song rose in volume. He frolicked over their formations, having a wonderful time.

The All-Council warriors who usually guarded the great stone hall of the healers had disappeared. Trainees raced around disorganized, flying with armfuls of instruments and healing tools, some hurrying toward the giant cave guardian to prepare for healing injured elites and others fleeing from the awesome creature.

Balim and Bella had a short window in which to enter and escape.

He pressed Bella to his chest and dove along the ground, skimming the rock. His fins pumped, rested and ready to move. She belonged pressed against his body. And she did not think he had an irredeemably dark soul.

He flew.

There, the unguarded back entrance led into the great hall of the healers. "Can you make your fins?"

She flexed her stubby feet. "Not on command. I'll practice."

"Pretend to be injured." He coached her to swim side by side with him. When satisfied that they would pass as two male mer, he led her through the cavernous carved stone of the hall.

Unlike most mer cities, which were comprised of organic Life Trees, the All-Council carved their city from immutable stone and cloistered their sacred plant inside a stockade. No warrior could enter its sanctuary.

Those who had seen it said it was disappointing and not worth the mystery. Living in such rocky, harsh conditions, it was spindly and weak, with few resin Sea Opals and never any flowers. The only warriors elected to be elders or representatives had long ago claimed brides and raised young fry. Their reproductive days were behind them. It was the same for All-Council generals and, until recently, the elite military. Any who held power had already met and discarded their sacred bride soul mates. So of course, the Life Tree of the All-Council never put forth any blossoms.

Balim flew across the barren stone.

Most of the guards must have been drawn off by Octopus Kong. Balim snuck along the empty colonnades flashing through the shadows. Other healers hurried to the entrance. None glanced at him or noticed Bella.

His mentor's voice boomed from his chambers at the end of the hall. "Go forth, my trainees! Rarely does the battle come to the All-Council. Do not let pass this training opportunity. There are warriors to heal!"

Balim reached his mentor's private chambers, confirmed they were alone, and pulled Bella inside.

The room was as he remembered. Empty of comforts, barren as the rocky halls, but filled with study tools, equipment, and small gardens of curative plants, cages of animals, and piles upon piles of rare healing materials in various states of growth or harvest.

His mentor, Great Healer Dalus, looked up from the

weave of one such flat plant. "I told you to—Trainee Balim." He straightened, noted Bella, and fixed on his former trainee. "I should say, Healer Balim. You are far from the rebel city."

"I was exiled." He positioned himself in front of Bella to disguise her appearance. "This is my apprentice. Bella."

"Bel-la," he repeated and folded his fingers over his thick abdomen. In the years since Balim had trained with him, the elderly warrior had grown older, wider, and balder. "Not rebel nor Undine."

"No."

"You have, of course, come to study Blue Ring."

Balim's belly lurched. He knew?

"Yes, yes, of course." Great Healer Dalus kicked at an easy pace out of his private study and down the empty hall. "This battlefield has seen great interest lately. General Giru has asked endless questions. He has ambitious ideas on how to end the rebellion."

"Did he share those plans with you?" Bella asked smoothly.

Dalus glanced back. "Only what was necessary to prevent contagion within his warriors."

Balim's belly fell further. "Then he was successful in removing a weapon from the cursed field?"

"I will show you. See with your own senses, Balim. Do not become lazy because you hold a title of Healer now."

Bella vibrated to Balim. "Is the battlefield honestly right outside?"

Healer Dalus answered her. "It is my favorite place to contemplate the limits of knowledge."

"It seems risky to live right next to an infectious hot zone for an incurable disease."

"Is it not natural? So many traveled to study the field, it

became an established meeting place of healers. A cursed, incurable battlefield is the most natural place."

They exited to the upper ledge of sheer cliffs.

Below, the battlefield spread out. Like the wrecked boats in Lake Eerie, broken tridents stabbed out of rocks where the bodies, abandoned even by fish, calcified into limestone skeletons.

The shouts of the living echoed along with the noise of Octopus Kong leading a merry chase. Here, the still water contained a deadly message for any who would sit and ponder it.

Dalus heaved himself onto a rock worn smooth on the ledge. He had often rested there to ponder this battlefield during Balim's apprenticeship. More lines etched his old face, and a deeper sadness mixed with the active curiosity that had safeguarded his permanent place as the highest healer of the mer.

"You still force your trainees to study it for lessons?" Balim asked.

"I ask them to consider what drives a male to continue to fight when his body breaks down around him, when sense should hold him back, when even honor has abandoned his fight."

His curiosity was legend. If anyone cured the disease, it would be Dalus.

"We're more interested in how to cure it," Bella said.

"Yes." His mentor's lip quirked. "And, perhaps, how it has spread from Oannes Field to Undine to Atlantis?"

Balim's stomach rolled. "You knew?"

"Not much passes by my eyes unnoticed, especially if a gifted trainee turns his gaze on my passion project."

Balim had thought himself so sneaky, stealing away

when the others were occupied and studying the field. Fanta-sizing how the old king would die and no one could stop it just as no one had stopped him from killing Balim's father.

Dark times were only a thought away.

Bella pressed her hand on his.

Her presence washed away the darkness in a soothing wave of light. He needed to trust and focus. The dark time was past.

"The ingenious method you used to remove the cursed items without contracting the illness is the reason new items can be removed." Dalus cast his eyes back at Balim, insulted by Balim's surprise. "I know the interests and occupations of my warriors, Balim. Although I am a healer, I am not a hermit."

"Why are others items being taken out?" Bella asked. "And where are they going?"

"First, to study. But it is impossible for mer to conduct such research without contracting the illness. So, in the end, we collected them for you to study."

"Me?" Balim repeated.

"You." He nodded beyond Balim to Bella. "Humans."

Balim gripped the pommels of his daggers. "Make any hostile move, and I will forget you are a great healer."

Dalus narrowed his eyes.

"Well, you got me." Bella hugged herself. "I guess I wasn't as sneaky as I thought."

He laughed. "I am trained to examine warriors for phys-ical illness. It would be a sad day for healers if I did not notice your particular deformities in the chest, hip, and fins."

She squished her breasts. "Thanks for the tip."

Balim's heart thudded as hard as when Dalus had

revealed he knew of Balim's crimes. "You will not summon your guards?"

"They are busy with a giant cave guardian that has arrived at the same moment." His suppressed smile told them he was no idiot. "To answer, I have no interest in engaging in another war where the two sides would rather die than allow the other to survive. We know how that ends."

They gazed out on the battlefield. Ghosts had come and gone. The past battles were long ended, deaths long forgotten, but still caused a powerful effect on the living.

"You should be on our side," Bella said. "We'll save your race."

"You will save nothing if you succumb."

"Is that why you surfaced and broke into Balim's hospital? So you could infect Pelan and the other humans?"

"Surface? No. I have too many responsibilities here. But you say Blue Ring infects humans? Do they get the bruising, the blue chains, the suicidal memories?"

"Suicide?" Bella and Balim both repeated the word at the same time.

Balim followed the thread. "The incurable disease kills by suicide?"

"It causes irreparable body decay unhalted by the Life Tree and wracks the warrior's soul with pain. Most commit suicide before the disease finishes its course, but make no mistake: the disease *will* finish its course. We have learned that much."

"What else?" Bella asked.

"What else have you learned?" Dalus pushed back, eager and interested.

"Tell us!"

Balim answered. "Human females and males are both

susceptible, but elixir slows the disease or cures it in females."

Balim shared the information about Roxanne and Mitch.

"At least one modern bride was immersed in the diseased fluid and suffered no effects, while the warrior now circles the last stage of illness."

"Fascinating." The healer's eyes glowed with great interest. "Then, I suppose it will not matter for long. I have lied to you, Balim."

He clutched his dagger and moved in front of Bella. "How?"

Dalus ignored his movement. "I teach that there were no survivors of this war. That is the lesson of the field and the wish of the All-Council. Not the truth."

"So there were survivors," Bella breathed.

"Two," Dalus confirmed. "They came not from this battlefield. As you know, the last kings carried the disease home in their dying corpses. The citizens, weakened by age and starving from the long war, succumbed also.

"Except in Derketo. A young male remained with his new bride." He nodded. "They survived."

Balim frowned. This contradicted everything. "How? Why did they survive?"

"They weren't starving," Bella suggested.

"His bride was fuller and more rested than her ragged husband, but by his account, he was quite ill. He even contracted the disease. She never did."

"And he recovered," Balim mused. "She healed him."

"Something, yes, healed him. I have spent my lifetime studying this field and this disease to answer how."

"She used queen powers."

Dalus tipped his head back, another smile on his face,

and raised a brow. "Legends do not cure diseases. Healers cure them."

"They are not legends. I have seen them, Great Healer."

His mentor tsked with disbelief.

"So how did the healer cure him?" Bella asked. "You have a theory."

"Very rudimentary. After consultation with General Giru, I have learned so many things. Humans classify their illnesses by the creature that causes them: parasitic, bacterial, and viral. They have promised me that once they have finished under their 'microscope' machines, they will tell me how to defeat the disease that annihilated the most powerful kings of history."

"Which is it?" Bella asked. "Animal, bacteria, or virus?"

"That, human, is something I hope your people will explain." He looked up again and rose, his fins descending as recognition filled his face with subdued welcome. "General Giru, I have held the intruders right at the lip of Oannes Field as you requested."

Bella clung to Balim. "A double-cross."

General Giru descended to their level.

He had a strange, unnatural coloration of pale skin and wore an unusual chest plate. Dark weave hid his shoulders and cushioned the skin beneath his daggers. Dark purple, iridescent tattoos tangled across his face like human blackberry vines.

Bella gasped. "The fake merman!"

"I am a true merman," he barked, his chest vibrations rough. "You poisoned your city. Destroyed your castle. Murdered your king. You and the warriors who compromise our proud traditions are pond scum."

Balim held Bella tight. His heart thudded out of control.

He was no warrior, and he could not fight off the

second-highest commander of the All-Council, who descended to their side, nor his warriors massed around him.

"There is nowhere to escape." General Giru vibrated with a gravelly tone in his chest. Congestion? But as he had proclaimed, he was no human. "Your weapons, Healer Balim, or I will cut you down where you float and leave your human bride without a protector."

Balim relinquished his daggers and trident. Although a central tenet of the mer was never to injure females or young fry, the All-Council had decreed rebel queens to be not female. Some generals still treated them with honor and others as rival warriors. General Giru's feelings were unknown. Balim would not risk Bella.

General Giru's elite warriors bound Balim roughly. They turned on Bella.

"Leave her," he begged. "Take her to the surface."

"We will." The general smiled coldly, his teeth white behind pale lips and semitranslucent skin. His soul was dark. He bit back great pain. "Great Healer. My draught?"

His warriors lassoed ropes to drag Bella without touching her.

Dalus gave the general a soft jelly flask filled with greenish-black liquid. He swallowed the inky substance. It must have been bitter because his throat muscles worked against his swallows, suppressing a gag. He finished the medicine, shuddered, and waited for it to take hold.

Dalus stood back watching. Just like Undine under the old king. Silent, judging, and leaving Balim to his punishment.

General Giru opened his eyes slowly. "Great Healer, bring the relic box."

"You require another cursed dagger?" Dalus brought him the equipment he requested.

"The humans have one request."

General Giru operated a modified metal version of Balim's lamprey to capture a crusty dagger from the battlefield below. He donned a thick mitt and studied his prize. The dagger resembled any other weapon lost to the ages. Although invisible to the senses, disease seemed to radiate danger.

Through the mitt, General Giru clasped the crusty pommel and brandished the dagger at an invisible enemy. "Ha! Ha..."

Imagining stabbing someone seemed to give him relief. His shoulders lowered, and his cheeks went lax. He blinked and straightened. His pupils dilated, and a strange dullness crossed his face. He shook himself and turned on the captives.

Bella watched the loosely held dagger with wide eyes.

Now he knew she was immune, Balim's fears eased. No matter what happened to him, she would survive.

General Giru focused on him.

Balim braced.

The general crossed the distance in a single, loose kick. He positioned the coral-crusted dagger against Balim's chest, just below the heart, and sliced a deep line.

"No!" Bella shrieked.

His chest radiated pain. Balim's nerves screamed, and his blood soaked the water. He thrashed, the cloud of disease growing excited as it interacted with his blood. Little stings like invisible anemones struck his veins, invisible sharks biting his body. Streaking, like the poison vial, into his chest and blackening his soul.

Bella moaned. "No."

"General, I am disappointed in you." Dalus sagged with a heavy voice. "Was injuring my trainee necessary?"

"Yes." The general wrapped the dagger in multiple layers of seaweed and placed it in a stone box. He secured his glove atop it and sealed the box.

"He was a good healer. Risk-taking but dedicated. Willing to pursue the truth no matter how deep into the wolf eel hole."

"Great Healer, a king killer, human sympathizer, and rebel cannot live. And do not forget that his injury is his own fault. If he had not shown how to acquire these cursed weapons, you would not have taught me, and I would not have made the allies I have."

Dalus peered into the battlefield. "But I only shared this with you so you could bring me a cure. And you have not."

"One is forthcoming. Failed Healer Balim shall again be instrumental in its discovery." The general nodded at his warriors. The elite guard dragged Balim and Bella for the surface.

"He will be cured?"

"No, but his sacrifice will serve the mer." General Giru turned away from the healing hall. "The Sons of Hercules need another test subject."

THIRTY-SIX

Bella tried to kick her fins to keep from being dragged by the warriors and to catch up to Balim.

His skin paled like Pelan's, turning translucent, and dark bruising spread out from the scabbed-over cut. His mouth opened and closed like a fish unable to breathe.

General Giru's warriors escorted them to a cable anchored to a distant rock. They clipped on to the same harnesses used on the Atlantis cable and ascended straight up.

The general sneered at Bella's anger. "Do you not enjoy the human marvels?"

"I thought the All-Council never surfaced," she snapped, repeating what Aya had told her. "I thought the ancient covenant restricted you to the sea."

"The founding of Atlantis destroyed the natural order. We must adapt until the order is restored." The general's lazy, complacent tone sharpened. "All will pay. Even me."

They ascended and then stopped, hovering at a specific mark on the cable to reduce the pressurization effects. Mermen did not get the bends, but apparently, other effects were reduced by pausing instead of rocketing for the surface.

Balim curled over and shuddered.

The general watched him with a dead gaze.

"Why are you doing this?" Bella demanded, furious. "The Sons of Hercules are your greatest enemy. You should hate each other."

"The enemy of my enemy is an untapped ally."

"Their goal is to kill *you*."

"They cannot poison the faithful," he scoffed. "Only rebels who deserve to die."

Balim clenched over his injury. "Does the All-Council know you made this treaty? That you have unleashed an ancient disease?"

"No one will question my results. When all mainland warriors are dead and Atlantis is a cursed boneyard, we will silence the rebel voices. Dragao Azul and Aiycaya will return to the All-Council. The mer will descend and revert to the natural order."

"Aiycaya?" Balim screwed open an eye. "Aiycaya has rebelled?"

"You would not have heard, would you? You were exiled before the news."

"What news?"

"Perhaps I will not tell you." His cold smile widened. "Comfort yourself by knowing Atlantis is emptied of its army, and it is too easy for my warriors to stow explosive vials in the remaining castles." He gazed at his cursed treasure. "Or worse."

The threat stabbed into Balim. He hunched over and moaned.

She hugged Balim, as powerless now as she had been to

soothe Jonah during his chemo when he'd cried because the insides of his bones ached.

Where were her queen powers?

"It'll be okay." She tried to channel something, anything, other than his pain-filled decline. "I'm here. This pain will pass. It sucks, but it will pass, and you'll be stronger because you endured it."

"He will grow weaker." The general smirked. "He will wither and die like all warriors who turn their backs on the ancient covenant."

This big, ugly bully poked at her furious heart.

Bella fired back at him. "No, he won't. I will heal him with my love. It's my queen power. I just have to develop it. You'll see."

"This human 'love' is a lie. Only resonance in the soul is truth."

"And we're soul mates."

"More lies."

"I transformed because of our resonance. Look at my fins."

"Any female destined to mate a warrior can transform. But modern females cannot speak true vows. Their minds are distracted, and their words are weak."

Balim's eyes cracked open, and his gaze fixed on her. The distinctive red of his tattoos and the matching threads in his irises darkened. He heard the general's words and believed them.

"No," she insisted to Balim. "I haven't loved anyone like I love you. It's not just words. Believe me."

But did he? His eyes closed again, and he slipped into unconsciousness.

Distant notes of discord filtered past their argument.

Her hope rose.

Octopus Kong? Nora?

The general tilted his head, rotating his chest in a circle to pinpoint the direction, and then frowned. "Spread out."

His elite warriors obeyed.

The noise faded.

The general's sharp gaze faded into the same lazy fog that had taken over his expression after drinking the medicine. He ordered his warriors to rise once more.

"You vow to love each other forever," the general taunted her. "But you are a modern human who will change her mind as soon as you meet another warrior more to your taste."

She hugged her unconscious warrior. "That will never happen."

"You think you are wise."

"Obviously you've never found your soul mate."

"Now you are the foolish one. I could not hold this position unless I fathered a young fry."

But doubt flashed in his eyes, and he turned away.

They approached the surface. The cable they'd been using ended at a floating buoy, and the warriors unclipped everyone, leaving Balim for Bella to handle. Close by, a long boat floated in the middle of nowhere. It pulled on its anchor chain, drifting on the current. She had never seen such massive metal. Each chain link was the size of her own body.

Satisfied that they were alone, the general broke through the water barrier and shifted to air-breathing. He looked even paler but less translucent. And the sunlight revealed marks of an old fight bruising his skin.

Bella knew nothing of boats but what she'd seen on TV, which wasn't much. The boat was painted a military greenish-gray and the massive deck was stocked with cranes, submersibles, and bristling with antennas and satellite dishes. It looked like a cross between a polar icebreaker and a scientific vessel, stable enough to cross the roughest, stormiest Atlantic swells in the middle of winter. How many people lived there? A hundred?

The general led them to the back end of the boat, ordered his warriors to hide beneath the waves, and yanked a long rope to signal his arrival.

A bell pealed.

They bobbed in the large waves.

The general frowned and pulled the greenish, algae-slicked rope again.

No one answered his summons.

He swam to a plunging ladder, clambered to the deck, and disappeared.

A platform descended to sea level. His elite warriors dragged Bella and Balim onto the crashing metal and then slipped beneath the waves.

The platform rose.

On the deck, the general stood with his trident out. He was nude aside from the weapons and armor, and his flaccid cock dangled between his legs. "Get off."

She obeyed, pulling Balim with her. They were both nude too. She never noticed that in the water but the instant she was on land, she shrank into a form small, vulnerable, and afraid.

The general sliced through her bonds with the deadly, sharp middle spine of his trident. He freed Balim, rotated the weapon, and nudged him with the rounded base.

Balim groaned.

The general grimaced. "Wake your so-called soul mate."

"He's sick," Bella protested.

"Wake him or I will."

She caressed Balim's pale, scraped cheek, murmuring her wish. It worked. His lashes fluttered, he blinked, and then rolled over and ejected the water. Gasping on his fore-arms and knees, he gathered strength.

His cut looked horrible. Purplish-green, festering, and bruised. A direct injury with a diseased dagger was much more virulent than whatever had infected Pelan. The ghostly blue rings hidden beneath his tattoos spread out across his body from the cut.

"Get him up. Walk with me."

"He's *sick*," Bella repeated, snappish.

The general's dead expression showed how he did not care.

Fine. Well, not fine, but Bella would try. She swung Balim's biceps around her small shoulders, hardening herself against his pained grunt and wince so she could be the caregiver he needed. "I've got you. You're with me. Everything's going to be okay."

Balim forced one half-human foot after another, stum-bling and dragging himself on her command.

They staggered after the general.

Bella was not a natural caregiver. She was too selfish. But for Balim, like for Jonah, she cared in sickness or health. And the way her spirit was firing for revenge, she'd be there fighting for vengeance long after they were parted by death.

THIRTY-SEVEN

Bella helped her soul mate stagger after the general.

The boat, which could hold hundreds of people, was empty. And that flummoxed the general. He wandered through passageways with no idea what to do.

"Hercules?" His gravelly call echoed down the hall. "Humans? I have your dagger and your test subject."

"Where is everybody?" Bella asked, looking up from focusing on her footing with Balim.

He raised his voice. "Where are you?"

No one answered.

The boat creaked. Distant waves splashed. It was strange and creepy.

They entered a room full of scientific equipment. The chairs were pushed back and the coffee was overturned, still a wet brown stain on the floor, as if everyone had abandoned the ship in a hurry.

"Something bad happened here," she warned him. "This is where they studied the dagger? We should go. Now."

He grunted. "The small boats are no longer attached."

"The lifeboats?"

A tank of blue water rested on a table. Inside rested a crusty dagger just like the one he had removed from the field and used to stab Balim. The general set his wooden box with the new dagger in it next to the tank, on top of a stack of papers, soaking everything and making the ink run.

"Make your people answer."

"How do I do that?" she asked.

He gestured at a flickering monitor. "Hercules conveys orders through this device."

She eased Balim into a chair, stretched, and then examined the computer station. A locked screensaver told her the company owner. NGMT Enterprises. The letterhead on the wet stack of papers spelled it out. Next Gen Mil Tech Enterprises. It was stamped with a government seal.

Next Generation Military Technology.

A government contractor? They had badly underestimated the Sons of Hercules' importance, influence, and reach. They were not "mere" college students, even though the active shootings and bombings had been performed by disgruntled college-aged men. They must be the expendable grunts. The true organization was obviously much, much larger.

She tapped the keyboard. It popped up a password field. She walked around the other computers. "They're locked."

He unsheathed the normal, non-diseased dagger strapped to his bicep. "Do not defy me. I will carve my dissatisfaction into your exile."

"I'm not defying you. Look." She wiggled the mouse and revealed identical password screens. "Do you know the password?"

"Pass...word?"

"The word to unlock them."

He considered. "Hercules."

She typed it. "No."

"Rebel."

"No."

"Anathema bride."

"Really?"

"The Sons of Hercules do not tolerate them," he replied, but of course it didn't work either, and the third attempt locked her out with a warning that the station had to be unlocked by the system administrator.

She needed Starr.

"We need to find an unlocked computer," she said.

The general made her shoulder Balim once more and follow him around the boat to the bridge.

It too was empty and filled with buttons, dials, switches, and gages. What did any of them do? Even the maps were strange looking, but a satellite image showed their position: the middle of the Indian Ocean.

And the date said several months had passed since she'd descended to Atlantis, putting home in midwinter.

Time dilation, Balim had called it.

Had Starr made much progress? She hoped everyone was okay. The journey through the undersea world had taken longer than she'd realized.

"Operate the satellite internet," the general ordered.

She eased Balim into one of the cushy seats and perused the mysterious instrument panels. "Which one controls that?"

"You are the human."

"I can read. But I can't understand most of these labels. I've never sailed on a boat."

"Do not defy me!" He lifted his trident to Balim's throat.

Balim closed his eyes and stiffened.

Bella felt so helpless. Balim was sick. She was imprisoned aboard an abandoned boat and held hostage by an unpredictable, violent, drugged general who didn't seem entirely sane. He was, hands down, the worst client she'd ever worked for.

Although he had yet to kidnap her child. So he was only second-worst.

What was wrong with her? Why was she able to cut off her emotions and have these ironic thoughts when Balim's life was on the line?

Her chest blazed. Because that was her strength. She could focus even when her loved ones were in a life-and-death fight. She could feel happiness and sadness and myriad other emotions. *I'm okay.*

"Operate it," the general ordered through clenched teeth.

"I told you, I can't." She lifted her chin. "You drove in a car. Did you learn how to drive?"

"The metal car drove itself."

"So, no. Don't be unreasonable. Sailing a giant metal boat isn't an intuitive life skill. I don't even know which button to push to turn it on."

The general lowered his trident. "How do I communicate I have upheld my vow?"

"Let me see..." She finished inspecting the deck and rummaged around in the pockets of the jackets the crew had left hanging over chairs next to opened cans of soda and half-eaten sandwiches. A square metal cell phone was her reward. She pulled it out. "Hold your breath."

General Giru eyed her suspiciously. "Why? Is it poisoned?"

"If I can guess the password, we can call anyone."

"How does holding breath assist with your guess?"

"It's just a figure of speech." She pressed the power button to wake it. "Here we..."

The phone showed a music player screen with the message, *Trusted device nearby. Safety lock disabled.*

Huh. Secret government contractors who'd set their phones to stay unlocked when trusted devices were nearby? Starr would love that.

She closed the music player and dialed, waited for it to connect, and prayed.

"I can release my air?" General Giru asked faintly, still trying to hold his breath and talk.

"Yes. Sorry. It's fine."

He breathed out.

How trusting.

The dial tone stopped.

Shoot.

"MerMatch," a clear female voice said confidently over the bridge loudspeaker, making them jump. "Hazel speaking."

"Hazel, it's Bella." Her heart thumped hard.

"Bella! Oh my god, I was just leaving the office, I almost didn't pick up the phone! Where are you?"

"A ship in the Indian Ocean," Bella said. "And right now, I'm afraid it's a plague ship."

"Stop this conversation." General Giru lifted his trident once more to threaten a half-conscious Balim. "Contact Hercules."

"Who's that?"

Bella looked at the general.

He straightened his spine. His pupils had returned to normal size, and he was showing the strain of whatever injury had caused him to demand medicine from Great Healer Dalus.

"I am General Giru, Second General of the All-Council armies. You will obey my orders, or I will eviscerate your friends, starting with the false healer Balim."

"E-eviscerate?" Hazel's tone edged into panic. "What? Bella? Are you okay?"

"For the moment." She kept a smooth, soothing lilt in her voice. "We just need to contact the Sons of Hercules."

"But how? We don't know—"

"I'm sure we *do* know." Bella smiled tightly at the general and then gazed at the intercom as she held the phone to her ear. "We didn't know how to call off this boat and now I'm talking to you, so it's a similar manner of working through the problem. Contact our contacts."

"Oh. Um. Oh. God. Okay. Here's, uh, here's Dannika."

The phone clattered, making them jump again, and Dannika's concerned voice took over the line.

"Bella, we're so glad to hear from you. You'll be pleased to know that Faier was found unharmed. He's even found his own bride. She's a—"

"Don't tell me too much. We're on a party line."

"Yes, of course. I'm making conversation while Hazel contacts someone who can help with your problem. General Giru, you said? I don't believe we've had the pleasure."

The chiseled general did not answer. Dark shadows around his eyes and hollow cheeks sickened his expression. He straightened by sheer force and looked as though he preferred to hunch over as Balim did.

"You do know him a little," Bella said, also trying to

keep the conversation easy. "He's the one who entered the mer hospital and infected everyone."

"How very brave," Dannika murmured. "He didn't worry about infecting himself?"

Oh.

Ohhhh.

"I think he did infect himself," Bella murmured.

He fixed on Bella for a long, hard moment. "I am a general of the All-Council. I do not collapse from weakness. The warriors of Oannes Field fought to death during their sickness. I will do no less."

"Bella, Hazel has almost connected you to your Starr," Dannika said, accidentally revealing her half sister's name. "Just hold on one—"

Clink.

Another voice intercepted the call and boomed through the loudspeaker. Not quite male, not quite female, and masked with computer distortion.

"What idiot forgot to abandon ship? Report to the bridge to be mocked by your superior."

General Giru straightened. "Hercules."

"Yes? Who's forgetting passwords and locking themselves out of their workstations instead of jumping overboard and paddling away like a little pup?"

"And what do we need to flee, Herc?"

A surprised pause ensued, and then strange admiration. "Why, Bella Taylor. Imagine you showing up on my condemned secret lab ship. You are more resourceful than I gave you credit for."

Her stomach soured, and fury filled her. "So are you. I assume this is the government lab you used to study the Life Tree blossom."

General Giru frowned. "Life Tree blossom?"

"Government?" He guffawed. "Private sector! The government pays so much more for the same biological weapon if it's developed by a company with black folders to contain its communiques."

"Packaging *is* everything," she agreed.

"Of course you understand. It really has been wonderful working with you, Bella Taylor. If only you had been more competent at your assigned task."

"You're the one who got impatient. You blew that poison vial, didn't you? I could have gotten you that blossom."

"I gave you weeks. You were betraying us. Don't deny it."

"The Life Tree doesn't blossom like a cherry tree. The last one was heavily guarded. And if you were thinking of synthesizing it into a cure, your premise was a mistake. Blue Ring is incurable precisely because it *can't* be cured by the Life Tree."

"That's what makes it so good," Herc corrected, sounding excited like a greedy collector. "Mermen can't fight it. But I digress. You have little time now. It's a shame we'll never meet."

"Yes, about that—"

"Hercules," General Giru interrupted. "As negotiated, I have brought you another test subject. Rebel Balim was infected with a fresh strain of the disease. We ascended directly. You may now test the progress on a living merman."

"Thanks, General Giru. As you can see, we're suffering from an unforeseen staffing shortage."

"I do not understand."

"Of course you wouldn't. Tell you what. Leave his body in the dissection lab. Someone will return to dissect his corpse."

"What about his female? She will not remain here."

"Lock her in the bridge."

"How?"

"The ship operates on electronic locks. Close the door and press the middle button on the keypad."

This was bad. She appealed to General Giru. "It's a trap."

The general dragged Balim through the door and closed the heavy metal, sealing it.

"He's lying!" She jiggled the locked handle and banged on the small strip of glass. "Don't do this. These people are your enemy. They want to kill you."

"Nonsense." Herc chuckled. "We want to kill *you*. And working together in a harmonious partnership, we will. Same goals."

"General." She tried to make him hold her gaze. "Your race is dying. I'm a bride. I could be pregnant with a young fry."

"You will be safe on your human ship. Hercules will release you after he returns." General Giru gathered up Balim and exited.

"He's not returning!" She smacked the glass. "You can't do this! This is crazy! The Sons of Hercules are our enemy! We're on the same side!"

"Bella Taylor." Herc tsked in that weird computer-muffled voice. "Don't you know better than to reason with an innocently childlike, easily manipulated monster?"

She let her hand drop and searched the bridge for an exit.

The seats were bolted to the floor. Heavy metal objects were bolted to the wall. There was a fire extinguisher. She yanked it out of its clip and banged it against one window.

It bounced off, leaving the metal extinguisher dented.

How thick were the windows? Feet?

"I could still get you a Life Tree blossom," she negotiated, stalking around the bridge and testing another window. Thud-bounce. "I can't do that if I'm dead."

"We're abandoning the project. Only a few hundred are infected, and it's not worth the money to develop a cure."

"You released a plague in New York City and it's not worth developing a cure?!"

"The CDC will handle it."

"That's so irresponsible."

"It's all your fault."

"I don't see how."

"You threatened to smear the reputations of my heroic sons. I had to act. We're *heroes*, Bella Taylor. We vanquish the monsters that spread their horrifying fish diseases across our pristine shoreline."

"It wasn't enough to focus on the mer 'stealing' women who would never become your girlfriend."

"Women are whores."

"That bullet point must delight the Ladies' Society."

"They don't even notice because they know, Bella Taylor. They fear the 'other.' The other skin color, the other country of origin, the other neighborhood, the other class. Hatred is a great unifier. It brings together very different people who have so much fear and so much hatred of each other and concentrates it on the ultimate other: the subhuman merman."

"There are greater unifiers than hatred."

"Yes, certainly. But as a marketer, you well know that adding in fear is effective. My messages of fear and hatred have even convinced a monster to do my bidding."

She crouched on her hands and knees and searched

beneath the consoles for tools while Herc congratulated himself.

"Preying upon doubts and catering to our worst impulses led my little experiment from a weekend hobby to sparking a movement across college campuses and now the world. Political figures consult me on the sly. Companies have lined up to throw money into my pockets, and they don't care if my work never passes an audit. Truly, it has been a success beyond my wildest dreams."

"And then you kidnapped my son."

His tone flattened. "I give him better care than a middle-class income such as yours could ever provide."

Her heart thudded. Jonah was still alive.

"And besides, any expanding company experiences setbacks. Less successful products fizzle while more exciting products come on the line."

"So the plague is a 'less successful product'?"

He grew more animated again. "Do you know an exciting illness? Ebola. Three days of brain hemorrhages and bleeding from your eyeballs. Nobody forgets that. Do you know an unexciting illness? Heart disease. Over half a million Americans die of it every year. One in four deaths. And yet do people exercise and eat right? No. Two Americans died in the last Ebola outbreak. Who fears Ebola? Everyone."

"Too bad for you Blue Ring doesn't make people bleed from their eyeballs."

"It takes far too long to kill them," he agreed. "And then one researcher tests positive for the disease when it's not clear how he got infected and the whole project has to abandon ship. He probably handled the dagger with a paper cut. They're supposed to be honing the ultimate weapon to fight back against a race that regrows limbs and survives bullets to the heart. I expect a man of science to show more grit."

"You know, you could have spent those resources figuring out how to regrow limbs for humans and let everyone survive bullets to the heart."

"Mmm. Benefit from the mermen? Not 'on message,' Bella Taylor. You can't unite the groups I have with positive thinking and miracles. We're talking Ku Klux Klan working side by side with ISIS."

"What a humanitarian."

"I'm a great unifier. You'll see when I'm accepting my Nobel Prize for annihilating mermen and safeguarding the sanctity of human life."

"Conveniently ignoring the biological weapon unleashed in a major US city and, apparently, on this ship."

"It will be dealt with. When your mortgage is underwater, there's only one thing to do, you know."

"Talk to the bank?"

"Burn the mansion and collect the insurance."

Nothing in this bridge would break her out. Bella pushed to her feet again. "That's dark."

"I'm a realist. And now, I'm signing off. I prefer to remember you like this, thinking you're so clever as you're debating, rather than screaming as you fruitlessly try to evade the fighter jets."

"What?"

"Don't worry. When the bombs hit, you shouldn't feel a thing."

"What about my son?" she demanded.

"He shouldn't feel a thing either."

"But where is he, Herc?"

"Closer than you might imagine." *Click.*

A screen embedded in the wall by the speakers lit.

It showed a blank part of the ship. Then, images rotated. Her in the bridge staring at the screen. An empty hallway. Her son, still alive, sleeping on a bunk in a locked room.

Jonah was here! On an infected ship about to be bombed by fighter pilots! She had to rescue him, find Balim—

The screen flashed again to show Balim stumbling back from General Giru. The general held a bloody dagger.

Balim clutched his belly. He'd been stabbed. His eyes rolled back into his head, and he collapsed.

THIRTY-EIGHT

Balim stumbled back and collapsed on the hard metal floor.

He barely felt his body. It seemed so far away. Even the new pain in his gut where General Giru had stabbed him fell away.

He was back in Undine, a trainee, gravely injured. His prince clasped his shoulders. Blood soaked the water, and dark pain circled his eyes. "You will survive this attack, little healer. Undine cannot go on without you. Your father will heal you swiftly. I will ensure he heals you first."

"No..."

His moan snapped him back to the present. He was lying half on his side on a human boat. General Giru stood over him.

Balim had been stabbed. He was bleeding.

He clenched the wound. Blood spilled over his fingers.

But somehow, he barely felt it. His infected chest pained him much more.

"Balim." His father's grateful, worried expression was the first thing Balim observed upon waking. Every thread of

dark wood and heartblood red in his irises focused on Balim with sharp relief. His features, his steady soul light, his patterns of tattoos were bright and clear. Balim's wounds pained him, but they were neatly sewn and bandaged, and he tried hard to be brave in front of his father. "I will never let you out of our safe castle again."

"Nghgh..."

General Giru advanced, orienting him once more in the present. Sympathy softened his harsh expression.

The memories pushed against his mind, forcing him to reenter them, pressuring him like a suppressed sneeze.

But Balim held them off. He couldn't get distracted. Not now. "You...stabbed...me..."

"I will again." He knelt beside Balim and wiped the blade on an abandoned human fabric. Cleaning it before dirtying it again with Balim's blood. "It is better to die swiftly than live with the pain of Blue Ring."

A commotion at the edge of the Life Tree dais drew his father's gaze away from Balim. The king's cry echoed. "My son!"

Balim moaned.

"Yes, I have suffered with this illness for many human months. It forces me to relive the same moments over and over." General Giru settled beside Balim. "Great Healer Dalus warned me that I would commit suicide. No! I was not so weak. But this memory torture is more excruciating than any physical pain. Only his draughts give me relief."

"Where is the healer? Why has he let my son, the city's prince, slip away?"

Balim's life leaked out between his fingers. "Bella..."

Her beautiful face turned to him in memory. Light shone from her chest. Her red hair floated like a cloud, and her green eyes glimmered with happiness.

Oh, that was good. Concentrating on her name pushed the terrible swirling blackness away. His belly hurt. He applied greater pressure to slow the bleeding.

"I too think of my soul mate." General Giru tipped his head back and regarded the ceiling. "We touched lips on the surface. She transformed for me and came into my castle. But then we could not progress." His chest heaved. "I, the most honorable warrior of Djullanar, destined to fight in the All-Council armies of the most elite warriors, could not sire a young fry with my sacred bride."

"Bella..."

"I secretly consulted with the only warrior I trusted. My then-closest friend, my second lieutenant. You can imagine my horror when he resonated with my sacred bride instead."

He tapped the blade against his chest and then set it aside and removed his coverings.

"I considered killing him. Revealing the truth would cause his and my deaths. Djullanar, like the All-Council, does not tolerate deviations from the proper order."

He set the chest plate aside and unwrapped his blades and the concealing cloths. The bruises and telltale blue rings emerged in the shadows of his atrophied muscles. His original strength had wasted away.

"I endured their secret trysts. Pretended his virility was mine. After that treacherous bride resurfaced, I thought we had reconciled as we jointly raised his outstanding young fry. I continued on to the All-Council and he took my place as a respected adviser to the king. But Blue Ring has forced me to realize that I have not moved past this betrayal."

He twisted the blade in the air before his emotion-clenched face.

"The moment I held my dagger to his throat—to *his*

throat, the male who saved my life uncountable times, who sacrificed his own father so I could live, who followed me without a moment's cloud of doubt—and I was so blinded by jealousy over an unworthy surface female, I threatened *his* life..."

His face blanked, lost in the tide of memories that sucked him under.

Balim oriented once more on Bella to keep from losing his own life. If he lost concentration now, he'd bleed out.

General Giru's words sparked a realization. He chased it. It was the key to curing Blue Ring.

Balim had thought his most painful memory was poisoning his king, but the memory that Blue Ring kept circling was when his father had healed Balim first. The king had cried in agony. *"Is not my son's warrior life worth a thousand of your weak healer's?"*

Yes. The prince was a greater warrior and a worthier male. If his father had healed the prince first, they would both be alive. Balim's life wasn't worth their loss.

Jonah was Bella's prince. She couldn't love her son and Balim equally. She had to love Jonah more.

But perhaps he underestimated Bella.

She said that she loved them both.

He focused on her memory. His life depended on it.

Her soul light connected with his, even separated by metal doors and glass, and the strength of the Life Tree flowed into him.

He was aware of himself. His sickness spreading from his chest and now his belly acids poisoning his blood. But he also held the answer. The cure.

The Life Tree could not heal Blue Ring sickness because there was more than one component. Dark memories clouded his soul and forced him to relive his worst moments repeatedly, killing his mind and weakening his body. Not even the freshest breeze could blow that sickness away. Nothing could shelter him from the onslaught of his past shame.

But Bella's love could.

The realization filled him with relief and then faded. Thinking of her was not enough. Her thought kept the memories back but did not cure him.

"Ah." General Giru jolted. His face blackened with shame, and then he steadied himself and focused on Balim. He lifted the dagger once more. "You will thank me before you pass into the blacknight sea."

"No. I will not."

"You say that now. But is not your supposed soul mate a mother of another male's human child? You know my pain even if you do not admit it."

He weighed the knife.

Balim was not strong enough to stop him. "There is a cure for Blue Ring."

General Giru hesitated. "You lie."

"There is."

"It is an incurable disease. Even the Life Tree does not cure it." He gestured at his injuries. "It will rot your body as it decomposes your mind. You will prefer this mercy killing."

"I will show you the cure."

General Giru lowered the dagger. Hope warred with disbelief. "Then show me."

"Bring me Bella."

"No." The warrior raised his dagger once more. "You have lied too many times. Now you will die."

———

Bella screamed and threw the fire extinguisher at the screen. It cracked—useless—but still projected the same images she was helpless to control.

Jonah on the ship. Alive. Sleeping.

Balim stabbed, lying on the floor, and the general kneeling over him to administer the fatal blow.

Jonah was in danger of being infected. Someone contracted the disease that shouldn't have, Herc had said. Jonah's compromised immune system was vulnerable.

They were all vulnerable to the bombs.

"Bella?" Starr's quiet voice sounded muffled with allergies coming from the loudspeakers. "Are you still there?"

"Starr!" She jumped. "Were you listening the whole time?"

"And recording. The cell phone you called is on the ship's Wi-Fi. There were hardly any protections. It's like I'm inside with you."

"Rescue Jonah!"

"You're a little, uh, closer than me, Bella."

"But I'm locked in!"

The cursor on the screen moved on its own. "There, I just popped the lock on your door. Jonah's locked in too." On screen, a light above his door turned green and his door swung inward. "Oh, not anymore."

Bella raced to the bridge door and twisted the handle. It moved easily, but the door didn't budge. "It's not opening! I'm pushing with all my might!"

"Did you try pulling?"

The door flew open with her tug, and she stumbled onto her bare butt. Laughter bubbled. "You're the real hero, Starr."

"I'm eleven thousand miles away and I haven't left this

computer screen since Jonah disappeared. You should really get him before the fighter jets."

Bella leaped to her feet. "I'll see you in New York."

"You better."

Bella ran out of the bridge as fast as she could. Where was Balim? They'd wandered all over the boat. She crossed the open deck and ducked into the science lab on pure adrenaline.

She had no weapons, and she was no match for a warrior on land or on sea.

But Jonah was alive and so was Balim. For now.

She had to save them.

Bella raced into the hall just as the general stabbed Balim for the second time.

She screamed.

———

BELLA'S SCREAM jolted Balim back from the brink of fuzzy memories. A sharp burning pierced his gut.

General Giru had embedded his dagger in Balim's belly. Again.

"No!" Bella pushed General Giru aside.

The general's grip closed on the knife, and he pulled it free, leaving Balim with a terrible seeping belly wound.

Bella cupped her hands over the dark blood. "No. No. Please no."

Her soul light flowed into his. Despite the new pain, old disease, and his other injuries, peace welled in his heart.

His wounds were deadly and incurable.

Bella would cure them.

He lifted his lips. "Kiss me."

"Balim." Tears dampened her cheeks. "You're dying."

"I need...your strength."

"Anything."

His words were draining along with his strength. "Happy, Bella."

"How can I be happy in this tragedy?"

"Happy. Kiss."

She didn't believe him but pressed her lips to his.

Their souls entwined and multiplied. Not ten times or a hundred times.

A thousand.

Her mouth fitted to his, and, sensing his response, she teased her tongue along his seam. He opened to her, welcoming her in and possessing her in return.

She loved him. His darkest time and his brightest. He was not a murderer to her. He was a warrior. A healer. A male.

Hers.

She pressed one hand to his belly while she nestled beside him. His heart beat with her blood, and his mind focused on their connection. His cock filled with their shared past. She had once invited him into her body while wearing a plastic, and she would do so again.

He connected to her. And her soul filled him with a fierce determination to live, to always chase the light, to heal others.

Now, he healed himself.

The stinging in his belly faded as his skin knit together, sealing his viscera away from the air. Her queen power shone. Because she had found her power. Happiness in sadness, sadness in happiness. The two coexisting in one.

Like them.

He pulled back, releasing her with a sigh. The bleeding had stopped. And so had the sickness. The dark bruises on his chest from the cursed dagger cut faded away. The rings disappeared.

That was why the first couple had survived.

And that was how they would fight the Blue Ring Disease.

"It is curable," Balim said to her, aloud. "Heal the mind and the body."

The shining in her eyes matched the brilliance glowing in her chest. "We can do that. Humans get a milder infection so if we catch it, give therapy along with whatever treatment, we can heal—"

"No." Behind them, the general growled. "No warrior survives Blue Ring. No one."

She fixed on the general's still-bloody dagger and lowered her voice. "We have to go. The Sons of Hercules are bombing this ship."

Balim was well familiar with their bombs. He groaned as Bella helped him to his knees.

The general brandished his dagger. "You are still infected."

"A queen could cure you," Balim replied.

"I am an All-Council general. I will never accept a queen."

Bella tried to reason with the general. "Your bride—"

"Never."

"If she knew you were sick, she could return to you and—"

"Others have fond memories of their brides. I do not."

"You were not soul mates." Balim took a deep breath and leaned on Bella. She helped him stagger to his feet. "When you meet your soul mate, you will know."

"Stop." He lifted his dagger in threat. "I had my bride.

That was more than many warriors receive. So, we die together."

"But my son, Jonah, is—"

"I have nothing worth living for. No one will cure me. And nothing will change my mind."

THIRTY-NINE

Bella had reached the end. She didn't know how to reason with the general. Didn't mer treasure their children? How could he wish death on her child?

The general was about to collapse. Could she attack him?

Balim held her tighter. Protectively.

They had no time. Something had to change the general's mind.

"Bella?" Nora stuck her head in, squinting at the abrupt change from bright sun to the dull interior and still coughing up seawater. "Are you in here?"

"Nora! Where've you been?"

"Oh, first I was following you, and then Octopus Kong and I had to keep a low profile, and then we had to chase off the warriors. I saw you run across the deck, and I didn't see the dick who captured you, so..." Her eyes adjusted as her gaze fell on the general. "Uh....oh."

General Giru stared at her, dagger raised, obviously threatening them. He blinked as though he were the one who couldn't see. "Who?"

"Great." Nora touched her chest. "I'm great. I mean, I'm Nora. Who are you? Or, wait. Do I know you?"

"He broke into the hospital and dosed the water with Blue Ring," Bella explained as she reviewed their options for sneaking out of the room unstabbed.

"Oh, I wasn't around for that. I was on a bathroom, well, a what-to-do-about-rent break."

"I would never have infected a female with Blue Ring," the general said nobly.

"Well, that's great. Because it would be awkward if you had."

"Awkward?"

"Yeah. Because..." She trailed off, shook her head, and waggled her index finger at Bella. "You were right. Totally right. I didn't believe you, but the knowledge is like, 'Bam!' and there's no mistaking it." Nora turned back to the confused general. "I'm your soul mate."

Wait.

What?

Balim made a startled noise. And the general looked the most shocked. Nora just nodded and laughed as if everything made sense.

"You are a human," the general stated as if that made any difference.

"Queen," Nora corrected. "And you're a dick. As well as terminally ill. And commanding a lot of warriors who lost to a giant octopus. But also you're my—"

"No." He lowered his knife and turned to her, Bella and Balim forgotten as Nora became his entire world. "No, no."

Bella edged Balim away from the arguing couple. Which direction would Jonah be? Could she leave Balim near the railing while she investigated?

"Yes!" Nora laughed again. "Admit it. You feel the same."

"I do not possess feelings."

"Sure you do. And you feel you're my—"

"I have had a bride." He raised a finger. "One. Taking a second defies the law of the ancient covenant."

"Oh, well, laws are made to be broken."

His mouth opened and closed. "But I am the second commander of the All-Council armies. I cannot speak with, much less claim, a modern rebel queen."

"And yet here we are speaking. Claiming is right around the corner."

"Then I cannot take that turn."

"You can't fight reality."

"Yes, I can." He held up his finger again, refusing Nora the same way he'd refused to succumb to his illness. With sheer willpower. "And I do. I make reality."

"Look, you're making yourself sick." She started toward him. "I'll heal you. I've got lots of practice, so I ought to be great at it."

He jolted back and stepped around a desk to keep it between them. "I do not need healing."

"You do. Look at you. I can't believe you're standing upright."

"I do not need you. I refuse you."

"What's your name? I'm Nora."

"No one. I have no name."

"General Giru," Bella offered, easing another step deeper into the hall.

Nora stopped and smiled. "Giru. I like it."

"You do? Nora. It is simple, like a proper name of the mer." He seemed to taste her name.

She smiled. "Yeah. But I have to warn you, that's about the only 'proper' thing about me."

He shook himself and backed away from her again. "I fought your people. Poisoned them. Stabbed your healer."

"Looks like he got better."

"We are enemies!"

Nora closed the distance between them.

He lowered his knife to protect her from its blade. "I enforce the order. Tradition. I uphold the propriety of the mer."

"And I got in trouble a lot as a kid." She rested her hands on his bare chest just below a row of blue rings. "Let's get this sickness off you."

"I uphold the past to safeguard the future of our young fry."

He did? All right, then!

"So help me find Jonah!" Bella raised her voice. "That's what I keep trying to tell you. They're sending fighter jets to bomb this boat, and my son, Jonah, is here!"

The two stopped and turned. Her words broke their private spell.

"Where?" Nora asked.

"Young fry Jonah?" General Giru frowned. "He is still here?"

So, General Giru knew Jonah. He *was* here. "Herc said so. And we have to find him before—"

"Mom?" Jonah stumbled out from a corridor. He yawned and shuffled in pajamas she didn't recognize, but in the crook of his elbow, he held his ragged bear. "Mom. Hi, Mom."

Her heart exploded.

"Jonah!" She rushed to him and threw her arms around him, squeezing him tight.

He was here. Really here. Awake, in her arms, and here.

And he had hair. Inches of puffy red hair. She stroked it. "You're awake. Are you all right? How long have you been awake?"

"Awhile." He yawned again. "You're naked."

"Uh, yeah." She hugged him. "I'll, uh, find a towel."

"You're all naked. All of you."

"It's a long story."

"The mer do not wear human fabrics in the sea," Balim told Jonah, unselfconscious about his nudity. "We swim naturally and do not require these fabrics for staying warm."

He seemed to accept that explanation. "Where's the doctor and everybody? Oh, General Giru."

"Young fry Jonah." The general frowned. "You did not exit the ship with the others."

"They never let me out. I heard shouting, but I was playing the Switch, and then it got quiet, so I took another nap."

She kept hugging Jonah, partially to shield her nakedness from him, and partially because she couldn't let him go. "Has General Giru been kind to you?"

"Yeah, we're friends." He squeezed the bear. "The doctors said I'm cured because of the Sea Opal elixir I drank and you just didn't realize it. I've been waiting to tell you a long time."

"I came as soon as I could." She swallowed and stood, still holding him. Had he always been so tall? All arms and legs and boy? "The doctors hid you away from me. They are not good men."

"General Giru is good."

The room grew silent.

Jonah looked at the general expectantly.

The general's brow wrinkled as he finally understood

that he was not standing on the side of right. Self-hatred flexed across his features. Horror crossed with denial.

"It is not too late to change," Balim told the decorated warrior. "Save this mother and young fry."

He frowned.

"General Giru?" Jonah asked.

"He's made mistakes too." Bella pulled Jonah to Balim's side and took his hand. "We all have. And we're getting out of here. If that's okay with General Giru."

Without a word, the general sheathed his dagger.

Balim let out a long breath and sagged against Bella. He was healing, but still terribly weak. She held him up, her own knees trembling, the single pillar of strength in their new family.

Jonah looked up at Balim. "Are you a general too?"

"No. An ordinary merman."

"Balim's a merman doctor." Bella squeezed Jonah. She would continue until the happy reality sank in. "He consulted with me on your treatment after Faier."

"Faier was cool." Jonah studied Balim. "He had more scars on his face."

"Scars are the marks of great heroes," Balim told Jonah.

"Like your chest?"

Balim looked down at the healthy red scab. "Hmm."

"Yes," Bella said. "Like his chest."

Jonah pulled up his shirt to display scars from his treatments. "I've got hero marks."

"You do." She hugged him. "I'm so proud of you."

His skinny arms went around her back. "Um, Mom? Why is everyone naked?"

"Ah." She released him and covered her bare chest and lower. "Yes. About that—"

Starr's voice crackled through one of the overhead

speakers. "Bella, can you hear me? Bella, they're bombing the boat. If you're still on there, get off now."

———

THE VOICE of Bella's Starr galvanized the group, and Balim hobbled with Bella and her child out of the room.

Jonah's eyes bugged. "Bombing?"

She ushered him across the deck following the general and Nora into the sunlight. Her words were for Balim. "Jonah's still human. He can't survive underwater like we can."

"Then he must not submerge."

General Giru's voice rang out. "He will not suffer an injury while I am here. I will operate the platform for you. Back, beast!"

The general raised his trident against the flailing arms of a curious, semisubmerged Octopus Kong. He had crawled up the side of the boat like a massive, squishy, friendly Kraken.

"Whoa." Nora forced the trident down. "That's Octopus Kong. He's our friend."

"Mer are not 'friends' with deadly cave guardians."

She lifted her chin. "Funny how you can be a merman your whole life and not know how friendly giant octopuses are."

"You will not endanger young fry Jonah with this giant cave guardian."

"Watch me."

Bella passed the arguing couple. "Jonah, how well do you remember your swim lessons from last summer?"

"That was two summers ago, Mom." He got onto the platform and settled, squinting in the sunlight and shivering as the sea sprayed him.

Bella noticed his physical reactions at the same time as Balim. "We have no life vests. Just keep your head above water. Oh, I need to grab a blanket."

Balim stopped her. "No, Bella."

"But he needs food and water. And I didn't check the cabin. I might find a first aid kit. At least a flare."

"We must go now, Bella."

She made a worried noise.

He calmed her with reason. "I will enter the water first and catch Jonah. Come next. We will travel faster together."

The platform reached the plunging waves, and Bella helped Balim jump.

Rough waves crashed over his head, shoving him into the safety of the deep.

He fought the shift from human to mer. His belly wound and chest laceration complained. He needed his healer tools.

Balim's head broke the surface, and he sucked in a deep breath of air, keeping his lungs while his sight shifted to human. "Jonah—"

Octopus Kong's tentacle wrapped around him and dragged him under once more.

He pushed on the giant cave guardian, releasing his air and shifting to vibrate. "No! I must catch Bella's young fry. He is human and must breathe air!"

The giant cave guardian rotated his dark plus-shaped eye to focus on Balim as though to ask him, skeptically, if he was serious.

"Release me," Balim insisted. "We must escape from the boat. It will soon explode."

Octopus Kong thrust him above the waves. He gasped and coughed as he shifted forms once more.

On the platform, Bella clutched Jonah to her chest. Her desperation eased as she saw him.

Above on the ship, Nora had to hold back the general from leaping in and attacking the giant cave guardian.

Jonah looked on with equal parts wonder and terror. "Wow. Did it try to eat you?"

"No," Balim gasped, the tentacle still wrapped around his middle. "A misunderstanding. Take my hand."

"Will it try to eat me?"

"No."

Far above in the sky, tiny whining wasps flew toward the boat. Were these the fighter jets?

"Hurry."

Bella moved smoothly despite her agitation. "Jonah, take Balim's hand. Got it? Good."

His hands were small and slick in Balim's grip.

Jonah fumbled his bear. "Mom?"

"I'm right behind you." She followed, sandwiching Jonah to the tentacle, trusting Octopus Kong as Balim did. She patted the giant cave guardian's exposed rubbery skin. "Let's go."

The giant cave guardian flew them across the ocean's surface, creating a monstrous ripple, while keeping chests and, most critically, heads above water.

Jonah shouted in surprise when they plunged through waves, and then he shivered.

Nora and the general disappeared from the platform into the water.

Octopus Kong slowed and then stopped.

"Is this far enough away?" Bella asked in concern.

Balim replied. "You know human weapons better than I."

"Maybe we should flee a little—"

Ker-ka-BOOM! Ka-BOOM! BOOM-BOOM-BOOM!

The ship erupted in a flash of light.

Balim's ears rang.

Jonah clapped his hands over his ears. Bella winced and clapped her hands over Jonah's so two pairs of hands were covering his young ears.

Balim covered hers.

The ocean cratered and surged. They dipped into a deadly wave. Octopus Kong shuddered.

The distant, whiny wasps sped away.

Jonah wiggled and Bella dropped her hands from his ears so Balim released hers. Jonah hugged his mother. She squeezed him back and threaded her fingers through Balim's.

The boat smoked a long, black tail into the sky. "There's our distress flare."

They watched for some time.

Jonah cried suddenly. "Aw, no!"

Bella startled. "What is it?"

"I left behind my Switch." He squinted at the fiery conflagration. "Can we go get it?"

"No," Balim said.

"We'll get another one," Bella promised.

Jonah's chin wrinkled, and he looked like he was trying very hard not to cry.

"It is disappointing to lose important tools." Balim drew his attention with sympathy. "I lost my first trident when I was about your age. A fish dragged it away and nearly hooked me as well. My father healed my injuries, and we set about making a new one. I missed my first trident for a long time."

Jonah's brows drew together with sadness but he

mastered himself and did not cry. "I was level seventeen in Street Warrior Twenty-Eleven."

"I'm sorry." Bella nudged his bear. "You still have this."

"Because it has your rock inside." He opened the bear to show her Balim's offering. "I was always cold at that other hospital, and the rock felt warm. And it stinks like you."

"Stinks?" Her lips quirked and water shimmered in her eyes. "Is Mom stinky to you?"

"Maybe a little," he admitted. "It's Mom stink, so it's okay."

She snuggled him so hard. "I'm getting my mom sink on you."

He pushed away, wiggling but also laughing, and his chest glowed bright.

Jonah might never be a merman because there was now only one mermaid of the sea, Queen Lucy's young fry Tory. But the elixir in his body had reacted with Bella's jewel. Balim resonated with Bella just as Bella loved Jonah and Jonah loved her. She was the nexus between them. The Life Tree had healed Jonah after all.

Nora popped up suddenly, startling them. "That explosion socked me right in the chest."

"The general survived?" Bella asked.

"For now. He wouldn't let me cure him." Nora pouted. "I think, and I could be wrong about this, that he's on the side of the All-Council because he's bitter about an ex and he never wants her to rejoin the mer."

"You are right," Balim said.

"No. I refuse to believe it. That would be too childish. He's second-in-command of the armies!" She shook her head. "Anyway, he said land is close, and if we drift this direction, we'll hit the shore. I'm going to nap in Octopus

Kong's shadow for now. It feels like I've been awake for six months. I'm just exhausted."

"We will let you know when we arrive."

"Great. After you get rescued, Octopus Kong and I will hunt down that general and clarify that he needs to be cured, and that he's an adult and my soul mate."

Bella's lips curved. "He's your one, huh?"

"Yes, definitely."

"How ironic that you have to convince him."

"Ironic? Or interesting?" She smiled and steepled her fingers. "Yes. I can't wait."

Balim was also exhausted but content, a feeling he never expected to feel while clutched in the tentacle of a giant cave guardian. Queen Elyssa was right to gift Octopus Kong with a special treat of rare food. He should join her next offering.

Oh. His contented glow faded. He could never return to Atlantis.

Bella squeezed his fingers, somehow divining his thoughts. "We'll go back someday."

"You may."

"We both will." She kissed their entwined fingers. "The mer and human worlds are only beginning to change. You've cured an incurable disease. Mitch and every other innocent person who's been hurt by this disease will be healed. You said you would atone, and I believe you. I'll be right there with you. Someday, you'll win a medal for that."

"For curing a disease my own twisted genius unleashed?" He shook his head. "I need no honors for stopping what my revenge started. Especially since the queens of Atlantis will star in the cure."

"Good." She smiled. "It will put a curveball into the Sons of Hercules destroy-all-mer pitch if the mer queens are curing everything. Of course, we have to stop the Sons of Hercules from recruiting another person. 'Hate is the great unifier' indeed."

"You will stop them," Balim assured her.

She grinned. "My marketing campaign of hope versus their smear campaign of fear."

"But you will not spread lies. Only truth."

"You have the utmost confidence in my marketing skills."

"Yes, Bella. You are exceptional in all you do."

She kissed his nose, closed her eyes, and rested against Octopus Kong. "Except for the acrid smell of burning metal, it's a beautiful afternoon for a nap."

He also closed his eyes, filled with her same warmth and confidence.

They had found her young fry son, stopped a health crisis, undermined the loyalties of an important All-Council commander, and thwarted a Sons of Hercules double agent. Soon they would be rescued. Bella's young fry would flourish. Balim would remain with Bella all his life.

On the surface, he would be okay. They were together. All that remained was to pledge the vows, sign the contracts, and make them a family.

He would live for Bella, for the father he had loved and lost, and for himself.

"You'll do great," she murmured, again divining his mind without him speaking. "And the answer is yes. When-ever you ask."

"Yes?" He fixed on the question. "Will you marry me in a human wedding ceremony with a white cloth, festive cake, and glittering tiaras?"

She smiled.

His heart soared. They were already soul mates. And he knew her answer.

Together, they would spread healing, hope, and love throughout the mer and human worlds. As husband and wife. Male and female. Warrior and queen.

"Yes."

<h1 style="text-align:center">EPILOGUE ~ BALIM'S NEW FATHERHOOD</h1>

"Young fry Jonah."

Balim stood in the doorway of the dark, blinds-drawn family room and squinted at the preteen huddled under the blankets playing on his replacement Switch.

"It is the daylight hour when human fathers play a sport with their young fry human sons. Come out, and we will throw a soccer ball."

Bella suppressed her smile as she listened for her son's response. She already knew from the short three months they'd lived in their house—nestled in Upstate in a good school district—what Jonah's response would be.

"You're not human," he replied, muffled and disinterested. "And I'm not your son."

"I would like to be your father."

"Why? Chaz is a jerk."

"I do not wish to be Chaz. I wish to be like my father was to me, but as a human. That is what I wish to be to you."

Bella melted a little and pushed the freshly washed towels into the cupboard. Balim had grown increasingly open with his emotions to the point of being able to express himself like this to Jonah. She knew what it cost him and how hard he still had to try.

"So stop." Jonah tossed the effort back in Balim's face. "You made me lose my level. Just go away. I don't want a dad, and I don't want you."

Balim looked down and trudged away.

Bella's heart squeezed.

She couldn't see the soul lights of the mer, but she could see how he was wounded by her child's simple, thoughtless words.

"Hey." She sidled up to Balim. "Jonah doesn't need you right now, but I do."

The shadows haunting him fell away. "You do?"

"I absolutely do." She took his hand and threaded his powerful fingers through hers, sealing their connection. "This way."

"Is it your marketing? The Sons of Hercules? Has Starr found their leader?"

"No, no. Something else, if you're up for it."

Intrigued, he followed her up the stairs.

Bella still ran marketing campaigns, but her passion project was undermining the Sons of Hercules. She worked remotely under Starr's digital protection and in a secure community.

Releasing her masterwork had caused an explosion in the media like a bomb.

The Sons of Hercules had paused their mainland attacks. Their military funding had come under scrutiny, the CDC had spoken out on the side of the mermen, and even the postal system had gotten involved. Postal Police Officers were aggressive, thorough, and relentless in prosecuting criminals who abused the mail. Bella had her fingers crossed.

The Sons of Hercules had stopped actively recruiting disgruntled college students to be their terrorists, but the airy confidence of the mysterious Herc couldn't be stopped by one campaign. He had too much power and influence. This was the calm before a storm.

But today was a Saturday, and she was finally living the dream, working on the week and enjoying a fun, loving family on the weekends. How funny that a dream she had never wanted with Chaz was now the biggest, brightest happiness in her life.

At the top of the stairs, she raised her voice. "Jonah, in five minutes, I want you upstairs cleaning your bedroom and sorting your socks!"

Silence followed.

"Jonah?"

"Okay, Mom!" he shouted with irritation.

"Don't play video games all day. We're going for a picnic at the lighthouse, and I need to shout at you if I think of more chores."

"*Okay*, Mom!"

She grinned at Balim and led him through the door of the master bedroom and clicked the lock. "He'll hide under the blankets with the earbuds on full blast. We'll have a little privacy."

"You do not wish for him to sort his socks?"

"Oh, sure, but he'll be playing frantically to beat the level before I bother him. He won't dare walk away from his game now."

"No?"

She rested her arms on Balim's shoulders and pressed

her full breasts against his hard, masculine chest. "I need you, Balim. I need you to inspect me."

He played along, walking her between piles of laundry toward the nice big bed. "Are you feeling well?"

"All hot, actually."

"Have you been feeling hot for long?"

"Ever since you followed me into the bedroom."

He grasped her hips and slid his skilled hands up, lifting her velvet shirt. "I will check every part of your body for injuries."

"I was hoping you'd say that."

"With my tongue."

She curled her calf around his iron-hard thigh. "I'm ready."

He dipped her onto the bed, straightened, and unbuckled his belt. "Take off your clothes, my queen."

Bella shimmied out of her shirt and jeans to reveal plain white panties. Balim's gaze gleamed, and the heartblood-red threads shimmered in his brown irises. He seemed to like her plain cotton more than her lace and so she'd worn more of them; something about the white color reminded him of their first time when she'd unwrapped a condom.

He kneed onto the bed and made good on his promise, searing her lips with his hungry kiss and then continuing downward, consuming her body in wet heat and flames.

She splayed her hands over the broad scar crossing his chest and the smaller dagger line on his rigid abdomen. He had regained his strength and health, and now he used both to lift her from the fluffy comforter, kissing over her panties to tease her trembling thighs.

He made her his queen. Over and over and over again.

Bella dipped her fingers beneath her waistband. "Do you want to unwrap me today?"

His red iris threads flared with inner heat.

He pinched the underwire at her chest. "Yes."

The fabric peeled away in his hands, revealing her breasts. He chased first one globe with his wet mouth and brought her to the peak of arousal, then the other.

Her channel slickened, and her sex lips turned slippery for him.

He rubbed her through the dampening fabric. She moaned. He smiled with cocky satisfaction at her readiness.

Two could play, and she liked games. Bella gripped his rigid cock.

He closed his eyes, sucked in a deep breath, and centered on her. Touching his forehead to hers, he finally hooked his thumbs in her soft cotton and unveiled her slick pink femininity. He stroked the visible beauty and kissed her mouth deeply, thrusting his tongue in time with his strokes because he knew it drove her wild.

And it did.

She urged him to cover her. Obliging, he knelt between her legs, opening her to him, and positioned his thick cock at her ready entrance. "Do you wish to wrap me today?"

Sometimes, he still liked to wear a condom because he enjoyed the friction and heat; he said it focused his pleasure. But she also liked the slippery length of him driven deep into her, joining them for eternity.

What did she desire today?

Bella simply entwined their legs and drew his bare cock into her channel to the hilt.

He rested there, his pelvis to hers, pubic bone to pubic bone, curly hairs nestled. Hers were the same fiery red as her hair, and his were darker chestnut-mahogany. His tattoos and her freckles colored their skin in intricate patterns. Every time they made love, he affirmed everything about her. He made her feel like they belonged.

Balim nuzzled her, centering her on this moment, joined with him, his scarred chest and abdomen to her smooth one.

She smiled. He wanted what she wanted too: the joy lifting her heart that they were here, together, joined. Although there was no guarantee of the future and they had seen too much pain in the past, this moment was perfect. Happiness wrapped in sadness, bittersweet and beautiful, like a fine square of the darkest chocolate.

He lowered onto his elbows and thrust into her pleasure spot.

She arched, meeting him with slow certainty, building to the climax they both loved. Sweaty, gasping, thrusting, moaning kisses and pleasure caresses. Promises, a thousand promises. His cock stroked her channel, kindling a fire in her that only he could quench.

She gasped her peak.

He jammed his arm under her waist and lifted her to meet his cock's thrusts, drawing out the pleasure.

She blazoned into light as the orgasm sang over her skin, endlessly delicious. He shuddered, synchronized with her soul, and burst his liquid seed deep into her soft womb.

They collapsed onto the bed beside each other, all tangled limbs and satisfaction.

He eyed her. "Bella. Are you happy here?"

"I love this house."

His smile twitched. "That is not my question."

Yes. She knew that. "I will be happy when the Sons of Hercules face consequences for their crimes."

Thanks to Starr's recording of the final call on the plague ship, their opportunity might come sooner than hoped. Dannika swore she'd met Herc. She never forgot a face or a name.

"The leader is a him," Dannika had said in the clean, private offices of MerMatch. "Ignore the vocal distortion. I know his way of speaking from those voice patterns. Herc's not a member of my inner circle, but I'm sure I've met him. Maybe he's a friend of my father's. Maybe I knew his sister in college. Our connection will come to me, and then we'll have him."

It was a happy thought in an otherwise uncertain time.

Balim could not go back to Atlantis because his return might cause unrest, and so Aya had continued his employment at the mer hospital. He also consulted with the CDC.

Doctor Kowalski worked for them as the prime researcher of Blue Ring.

Sea Opal elixir arrested the illness, and a combination of therapy, antidepressants, and a visit from Queen Elyssa had cured everyone infected in the first outbreak. Mitch had made a full recovery with the support of his loving wife and two daughters, and was now back at work in the new mer hospital with Balim. But occasionally, patients still turned up in hospital emergency rooms, and that was when Balim's team activated.

Bella turned the question around on Balim. "Are you happy?"

His mouth flattened. His gaze drew to the locked door leading out of the bedroom. "I still have much to learn about young humans."

She cupped his hard cheek. "Jonah likes you, and he's interested in forming a relationship. He's just also a typical ten-year-old boy who skipped almost an entire year of his life and has to make up for it. And preferring to snuggle under blankets is a family trait."

"I wish to act honorably and earn his respect."

"Maybe instead of trying to do human bonding activities, you should try mer."

"But he is a human son. I must give him the human experience he needs to develop into a strong man."

"You're attentive and that's kind. But he knows you're not human, and he doesn't want you to be. What merman things can you both do? That's where you'll make the compromise."

Balim thought hard. "Hence the trip to the lighthouse?"

"Yes." She jammed a hand under her head. "I thought you both enjoy the seaside—"

The doorknob jangled.

Bella dove under the covers, scrambling to hide, and then tossed sheets over calm, naked Balim. "J-Jonah?"

"Mom? The door's locked."

"Yeah. Sorry. Did you need something, hon?"

"You have my socks."

She clutched the sheets higher, her heart thumping a million times a minute. "Weren't you playing video games? Loud?"

"I beat the level, and I want to go to the lighthouse after lunch with you and Balim."

Balim brightened and headed to the door. "Very good."

"Stop!" she hissed. "Where are you going?"

"To let him in."

"You're still *naked*. I'm still naked. Stop it!"

"He saw us naked on the ship."

"Yeah, but we're not on the ship. Balim!" She jumped out of bed and wrapped the top sheet around her body.

Balim opened the door.

She stood gross and sweaty and disheveled. "Sorry. Mom decided to, uh, exercise and get in the shower, so..."

Jonah's nose wrinkled. "Okay."

"Right. Sorry. The socks are over here. I'll run away to the shower."

Jonah bobbed in, nodded to Balim, who was calmly half-dressed, and picked up the basket of socks. "Okay, Mom, but your body is normal, so don't feel bad about it."

She checked. "I'm sorry?"

"Balim told me." Jonah's bare arms still showed the marks of the many, many IVs he'd had during his treatments. He displayed them unselfconsciously. "Mermen swim naked because bodies are natural when you don't need clothes to stay warm."

Balim beamed. "Correct."

"But humans do." Bella eased toward the master bedroom shower. "And with that in mind, let's put clean clothes on so we can enjoy our picnic."

And so they went on their picnic and enjoyed the fresh spring afternoon in Upstate. The weather didn't know whether its dark-bottomed clouds skiffing across the blue sky would pass over or dump rain. They scarfed snacks just in case. Jonah played cards with Bella, and then, while her back was turned, he stripped to his water socks and raced Balim into the water. Their polar bear run and Jonah's subsequent frigid shrieking startled the other families at the park and inspired a few brave children to do the same, much to their parents' chagrin.

Jonah's hair was longer now. Shaggy to the point of needing a trim.

Once, she'd feared he'd never make it to his eleventh birthday. She'd been so angry at Chaz for abandoning Jonah a second time a decade after his first exit.

But even that difficult visit had turned out a surprising, happy result.

Upset by the vision of Chaz abandoning his other sons in a time of medical need, Caro had marched him to the local registry the next day and gotten them both swabbed. She was not a match.

Chaz was.

Surprisingly, his fears of the procedure hadn't been completely unfounded. He'd donated and experienced a rare side effect that caused a slight limp.

The limp was expected to wear off. His celebrity status as a local businessman who'd given a little girl on the West Coast a second chance at life was not.

According to their church gazette, Chaz had joined the bone marrow registry because he "knew it was the right thing to do," and once he'd been matched, he'd "never had a doubt in his mind that he would save that little girl's life." Also, "anyone who refused to test should be ashamed of themselves. Don't call yourself a Christian or a man."

The article had made Bella's eyes roll so many times, she'd nearly gotten dizzy. But she would roll her eyes a hundred thousand times more if even one more child was saved from leukemia by a pompous, arrogant man. To that little girl, Chaz *was* a hero.

And for Bella, that was the true happy ending.

Now, she packed up the picnic supplies, a protective eye watching over her child.

Jonah hadn't needed Chaz then, and he didn't need him now. He had her. Now he was laughing, shrieking in the frigid waves, seizing what life offered. And, when he got too deep, he had Balim's helping hands to guide him safely back to shore.

She wrapped Jonah in a thick towel she'd packed in the minivan just in case. He shivered under the thick weave and struggled in his dry clothes. On the way home, she stopped at a drive-through and bought hot chocolates.

Balim eyed his. Although they felt safe here, his iridescent red tattoos were still identifiable, and they knew someday that this utopia would end.

She sipped his chocolate, waited a moment, and swallowed. "Look, no Rotenone."

His mouth tugged into a smile. "You have a line of chocolate on your lips."

She licked it away and tilted her chin to follow it with a kiss. He tasted of cocoa with cinnamon. Yummy.

This was the life she'd wanted. Trips to the local beach, stopping to savor the cocoa, and watching movies on the couch while her son struggled to keep his eyes open and her husband passed out, mouth open, snoring through the end credits.

She rested her hand across her belly.

There were more consequences than just sensation when she'd decided not to wear condoms. Another child could get sick. Be targeted by the Sons of Hercules. Bella could live in fear and grief.

Or she could cling to hope. Accept the gifts of happiness while not blinding herself to a multifaceted reality.

She had so, so much happiness.

Sadness existed. It was a sand kernel inside the pearl of her blessings. She and Balim had a long road to free the mer from the tyrannical hold of the All-Council and to make the surface safe for them from the Sons of Hercules. But so long as she drew breath, Bella would walk that road.

And when she could no longer draw breath, she'd dive in the water and breathe there.

Bella turned off the movie and roused the boys for bed, kissed Jonah good night, brushed her teeth, and joined

Balim under the covers of her newly made bed. He nodded off again; he worked long hours in the hospital, and weekends were his time to catch up. She closed her eyes beside her husband, near her son, in the house with the extra bedroom for a child that might grow into a son or a daughter.

She chose happiness.

She chose strength.

She chose love.

Queen Bella, double agent to expose the Sons of Hercules and protect Atlantis, dreamed of how her new family would change the world.

Dear Reader,

Thanks so much for reading!

Did you miss the first book in the series? Pick up *Seduced by the Sea Lord*.

The next book in the series is *Shattered by the Sea Lord* starring Ciran and Dannika.

Would you like more mer shifter goodness? Join my newsletter and receive supersecret bonus epilogues full of yummy mer warriors + the women who tame them. It's like the happy ending to the happy ending.

This time, I included Bella and Balim's epilogue inside the book because, first of all, I finished it early enough to include (yes!!! This never happens; I am always finishing the epilogue the night before the book releases) and second of all, I have two additional awesome newsletter-exclusive bonuses! Enjoy a supersweet excerpt of Pelan awakening from his terrible illness in "Pelan's Bride." Next, rebellious queen Nora refuses to give up on her soul mate in

"Claiming Her Sea Lord." Two special exclusives just for newsletter subscribers!

Subscribe here: http://smarturl.it/StarlaNewsletter

See you next time!

Sincerely,

Starla

ABOUT THE AUTHOR

USA Today bestselling author Starla Night was born on a hot July at midnight. She hikes, scuba dives, and swims naked in the ocean. She writes about smokin' hot dragons and tattooed mermen at StarlaNight.com.